Cengage
2/15
3/-

W9-CAA-873

MADAME PICASSO

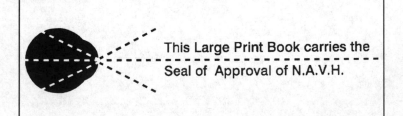

This Large Print Book carries the
Seal of Approval of N.A.V.H.

MADAME PICASSO

ANNE GIRARD

THORNDIKE PRESS
A part of Gale, Cengage Learning

GALE
CENGAGE Learning·

Farmington Hills, Mich • San Francisco • New York • Waterville, Maine
Meriden, Conn • Mason, Ohio • Chicago

GALE
CENGAGE Learning®

LIBRARY OF CONGRESS CATALOGING-IN-PUBLICATION DATA

Girard, Anne.
 Madame Picasso / Anne Girard. — Large print edition.
 pages ; cm. — (Thorndike Press large print historical fiction)
 ISBN 978-1-4104-7593-0 (hardcover) — ISBN 1-4104-7593-X (hardcover)
 1. Gouel, Eva, 1885-1915—Fiction. 2. Picasso, Pablo, 1881-1973—Fiction.
 3. Large type books. I. Title.
 PS3607.I46927M33 2015
 813'.6—dc23   2014038099

Published in 2015 by arrangement with Harlequin Books S.A.

Printed in Mexico
1 2 3 4 5 6 7 19 18 17 16 15

For Stephen Robert

■ ■ ■ ■

PART I

AMBITION, ART, PASSION

■ ■ ■ ■

We knew very well that we were damned,
But hope of love along the way
Made both of us think
Of what the Gypsy did prophesy.
                    — Guillaume Apollinaire

CHAPTER 1

Paris, France, May 1911

Eva dashed around the corner, whirling by the splashing fountain on the place Pigalle at exactly half past two. Intolerably late now, she clutched the front of her blue plaid dress, hiked it up and sprinted the rest of the way down the busy boulevard de Clichy, in the shadow of the looming red windmill of the Moulin Rouge. People turned to gape at the gamine young woman — ruddy cheeks, wide, desperate blue eyes and mahogany hair blowing back and tangling with the ruby-colored ribbon on the straw hat she held fast to her head with her other hand. Her knickers were showing at her knees, but she didn't care. She would never have another chance like this.

She darted past two glossy horse-drawn carriages vying for space with an electric motorcar, then she turned down the narrow alleyway just between a haberdashery and a patisserie adorned with a crisp pink-and-white awning. Yes, this was the shortcut Sylvette had told her about, but she was slowed by the cobblestones. Too far from the sun to fully dry, the stones were gray and mossy and she nearly slipped twice. Then she splashed through an oily black puddle that sprayed onto her stockings and her black button shoes the moment before she arrived.

"You're late!" a voice boomed at her as she skittered to a halt, her mind whirling in panic.

The middle-aged wardrobe mistress looming before her was ominously tall, framed by the arch of the backstage door behind her. Madame Léautaud's bony, spotted hands were on the broad, corseted hips of her coarse velveteen black dress. Her high lace collar entirely covered her throat, lace cuffs obscured her wrists. Beneath a slate-colored chignon, her large facial features and her expression were marked by open disdain.

Eva's chest was heaving from running, and she could feel her cheeks burn. She had come all the way down the hill from Montmartre and across Pigalle on her own. "Forgive me, madame! Truly, I promise you, I came as quickly as I could!" she sputtered, straining to catch her breath, knowing she looked a fright.

"There can be no simpering excuses here, do you understand? People pay for a show and they expect to see a show, Mademoiselle Humbert. You cannot be the cause of our delay. This is *not* a particularly good first impression, when there is so much to be seen to just before a performance, I can tell you that much!"

At that precise moment, Eva's roommate, Sylvette, in her flouncy green costume, and thick black stockings, tumbled out into the alleyway beside her. Her face was made up to resemble a doll, with big black eyelashes and overdrawn cherry-red lips. Her hair, the color of tree bark, was done up expertly into a knot on top of her head.

One of the other girls must have told her of the commotion, because Sylvette was holding an open jar of white face powder as she hastened to Eva's rescue.

"It won't happen again, madame," Sylvette eagerly promised, wrapping a sisterly arm across Eva's much smaller, slimmer shoulders.

"Fortunately for you, one of the dancers has torn her petticoat and stockings in rehearsal and, like yourself only a few moments ago, our regular seamstress is nowhere to be found or I would send you on your way without another word. Oh, all of you wide-eyed young things come down here thinking your pretty faces will open doors only until you find something better, or you trap a gentleman of means from the audience to sweep you off your feet, and then I am abandoned."

"I am a hard worker, madame, truly I am, and that will not happen. I have no interest in a man to save me," Eva replied with all of the eager assurance that a petite country girl with massive blue eyes could summon.

Madame Léautaud, however, did not suffer naïveté, ambition or beauty gladly, and her halfhearted protestation fell flat. Sylvette this morning had warned Eva — she could be out on her delicate backside and returned to their small room at la Ruche (so named because the building was shaped like a beehive) before she could conjure what had hit her if she didn't convince the woman of her sincerity. Sylvette had worked here for over a year and she herself was only a chorus girl in two numbers, an anonymous background figure — one who never made it anywhere near the bright lights at the front of the stage.

Three dancers in more lavish costumes than the one Sylvette wore came through the door then, drawn by their mistress's bark. They were anxious to see a fight. In the charged silence, Eva saw each of them look at her appraisingly, their pretty, painted faces full of condescension. One girl put her hands on her hips as she lifted her eyebrows in a mocking fashion. The other two girls whispered to each other. It brought Eva back swiftly to the cruel Vincennes home-town rivals of her youth — girls for whom she had not been good enough, either. They were one of the many reasons she had needed to escape to the city.

For a moment, Eva could not think. Her heart sank.

If she should lose this chance . . .

She had risked so much just to leave the city outskirts. Most especially, she had risked her family's disapproval. All she wanted was to make something of her life here in Paris, but so far her ambitions had come to very little. Eva looked away from them as she felt tears pressing hard at the backs of her eyes. She could not risk girls like these seeing her weakness. At the age of twenty-four, she could let no one know that she had yet to fully master her girlish emotions. There was simply too much riding on this one chance, after an unsuccessful year here in Paris, to risk being seen as vulnerable.

"You hope to be a dancer perhaps, like one of them?" Madame Léautaud asked, indicating the other girls with a sharp little nod. "Because it has taken each of them much work and hours of practice to be here, so you would be wasting more of my time, and your own, if that is your intention."

"I am good with mending lace," Eva pressed herself to reply without stuttering.

That was true. Her mother had, in fact, fashioned wonderful creations since Eva was a child. Some of them she had brought with her to France from Poland. As a legacy, Madame Gouel had taught her daughter the small, careful stitches that she could always rely upon to help pay the bills once she had married a nice local man and settled into a predictable life. Or so that had been her parents' hope before their daughter had been lured into Paris just after her twenty-third birthday. This was the first real job opportunity Eva had managed to find, and her money was nearly gone.

Sylvette remained absolutely silent, afraid to endanger her own tenuous standing here by saying a single word more in support. She had given Eva this chance — told her the Moulin Rouge was short a seamstress because, with all of the kicks and pratfalls, the dancers were forever ripping or tearing something. What Eva made of it now in this instant was up to her.

"Very well, I will test you, then," Madame Léautaud deigned with a little sniff. "But only because I am in dire straits. Come now and mend Aurelie's petticoat. Make quick work of it, and bring me the evidence of your work while the others are rehearsing."

"*Oui,* madame." Eva nodded. She was so grateful that she suddenly felt overwhelmed, but she steadied herself and forced a smile.

"You really are a tiny thing, like a little nymph, aren't you? Not altogether unattractive, I must say. What is your name again?" she asked as a casual afterthought based on what Sylvette had told her.

"Marcelle. Marcelle Humbert," Eva replied, bravely summoning all of her courage to speak the new Parisian name that she hoped would bring her luck.

Since the day she had arrived alone in the city wearing her oversize cloth coat and her black felt hat, and carrying all of her worldly possessions in an old carpetbag, Eva Gouel had been possessed by a steely determination. She fully meant somehow to conquer Paris, in spite of the unrealistic nature of such a lofty goal. Hopefully, this first job

15

would mark the beginning of something wonderful. After all, Eva thought, stranger things had happened.

Madame Léautaud tipped up her chin, edged by a collar of black lace, turned and walked the few steps back toward the open stage door, beckoning Eva to follow. It was then that she caught her first glimpse of the hidden fantasy — the inside of the famous Moulin Rouge.

The walls beyond the door were painted entirely in black, embellished with gold paint, in flourishes and swirling designs. Red velvet draperies hung heavily, flanking the walls, so that from this distance the place had the appearance of a lovely, exotic cave. It was a strange, seductive world into which Eva was so tentatively about to step and, in that moment, her heart raced with as much excitement as fear.

She tried not to look around too conspicuously as she followed. She was ringing her hands behind her back and her heart was pounding. She was not at all certain how she would steady herself enough to guide a thread through a needle.

Behind the stage, it was a dark and shadowy space even though it was mellowed by the light of day. She smelled the odor of spilled liquor and faded perfume. It was actually a little ominous, she thought, but that made it all the more exciting. As more costumed dancers passed her, coming and going toward the stage, she began to recognize them from the posters that were plastered brightly throughout the city. There was la Mariska the ballet mime, Mado Minty the principal dancer and the beautiful *comedienne* Louise Balthy, who was both Caroline the Tyrolean Doll and la Négresse. There was Romanus the animal trainer, Monsieur Toul with his comic songs and the troupe of Spanish dancers in their short red bolero jackets and black fringed hats.

Eva had never been sure what she would do if she actually ever saw one of these celebrated performers up close, much less met them. The prospect was frightening and yet thrilling at the same time.

What if Madame Léautaud rejected her now that she had come this close? Would she be forced to return to the city outskirts? No, she would not let that happen. She would not go back to Vincennes. But if she stayed in Paris with no job there would be little else for her. Louis's proposal that they become lovers, and he would therefore take care of her, might become her only option.

Poor Louis. He had been her second

friend in Paris. Sylvette had introduced them. Since he was Polish, and her mother was, as well, and they all lived at la Ruche, their friendship had been quickly cemented. The three of them had been inseparable since.

Eva was with Louis earlier that day when she had to sneak away for her interview at the Moulin Rouge. She had made a weak excuse about having forgotten something she needed to do, just before she left him, and dashed around the corner. He was standing there unfastening his portfolio of watercolors outside the door of Vollard's shop barely hearing her for anxiety over a fortuitous meeting of his own. Ambroise Vollard was the famed art dealer just up the hill on the cobblestoned rue Laffitte and, after months, he had finally agreed to see some of Louis's work.

Louis, whose real name was Lodwicz, had been studying at the Académie Julian, painting in the evenings and selling cartoons to *La Vie Parisienne* to pay his rent. The fact that his wonderful Impressionist-style watercolors did not sell, but his cartoons did, was a source of frustration to him.

Louis had loaned Eva money and regularly bought her dinner this past year to help see her through financially. She did not want him as a lover but she did not want to let him down, either. Loyalty meant everything to her.

Now, Eva stood before Madame Léautaud in the dressing room behind the stage as she examined the hem Eva had just mended.

"I can't even see the stitches or the rip, your work is so fine," she exclaimed with a mix of admiration and irritated surprise. "You may begin with us this evening. Be back here by six o'clock and not a moment later. And do not be late this time."

"*Merci,* madame," Eva managed to utter in a voice that possessed only a modest hint of confidence. A group of theater technicians and stagehands walked past, chuckling.

"During the show you will stand in the wings. Sylvette will show you where so you will be out of the way. If one of the performers needs a costume repair you shall only have a moment to mend a hem or reattach a button, cuff or collar. You're not to tarry, do you understand? Our patrons don't pay good money to see torn costumes, but they don't like an interruption in the flow of the acts, either."

Then Madame Léautaud leaned a little nearer. In a low tone, she murmured, "You see, Mademoiselle Balthy, our wonderful *comedienne,* has put on quite a bit of weight. We can only draw the corset in so tightly, yet she can be relied upon to split her drawers during one of her exaggerated pratfalls." Madame Léautaud bit back a clever smile and winked.

A moment later, Eva was back in the grimy alleyway, feeling the utter thrill of victory for the first time in her life. As she hurried back to the rue Laffitte to catch up with Louis, she thought the sensation she had felt was a little like flying.

Eva took the funicular up the hill and dashed as quickly as she could back to Monsieur Vollard's shop. It had been wonderful to have a Polish confidant in Paris these past months — someone who understood her thoughts and her goals in ways that did not require French words, and she had no wish to endanger that now by abandoning a friend.

Louis was like a brother to her, though she knew he wished it to be more. But they were too alike to be suited for one another. He was reliable and kind, and since she'd been in Paris, Eva needed that far more than romance.

Poor Louis, tall and pale with dust-blue eyes, living in the shadow of Eva's potent dreams. He still had not lost his thick Polish accent. Nor did he long for the sense of city style as she did. He still carefully waxed the ends of his beige mustache, wore a stodgy top hat when he went out, his favorite single-button cutaway jacket and two-tone ankle boots, which had all been fashionable a decade ago.

Still, it was Louis who had created the name Marcelle for her and she would be forever grateful because Marcelle had clearly brought her luck. Over wine at a small country brasserie, Au Lapin Agile, tucked cozily on a little hill in Montmartre, Louis had playfully proclaimed her to be thoroughly Parisian by giving her a name that sounded entirely French.

She had giggled at the new incarnation, but she had instantly liked it, too. It felt whimsical and freeing to be someone else, and there was such exciting power in that. Marcelle could possess an air about herself that Eva could not. Eva was cautious and meek. Marcelle would be carefree and confident, even a little seductive. She had even mastered the proper singsong city accent and altered her wardrobe with little touches to reflect some of the newer fashions, like calf-length skirts and high-waist belts.

Louis told her that she had a nose like a button, small and turned up at the end. She knew her blue eyes were bold and big, and that her long dark lashes framed them. She was petite and slim and he told her the overall effect was an alluringly innocent quality. But Eva did not feel innocent at all. Inside she was a powder keg of determination just waiting to experience life.

She longed to be a part of the vibrant new age in Paris, the Moulin Rouge and the Folies Bergère. The famous Sarah Bernhardt and Isadora Duncan were both drawing huge crowds at the Trocadéro, and two years earlier, the well-known dance hall performer Colette had kissed another woman so passionately onstage that she had nearly caused a riot. Ah, to have seen that! Paris was positively alive, Eva thought, a place pulsing with brash young artists, writers and dancers, all as eager as she was to make their mark.

Everyone was reading de Maupassant or Rimbaud, for their realistic portraits of life, and also the radical work of two new Parisian poets, Max Jacob and Guillaume Apollinaire. Eva loved Apollinaire's work best for how daring and edgy it seemed to a conservative girl from the suburbs. A passage from his poem "The Gypsy" long had contained her fantasy of a wild, exciting life in Paris.

> We knew very well that we were damned,
> But hope of love along the way
> Made both of us think
> Of what the Gypsy did prophesy.

In spite of the steady uphill climb back to Montmartre, Eva was skipping past the string of little shops along the cobblestoned rue Laffitte, beaming like a child as she arrived at Vollard's shop. Louis saw her through the street-front window. A little bell tinkled over the door as he opened it and came outside.

"My meeting is already finished — I couldn't even introduce you as my good-luck charm. You knew what this meeting meant to me. Where the devil did you go?"

"I found myself a proper job! It's only a seamstress job but it's a start. I wanted to surprise you."

All seemed instantly forgiven as he drew her up into his long slim arms, and twirled her around so that her plaid skirt made a bell behind her.

"Oh, I knew you would find something eventually!"

When Louis set her down he drew her to

himself and held her tightly against his bony torso.

She sensed him remembering the boundaries of their friendship as he took a single step backward, the color rising in his pale cheeks.

"That's such wonderful news. And, as it happens, I have a surprise for you, too — now we must celebrate!" He smiled, revealing crooked yellow teeth.

He held up two tickets as his dim smile broadened. "They are for the Salon des Indépendants tomorrow afternoon," he said proudly.

"How on earth did you manage them? Everyone in Paris wants to go to that!"

The coveted tickets were nearly impossible to find. Eva had always been too poor and too common to partake in much of what Paris had to offer, so it was all just a fantasy, the glamorous life only a fingertip away. Though she wasn't entirely thrilled with having to spend the afternoon alone with Louis, now she had the chance to attend the famous Salon des Indépendants! It was one of the most important art exhibits every year and all of the young artists in the city vied to have their work exhibited among the paintings of those who were more well established. Anyone who was anyone in

Paris would be there.

"My boss at the newspaper got the tickets for his wife. It turns out she finds some of the artists too vulgar for her taste."

Eva giggled. She would be the absolute envy of Sylvette — and everyone else at the Moulin Rouge. It was simply beyond her to turn down the offer.

They walked along the Parisian lane that snaked its way around the butte de Montmartre, its gray slate roofs and peeling paint welcoming them as a light mist began to fall. Strolling happily, they passed a stall brimming with boxes full of lush, ripe fruit and vegetables. The sweet fragrance mixed with the aroma of freshly baked bread from the *boulangerie* next door.

Eva glanced up at the Moulin de la Galette beyond, with its pretty windmill. Yes, all the pretty little windmills, and the secret cobblestone alleyways around them, hiding the dance halls and brothels of that seamy neighborhood that shared space with vineyards, gardens and herds of sheep and goats. Up the other way was the place Ravignan, which had become quite famous for the many artists and poets who lived and worked up there at that crumbling old place called the Bateau-Lavoir.

She pushed off a shiver of fascination.

"Shall we pop over to la Maison Rose for a private little celebration before we head home?" he asked. "And afterward, perhaps you'll allow me a little kiss."

"We've been all through that. You really must give up the idea." She laughed, making sure her tone was sweet.

"Well, then you shall become my muse, at the very least, if not my lover." He smiled. Nothing, not even her rejection of his advances, could seem to spoil their two personal victories today. "I need one now that Vollard has actually bought one of my paintings. That is my other big surprise."

"How wonderful!" she exclaimed. "Then a French muse is fitting. Not a Polish one, at least," she countered with a happy little smile.

"*Tak, piękna dziewczyno,*" he answered her in Polish. *Yes, beautiful one.* "A *French* muse. Every good artist needs one of those to inspire him."

By night, the Moulin Rouge was a different world than what Eva had seen earlier that day — the glitter of bright lights, the strong smell of perfume and grease paint, the hum of activity. It was thrilling to be even a small part of the backstage enclave.

Trying to keep out of the way as stage-

26

hands and actors dashed back and forth past the racks of costumes, Eva stood in the wings with wide-eyed amazement. She was struck by the diverse crowd of performers, everyone chattering, whispering, gossiping, and many of them drinking. To ward off stage fright, they laughingly declared.

Eva noticed that their brightly colored costumes were surprisingly garish. They were certainly cheaply made and sewn. Her mother long ago had taught her to know the difference. Close up, she could see the patches, the repairs, the soiled collars and dirty stockings. It was a disappointment, but she did not let it detract from the absolute thrill she felt at merely being here. It was all so exciting, this vibrant, secret world of performers!

Eva tried to be inconspicuous as she waited for her moment to be called upon. She clasped her hands to keep them from trembling, and her heart was pounding. She recognized all of the performers. Mado Minty breezed past her first, in an emerald taffeta costume with flared hips, cinched waist and a tight bodice. Across the way, near a rack of hats and headdresses, stood the celebrated *comedienne* Louise Balthy, with her distinctively long face and dark eyes. She was eating a pastry.

As Madame Léautaud had predicted, Eva was called upon several times during the performance to dash in with needle and thread.

Suddenly, she felt someone stumble over her foot.

"Hey, watch what you're doing! Do you not know who I am?"

Eva jolted at the sharp voice when she realized that it was directed at her. She glanced up from her sewing basket and saw a beautiful woman wearing an elegant costume, rich in detail. She looked just like her posters and Eva would have known her anywhere. This was Mistinguett. She was the current star of the Moulin Rouge.

"I — I'm sorry," Eva stuttered as the tall, shapely performer glowered down at her.

"Where *do* they find these people?" The young woman sniffed as she straightened herself and brushed imaginary lint from the velvet bodice of her costume.

"Two minutes, Mistinguett! Two minutes till your next act!" someone called out.

"Sylvette! Where the deuce are you?"

Her harsh tone turned heads and, an instant later, Eva's roommate dashed forward, clearly mid costume change herself, but bearing a full glass of ruby wine.

"I'm sorry, mademoiselle, I was just in the

middle —"

"Sylvette, I don't give a rat's tail what you were in the middle of."

Eva did not move or speak as she watched her roommate reduced to blanch-faced subservience. When the moment passed, she lowered her eyes and, feeling a bit shaken, went back to her needle and thread.

The performance went on, and Eva continued to make costume repairs. A torn sleeve, a popped button. But in the end it was Mistinguett, not Louise Balthy, who split her drawers in a high kick. She stormed off the stage and cast an angry glare at Eva.

"And what are *you* staring at?"

The sudden question hung accusingly between them. Oh, dear. She hadn't been staring, had she? Eva could not be certain. Mistinguett glowered at her as a young wardrobe assistant held her hand so she could slip the torn drawers down over her lace-up black shoes.

"Forgive me. I was only waiting," Eva replied meekly.

"Waiting for what?"

"For your drawers, mademoiselle. So that I can mend them."

"You? I've never seen you here before!"

"I may be new here, mademoiselle, but I am experienced with a needle and thread."

Mistinguett's fox-colored eyes widened. "Are you *mocking me*?"

"No, certainly not, Mademoiselle Mistinguett."

Eva could feel the heavy weight of stares from some of the other performers, in their many varied costumes and headpieces, as they passed by her. They knew better than to stop, however, when the temperamental star was angry.

"Well, see that you don't!"

Mistinguett pivoted away sharply. "Do be quick about it. I have my big number in the second half."

Eva thought, for just a moment, that she should sew the drawers loosely so that Mistinguett would split them a second time in the same evening. But she quickly decided against the clever tactic. She needed this chance too desperately. For now, a reprisal would have to wait.

Once the crisis had been averted, Mistinguett went off with a tall young man with thick, thick blond hair that was slicked back from his face in a wave. "Who is that?" Eva asked Sylvette as she waited to go on for her second number.

"His name is Maurice Chevalier. He dances the tango with her late in the second half. But talent certainly isn't how he got the job." She winked and Eva bit back a smile.

There was so much happening in this glorious place. So many acts, so many personalities and so many names to memorize. For the moment, Eva was holding her own. All of the sewing mishaps had been seen to for the moment.

As the performers filed backstage to relax during intermission, Eva dared to steal a peek around the heavy velvet stage curtain.

Her heart quickened to see such a huge audience crowded into the theater. She looked over a sea of silk top hats, stiff bowlers and fedoras. There wasn't an empty seat in the place.

As Eva scanned the well-dressed crowd, her gaze was drawn to a group of dark-haired young men, exotic looking and dressed in varying shades of black and gray. They were seated prominently at the table nearest the stage. The tabletop was littered with wine and whiskey bottles and a collection of glasses, and she could hear from their animated conversation that the group was Spanish. They slouched in their chairs, periodically whispering, drinking heavily and trying, like errant boys, to behave themselves until the show resumed. There was a heated air of something tempestuous about them.

But one stood out boldly from the others. He was a powerful presence, with his long, messy crow-black hair hanging into large eyes that were black and piercing. He was tightly built with broad shoulders, and he wore wrinkled beige trousers and a rumpled white shirt with the sleeves rolled past his elbows, revealing his tan, muscular arms. His jacket was slung over the back of his chair. He was incredibly attractive.

Surely the man was someone important since he was sitting at the front of the dance hall. As she turned away from the curtain, Eva thought how interesting it was that there was no beautiful woman beside him. A man who possessed such a powerfully sensual aura, and such penetrating eyes, must have a wife. A mistress, at least.

She almost asked Sylvette if she knew his name, but then suddenly the orchestra music flared for the second half of the show, and she heard Madame Léautaud shouting for her. Fanciful thoughts would have to wait since there was work to do, and Eva was determined to make a success of this job.

CHAPTER 2

He stood barefoot and shirtless before the easel wearing only beige, paint-splashed trousers rolled up over his ankles and holding a paintbrush in one hand. Morning light streamed into the soaring artist's studio in the ramshackle Bateau-Lavoir. There was an easel planted in front of a window that overlooked a sloping vineyard where sheep grazed. Beyond it lay a sweeping vista dotted with the slate-gray rooftops and chimneys of the city.

In the humble space, the cold tile floors were littered with rags and jars of paint and brushes. The plaster walls were papered with art. Here, Pablo Picasso was free to be much more than a painter. Here he was like a great Spanish matador, the wet canvas like a bull to be finessed into submission.

The act of painting was all about seduction and submission.

Finally now when the private thoughts

were put aside, the canvas yielded at last. Once he knew he had won control, Picasso was humbled before his opponent. It opened to him like a lover, took hold of him — possessed him as a sensual woman would. The comparisons always mixed freely in his mind. The work after the surrender, once his challenger, became his most exotic mistress.

Paint stained his fingers, his trousers, the inky dark coils of chest hair, his hands and his feet. There was a streak of crimson slashed across his cheek, and another across a swath of his long black hair.

It was quiet in his studio at this early hour and there was a hazy stillness around him. Picasso savored moments like these. He gazed at the wet canvas, the cubes and lines speaking to him like poetry. And yet the quiet brought thoughts of other things, too.

Fernande had drunk too much again last night after their quarrel, so he had gone off to the Moulin Rouge, taking solace in the predictable company of his Spanish friends. Feeling increasingly celebrated here in Paris eased a little of his disquiet. But he knew that when the night was over, Fernande would be at home in their new apartment, and last night he was still too angry to return to her. So he had come to his studio.

He loved Fernande. He did not doubt that. She'd had a difficult life before him, married to an abusive husband from whom she had escaped, and who she was still too afraid, even now, to divorce, and Picasso always had an overwhelming need to protect her because of it. They had been together through the hungry years, living the life of an unknown and struggling artist in Paris, which had strengthened their bond in spite of their ongoing inability to marry.

Yet lately he had begun to question whether that was enough; and his ambivalence about their relationship was extending to other things in his life. In the increasingly looming shadow of his thirtieth birthday, he felt deeply that something was missing. Perhaps it was only that he felt this concerned him.

Picasso picked up a smaller paintbrush and plunged it into a pot of yellow paint. Beyond the smudged windows, the sun was shining. He focused for a moment on the grazing sheep that made the little corner of Montmartre seem like countryside. He thought suddenly of Barcelona, where his mother remained, worrying about him every day.

Thoughts of family, and the simplicity of childhood wound themselves like thread in

35

his mind. He thought of his little sister Conchita, with her wide blue eyes and precious innocence. Even after all these years, Picasso missed her so dearly, but forcefully he pressed the memory away and urged himself to think of something else. He could not change what had happened. All it ever did was bring him pain laced heavily with guilt.

The sound of someone knocking sent the memories skittering into the back of his mind. The door opened and two young men staggered inside. They were his good friends Guillaume Apollinare and Max Jacob. They were laughing, their arms draped fraternally around each other, and they carried the strong scent of alcohol.

"So much for Pablo's promises," Apollinaire slurred, and his flamboyant gesture filled the room. "You said you would meet us at Au Lapin Agile last night right after the Moulin Rouge show."

"I say a lot of things, amigos," he grumbled, and returned to his painting. But as annoyed as he was by the interruption, he was relieved that it was his friends who had come and not Fernande.

Picasso loved these two misfit poets as if they were his own brothers. They stimulated his interest in ideas, in poetry, in thought — and that encouraged him always with his art. They talked together, drank, argued wildly and had built a deep trust that Picasso greatly valued now that he was beginning to find the first hint of real fame. He was not always certain any longer who he could depend upon to like him for himself. But Max Jacob and Guillaume Apollinaire were beyond reproach.

Max, the smaller of the two men, was the trim, well-read and exceedingly witty son of a Quimper tailor. He had been Picasso's first friend in Paris. That winter, ten years ago, Picasso was so destitute that he had been reduced to burning his own paintings as firewood just to keep warm. Max had given him a place to sleep, the two of them taking turns in a single bed in eight-hour shifts. Max slept at night while Picasso worked, and Picasso slept during the day. Max had little but he always shared with Picasso what he had.

It was generally assumed that Max led Apollinaire in their flights of fancy, but that was no longer true. Max's addictions to opium and ether set him at a disadvantage to the charming and clever Guillaume Apollinaire, who now ruled their social engagements.

"Where's your whiskey?" Max slurred.

"Haven't got any," Picasso grunted in reply.

"Fernande drank it all?" Apollinaire asked.

"As a matter of fact, she did."

"Oh, bollocks, that's a lie. She rarely comes slumming up here anymore now that you've gotten her that elegant place on the boulevard de Clichy, and we know it," Max countered.

"Well, she came yesterday. We fought, so she drank the whiskey because I had no wine," Picasso replied in French, but with a voice thickly laced with the melody of his Andalusian roots. Everyone always told him that his French was a dreadful mess of improper verbs and tenses and he knew it, but so early in the morning like this, he didn't care.

"Ah," Apollinaire said blandly, dabbing a single long finger at the canvas to check for wet paint. He did not always believe Picasso's stories. "That *does* explain a multitude of things."

"Well, whatever she's done, you will forgive her. You always do," Max said.

Pablo felt the squeeze of anxiety make a hard knot in his chest. It was all starting to feel like an inescapable cycle. Best just to work and not to think. Of her, of the futility, of the wild restlessness that was invading his heart more strongly every day. He must bury it just as he did his thoughts of his sister, and how she'd died.

Max looked around the studio, taking stock of the new canvases. Then he paused at the two rough-hewn Iberian stone heads sitting just behind the little drapery that hid his single bed. "You still have these?"

"Why wouldn't I have them? They were a gift," Picasso snapped of the antiquarian busts he used in the studies for several pieces of his work.

"A peculiar gift, I always thought. They always looked to me like something from a museum," Max dryly observed. He ran a finger over the throat of one bust and touched the head of the other. "Where on earth does one find something like these? Legally, that is," he asked.

Apollinaire replied. "How would I know? I got them from my secretary who was trying to bribe me to introduce him around Paris. Apparently, he thought they would impress me. I gave two of them to Pablo. Simple as that. It has never been my habit to question where gifts come from."

"Or where the women come from," Max quipped with a smirk and a clever flourish. "And yet, they *do* come to our dear Picasso — and both rather generously."

39

"Are the two of you quite finished?" Picasso growled as a stubborn black lock of hair fell into his eyes.

"What, pray tell, is *this* meant to be?" Apollinaire asked, changing the subject. He was looking at the wet canvas on Picasso's easel.

Picasso rolled his eyes. "Why must art always *be* something?" he snapped.

"That circle there reminds me of a cello," Max said playfully. He was rubbing his neatly bearded chin between his thumb and forefinger as he and Apollinaire looked at the painting and then exchanged a glance.

"It reminds *me* more aptly of a lady's *derrière,*" Apollinaire offered with a devilish little smirk.

"Not that *you* have actually ever seen one, Apo, my good man," Max quipped, using the endearing nickname they all had adopted for him.

"Well, *you* most certainly haven't."

"Do you not *feel* things when you look at the painting, or do you only see with your eyes?" Picasso asked, annoyed that they had disturbed him at this sacred hour, and irritated that now they were poking fun at his work. "*Dios mío,* sometimes I feel as if I am surrounded by a gang of idiots!"

"What *I* feel is confused." Apollinaire

chuckled, pretending to further inspect the canvas. "Pablo, your mind is a mystery."

"I feel thirsty just talking about it. Shall we all go find a drink?" Max asked.

"It's not even noon," Picasso snapped.

"Morning is always a fine time for a beer. It will set your day to rights," Apollinaire answered as he loomed over the two of them like a lovable, slump-shouldered giant.

"You two go ahead. I'm going to work a while longer, then I am going to take a nap." Picasso nodded toward the little iron-frame bed in the corner of the studio. It was covered with a fringed apple-green quilt embroidered with red roses that has mother had sent from Spain. He pressed his hair back from his eyes.

"Sleep here?" Max asked with a note of surprise, since Picasso was well beyond his hungry years in Montmartre. There was no reason for him to spend more time up here in this frigid tumbledown place than was absolutely necessary. "Will that not make things worse at home with *La Belle* Fernande?"

"Fernande and I will be fine. We always are," Picasso assured his friends as he picked up a paintbrush and turned away from them. "Go on ahead. I will see you both Saturday evening at Gertrude's, as usual," he assured them as he began to stir a pot of paint.

He looked forward to Gertrude Stein's Saturday evening salon. He craved the young minds there, and his intellectual arguments with Gertrude herself, who was always up for a debate. She challenged him. She made him think, and she questioned every single societal rule there was to question. That woman was a force of nature! If only he was attracted to her physically.

"Now let me get back to work."

"Aren't you forgetting? You promised to go to Apo's reading at the Salon des Indépendants tomorrow," Max reminded Picasso in a whisper as they arrived at the door.

"I haven't fogotten," Picasso said.

But he had forgotten entirely.

For a moment, with her eyes still closed, and the fog of sleep just beginning to leave her, Fernande had a vision of her husband, the man who had beaten her. She opened her eyes in a panic, but all she saw was a little toffee-colored capuchin monkey dressed in a smart red jacket with a necktie sewn to the lapel. The creature was peering at her with beady black eyes as Pablo stood behind him, smiling.

"The monkey from the café?" Fernande asked, trying to make sense of the little thing perched on her chest, busily cleaning himself. The moment seemed absurd, especially with the fringes of such an awful dream still playing at the edges of her mind.

"I bought him on the way home from the studio this morning. Granted, he is unique but he is better here with us and our little menagerie than how he was being treated."

Fernande glanced around at their shaggy dog, Frika, a huge shepherd mix, Bijou the Siamese and a white mouse they kept in a wooden cage near the window. Yes, it was becoming a menagerie indeed.

She sat up and the bedcovers fell away from her bare chest. Her long auburn hair tumbled down over her shoulders highlighting her green eyes. The animal leaped from her lap and up onto the dresser, then onto the floor, in skittish bursts of movement. "But a monkey, Pablo?"

He sank onto the edge of the bed beside her. "He was being abused and neglected. You know me, I could not resist rescuing him. I didn't have enough money with me so I made a sketch for the organ grinder. He seemed quite happy to make the trade."

The apartment was now flooded with bright morning sunlight and Fernande

43

looked around at all the rescue animals Picasso had always insisted on taking in. "Besides, it is an investment," he continued. "I can use him in some of my new studies. Monkeys have been symbolic in art back to the Middle Ages, so he might actually prove useful."

"When he is not soiling our floors or our furniture."

Fernande sighed as she watched the little creature leave a puddle on the carpet, then scramble across a bureau. Picasso pulled a piece of a croissant from his jacket pocket to give to it. Bijou and Frika lay together on the rug, watching the encounter with bland acceptance.

Fernande sighed and finally got out of bed to dress. She loved Pablo's tender nature most of all. Perhaps one day, if she loved him enough, God would bless them with a real child. She knew he wanted a family most of all, just like the one he had as a boy in Barcelona.

As she drew on her chemise and buttoned her blouse over it, she saw his eyes narrow. Peeking out from behind her pillow, he had found the pencil sketch she had posed for yesterday while he was in Montmartre. She knew how Picasso felt about her modeling for other artists but she had done it, anyway.

The days were long here in this lovely apartment, and he was not the only one who deserved fame. His success kept getting the better of her.

"What is this?"

"You know what it is."

She knew he immediately recognized the style. "You posed for van Dongen?"

"Pablo, be reasonable. You are gone for hours at a time most days, and Kees is one of our friends from the old days. We know his wife and little daughter, for God's sake."

"He's still a man and you posed for him with your clothes off." He stalked across the room toward her as she buttoned up her long black skirt. Picasso took her wrists and pulled her forcefully against his chest, stopping her. There was desperation in the movement. "Have I not given you everything you have ever asked for? This apartment, elegant clothes, a wardrobe full of hats, gloves and shoes, and an entrée into any restaurant in Paris you like so that you don't have to do that demeaning work any longer?"

"It's not work to me, it's freedom."

A silence fell between them, and Fernande turned her lower lip out in a little mock pout and her green eyes grew wide. "Does this mean we are fighting again today, too?"

she asked.

"It's a disagreement. Only that."

"We quarrel too much, I fear."

He pressed a kiss onto her cheek and released her wrists. His hands snaked around her then and moved down to the small of her back, drawing her close against him. He was so good at seduction, Fernande thought, and she tried not to think again of the blinding number of women on whom he had honed his skills. She was good at manipulation, but they both knew he was better.

He tipped her chin up with his thumb so that she could not look away from his eyes. "Yet, we always reconcile, which is the enjoyable part," he said.

It was difficult to feel angry about how forceful Picasso could be when her desire for him had already claimed her. She wanted to be right back in that big warm bed with him, even if there was an element of predictability to their relationship now. After all, they loved each other, and at the end of the day that was enough for her. It had always been enough for him, too.

"I want you to tell van Dongen you can't pose for the painting."

"You don't trust me?"

"It is not a question of trust."

Fernande could hear the sudden edge in his voice, and she wondered how much he knew of what she did during the long hours when he was up in Montmartre working. "Of course it is."

"I will not say I am sorry for trying to protect you all of these years, after what your husband did to you. You deserved much better than that."

She thought of saying that she did not deserve to be so high on the pedestal upon which he had placed her five years ago. But she could not bring herself to because some part of her still craved his adoration. Instead, she pressed a hand to his chest, knowing the curves of him so well, knowing what would make his body respond. It surprised her when he gently brushed her hand aside and turned to look at the little monkey, who had perched on top of the dog's large, shaggy back. Watching Picasso, Fernande's heart felt heavy all of a sudden. She was not certain why.

"Let's go across the street to L'Ermitage for lunch. Just the two of us, hmm?" she asked, trying to sound kittenish. She felt a strange new barrier between them and she did not like it.

"All right. But don't give me a hard time

when I want to bring the leftovers back for Frika."

"Sometimes I think you love that dog more than you love me."

"*Dios mío,* Fernande, I am still here, aren't I?"

CHAPTER 3

"I can't do it! I won't!"

She heard her own voice first, when she remembered what had happened the last time before she left home, and the memory of the scene was quickly vivid again in her mind.

Eva's parents did not react to her protest. Her mother stood silently at the stove stirring the iron pot full of beet soup. Her father sat across from her at the small kitchen table, his elbows heavy on the table and his meaty hand clenched around a half-full mug of wine. He was always so irritable when he drank that sour-smelling cheap wine but no one dared to tell him.

"Kochany Tata," Eva pressed, hoping that the tender term of endearment would soften him. Yet she knew there was a note of something more harsh in her voice that she could not contain. It was something he would hear because he knew her so well.

The scent of pork, ginger and sour wine was bitingly strong with the tension.

"And what is wrong with Monsieur Fix?" her father asked. He was hunched over and looking up from his glass with glazed, heavy-lidded eyes, as though life itself had gotten as burdensome for him as it had for her mother. He was not yet forty. "You're too good for the man, are you?"

"I don't love him, *Tata.*"

"Opf, love!" he grumbled, batting a hand in the air. "It has all been settled with his family. A girl like you should have a husband, a house full of children and a secure life here near your parents."

She cringed as though he had pronounced a death sentence on her. *A girl like you.* What he meant was a plain sprite of a girl, still unmarried at the age of twenty-three, still untested by men, relationships and the world. How she should respond so as not to ignite his anger, Eva did not know because she was not desperate for marriage. The only desperation she felt was to make something of her life. Her mother continued stirring the soup.

"I won't marry him, even if he is the only man in the world who ever wants me."

"You will."

"You don't understand me, Papa! That life would kill me, I know it would!"

"He is the first serious offer you've had. By God, you will marry him."

"I'm a grown woman! You ask too much."

"You will always be my child, Eva Céleste Gouel — you do as you are told, and there is nothing more to understand," her mother declared, finally breaking her silence as she tossed down the wooden spoon and it clattered onto the tile floor.

"No! I tell you, I won't!"

Suddenly her father slapped her and the force of the blow to her cheek turned her head. She felt the sting of surprise, since her father had never in her life struck her before. Her parents loved her. They had always loved her. As she turned slowly back to face her father, she tasted the trickle of blood from a crack in her lip. "You are our daughter, you owe us for that, and by God in His heaven, you will be Monsieur Fix's wife, if it kills you!"

Finally her mother spoke. There were tears shining in her eyes. "Eva, please. He is stable enough not to abandon you if you fall ill again. That pneumonia last winter nearly took you. You have always had a weak constitution, your lungs especially. Something bad will happen to you if you go off where we cannot protect you. Something awful, I know it!"

"Eva? Are you listening to me?"

The memory still had the power to claim

51

her. It slipped like a phantom back into the corner of her mind as she gradually heard Sylvette's voice again. The room they shared was dark so Sylvette could not see the tears in her eyes. The sound of crickets flooded the room through the open window as she realized Sylvette had been telling her a story she had not heard.

"Were you thinking again about what happened with your parents?" Sylvette carefully asked.

"It's just a vivid memory that comes to me at nighttime, that's all. I'm fine."

"Do you want to talk about it?"

"That won't help." She felt the tears fall and then dry on her cheeks. She did not bother to wipe them away. There was a quiet stillness between them after that for a time.

The small room they shared was lit by a moonbeam. Both girls lay on their backs looking up at the ceiling, and Eva could hear Sylvette's rhythmic breathing. It was soothing, she thought, and the assurance of it calmed her. She looked across the little wooden dresser with porcelain knobs that separated their two beds. A moment later, Sylvette tried to lighten the mood between them.

"Did you see Mistinguett's face when you said that *you* were going to mend her drawers?" Sylvette asked, beginning to chuckle. The sound reminded Eva of the tinkle of bells.

Eva felt herself smile and then they both laughed.

"She hates me." Eva groaned.

"She hates all women who are a threat to her."

"I'm not at all beautiful, or talented like her, so I should be no threat."

"But you do have a certain quality. People can feel it. And men look at you differently than they do a woman like her. You are sweet and innocent. They want to protect you."

"I'm not so innocent. Certainly not all that sweet."

Sylvette giggled. "Oh, believe me, yes, you are!"

Images of how she had left home crept back into her mind. Her defiance with her family haunted her. A week after the argument with her parents, Eva had summoned the courage to buy a Métro ticket to Paris, and she did not even tell her parents she was going. She was too terrified that they would change her mind.

Her parents were not terrible people. She knew her mother had struggled to find a way out of the poverty she had known in

53

Warsaw, and she dreamed of marrying and having a child in the peaceful suburbs of France. But Eva did not share the same dream. Eva had dried her tears as she'd stepped onto the Métro car in her only pair of button shoes. She knew how badly she was hurting her parents, but she had craved excitement. And the powerful hope for something more than she could find at home.

"Sylvette?"

"Hmm?"

"What happened to the seamstress before me?"

"Mistinguett didn't like her," Sylvette answered after another small silence.

"She is so awfully intimidating."

"I probably shouldn't tell you this, but it might make you feel better. Mistinguett's real name is Jeanne, but no one dares to call her that."

"Why not?"

"Because her own mother was a seamstress. I think she wants to distance herself from her past, as you do. Throwing her weight around helps her do that. It is her one weakness, I think, that those days still can wound her and she flares up in defense."

"Sylvette?"

"Hmm?"

"Thank you for helping me get the job," Eva said, feeding the next little silence.

"It was nothing. I only told you about the opening. You got the job all on your own," Sylvette replied with a yawn. "Besides, you will be able to repay me one day. I feel certain of it."

The next afternoon, Eva and Louis made their way together along the busy quai d'Orsay beneath a wonderfully warming spring sun. Everyone in Paris seemed to be out enjoying the lovely weather — parasols open, wide-brimmed hats, their plumes fluttering in the breeze. The sidewalks were ornamented by shabby little bookstalls filled with ragged leather-bound treasures. Brightly painted boats bobbed on the shimmering Seine beyond.

This was her favorite part of the city, and today, with the sunlight playing through the Tour Eiffel and the Parisian rooftops on the horizon, it all looked positively magical.

Ah, how she loved the vibrance of this city!

Next, they cut through the shaded luxury of the Luxembourg Gardens, with its broad sun-dappled walkways, manicured lawns, Grecian urns and magnificent fountains luring them beneath its lush bower of trees. Young bourgeois couples strolled hand in hand casually with them past the Medici Fountain, the ladies twirling their parasols, the men in high cravats and bowler hats or crisp boaters, and fashionable walking sticks. Other couples sat on green park benches scattered along the walkways, some of them feeding the pigeons.

As they walked, they spoke of the latest news. Everyone was talking about what the newspapers called the World's Largest Ocean Liner, being nearly completed across the channel in Ireland. They were going to call it the *Titanic,* excitedly heralding it unsinkable.

Now *that* seemed a sure way to tempt fate, Louis said. The prospect of going all the way from England to America on her maiden voyage seemed absolutely terrifying. Yet, was life not really all about doing the things that frightened one the most?

The greater the risk, the greater the reward. Ironically, it was her father who had always said that. "Would you take a voyage if you had the fare?"

"Not in a million years." Louis laughed. "I despise the ocean. It's too big and black and unknown!"

"It's the unknown in life that's the best part," Eva countered with a broad smile.

She was happy finally to merge then with

the large crowd moving past the Grand Palais on the broad avenue Nicholas II, and up the dignified staircase into the great white stone Petit Palais, where the exhibition was being held. She could put her concern about Louis's intentions aside for a while and allow herself to be excited about the artwork everyone was talking about. She tipped up her chin proudly as he handed the two tickets to the man at the entrance.

The building itself was magnificent, and inside there were massive murals covering the walls along with a soaring stained-glass rotunda. There were different rooms all dedicated to various styles of art, and Eva and Louis made their way steadily through the crowd into one of them. Eva noticed that the men and women were holding their gloved hands to their mouths. She quickly realized why and giggled with embarrassment. She had wandered into a room celebrating the work of Henri Matisse.

Eva's senses were bombarded by bold color, crude styles and raw designs she could not have imagined. She had no idea what she was meant to think or feel about any of it, but some of it was shocking since his work lacked all convention. Several people openly laughed and pointed at a portrait called *Woman with a Hat*. Eva thought the work was a torrent of confusion with boldly colored brushstrokes slapped onto the canvas as if by a bricklayer's trowel. It seemed wild and forbidden.

She was fascinated by the naked women in the other paintings around it — the bodies, the great sensual gobs of oil paint on canvas. Eva needed to catch her breath.

"*This* is the sort of thing artists are doing?" she asked, feeling her body stir as she gazed up at bare breasts, legs and torsos seemingly on every other canvas.

"This was the style a few years ago. They do this and much more that they would not dare to display here. Much of it far more blatantly erotic even than all of these nudes." Louis sniffed reprovingly.

"You've seen worse?" she asked.

"Of course. But now that drivel they call Cubism is the new thing, leaving all this flesh to a retrospective collection in favor of something even more wild. Come, you'll want to see it. It's in the next room." He took her hand and led her through the crowd. He was so stodgy, and his description was the perfect example of that. She hated his moist hand almost as much as how predictable he always was. But even that could not dampen the thrill of this moment. Being here, amid this elite crowd at such a glamorous exhibition, was the most exciting thing that had ever happened to her, and her heart was soaring.

"Last year a Parisian donkey made a painting with its tail and they showed it at the exhibition here. That trash sold for four hundred francs, and an artist like me can barely make a decent sale," Louis droned, doing his best to assert his knowledge and dampen the thrill she felt.

As they made their way to the next room, Eva wasn't certain what she had expected to see but the new sensory barrage stunned her even more. The vast room, with its colored play of light and all of the people, suddenly made the space seem extremely warm. There were so many huge canvases covered with lines and angles. All of them seemed like sharp pallid cubes with human beings trapped inside trying to escape. Eva felt a shiver at the evocative paintings as she wondered what some of the artists might have been trying to say. There were too many people milling around her to pause long enough to hazard even a guess, but each one was oddly stirring to her.

"These are the damned artists who should be called the Wild Beasts, not the Fauvists. There's not a thing artistically sacred to any of them. Just look at all of the nonsensical shapes," Louis grumbled.

"One of them is actually making something of a name for himself at it, although apparently now he's too much better than everyone else to exhibit his work here. Some Spaniard called Picasso. Wretched Spaniards."

He rubbed his chin as he looked up at a huge canvas of gray and beige cubes. "I'd like to meet him, though. Maybe some of that dumb Spanish luck of his would rub off on me. At least I know I can paint better than a donkey's tail!"

She'd heard the name Picasso, of course. Everyone who was anyone in Paris was talking about him, saying he was a true renegade. She had read recently that he had become known for leaving the style of Matisse, and for embracing this new linear style Louis despised. Eva knew nothing about art, but she knew that these paintings fascinated her.

When Louis was distracted and began speaking to a couple he seemed to know, Eva wandered alone back into the first room and to a corner adorned by a large canvas depicting a nude, recumbent woman. She leaned nearer. Henri Matisse, *Blue Nude*. There was no disguising how erotic it was. Beside it, a few feet away, *The Joy of Living*, also signed by Matisse. On that canvas there were naked people lounging everywhere painted in vibrant tones of yellow, red, pink and blue. One couple was even depicted . . . Oh, dear! Eva tried her best not to gasp.

It was at that moment that she saw him.

He gazed up at the vast canvas on the wall before him. He was a rough-looking sort. Like a hoodlum, she thought, a true shabby bohemian. He looked dangerous in his sensuality, not neat and proper like Louis. He wore a casual black corduroy jacket, black turtleneck sweater, wrinkled beige trousers, a slouchy blue cap and scuffed shoes. His thick fingers were stained with paint. He was tightly built and stocky, like a prizefighter.

And then she remembered.

It was the man from the Moulin Rouge last night. There was no mistaking those eyes; they were black as midnight and looked as though they could burn right through the painting. There was a brooding sensuality about him and she felt her body stir. He was looking at the same Matisse canvas, full of lounging nudes. To her horror, he turned sharply and caught her staring at him.

Eva's heart vaulted into her throat, and suddenly she felt foolish. Then, as if they were the only two people in the room, his lips turned up just slightly in a casual smile and he nodded in acknowledgment of her.

Time lengthened as the energy between them flared. Her imagination betrayed her and as they assessed one another, Eva thought she could almost feel his hands running down the length of her back, drawing her against him. As she watched his gaze travel downward, she knew his thoughts were mirroring hers. His eyes were angling from her neck down along her torso with the skilled appreciation of a lover. Thankfully, no one in the crowded room seemed to notice how they had captivated one another, and Louis was still back in the room with the Cubist works.

Eva bravely returned his smile. She felt so brazen! She knew well enough that she was not a grand beauty — not like the dancers at the Moulin Rouge — but this stranger looked at her with desire.

"Curious art," he casually remarked of the piece they both were observing. He spoke with an accent so thick that at first she wasn't certain what he had said.

"I don't understand it."

"Do you suppose the artist does?"

"Well, Monsieur Matisse painted it, so he must."

"What do you imagine he is trying to convey?" he asked.

"Chaos. Daring. Certainly a wild heart," she said thoughtfully. "His mind must be a frenzy."

"Along with his love life," he replied, gazing back up at the piece.

She was as intrigued as she was embarrassed as he clamped his own chin with thumb and forefinger and she, too, looked back at the canvas with a restrained smile.

"What if it is his soul that has control of him when he paints, and not his mind at all?"

She couldn't quite imagine what he meant and considered for a moment how to reply. "I just don't see why he wouldn't paint pictures like everyone else. Even like Toulouse-Lautrec did, or Monsieur Cézanne. They were innovative, and yet they were masters."

"Not when they were alive, that's for certain.

"Perhaps Monsieur Matisse craves the freedom to be defiant about how he sees the world."

"How do you mean?"

"Perhaps he wishes to paint objects as he *thinks* or feels them, not as everyone else *sees* them."

Suddenly she understood what he was saying. It was the very reason why she had run away from Vincennes, because she wanted the freedom to see the world differently than her parents did. Because she wanted to *feel.* She wanted to be like Apollinaire's Gypsy.

"It is a terrible thing to be swallowed up by the world and be forced to see it as others do," Eva finally said as their eyes met again. "Not to do what one feels."

"I could not agree more — señorita. For many of us, conformity is impossible."

"Picasso! *¡Aquí!*" someone called, extinguishing their moment, and a young dark-haired man approached them. "You have been discovered here and there's a photographer on his way to you!"

Eva felt a warm rush as they quickly left the room. *He* was Pablo Picasso? She had just flirted with a famous artist.

Needing a breath of fresh air, she made her way outside and leaned against a white stone pillar. Their little game of seduction had overwhelmed her. As much as she always said she was not an innocent, Eva was naive and out of her league with this man.

She stood still, trying to catch her breath as her mind swam with the potent mix of excitement and uncertainty. Eva had never felt so alive as she did at that moment. It really had been the most extraordinary couple of days and she did not dare to imagine what might lay ahead.

CHAPTER 4

That mysterious, spirited young woman from the museum had captured Picasso's imagination and he could not get her out of his mind. Since the Salon des Indépendants two days ago, he had become obsessed with her. He had not thought to ask her name, but her face and small frame were as deeply etched into his mind now as if he had already had her in his bed. Or painted her.

He had stood there staring at her, and as she looked back at him with those guileless blue eyes and such a rosebud of a mouth, he had wanted to devour her.

But he must stop this. He was not a single man. He loved Fernande, and he was trying to remain faithful to her. And anyway, that girl was not his type. Fernande was statuesque and elegant, with her mythic beauty and luxuriant mane of flaming auburn hair. She was a woman who commanded every room she entered and possessed every man's ardor. Voluptuous, worldly.

That little nymph was none of those things.

It made him smile to think how deliciously awkward the encounter at the exhibition had been. She was clearly not a sophisticated girl. By the look of her simple dress, she was probably from the countryside. Her eyes that flickered at him in the open light of the vast gallery were as bright and unassuming as a blue September sky. How refreshing simplicity did seem to him in the midst of the complicated world he lived in with Fernande. At the moment, he was questioning everything in his life.

Picasso stood barefoot and shirtless — as he always did when he worked. He stared blankly at the unfinished painting on his easel, the scent of wet paint and turpentine filling the air.

Fanny Tellier lay naked before him, posing on the bed beside his easel. She was a professional artist's model and she had not moved for the better part of an hour. The painting should have been finished by now with such a compliant subject, but he could not stop thinking of the girl. He had felt sullen and unproductive for weeks, and this new distraction was not helping matters.

What a good thing that his abstract style

hid the things he was really painting because today that girl was working her way into every brushstroke.

Cubism made him the master, with the power to represent people and objects as the sum total of their parts, and to place them in any order he liked. Picasso found it almost a Godlike power. He could have painted the status quo, kept on with his melancholy blue paintings, or his fascination with harlequins. That would have been far easier. He certainly knew, artistically, how to give people what they wanted. He could paint the beautiful pictures people expected like a child repeating his alphabet, and then reap the rewards. He had imitated the very best museum oils. His painting *Science and Charity* was right up there with the best of them, he thought smugly. And that he had painted at the age of fifteen. But realism had been such a hollow exercise since then. These days, he needed to explore, hunt, create, and he needed to matter to himself, not the critics.

The shadows lengthened on the wall as a slanting ray of first morning sunlight grew red, then mellowed to gold at dawn. It began to shimmer as it crept farther, slowly taking the space over, flooding the room. His candles flickered as they dwindled, wet wax pooling at their bases, and the glow still shone on the paint pots, brushes and rags. *Ma jolie femme,* he thought of the mysterious girl. How innocent she seemed, how unaware yet of the complexities of life that plagued him.

Through the windows, Picasso could see that the light over Montmartre was changing. Morning was fully breaking now. The steel-colored Paris sky was threatening rain and steadily muting the sunlight. Bathed in a shimmer of perspiration from the coal fire burning crimson beside her, Fanny finally moved her arm on the collection of pillows beneath her head. Her movement drove Picasso from the moment and frustrated him. He simply couldn't put on canvas what he felt.

"That's it for today."

"Shall we get to it, then?" she asked, rising from the bed and approaching him.

Still naked and willing, she wound her long fingers seductively across Picasso's shoulder, then down along the side of his arm. Fanny had a reputation for sleeping with her artists, and he knew that much, personally. This was not their first time. She kissed him then and he let her. For a moment, as he tasted the warmth of her mouth, he considered it. She was not all that different in form or age from the girl at the exhibition. They had similar hair and the same bright blue eyes, but his gut told him the similarities ended there. Gently, Picasso drew her hand from his arm and handed her a dressing gown.

"Not today."

"Really, Pablo?" she declared with a note of effrontery. "That's not like you at all."

"You're right, it wasn't. But it is now." He gently tied the silken sash at her waist.

"You've given up women?"

"Perhaps for a while. We shall see." He shrugged.

"Does Fernande know that?" she asked as she moved across the cluttered studio to gather her clothes.

"I haven't given her up, if that's what you mean. I owe her too much for the years of poverty I forced her to endure with me. Or so she often reminds me."

"You are staying with your mistress out of loyalty? How positively bourgeois," she said with an amused smile as she began to dress. "Only love is a reason. Other than that, dear Pablo, you are fooling yourself."

"I love Fernande very much. I always will."

"Then why isn't she the one posing for you as she used to? We're old friends, you and I. You can tell me the truth. It would probably make you feel better if you did. You've worn that nasty frown the entire time I've been here so something is clearly troubling you. Why not get it off your chest?"

"All right, the truth is I'm not sure anymore that I am meant to be with her forever."

"What has changed since the last time we spoke?"

"That's just it, I don't know for certain. We fight too often, and she seems never to have enough of my money to make her happy." He raked his hands through his hair. "I'll be thirty years old soon, and sometimes I feel like she and I want different things out of our lives. So much has changed since we met."

She tipped her head and thought for a moment. A hint of a smile turned up the corners of her mouth. "You surprise me. You're a deeper, more serious man than I thought. It's a lot different than all that puffed-up bravado. I like it."

After Fanny had dressed and put on her coat and hat, she returned to where Picasso was cleaning his paintbrushes. She was slipping on her black gloves as she approached him.

"Look, Pablo, maybe it's none of my business, but the gossip in Paris is that she's not all that loyal to you."

He smiled and pressed a kiss onto her cheek, gently refusing the bait because, in a strange way, he cared about her. "I appreciate your trying to help, but our relationship is complex. We have both been unfaithful through the years," he replied as he drew several francs from a ceramic jug on his working table where a clay pot of clean paintbrushes was sitting.

"Not that it's altogether unappealing, mind you, but you're also a complicated man, Pablo Picasso," she said with a wan smile.

"Unfortunately, my dear, you don't know the half of it," he replied as he saw her to the door, eager to have her out of his studio.

After she had gone, Picasso gazed over at the half-finished canvas, much of the paint still wet. He needed solitude — the isolation to make this piece into what it was inside his mind. There was a heaviness within him, and he stood there for a long while, basking in the silence that had been returned to him.

There had been too many voices in his head. Too much of the past.

His heart was not bound up enough by the work on his easel, and he needed it to be. But he was stuck. For Picasso to complete it, he knew he needed inspiration. What he needed was a muse.

CHAPTER 5

Saturday evening at the Moulin Rouge, Eva was busier with mending than she had been the first night. She waited with needle and thread just offstage, behind the edge of the heavy red velvet curtain, with her fingers trembling. She so very much needed to get this right.

"Be quicker about it than you were last night!" Mistinguett growled, thrusting a torn stocking at Eva as a wardrobe assistant approached them bearing a long-handled hairbrush to smooth the star's hair back into a tight mahogany wave. "What *are* you staring at, you imbecile? Sew!" she barked when Eva did not move quickly enough.

Shaken from the moment, Eva realized that she had been transfixed by the glamorous star. She hadn't noticed how openly she was staring until she caught a glimpse of Sylvette standing behind her, wearing a stricken expression. Quickly, Eva cast her own gaze downward and set back to work. It was easy enough to fix the tear, and Eva quickly offered the stocking back up to Mistinguett, who snatched it from her without a backward glance or a thank-you.

After the music began again and the actress burst onstage to thunderous applause, Eva tucked the needle and thread into the pocket of her skirt and peered out past the heavy curtain.

He hadn't been there during the first act but he was there now. Picasso sat at the front table, along with the same group of boisterous Spaniards. Tonight, however, she saw that Monsieur Oller, the barrel-chested owner of the Moulin Rouge, was seated prominently beside him. He wore a stiff black suit and bow tie, with a heavy gold watch chain over his chest, and he and Picasso were conversing intensely with each other, heads together. Eva was duly impressed, but she knew she shouldn't be surprised that the two appeared to be well acquainted.

Eva scanned the tables around him looking again for a girl who might be Picasso's companion. It occurred to her that there just may well be a Madame Picasso, and she cringed at the thought. She realized then that she knew so little about him other than that his strange new style of painting had set the French capital on its ear. He was a bohemian renegade, and he was the talk of the town. Although there were several young women in the row behind him giggling and pointing sheepishly at the handsome young man, there was no woman seated prominently nearby him. Eva shook her head and smiled in self-reproach. Someone like Picasso was so far beyond her reach, even for a fantasy.

Busy with mending, Eva returned to her work, and by the time she managed to steal another glance, Picasso and his band of friends were gone.

Near midnight, after the show was over and they had returned to their room, Sylvette brushed out her long hair and sighed. Eva lay back against the pillow wearing her mother's bright yellow kimono, the only bit of her mother she had brought away from Vincennes. She was watching the nightly ritual and thinking about the evening.

"She will have me fired, too, won't she?" Eva asked, speaking of Mistinguett.

The fear and the possibility had been on her mind all day.

Sylvette stopped brushing her hair and glanced at Eva through the mirror's reflection. "Not if she feels loyalty to you."

"How on earth am I going to accomplish that?"

"A gift, perhaps?"

"I have nothing someone like her would value."

"Where did you get that kimono?"

"My mother brought it with her from Poland. Her own mother made it."

Sylvette turned around on the stool. "It really is lovely. And just the sort of exotic thing Mistinguett likes. Make her a gift of it."

"It's the only thing of my mother's I have with me." Eva again felt the swell of betrayal toward her parents. The days she had spent with them — the good ones, and far fewer bad — seemed sharper now in her mind since she no longer had them in her life. From her mother, she had taken a kimono, and from her father, a pinch of his pipe tobacco that she had sewn into one of the sleeves so that when she wore it, she would be reminded of them both.

"Well, then that's a pity," Sylvette replied. "Because I can think of no other way. I suppose it comes down to whether you want to live in the past, or secure your future. You said being here in Paris meant everything to you."

"Of course it does."

"You can always make another kimono. You won't ever have another chance at a place like the Moulin Rouge."

It would not be the same, of course, but Sylvette was right. After all, it was really just a robe and Eva could not afford *not* to make an offering in order to secure her job. She was beginning to understand that maturing really did mean letting go of a great many things from one's youth, and Paris could not protect her from the reality in that.

The next afternoon, Eva and Sylvette were in the dressing room as the actresses and dancers slowly filed in past the racks of costumes and the littered makeup tables. Their faces were yet to be painted, and they were still wearing their street clothes. The girls who graced the stage at the Moulin Rouge all possessed an air of confidence, and Eva studied them with awe.

She had told Madame Léautaud she had no ambitions for the stage but of course that was not entirely true. What girl would not relish being the center of attention, adored and desired by audiences filled with handsome young men? Eva thought of Picasso and felt her cheeks warm. He fascinated her — for his celebrity, of course, but also for his bravado, and for the sensuality that seemed to pulse through him even when she saw him at a distance. She had never known anyone like him. She couldn't tell Sylvette they had briefly met. Sylvette wouldn't believe her, anyway. Besides, a man like Picasso — least of all a famous one — would never have real interest in a girl like Eva. Or so she thought. Steady, predictable Louis was the best she would likely ever have.

Poor, dear Lodwicz. Eva would never love him. Not if he were the last man on earth. If she wanted to settle for that sort of life, she could have stayed in Vincennes and married old Monsieur Fix.

"What the devil do you think you're doing in here?"

Mistinguett's harsh tone startled Eva, and the door slammed like an exclamation mark. Mistinguett stormed across the dressing room toward Eva, who had come in early to keep Sylvette company as she prepared for the show. Eva glanced up from Sylvette's makeup table at the actress who stood with a half-full glass of champagne in one hand and the bottle in the other. Sylvette's face paled as she shot to her feet.

"And what the deuce are you wearing?" Mistinguett asked, scanning Sylvette from head to toe.

Eva had brought the kimono to the Moulin Rouge that afternoon and, while they waited for the actors to arrive, Sylvette had playfully tried it on.

"It's a kimono," Sylvette volunteered sheepishly as Mistinguett poured more champagne from the bottle. "Isn't it a lovely thing? It's from the Orient. So exotic, sewn by monks! It has been in Marcelle's family for years."

"Is that true?" Mistinguett asked Eva suspiciously as she sipped from her glass.

"Of course it's true," Sylvette inserted.

"How did your family come by such exquisite fabric?" she asked as she set the bottle down, then reached out to finger the silk as though it were something precious.

"My grandfather brought it back from a trip to Osaka."

"I would love to go somewhere so enchanting." Mistinguett sighed as her lips turned up in a winsome smile — the firm wall of her hauteur slipping just slightly.

"Me, too," Eva replied, meaning it, since she had never been anywhere but here to Paris.

"May I try it on?" she asked. Her tone was beginning to sound surprisingly friendly.

"Of course!" Sylvette intervened again,

slipping off the kimono and handing it to the star.

Mistinguett slipped into the luxurious garment with the grace of a dancer, then sank into her own makeup chair. As she fingered the sleeve, she looked at Eva.

"How much would you take for it?"

"Oh, it's not for sale but —"

"Everything has a price, *chérie.* So does everyone."

"I don't feel that way," Eva bravely countered.

"You will one day, after you have been in Paris for a while . . . Martine, is it?"

"Marcelle. But my real name is Eva. Eva Gouel."

She was not certain why, but suddenly Eva felt compelled to tell the truth. Perhaps it was because she knew Mistinguett had also created a new persona. It was something they shared.

In response, Mistinguett smiled. "I changed my name, too, when I first arrived here in the city. My real name is Jeanne Bourgeois. My mother was a seamstress on the Îsle de France, but I shall deny that to my death if you tell anyone. Perhaps that is why I like you. You should think about keeping your real name. It's rather pretty. You're actually quite a lovely creature yourself, with such a delicate face. Like a little geisha." She smiled at Eva as she began to paint her own face with stage makeup. "Yes, that's it, a mysterious Osaka geisha who hides everything behind her shyness. Especially because of the kimono. Take care around here, Eva. Or Marcelle — or you'll be eaten alive."

"I shall bear that in mind." Eva smiled shyly.

"See that you do."

"Mademoiselle Mistinguett! Five minutes!" a stagehand called out past the closed door, warning of the opening act.

"You are welcome to borrow it, anytime you like, though," Eva said.

The actress slowly rose and slipped out of the kimono as artfully and elegantly as she had donned it. As they spoke further, she transformed herself into Titine, a comical stage vagabond, a character she had invented. "Perhaps in such a garment Maurice would actually notice me for a change."

They both knew she meant the handsome young singer Maurice Chevalier, who had clearly captured Mistinguett's attention, yet so far seemed to have eluded her charms.

"Besides, I don't borrow things, *chérie* — only, on occasion, other women's men. I have never found one worth keeping, anyway."

A few moments later, Mistinguett clopped onto the stage as the comical vagabond Titine, wearing mismatched boots, an overcoat and a beret. When she was gone, Eva and Sylvette glanced at each other, and Eva dared herself to take a sip from Mistinguett's champagne glass. Sylvette drank a swallow straight from the expensive bottle, then both of them broke out in peels of laughter.

It was no surprise to either girl when Mistinguett, in a swirl of diaphanous peach-colored chiffon, needed to be helped off-stage after her final number that evening. She'd clearly had far too much to drink at intermission and throughout the night. How she had managed to make it through her vagabond number and then her tango with Maurice, Sylvette and Eva could not guess.

Eva and Sylvette watched from the wings as the final cancan was being danced to raucous hoots and hollers from the crowd. They hoped they could intercept Mistinguett as she exited the stage before Madame Léautaud — or worse yet, Monsieur Oller — could see her staggering. Eva wasn't exactly certain why, but she was beginning to grow fond of the temperamental star, who was clearly more complex than she at first had seemed.

Offstage, Mistinguett sank onto the velveteen-covered divan across from her dressing table, leaned back and promptly vomited. Sylvette dove to press the actress forward, but the delicate skirt of Mistinguett's tango costume bore the brunt nonetheless.

"Pour l'amour de Dieu!" Eva cried.

"Quick, find her something else to wear!" Sylvette called out as she frantically wiped the small amount of vomit with a scarf. "Monsieur Oller always comes backstage to congratulate everyone after the performance and he usually brings guests. We could all be sacked for this!"

Eva felt a mounting panic. She couldn't lose this job, not when she'd only just gotten it.

"Grab your kimono while I get her out of the costume! And shake some perfume on it to block that horrendous odor!"

Mistinguett was moaning and had seemed for a moment not to know where she was.

"I need more champagne," she mumbled.

"What you need is a *café* and a bath," Sylvette snapped. "Eva, go tell the stagehand to bring a *café* as quickly as he can! In the meantime, I'll help her change."

Eva ran off and returned a few minutes later bearing a cup of coffee. Mistinguett was sitting more alertly and wearing Eva's yellow kimono. The fabric draped around her body in waves and fit her far better than it ever had Eva. She felt her heart squeeze with longing and regret for all she had given up in a life with her family, and now, at this awkward moment, she dearly missed her mother especially.

"Marcelle, can the costume be cleaned? It's such delicate chiffon," Mistinguett asked sadly as she rubbed her temple.

"I am a seamstress, not a laundress."

"Handiwork is handiwork," she snapped back uncharitably as panic took control.

Eva knew she could clean it since her mother had patiently taught her that a combination of baking soda and French Javelle water would work even on the most delicate fabric. Tears pricked the backs of her eyes at the memory. But she knew she deserved to feel sad. Eva certainly no longer deserved her family's love for the way she had left them. Perhaps she could make a difference that would somehow begin to make amends. "I will have it good as new for the show tomorrow," she promised as Mistinguett sipped from the demitasse of coffee, her pale face brightening slowly.

"You are a wonder, Eva. I'm sorry I misjudged you. All right, I've said it," Mistinguett murmured just as the dressing room door burst open.

Wreathed in a plume of cigar smoke, a group of young, dark-haired men strode in led by the stout, white-haired Joseph Oller, clenching a cigar between his teeth. Though the owner's presence was predictable after the show, tonight the girls were all a bit startled by it. Eva and Sylvette stepped back as Mistinguett rose from her divan. The length of the yellow kimono fell around her like a pool of water, hugging the ample curves of her tall willowy frame.

"I brought a few gentlemen I would like you to meet. Mistinguett, may I present the noted poet Guillaume Apollinaire, his friend Ramón Pichot, and *this* is the man of the moment here in Paris, the artist Pablo Picasso."

Eva felt a jolt of surprise seeing him. Standing at the back of the room, she was hidden by the piles of costume pieces, shoes and hats. Nevertheless, she felt a tremor surge through her and she reached out her hands behind herself to clutch a dressing table for support. It wouldn't do at all to go weak-kneed now.

86

Picasso was as alluring as she remembered, and in the evening's buttery-rich gaslight, he appeared even more exotic with those great coal-black eyes above a cleverly quirked half smile.

Unlike the last time she had seen him, tonight Picasso looked every bit the confident and celebrated artist. He was wearing neatly creased black trousers, a black sweater that seemed to hug his tight chest and broad back and well-polished black shoes. A forelock of hair that fell untamed onto his forehead was the single element that hinted at what his dark eyes promised.

"Monsieur Picasso, it is a delight," Mistinguett said flirtatiously.

As she extended a feathery hand to him, the elegant sleeve of the kimono slipped back from her wrist revealing her slim, pale forearm. Eva did not believe anyone had a right to be quite so beautiful.

"What the devil have you got on?" Oller huffed with exaggerated indignation. "You don't receive gentlemen in a dressing gown like that! Monsieur Picasso, Monsieur Apollinaire, Monsieur Pichot, my apologies. Apparently, my star here —"

"I was fitting her new costume," Eva blurted, hearing her own voice tumble out as though it had come from someone else.

An awkward silence pulsed through the group as Oller scowled at her. "A costume? *That?*"

"Yes, for a geisha number I'm working on," Mistinguett responded with a believable smile, retrieving the moment.

Eva felt her face flush as she stepped back, bumping into the dressing table. She heard the bottles clatter behind her and gripped the top of the table again to steady them. She felt as though she would collapse from embarrassment.

"That is definitely creative," Oller at last proclaimed. He clenched the cigar in his teeth more tightly and his smile lengthened.

Finally across the room, Eva's gaze met Picasso's.

As the chatter about the geisha act faded to the background, Eva watched Picasso close the distance between them.

"So we meet again," he said with a seductive half smile. She felt her body weaken. "Clearly, it is fate."

"But we have not really met, have we?"

"It was my great mistake not to have asked your name the last time."

"I am Marcelle."

"And I am Picasso."

"Yes, I know," she said, smiling awkwardly at her own response.

"But did you *know* also, mademoiselle, that I am going to paint you?"

"Are you?" she asked as the others continued to talk and laugh, which helped to shelter their quiet conversation. Eva had been thrown off balance by his bold declaration and she was doing her best to hide that fact.

"Oh, most definitely."

"And when might that be, Monsieur Picasso?" She bit back a soft laugh, suddenly enjoying their flirtation.

"Tonight, if you shall permit me," he answered. "I am too inspired by your beauty to wait any longer than that."

Eva caught a glimpse then of the very tall man beyond Picasso who had been introduced as Guillaume Apollinaire — a man she had always wanted to meet because of his evocative poetry. But at the moment there really was no one in the room but Pablo Picasso — even if his advances sounded like lines from a penny novella.

"So then tell me, is Marcelle your real name, or just the one you use in Paris?" Picasso asked her beneath the chatter of the others around them. "So many people I meet here want to be someone different."

His magnificent Spanish accent and his potent gaze had swiftly shut down all of her defenses. How could he have guessed?

"I haven't quite decided that yet," she answered, trying her best to sound nonchalant.

"Care is good. Caution, less so."

"You speak now only of names when you speak of caution?" she asked coyly.

"I speak of whatever moves you not to take too much care with me, mademoiselle," he said huskily. "Perhaps I should have asked your given name."

Saints be preserved, but he was quick with a parry! Clever, forthright *and* handsome. She was not at all certain she could keep up but it was exciting to try. Especially with those huge black eyes seizing all of her attention and making her blush.

"If you must know, it's Eva — a most unglamorous Eva Céleste Gouel," she confessed.

Picasso gently placed a hand at the low point of her back. No one in the room noticed the gesture, which made the moment even more deliciously intimate.

"When I slip out of the dressing room, follow me a moment later," he said matter-of-factly in a way that made it beyond her power to object. She felt herself grow excited by the danger of his request.

It seemed only a moment later that Picasso

90

was clutching her hand tightly and they were running together like children through the lamplit streets up toward the foot of Montmartre, the glorious vista of Paris and all of the city lights shining brightly behind them.

Laughing and holding hands, they trudged up the many steep steps of the rue Foyatier. Then they hurried across the rue Lepic and down the cobblestoned rue Ravignan toward the artist's enclave at the Bateau-Lavoir.

Picasso squeezed Eva's hand when they finally arrived at the ramshackle building in the center of a sloping square, lush with rustling chestnut trees. She knew this shabby old place, with its sagging roof full of filthy glass skylights, was a haven to impoverished painters, models and thieves. She and Louis had passed by it many times on their way to Au Lapin Agile or la Maison Rose. She had found it distinctive, too, and even a little charming, because it seemed constantly peppered with pigeons, stray cats and fat gold leaves.

There was usually a crowd of Spaniards gathered there, sitting on overturned crates and stools, one of them invariably strumming out a tune on a battered old guitar. But tonight they were alone. Only the gaslight from the streetlamps kept them company.

"You are stunning," Picasso said.

It took all of her effort not to squirm childishly beneath his potent stare. He smelled faintly of pipe tobacco, wine and the distinctive scent of his maleness. The combination was strangely intoxicating, and Eva could feel that her throat had gone dry. He looked at her with a rich expression of expectation. Yet it was not rude or arrogant. She felt the inevitability in it.

"You do know how to flatter a girl," she said. Her knees were impossibly weak. "More men in Paris really should learn how to do that."

"It is a thoroughly Spanish trait, mademoiselle, I assure you," he said as he encircled her with his arms. Then he pulled her back with him against the crumbling wall of the house, pressing himself up against her. Eva gasped as he covered her mouth with his.

A soft moan escaped his lips and Eva squeezed her eyes shut. She was fighting a dizziness that was engulfing her as they kissed, as she felt his rigid body against her wanting more. Her defenses crumbled and a moment later he was clutching her hand tightly in his own again and leading her inside the old house.

Someone was cooking in one of the studios and the strong aroma of spices was sensual and inviting. The floorboards and stairs creaked beneath their footsteps as they made their way through sounds of guitar music and chatter behind closed doors. All of it — this odd place, her innocence and desire — mixed together in her mind along with the excitement and fear of something she had never done before, disarming her. It was then, as if he sensed it, that he squeezed her hand more tightly, warm, powerful and commanding. His touch reassured her and eased the fear. Eva let him lead her the rest of the way. She wanted to be here, she reminded herself. She had come away willingly.

Picasso's studio was at the end of a corridor. He turned a doorknob and pressed back the door, which made a long, low squeal. Then he held out his arm with a gallant flourish, issuing her inside.

Eva took two steps and was stopped by the profusion of work that lay scattered before her. The room, with giant windows and peeling plaster walls, was littered with canvases, large and small ones, hanging in a riotous jumble on the walls. The color, the light and the clutter, all of it together, made her gasp. Her hand flew to her lips but not in time to stifle the sound of surprise. Picasso bit back another smile, which he meant for her to see.

"Bienvenida," he said as he closed the door behind them.

The odor of paint and turpentine in the small space was bitingly strong.

Picasso's smudged windows, full of badly painted panes, dominated the space and ushered in the silver light from a shimmering full moon. He lit an oil lamp on a table in the center of the room, illuminating the many canvases with mellow light.

Some of the works hung crookedly, some were straight — all vying for a cramped bit of space. Other canvases were propped against the walls, three- and four-deep; they were stacked on tables on top of loose pages filled with sketches. More were tossed onto the studio floor like litter, along with paint boxes, jars, squashed tubes of paint and rags. The sheer volume of work was astonishing. It seemed to Eva like a great creative explosion.

But there were finer details of the place that came into focus once Eva allowed herself to breathe in and see it all. There was a small wooden animal cage on the floor, and beside it were two roughly sculpted stone heads, perched on wooden pedestals, remarkable to her for how antiquarian they appeared. The only real piece of furniture, besides an easel, was a small iron-frame bed covered over with a pretty apple-green quilt embroidered with red roses and red fringe.

"You . . . *live* here?" she asked. She turned back to him and their eyes met.

"Once. But not any longer. Yet, it *is* still the place where my soul resides."

Not quite knowing what he meant by that — or how to react to any of this evening — Eva picked up a sketch that was lying on the table. It was boldly erotic — two women open to an animal-like male figure with a dark forelock of hair. She had never seen anything so carnal and she felt embarrassed. Picasso looked at her unfazed.

"It is a satyr and his nymphs," he said.

Eva glanced up at him, pressing back her naive shock. She could feel the hesitation in her own expression. "Is the satyr supposed to be . . . *you*?"

"If you wish."

"I don't understand."

Picasso shrugged and flashed his disarmingly sheepish smile. It was a response of equivocation. "I see life differently," he said with a charmingly casual simplicity.

"Clearly, you do."

Oh, dear, she should not be here, she thought, no matter what she had told herself earlier. This place was cold and plain and it felt wildly dangerous. Eva was suddenly terrified of her own innocence — of displeasing him. *But there must be a first time for everyone,* her conscience silently argued, and her heart raced. Her first time, here now with a great artist, would be something she would never forget. She trembled and tried her best to look mature. She felt herself being drawn into him so powerfully that she couldn't run even if she wanted to.

Eva pushed away the thoughts competing in her mind. Trying to buy time to process the moment, she focused on a stack of large canvases propped on the floor beneath the window. The collection of paintings had been done in rich shades of dark blues and grays, and the images at the center of each were absolutely haunting, gaunt, bereft characters. They were nothing at all like the charismatic, carefree man who had brought her here. Rather, they were people who all exemplified some dreadfully sad tale, and Eva could feel the human tragedy in each of them.

Eva knew nothing about art. But she knew what moved her. These were powerful images, all so raw, and very different from the Cubist works at the exhibition of a sort she was told he, too, painted. Her body reacted to the drama in these before her mind could. What did it mean that he could create in two such different styles? Was there a story? Her head throbbed with a jumble of questions and emotions and it made her feel insecure to wonder about them. Clearly there was more to Picasso than what he had allowed her so far to see.

Next in the stack of canvases was a portrait of a young, dark-haired man, clothed all in black with a glowing backdrop. His pale face, looking directly at the viewer, black eyes wide and plaintive, was rendered almost cadaverously white by the intense blue of the background. The face had a poignant sadness that drew her almost as profoundly as the women had.

"Yet like the satyr, that is me also," Picasso said, breaking the silence between them. His tone suddenly was disarmingly tentative. She felt the vulnerability in it, which was something she certainly had not expected. "Another side of me."

Such two starkly different sides of the same man, Eva thought — a confident young painter, handsome and sensual, and yet something far more vulnerable — as she compared the whimsically erotic sketch on the table with this self-portrait. Picasso waited patiently for Eva to react, but instead she looked away and returned her attention to the rest of the canvases against the wall. The final painting at the back of the large stack bore an image of a man's face and head, eyes closed, painted in profile. The figure was illuminated by the stark yellow glow from a single candle. There was a bullet wound visible at his temple.

Startled, Eva glanced back at Picasso. His wry smile had disappeared, replaced by something deeper and more somber. The anguish in his wide black eyes said that he had not wanted her to see this painting. Perhaps he had forgotten it was there.

"Who was he?" she asked cautiously.

"His name was Carlos Casagemas. We came to Paris together from Barcelona. He was my best friend . . . before he committed suicide," Picasso replied grimly as he approached her. He changed the subject by putting his hands firmly on her upper arms and clamping them tightly.

There was tremendous force in his grip. He was holding on to her with possession now, and his face was full of a brooding sensuality. Eva could no longer think as the sound of her own heart pulsing filled her ears.

Picasso released one of Eva's arms and began to slowly unbutton her white cotton blouse as he locked his gaze onto hers again. He was nothing like the boys she had known in Vincennes. Nothing at all like Louis. He pressed the full length of his body against her then as he had done outside. He breathed softly against her neck as his warm fingertips met the skin of her bare breast. He withdrew slightly and challenged her to look away from his gaze.

"I'm not an expert but the way you are staring at me right now is not how an artist properly assesses a model. I live with enough artists around me to know that much," she nervously murmured. Yet the words came as a weak refrain. "Was that not, after all, why you invited me here, to model for you?"

She tried desperately to press back her deepening arousal. She glanced at the bed in the alcove. When she turned back, Picasso closed the gap between them with a sudden, sensual kiss and Eva moved willingly into his embrace.

His fingers ran over the hard point of one nipple and then the other as he kissed her more deeply, filling her mouth with his tongue.

"I want to see all of you," he said in a throaty Spanish whisper.

Was it his fame, how shatteringly attractive he was or his surprise possession of her that was most alluring? She had not fully imagined any of this an hour ago as she had stood in the actress's dressing room. What was happening was so forbidden — surely a sin. It was certainly wrong, yet she wanted it just as much as he did. They moved together as one — still kissing, touching, bound by each other — to the little bed in the corner of the room. Their kisses grew more urgent and Eva lost sight of the paintings, of their conversation, of all rational thought. The rough need flaring through Picasso's warm lips finally took total control of her. She felt her body open to him even before either of them were bare. She was aware of the ache for him deep inside herself as he stripped off her skirt, her stockings, her camisole and her drawers, as he caressed her body, lingering skillfully on every tingling curve and rise of flesh. *Please let me be good enough for him,* she desperately thought.

He released himself from her for a moment to draw off his own clothes. Then, with moonlight shining through the window on him, he paused before her, naked and unashamed.

They did not speak further. There was no need for it.

Arched over her a moment later, yet still restrained, Picasso ran his hand along her supple body with the precision of a sculptor. His fingers were an artist's tool moving deftly along the lines and curves of her. He moved until all of her senses were wildly alive, tender and achingly sensitive. She was trembling as his fingers finally found the untouched place between her legs. As he kissed her again Eva tasted a moan of desire deep in her own throat.

In the flickering light of the oil lamp, Picasso forced Eva to lie still beneath him. With exploring kisses and languorously patient caresses, his tongue moved as his fingers had done, until desire blotted out all of her remaining sense of reason, touching her in ways she had never even known how to fantasize about.

He finally clamped his hands on her hips to mount her, and the pleasure turned to a swift sharp pain in a place deep inside her. Only then did she remember how fragile innocence was. He was rough and frenzied with his own need, unaware still, in that passionate moment, of her virginity. She tried her best to open to him as he moved, but

101

her body resisted and she arched her back as he pressed hard into her. A moment later as he groaned into her ear, the pain disappeared and she rocked with him into oblivion, forgetting everything else in the world but this dark-eyed stranger and how he had just now changed her life forever.

CHAPTER 6

"Marcelle Humbert, I tell you, you are absolutely brilliant!" Sylvette squealed dramatically after Eva tried her best to slip silently into their room early the next morning.

She was unable to think of anything but Picasso: his warmth, the way he tasted. Her skin still tingled from his caresses. Not wanting the fantasy to end, she had left Montmartre while he was still sleeping. She had gone away so swiftly before dawn because she could not have borne Picasso waking and asking her to leave. He was too famous for it to have ended otherwise.

She knew it would be better this way.

Sylvette knelt beside Eva's bed, her eyes wide with excitement. "Mistinguett is going to do a number as a geisha, and Monsieur Oller loves the idea! She thinks you are her savior after last night. She has even invited us to lunch today before the show. Can you imagine, she wants *us* to meet her friends? And all of this because of your lovely little kimono. What an impression you have made at the Moulin Rouge!"

Eva thought again of how her mother had given her that kimono, and regret seized her for a moment. *I'm sorry, Mama,* Tata, *for disappointing you both,* she thought, and her heart squeezed. It felt like a lifetime since she had seen her parents. Still, how could she turn back to them now? What would they think of her especially after what she had done last night?

Sylvette paused and looked at Eva more critically. "Where were you last night, by the way? You didn't come home. Were you downstairs with Louis, finally?"

Eva was uncertain why but she still didn't feel she could tell Sylvette the truth about Picasso. But her friend would not have believed her, anyway. She could barely believe it herself. Eva grinned coyly and sank onto the edge of her bed.

"Why you little minx, you!" Sylvette giggled, and Eva did not deny it. "So, will you join us for lunch, then? Please? You won't back out on me, will you? Mistinguett is bringing a friend apparently, and it would be so exceedingly awkward just the three of us without you."

"All right, yes, I'll be there, if it means that much to you." Eva rolled her eyes and smiled. "But only because you helped me get the job in the first place."

"Oh, splendid!" Sylvette sank back on her heels, the glow of victory shining on her pretty face. "And she really does like you now, you know. You positively saved her with that geisha idea. I never asked you how you thought of it."

"I learned to be resourceful growing up with little money," Eva replied as she slipped off her shoes and rubbed her toes, sore from the walk out of Montmartre. She hadn't wanted to take a trolley and the route was long even just from the subway stop.

"This is going to be exciting!" Sylvette steepled her hands and tucked them beneath her chin. "There's no telling what can happen with a woman like Mistinguett once she likes you and offers to take you to lunch in *her* glamorous Paris."

Eva didn't have anything suitable to wear for a luncheon with anyone important, which should have concerned her. Secretly, though, her mind was still humming with thoughts of what she and Picasso had done together, and she couldn't have cared less about dresses or hats or gloves. She was beginning now to regret having left so swiftly before she'd given him a chance to tell her if he had feelings for her, and she wondered what it would make him think of her. Was that not what loose women did, leave before dawn? He was probably accustomed to that, so many women at his feet. Of course he was. He was young, handsome and nearly famous. He had probably forgotten her already.

"Why on earth are there tears in your eyes?" Sylvette asked, bringing Eva back to the moment. "Oh, I will kill Louis if he's hurt you!"

"He didn't." Eva sniffed, brushing her eyes with the backs of her hands. She nearly added that it wasn't him at all but she thought better of that. "And I would appreciate you not mentioning it to him, either. I'm sure he would be embarrassed that I told you."

"Your secret, pretty Marcelle Humbert, is safe with me — your very dearest friend," Sylvette solemnly promised.

Eva stood, feeling the need to freshen up. Suddenly she didn't want to be reminded of what she had done. As much as she had enjoyed it, she was also a little ashamed. In spite of how dispassionate she was trying to be about it all — and how adult — at the end of the day, Eva could not let go of the reality that she had given her virginity to a virtual stranger. The little girl who still lived inside of her heart wept over her precious surrender, even as Eva smiled and laughed with Sylvette.

Perhaps he would call on her again at the Moulin Rouge. After all, there were such things as romances. But she felt vulnerable and silly for even thinking about it.

Eva gathered up her soap and a towel, getting ready to go down the hall to the bath. Before Sylvette could say anything else a knock sounded at the door. She wasn't certain why, but she hesitated a moment before she opened it. On the other side was a young deliveryman. Freckles and a driver's cap met her, along with his dutiful expression. Not many people sent deliveries to a humble place like la Ruche, she thought.

"Mademoiselle Gouel?" he asked with an adolescent lift of his heels.

There was a red leather-bound book poised before him in his hands. The title was displayed in prominent gold lettering: *Satyrs, Pan and Dionysus: Discussions in Mythology.*

She nodded and the man handed the book to her. There was no note, but she knew where it had come from. To know that he thought of her as something more than a night's dalliance filled Eva with more excitement than she knew how to process. For an instant, she hugged the book to her chest. Then she closed the door and reluctantly turned around. She knew she was beaming.

"What the devil is that?" Sylvette asked.

"Oh, nothing important. You should wear that violet-colored dress today, the one with the little pearl buttons. The fabric brings out the color of your eyes," Eva said divertingly.

"Do you really think so?"

"Absolutely. By the way, who is joining us today?"

Sylvette laid two dresses across her bed and looked at them with her hands on her hips as she answered absently. "I'm not totally certain other than that Mistinguett said her name is Fernande Olivier."

Le Dôme was the best of the four cafés on the corner of the bustling boulevards Montparnasse and Raspail. It was shaded by an elegant bower of horse chestnut trees and had a butter-yellow awning. Le Dôme was a lively spot, harboring a tangle of closely packed tables with chairs spilling out onto the sidewalk. All of it was full of such life, young Parisians chattering endlessly about politics, art and literature. The newly opened la Rotonde across the street was swiftly becoming its main rival, and there was always someone interesting among the crowds, drinking, smoking, laughing and debating. Progress and possibility was every-where.

Once, Eva had passed by and caught a glimpse of Isadora Duncan, the beautiful and famous dancer. She had been not two feet away, impossibly striking in a white turban, white dress and man's black silk necktie. Her spider-long legs were crossed and she held a cigarette poised in an ivory holder, allowing it to punctuate her thought-ful dialogue as she conversed with a group of young people collected around her.

Eva secretly craved an opportunity to be back at that café, near people like that. Fame really was so intoxicating, and she was absolutely starstruck. Just to sip an aperitif, and listen to conversations around her there, was to drink in the pure magic of this city.

Today, Eva felt almost confident in a pale blue dress, ornamented by a delicate string of seed pearls, a beige cloche hat and beige high button shoes. She walked along the boulevard toward the café with Sylvette, who was wearing the violet dress Eva had suggested. Eva had borrowed her own ensemble from a girl down the hall at la Ruche who modeled frequently for an artist named Maurice Utrillo. Fortunately, it fit Eva as if it were her own. In it, she felt for the first time prettier than her tall, willowy roommate, for this one day at least.

When Mistinguett saw them approach, she stood and waved them over. She was seated at a banquette at the back of the café, up against a wall of mirrored glass. Waiters dressed in black-and-white wearing long white aprons wove through the noisy place, full trays aloft. The other young woman with Mistinguett sat with her back to the door. From her reflection, Eva could see that she was tall and her bearing bespoke a relaxed grace that was intimidating. She wore a large hat decorated with a rose-colored ribbon and large pearl-and-garnet earrings. She glanced up but did not stand as Mistinguett embraced each of them warmly.

"Oh, isn't this delightful! These are the two girls I was telling you about who positively saved me with Monsieur Oller."

Eva saw the young woman's face now as she turned her head on a long slender neck. She was lovely with such expressive, wide, olive-colored eyes, full lush lips and long auburn hair in a smooth fall beneath her hat. She extended her own silk-gloved hand to Eva's bare one as their eyes met.

"Ah, yes, the seamstress with the kimono," she said in a strikingly seductive voice.

"I am Marcelle Humbert."

"And *I* am Madame Picasso," she said. A reserved smile slipped onto her beautiful face in the same graceful way as all of her other movements.

Eva felt her knees buckle beneath the weight of her slim legs. Her stomach seized with a wave of nausea that, for a moment, was overwhelming. The wife of Picasso's brother, she hoped. Oh, please, yes, let that be the case! Or a cousin of the artist, perhaps? But no, this woman — this Fernande Olivier — would never have spoken the title with such boastful pride if that were so. Breathless, Eva sank onto the empty chair beside Fernande as Sylvette now extended her hand to her.

"Madame Picasso, it is an honor," Sylvette gushed, wide-eyed, with dimples showing. "I have seen your husband at the Moulin Rouge. He is terribly talented. They say his work is genius."

"Indeed." Fernande nodded noncommittally as she tapped her cup with her finger.

Mistinguett's expression was more reserved suddenly, and Eva saw the two women exchange a glance. She seemed to

111

want to say something but then the waiter approached to pour the wine. Fernande leaned back in her chair.

"It's a pleasure to meet someone so resourceful," Fernande said to Eva. "I respect that in a woman. That is certainly what it takes to achieve anything worthwhile in this very competitive city."

"Merci." It was all she could manage to say. She still could not process what was happening. He was *married*? She felt like such a fool. Why hadn't she suspected? Assumed? Even the thought of it. And of course the wife of a great artist would look like this: tall, elegant, confident.

Eva hated this woman suddenly. But she hated herself more. She longed to give in to her tears and run out of the restaurant, but that would be to reveal everything, including her stupidity. He had taken more advantage of her than she had even guessed possible. Captivating or not, Pablo Picasso was a bastard! Eva drank half her glass of wine in one swallow.

"So, have you been married long?" she asked, suddenly wanting to know.

Mistinguett and Picasso's wife exchanged another glance.

"We are not *technically* married, Mademoiselle Humbert. Although, I have been

112

with him long enough, and suffered enough of his failures and his poverty, to claim the title. So, unapologetically, I have taken it."

Eva looked at Sylvette, who seemed perfectly charmed by the explanation. "We women need to claim what we want. If we don't, we will never get anything."

"We *will* be emancipated one day, after all. The suffragette movement is growing everywhere," Mistinguett agreed. "It's important to remind our men that there is no going back. It *is* the wave of the future."

Fernande sipped her wine gracefully. "Yes, well, Pablo, Monsieur Picasso, is quite a traditionalist. He's a Spaniard, you know. He prefers the old ways in spite of himself, and he fights me on all of it."

"But he's such an innovator in his art," Mistinguett pointed out. "There's not much traditional about that."

Remembering the sketch of the smiling satyr, Eva thought how true that was. He was a cad. He had deceived her and then used her. She must keep that foremost in her mind now.

"So, tell me about yourselves. Where are you from?" Fernande asked casually.

As Fernande spoke, Eva noticed that her skin was practically translucent, flawless. With her thick red hair, exotic almond-

113

shaped eyes and deeply sensual voice, she really was an uncommon presence. It was easy to see how Picasso had been attracted to her.

Who wouldn't have fallen in love with her?

They could not have been more different. Eva, with her slim shape, delicate features, wide blue eyes and glossy mahogany hair pinned tightly into waves, suddenly felt like an adolescent compared to this stunningly beautiful woman.

"I am from Vincennes originally," Eva finally managed, executing perfectly practiced Parisian French. No one would ever suspect her mother's more humble Polish origins.

"And what about you?" Fernande asked, glancing over at Sylvette. "You are in the chorus?"

"But I hope to make it more one day. I would like to become an actress."

Fernande smiled, and there was an element of the Cheshire cat about her expression. Eva felt a strange chill just before she looked down at her menu.

"I recommend the fricaseed chicken here. Although I am an absolute slave to their simple plate of Yorkshire ham, a slice of cheese, and to have it with a pint of dark beer. Those penniless days for Pablo and

114

me never do quite fully leave either of us, I'm afraid, and we both have begun to remember them rather fondly."

How could I have been so naive? Eva thought frantically, her stomach as tied in knots as her heart was. This was the man — another woman's man — to whom she had foolishly given her innocence. How could she think he might fall in love with her?

Still, lunch was cordial. Eva did her best to participate in the conversation, in order to keep above any sort of suspicion. She would have preferred to keep hating Fernande Olivier, but she found that she could not. For the most part, other than that hitch in her tone, Fernande seemed an intelligent, funny, if slightly quirky, young woman with a bit of a flair for the dramatic. By the end of lunch Eva had no difficulty seeing how Picasso — or any man — could have fallen completely, hopelessly, in love with her.

After the lunch, the women stood out on the boulevard waiting for a cab. Eva now noticed Fernande's trendsetting hobble skirt. She had seen ads for them from the Maison de Poiret. It was the height of fashion. "You really didn't need to pay," Eva said as a coal-laden cart trundled past them, along with several shiny black automobiles.

"It was my pleasure," Fernande replied. "Anyone who would risk their own employment in order to help my dear friend is certainly a friend to me."

"Sylvette and I are off to the theater for rehearsal. How about the two of you?" Mistinguett asked.

"Back to the passage Dantzig," replied Eva, not wanting Fernande to know about the humble artists' colony at la Ruche where she and Sylvette had their room.

"Same direction," said Fernande. "Please do share my cab."

There was no way she could have refused the offer. And she didn't want to, anyway. A curiosity about the young woman so different from herself but who had attracted the same man had begun to build inside of her.

It was the first time Eva would be riding in a motorcar, so she stepped tentatively onto the running board, fearing it might move suddenly and carry her away. Motorcars had always seemed rather loud and a little frightening as they chugged up and down the busy Paris boulevards. Yet they were clearly the wave of the future and she was excited to experience now what so many others already had. Even though it was a vehicle for hire, when she stepped inside, it seemed to Eva the most elegant conveyance in the world.

"You wouldn't know it to look at me now, dressed up in all this finery, but I came from the *banlieue* myself," Fernande suddenly admitted as the cab merged out into busy traffic. "When Pablo found me, I was modeling for two francs for an eight-hour day and he was a starving artist who could barely speak French. And when he did it was comical. He really seemed quite the caveman to me."

Eva looked over at her as she spoke but she didn't respond. She wouldn't have known what to say, anyway. She had never been so confused by her emotions or all that was happening.

"I'm not sure why I am telling you this," Fernande admitted, feeding the silence that had suddenly fallen between them.

"I can confess something, too." Eva was surprised at herself but she continued. "I ran away from my home."

"So did I."

"Marcelle isn't even my real name," Eva went on, feeling as though she needed to share something after Fernande had confided in her. She hoped Fernande would reveal something more about herself and Picasso. "It's Eva, Eva Gouel. I'm half Polish, half French. Not Parisian at all."

117

Fernande smiled at her and a spark of understanding flared between them. "My given name is Amélie Lang, but I have been using Fernande Olivier since the day I arrived in Paris. I use whichever name the moment dictates. I like the sound and the feel of each, for different reasons, I suppose. . . . It seems like we have quite a lot in common, you and I."

"It would seem so," Eva agreed.

When they arrived at la Ruche on the passage Dantzig, the motorcar chugged to a stop, the glass front windshield clattering. A moment later, the driver came around to open the door for her. Eva was glad that the humble beehive-shaped building was hidden behind an ivy-covered stone wall.

"Do you like the circus?" Fernande asked as Eva was exiting the car. She turned back to Fernande.

"I'm not sure. I've never been."

"You've never been to the circus? Oh, heavens, we go to the Medrano all the time. Pablo was keen on it for a while so he could paint the performers — the harlequins and clowns. He found the ragtag lot of them appealingly vulnerable, he said. For me, it's just a night's diversion, but I confess, I'm weary of it all. You would spice things up a bit if you joined our regular group."

More than you know, Eva thought as she smiled innocently at Fernande.

"Have you a gentleman you could bring along? A suitor, perhaps?"

Louis came to mind. Eva knew she could not very well agree to join Picasso and his lover without a man beside her. At the very least, Louis would give her strength to go through with such an absurd proposition. She was still angry with Picasso for deceiving her, and yet it was beyond her to decline an invitation that would permit her to see him again. And to see how he would react.

"I suppose so," she finally replied.

"Not one you're mad for, then?" Fernande asked inquisitively.

"He's only a friend, so far." Eva shrugged as the driver waited at the open car door. She knew she was batting her eyes with rather irritating frequency, but she was doing so intentionally. The theater had already taught her many things.

"Good, then, so you are open to a new suitor. Because we generally bring friends, and Monsieur Picasso and I have been trying for ages to set up our friend, Guillaume Apollinaire, who has recently separated from his lover. He would like you, you're just his type. He's something of a noted poet. You may have heard of him?"

119

"The name sounds familiar," she demurred, not wanting to sound like the outright fan she was, since that would set her at an obvious disadvantage.

"He's Polish like you, so the two of you should get on like a house on fire."

"Thank you for the invitation, Madame Picasso."

Eva nearly choked on the title, but since they had only just met that day, it seemed the appropriate way to address her until she was invited to do otherwise. She certainly couldn't call her Mademoiselle Olivier, after the stand she had made for Picasso. Fernande reached out of the cab and took Eva's hand.

"Monday evening, then. It's all settled. It will be great fun. And you must call me Fernande. All of my real friends do. I shall leave two tickets for you at the door and there will be someone to see you to our seats. Perhaps we can all go for a drink afterward."

"I look forward to it," Eva forced herself to say while she smiled as sweetly as she could. But her anticipation of the Circus Medrano was for very different reasons than Fernande ever could have thought. She looked forward to it only so that she could see Picasso again, and confront him.

120

■ ■ ■ ■

"Believe me, Fernande Olivier cares far more for the title than the man. They have grown apart. She is already married, you know, so she can never truly be Madame Picasso, but that doesn't stop her from going about posing as if she were."

Mistinguett spoke the revelation in a low gossipy tone. It was an hour before the Friday night show and they were in the dressing room. Mistinguett stood, statuesque, wearing Eva's yellow kimono for a fitting, the garment melting across her distinctive curves. Her hair was done up under a black wig, and her face was powdered and painted white, her lips made red, in a cliché imitation of a geisha. She was going to try out the new number tonight in the first act.

Something was missing however from the kimono. It lacked the dramatic flare it needed to compete with the other glittery costumes. But what? Eva silently inspected her beloved garment as she stood facing the star. She assessed the hem, and then the long, bell-shaped sleeves, remembering the small sachet of her father's pipe tobacco that she had sewn inside the cuff. She felt the familiar guilty tug at her heart.

But then she knew.

She went to a large box of old costumes, bits and pieces in a nook behind the stage, and drew out a long strip of vermilion silk she had seen there. A moment later, she held up the glittering red fabric for Mistinguett's approval.

"What if we cuff the sleeves and collar with something more dramatic like this? The contrasting fabric beneath the lights should make it look quite remarkable."

Mistinguett gave a pleased smile. "That's brilliant!"

"Thank you." Eva nodded.

"I had no idea you were a designer."

"Nor did I."

"Well, you certainly are now! Let's do it!"

Full of the heady new sensation of success, Eva dared then to change the subject. But even as she did, she was terrified to ask the question for what she feared they would discover.

"So, why is Monsieur Picasso still with Fernande if she is so contrary to his Spanish roots?"

"A great mystery in Paris, I assure you. He's had quite a reputation for some time with the ladies. And he took up a new studio in some derelict old building in Montmartre where he used to paint when he first began. They say it's to get away from Fernande's demands. Personally, I bet it's a place to take women."

"I thought she was your friend," Eva said, thinking that with friends like her, Fernande Olivier most certainly did not need enemies.

"With her growing new sphere of influence here in the city, because of him, I would be foolish *not* to be her friend," she replied. "But there is a desperation about Fernande that is off-putting, at least to me. I think she would fight to the death over anything that mattered to her. It's as if she's never quite certain if she is happy or if she's on the verge of some great tragedy."

Eva nodded in agreement, though she didn't really see Fernande as anything but confident and beautiful.

"And do be careful of Picasso," Mistinguett added as she ran the slip of red silk through her fingers. "He's broken more than a few hearts around here — pretty girls who actually thought they might have a chance against Fernande."

"I will bear that in mind," Eva replied in a tone that said such a thing were beyond the realm of possibility.

She took the kimono back from Mistinguett then and began carefully taking apart the cuffs of the sleeves, wishing that she could take apart the love affair between Picasso and Fernande just as easily, if she were given half a chance.

Eva still longed to tell Sylvette the whole story.

She almost did a number of times as she dressed for the Circus Medrano Monday evening. She had chosen the same pale blue dress she had borrowed for the luncheon with Fernande because of how confident it made her feel, and tonight she certainly needed all of the confidence she could find.

The Moulin Rouge was closed on Mondays so this was the only opportunity to attend such an event. She knew she should be excited to have been invited, but she was also nervous about seeing Picasso again.

Louis held her arm as they approached the crowd gathered in front of the circus building. Neither one of them knew quite what to expect.

"I still don't understand how you managed such an invitation," he said excitedly, taking in all of the activity and the rollicking circus music spilling out from inside.

"Well, I owed you, certainly, after you took me to the exhibition. You told me that you would be pleased to meet such a celebrated young artist as Picasso, so I thought this might be fun. Everyone in Paris talks of him."

"Of course I am pleased. I'm hoping he might be able to give me a few pointers about my own work since they say, for all of his success, he, too, had a rough go of it in the beginning."

Eva cringed inwardly at the note of desperation in his voice. Louis had painted some beautiful watercolors but his work did not come from the place of passion Picasso's did, and he certainly had nothing of the celebrity about him. Louis was a man who played at art. Picasso was a man who lived it.

Once Eva had given their names at the box office they were ushered inside by a young man dressed in a red-and-black harlequin costume. They passed a clown, a juggler and two girls in scanty dresses, each with huge bobbing feathers attached to their headdresses. Eva could tell from their expressions that only important guests were seated by a host.

Her heart began to race as they neared the front row. She spotted Picasso, Fernande and their group of friends prominently seated there. Suddenly she was not sure that she could go through with this. Her stomach squeezed into a tight knot and rocketed into her throat. Fernande stood, smiled broadly and waved to call them over.

"I'm so pleased you made it. I know you will love the show," she said, embracing Eva as if they'd known each other for years, not days. "Pablo, this is Marcelle Humbert and her friend. Both of you, may I present, Pablo Picasso."

She felt a brief spark of defiance and almost announced that they had already met, but her nerves overcame her and, beneath Picasso's bold, dark gaze, she simply nodded.

"I'm Louis Markus," Louis offered affably.

"And these are our dear friends, the very beautiful Germaine and her husband, Ramón Pichot, a wonderful artist himself," she said of the attractive young couple with them. "And of course *this* is Guillaume Apollinaire."

Apollinaire stood to greet them. He was exceedingly tall with a long heavy chin and sloping shoulders. Reading his poetry in Vincennes, Eva had always envisioned someone entirely more dashing and modest-sized. Still, he was a man with a likable aura and with the most wonderfully warm smile, she thought. He looked like a gentle giant.

"What an interesting beauty you possess,"

Apollinaire remarked with a noticeable lisp, and she could hear the familiar Polish accent behind his words. He did not seem to remember having met her backstage at the Moulin Rouge.

"Listen to nothing he says. He is a dreadful flirt, and currently on the rebound. But of course they will reconcile — like everyone else in our little group. We are all bound together for eternity," said the pretty young woman called Germaine as she extended her hand to Eva. Her hair was a similar shade to Fernande's and she had the same striking green eyes. Eva thought they could have been sisters. "It's a pleasure to meet any friend of Fernande."

"Thank you," Eva said. She glanced at Picasso then and saw that he was still staring at her. She was not certain what his strong gaze was telling her but she reveled in how awkward the situation must be for him, too. It was the only power she wielded over him and she wanted desperately to enjoy it. Was that not what a worldly woman did in a situation like this?

"Oh, it's starting! Monsieur Markus, come sit beside me. Pablo loves to chatter on about all of the acts, and I, of course, have heard it all before," Fernande instructed as if she were directing servants at a dinner party. "I'm told you're a painter. Louis Markus, hmm. Did you ever consider changing your name? If you're going to be a great artist in Paris, you really should be called something far more grand and memorable."

Eva heard him chuckle since he had changed it once already. Louis Markus had been a vast improvement by Parisian standards. "Have you anything in mind?"

"Not yet, but I will," Fernande announced.

Eva sank awkwardly into the only seat left open, the one beside Picasso. There was a railing right in front of them and the scent of sawdust and manure was disarmingly strong. A trumpet sounded, announcing the beginning of the show, and Picasso leaned in close to Eva.

"We really must stop meeting like this," he said softly into her ear.

"I'd be happy to accommodate you if you would kindly stop cropping up everywhere."

Fernande was happily chatting with Louis and pointing at the elephants, who were lumbering out into the center ring to great fanfare.

"That was unwarranted."

"Was it?" Eva asked curtly, holding fast to her hauteur.

"There's not a day this week I have not thought of you."

"I'm sure Madame Picasso would not appreciate knowing that."

"I have no wife."

She cast a wary glance at Fernande. "She calls herself that so it is the same as if you did."

"Perhaps that's true," he conceded with an uncomfortable shrug. Two great gray elephants in red-and-gold collars were paraded in front of them then by a man in a red coat and black top hat. He snapped a huge bullwhip. "I swear to you, when we met I had no intention of deceiving you."

Eva could hear a slight hitch of regret layered beneath his whispered words.

"Once the milk is spilled it is spilled."

There was a silence between them as the ringmaster bellowed in his loud, showy baritone. Picasso washed a hand over his face. He drew in a breath, exhaled, then looked out into the sawdust-covered center ring.

"I would not have expected such a harsh tone in your words."

She stiffened, looking as well to the center ring and the two scantily clad female performers with feathered headdresses who had come out to ride the elephants. "They are

129

not merely words, *monsieur.* The tone cannot be helped because they are the thoughts of my heart, meager and naive though they may well be to someone like you."

"They touch me. *You* touch me. In a way I have not felt in a very long time."

"And you insult *me* as we sit here in the presence of your wife."

"*Dios,* she is *not* my wife!"

"Continually making that distinction is beneath you."

"How have you any idea what is beneath me or what I am capable of?" he snapped at her.

Fernande was momentarily distracted by the rise in Picasso's tone, and she glanced over at them. Eva felt herself flush. Her heart quickened. Perhaps she was not ready for this. She had never been so confused or humiliated. If she could take that one night back, *ah, if . . .* But she knew, even as the thought whispered through her mind, that a thousand times over she would still have given herself to Picasso. It truly had been the most exciting night of her life.

Neither of them spoke again until after the circus was over and they all walked together out onto the busy boulevard de Rochechouart with the rest of the crowd. The streetlamps were lit by then, and each

130

one cast an amber cone of light through which they all passed. It was a warm evening and there were people strolling everywhere. Louis put a casual arm across Eva's shoulder as they walked onto the rue des Martyrs and she felt herself seize up at the possession behind his touch. She forced herself not to shrink from him, however, since suddenly she wanted Picasso to feel jealous.

"You should all come to the apartment for a drink," Fernande said blithely as she walked just ahead of them, linking her arm with Apollinaire. "It's such a grand place we've got now, and I do love to entertain. Did you know Pablo rented me an apartment on the boulevard de Clichy? Everyone who is anyone lives there."

"I don't think that's a good idea," said Picasso.

"Ah, the master has spoken!" Fernande snapped with a dramatic flourish. "Picasso does not *think*! Which in itself is a statement not so far from the truth."

"Easy, Fernande," Germaine warned.

Eva perked at the exchange between the two women, realizing how much better they knew Picasso.

"That's all right, perhaps another time."

"Oh, come now, Mademoiselle Humbert. There is nothing like the present! In Paris, one must seize opportunity. Pablo is a master at that. Tell them, Pablo. Tell them about being a master!"

"Stop it, Fernande," he groaned in response.

"*Con calma, mi* amigo," said Germaine's husband. Eva knew even without understanding Spanish that Picasso's friend was urging him not to make a scene, which the group had clearly been privy to more than once before.

"Spoilsport," Fernande muttered beneath her breath.

"You mustn't always bait him like that," Germaine urged her friend, and suddenly Eva wished to be anywhere but here.

It all felt so exceedingly awkward. Louis tightened his fingers around Eva's arm. Both of them could feel a battle brewing.

"Shall we not talk of how *he* baits *me*?" Fernande whispered back urgently.

"*Bait you?* I have given you everything you have ever asked for!" Picasso shouted, seemingly unleashed as he sped up to walk beside her.

"Let's calm down, everyone, before this gets out of hand," Ramón suggested, trying to ease the tension between them. "I think we are all in need of a drink."

"Brilliant idea," said Apollinaire.

132

"I'd prefer opium," Fernande said in a kittenish mewl.

"You know perfectly well *that* is not going to happen again."

"Don't be too sure what is going to happen with me, Pablo," Fernande said.

"I could say the same to you, *mi corazón,*" he shot back.

Instead of their apartment, they settled for la Closerie des Lilas on the boulevard du Montparnasse, a stylish café crowded most nights with young intellectuals. They collected at the long mahogany bar, where a group of men in white tie and tails, and women in elegant gowns, were enjoying a drink. They were likely going to or coming from the Opéra de Paris.

Picasso leaned in toward Eva. "I began the painting of you after you left," he said in a low tone, breaking the din of animated conversation and the clatter of dishes around them.

"You are wasting your time," Eva replied, refusing to look at him.

"Oh, I never do that," he countered, biting back a smile as he glanced around. "Did you like the book?"

Fernande was openly flirting with Louis now, and she seemed to Eva to be rather drunk already. "Sylvette is using it as a doorstop."

"Ah, Sylvette."

"Have you seduced her, as well?" Eva asked baitingly just as Apollinaire approach them.

"I'm told you like my work," he said affably as he barged between them as everyone was doing with one another in the crowd.

"I do."

"Any poem in particular?"

" *'We knew very well that we were damned, / But hope of love along the way / Made both of us think / Of what the Gypsy did prophesy.'* That one has always spoken to me the most."

Eva saw a spark of jealousy flare in Picasso's eyes and she reveled in it.

"You memorized it?"

"Several of them, actually. *'I have picked this sprig of heather. / Autumn has ended, you do remember. / Never on this earth shall we meet again. / Scent of time, sprig of heather / Remember always, I wait for you forever.'* "

"I'm duly impressed, mademoiselle."

"Apo, go see if our table is ready yet," Picasso grumbled with an authoritative air. He seemed to be completely ignoring Fernande, and what was happening between her and Louis, half a bar's length away.

134

"I must see you again. You must allow me to paint you."

"Sit for you, like last time? Oh, I think not."

"Was it really so bad between us, Mademoiselle Gouel?" Picasso pressed as he leaned in close enough that she could feel the warm, primal attraction between them, and his breath near her throat.

Eva drew up her wineglass and took a sip. When she realized her hand was shaking, she slowly set the glass back down on the bar, hoping he had not seen it.

"I certainly didn't know you were living with someone," she said.

"And I didn't know you were such an innocent to the ways of the world. So we each have had the other at a disadvantage."

She never expected him to be so clever, or so disarming — particularly now in a crowd of people in which his lover was mere steps away. Eva might be out of her league with him but she was just angry enough not to submit to his artful ploys again.

"Forgive me, I don't mean to toy with you," Picasso said as he trapped her fingers in his own beneath the bar. "Only say you'll allow me to see you again."

"And Madame Picasso?"

"Fernande has a new lover, as it turns out,

a strapping young German boy. My friends think I don't know. They are trying to protect me so that I will keep painting. Anything to keep the peace, and keep the money rolling in. But I know."

"It is all just too dangerous for me," Eva shook her head. "I really cannot get caught up into this."

"Alas, it seems to me, *mi belleza,* that you already are."

When their table was finally ready, Apollinaire insisted that Eva sit beside him so that they might speak further of poetry and the poets she liked. Then, in turn, he would reveal how he had come to write some of his own intentionally cryptic, often gritty, verses. It was such a joy, he said, to speak to anyone who respected the art. Picasso sat across from her at the table between Germaine and Ramón. Throughout dinner, in spite of their distance, Picasso's gaze never strayed far from Eva. She could feel it even as Apollinaire chattered on about poetry and drugs.

"Do you not ever write about love?" she asked as they were served a course of terrine.

"I've never been in love. Only lust." He sighed. "And I make a point only to write what I know."

"Seems prudent. I don't think I have been, either." Eva chuckled, knowing she hadn't.

"So Fernande tells me you, too, are from Poland, Mademoiselle Humbert?"

"My parents met there. My father is French, my mother Polish. We lived there only when I was a small child, until my father brought us all back to live in France."

He really was surprisingly easy to talk with for someone whose work she had so long admired. "My real name is Eva Gouel, but I'm putting it aside for now to see what else is out there for a Parisian girl who goes by the name Marcelle Humbert."

"Ah, yes. That *is* much more Parisian. Not clearly quite so authentic, though, for your lovely Polish smile. I'm really the very unpoetic Wilhelm Kostrowicki, but, as a fellow Pole, I will trust you not to spread that around." He chuckled.

"Fernande told me she, too, has called herself many different things here in the city."

"Including Madame Picasso."

"You don't approve of her calling herself that?" Eva asked.

"I wouldn't dare say so if I didn't. Fernande Olivier is a force with which to be reckoned. Certainly not one to be crossed."

And into the mix suddenly came Fernande's lovely voice from across the table. She was telling Louis that she had come up with a name for him and that after tonight he must be known in Paris as *Marcoussis*. That, she decreed, was a wonderfully artistic name that was sure to bring him luck.

"I will consider myself warned," Eva said to Apollinaire.

"But you are her new friend, so there is nothing in the world to worry about," he said with a throaty chuckle, and he lifted up his knife and fork. "As long as she likes you."

CHAPTER 7

"Why, Pablo Diego Ruiz y Picasso, what the devil has gotten into you? I'll be damned if you aren't stone drunk!" Max Jacob chuckled as he stepped back from the open door of his brick apartment building on the boulevard Barbès.

"Not drunk enough," Picasso grunted as motorcars and carriages moved past in the street behind him. His eyes were bloodshot and unfocused. "Where's your wine?"

"Haven't got any, I'm afraid, ol' chum. Sound familiar?" Max quipped tauntingly. He never missed a chance with his old friend to give as good as he got. He had given Picasso the first roof over his head here in Paris, lent him a few centimes when he needed it and bought him food. Max felt that gave him license that few others had.

"Where's your ether, then? I *know* you've got that," Picasso slurred.

"Now what kind of a friend would I be if

I told you?" Max put a hand on his arm as Picasso lunged for the dresser drawers. "I've gone cold turkey this time, amigo. I woke up two days ago in front of my house in a pool of my own swill, with a stray cat licking my face. Nothing quite so poetic to set you right as that. It put me off the stuff for good. I swear it."

Max spoke it as a musing but he had battled a drug problem for years. When Picasso and Fernande had given up smoking opium two years ago, Max had gone on with a vengeance, adding ether to his ever-growing list of addictions.

"I need to speak about Fernande and, of all our friends, you're the least biased in her favor so I know you will be honest."

"You mean, I'm the one who is the least captivated by her seductive charms." Max chuckled as he closed the door.

"*Sí,* if you like."

"That may have more to do with my sexual preferences than my powers of discernment, *mon ami.* She's just never held sexual sway over me. But like everyone else, I do acknowledge her undeniable beauty."

"I'm not sure she holds that sway over me any longer, either."

Max stepped back as if he'd been struck. Then he sank into the shabby wingback chair beside his coal fireplace. "*Merde.* That's something I truly never thought I'd hear you say."

"Me, either."

Picasso washed a hand wearily over his face, and a deep mournful groan escaped from behind it. He was confused, and so tired. Certainly he was frustrated. They were all things he loathed being for how pathetic it made him feel. Power was the only true aphrodisiac worth its while to him.

"Is Fanny Tellier modeling for you again?" Max asked suspiciously as they sat together in the quaint drawing room bountiful with decorative ferns. Heavy fringed draperies hung from the windows and books lined the walls.

"It's not her. It's no one," Picasso lied. To speak of Eva seemed a betrayal of a gentle young woman, albeit one with an alluring spark of fire.

"No, it's not her at all. It's me. The predictability of life right now, the way we've all been so wild, and will go on being wild." He sighed. "I don't know. And then there's the work. No one but Kahnweiler seems to understand my new paintings. Everyone wants a bite out of my growing success, but no one really cares for the taste of what lies beneath."

"You're twenty-nine years old, *mon ami,* hardly ready for such somber reflection and self-pity."

"Well, lately I feel quite old and just as frustrated by this path, as if I were ready for all of that."

"Good Lord, Pablo, what the devil has brought this on? Fernande has always been your muse, your great love."

"That's just it!" He held his palms out in a pleading gesture. His face quickly reddened with frustration. "What if she isn't my muse? What if it's someone else who is meant to inspire and support me? Will I be trapped in this strangling world unless I break free to claim her? *Dios mío, ayudame,* where is that ether?"

Max exhaled and shook his head. "It's the German, isn't it? Apo told her to be careful but she never listens. . . . I don't know which one of you is worse. Maybe the two of you need to get away. It's nearly summer. Why not leave Paris for a while. Go down to the South, gain some perspective again, hmm? Take your animals. You know how your little menagerie cheers you. Paint, make love. The boy will wither away."

But would his interest in Eva wither? Would he outrun that curiosity for something different that he could not chase away? Was such a thing possible now that he had become fascinated by her?

The more he thought of Eva, the more he needed to be with her again.

"Think this through carefully, Pablo. Fernande is one of us. The group won't easily accept another woman after all these years, I warn you. Come to think of it, nor shall I. Fernande might be a bit of a nuisance right now, but she's our nuisance, *mon ami,* remember that."

Chapter 8

"The bright red cuffs are just what the costume needed so the audience can follow my movements without words, which is how I plan to captivate them. Marcelle, I owe you everything," Mistinguett pronounced as she pulled Eva into a dramatic embrace before the show.

"Whoever thought our little sprite here could become a costume designer at the Moulin Rouge," Louise Balthy chimed as she rounded the door toward them.

"I didn't actually design it," Eva demurred, blushing at the praise that she wasn't accustomed to, and which she did not entirely trust. "I just enhanced it a little."

"Modesty won't get you very far in *this* city," said the chubby *comedienne.* "We all must use what we've got. For heavens sake, look at me!"

"She's absolutely right, you know. You

have certainly proven yourself to all of us," Mistinguett decreed.

"And you saved *me* with my torn stockings and drawers more than a few times these past weeks, so my loyalty knows no bounds," Louise concurred faithfully.

"I'm glad." Eva smiled. "But the creation of one costume does not a designer make. It's a bit premature to give me a lofty title like that. Especially without Madame Léautaud's approval."

"True. But you have caused everyone here to stand up and take notice. Some new title is only a matter of time," predicted Louise.

"So then, what time shall I call for you Saturday evening for Gertrude Stein's salon?" Mistinguett asked. "You are still going to accompany me, aren't you?"

Deep inside the pocket of her skirt, Eva touched the little sachet of pipe tobacco she carried with her always now, in this new place, feeling comforted by it when so many things in her life were so swiftly changing.

She knew it would be suspicious if she did not go now that she had been formally invited. She could not risk offending Mistinguett, either, so she was relieved that Louis had been invited, as well, for fear of running into Picasso there.

The whole thing would be over soon

enough. That, at least, was what she was telling herself as the show began, though she couldn't help but steal a glimpse from behind the stage curtain at the table where she had seen Picasso and his friends. Eva hated the disappointment she felt not finding him in his usual spot. There, in his place instead, was a stout, silver-haired woman wearing a prominent hat ornamented with an ostrich feather, her fan wide open and fluttering. Beside her was a man with a ginger-colored goatee who looked entirely bored.

Just as well, Eva thought with a sigh of resignation. Pursuing Picasso was like playing with fire.

She watched the geisha number from backstage, and then Louise's Spanish dance after that. It was a more serious turn for the *comedienne* as she twirled her bright fringed shawl and tipped her black bolero at the crowd to a round of thunderous applause. Surprisingly enough, there were no mishaps tonight for Eva to tend to. It was something of a relief, Eva thought as she absently fingered the little pouch inside of her pocket. Tomorrow was Saturday. It had crept up swiftly and she was not at all certain she was ready for it. She still had no idea what to wear.

146

"Something on your mind?" asked Mistinguett as Eva helped her out of her headdress and kimono at intermission.

"I don't know."

"You and Louis not getting along?"

"We're just friends, I've told you that."

"Ah, but he would like it to be more. It's written all over his face. That boy is crazy about you. But alas, I can see that the feeling is still not mutual."

Eva shook her head. "I just don't want to hurt anyone."

"The heart does have a way of getting what it desires."

"Not this time, I'm afraid." Eva sighed.

"What will you wear tomorrow to the Steins' salon?"

"I seriously have no idea," Eva managed a laugh. "I'm sure I don't have anything chic enough."

"Clearly you haven't met Gertrude! She is the epitome of avant-garde. She goes about most of the time in a loose black kaftan and open-toed sandals, like a monk! You really do have to meet her to understand."

"Will Monsieur and Madame Picasso go for certain, do you think?"

"Undoubtedly. Pablo really was Gertrude's first great friend in Paris and without her patronage, and her brother's enthusiasm

147

for the paintings, it's possible Pablo Picasso would be back in Barcelona painting on a street corner for a handful of pesetas."

Eva knew very little about Gertrude Stein other than that she was a wealthy American, and enormously influential here in Paris. She had never actually met an American before but she had seen them from time to time around the city, pointing and chattering — most of them dressed a little too garishly for her taste. But everyone said the Steins were different. Their love of art and culture bordered on faithful obsession. Eva loved the idea of obsession for the intensity behind it. The question was, could she ever have an obsession — one that would not entirely consume her, like the one that felt, at the moment, far too close to doing just that?

The large studio on the rue de Fleurus was already packed with guests by the time they arrived. The whitewashed walls were cluttered with art and the room, crowded with heavy baronial mahogany furnishings, was blue with cigarette smoke. Mistinguett was warmly received by the man tending the door and Eva and Louis were ushered in along with her, past a crowd of American tourists waiting to get inside. She could feel

Louis's spine stiffen with pride as he clutched her hand and they moved past the crowd. Her own heart was racing, although for a much different reason. She warned herself not to look around too obviously so as not to appear a complete bourgeoise.

Once they were inside, Eva drank in the moment, not wanting to forget it. She saw Apollinaire and an animated Sarah Bernhardt arguing at a large table in the center of the room. From the posters around Paris, Eva would know the diva anywhere. She wore a bright green dress with puffed sleeves, and had hair as wild as her reputation.

Someone else nearby them was reciting Verlaine with great dramatic flourishes, while another was defending the work of Baudelaire. Other guests were pointing at the art-covered walls as "Alexander's Ragtime Band," a spirited new tune by a rising young wonder called Irving Berlin, blared from an unseen Victrola.

Eva couldn't believe that she was here among the brightest of their generation — so far above the world she had left behind at home. Here, she really *could* be anything she wanted to be!

And then, as if he had simply appeared, there he was, across the room.

Picasso was seated alone in a corner, yet to her he was the center of the crowded space. He sat on an ottoman, slumped-shouldered, chin propped heavily by a fist. The wall behind him was covered in art of all shapes and sizes. Well, *this* was something new. Not the clever and charismatic artist, but at the moment a man who looked as if he wanted to be anywhere but here.

The brooding genius, she thought. She was as drawn to him as ever.

A woman approached him. She was wearing a black caftan, a chunky necklace of amber beads and sandals. Her pale brown hair was drawn away messily from her face, and she had the ruddy pink cheeks of a young woman. Gertrude Stein, of course. Mistinguett's description fit her to a T.

She sat on the ottoman beside Picasso and draped an arm over his shoulders. A moment later, Eva could see them deep in conversation.

"Thick as thieves, those two."

The voice came suddenly from behind her. Eva turned with a start.

"Leo Stein," said a slim, balding young man, by way of introducing himself. He was rocking back and forth on his heels, wearing a brown frock coat and spectacles, with only a skein of hair on top of his head. He was holding a drink and smiling affably. "I am Miss Stein's brother. And who might you be?"

"Marcelle Humbert."

"Another friend of Picasso's?"

"We are here with Mistinguett."

His smile broadened. "Ah, from the Moulin Rouge. I caught you staring at him, so I assumed. But you wouldn't be the first. Such a charming chap, our Pablo. So talented."

"And *so* married," she added with a smile of her own, forcing up a necessary spark of confidence. It felt important to her to make clear she knew Picasso was taken so he did not misinterpret. "I'm sorry if it seemed that I was staring."

Leo Stein tipped his head and looked appraising at her through his thin, gold-rimmed glasses. "Well, not really married, in the strict sense of the word. But you're right, he might as well be. There's quite a history there with those two. They fight like cats and dogs. Sometimes it seems like they want to kill each other. Everyone hears they've broken up, all very grandly, and then what do you know, he pops back in with her on his arm, as if nothing ever happened."

Eva could feel her stomach seize up at the

thought of such powerful history between the two of them. Only then did she realize Louis, beside her, was listening to the exchange. She straightened her back and relaxed her smile as she glanced over at him.

"Picasso is *married* to Mademoiselle Olivier?" Louis asked with obvious interest. "No one said a word."

"She calls herself Madame Picasso around town. I suppose she thinks she's earned the title," Leo offered. "I like her quite a lot, as it happens, so I'd be forced to agree."

"But if they're not really married, it's just for show, isn't it?" Louis asked, suddenly interested in what sounded like quite a scandal.

"I don't know about that. A mate is a mate, the law be damned," interjected a female voice with an American accent. When Eva turned around she saw a curious little woman with crow-black hair, a prominently long nose and a very unfeminine mustache.

"Eva, this is Alice Toklas," announced Leo Stein. "This is my sister's . . . companion."

"So what's your story?" Alice asked.

"My story?"

"What brought you here? There's always a story. They want to be an artist, a dancer. . . . Everyone comes here to Gertrude's collection hoping that the talent might rub off. Everyone wants something."

What I want is to take another woman's lover, was the pointed reply that moved its way into Eva's mind. But, doing war with her tongue, she refused it.

Even with her mind's ardent protest stunning her, something made Eva cast another quick glance at Picasso when Leo Stein was not looking. Picasso had risen from the ottoman and was making his way toward her through the crowd. Her heart began to slam against her ribs. His hands were shoved into the front pockets of his trousers and his huge black eyes had settled on her.

"Ah, speak of the devil," Leo said with a smirk. "Mademoiselle Humbert, this is Pablo Picasso. A year ago, I would've introduced you as a master, Pablo, but that Cubist drivel you insist on doing now has seriously made me doubt your sanity — and your talent — altogether."

"*Mi* amigo, we've been through this," Picasso acknowledged grudgingly as he nodded blandly to Eva.

"Apparently you're quite the renegade, Monsieur Picasso," she said. She managed a surprisingly confident smile, which surprised her.

"We're all a bit renegade around here,"

Alice added. "It's just that Gertrude and Leo were so fond of your earlier works, Pablo, they've taken this new phase a bit hard, I think."

Leo lifted his eyebrows and shrugged in agreement.

"Well, I've heard it said somewhere that repetition is the first nail in an artist's coffin."

"That's exactly it." Picasso smiled at Eva in agreement.

"Well, while you two admire each other's acumen, I am going to introduce Leo to Sarah Bernhardt over there. Your friend here may join me if he wishes to meet a legend in the making. That's what Sarah calls herself."

Alice gestured to Louis, who turned and followed her without needing to be asked twice.

"It's so good to see you," Picasso said quietly once the others had melted back into the crowd.

"It's good to see you, too," she replied, her heart quickening.

"I'm so sorry about everything," he said deeply. Eva could see that he meant it.

She shrugged, offering him a weak grin, feeling certain that whatever she said next was going to be childish or silly. "How often can a girl say she allowed herself to be swept away in the moment by a famous artist? Come to think of it, when it comes to you, I am probably not so rare."

"Oh, but you are. You are as rare as the sapphires I see in your eyes."

She scoffed at his wildly clichéd compliment and the tension softened between them.

"Who said that, about a nail in an artist's coffin?" he asked.

"I don't actually know, but I'm sure someone did."

"Finally, a quick-witted girl."

"My mother was the true quick wit, not me. I could never quite keep up with her."

"If you are anything like her, that would make her quite an exceptional woman."

"She is an exceptional woman," Eva agreed, and she could hear the sadness in her own voice, missing her parents more every time she thought of them.

"Your family is in Paris?" He shifted his body subtly to close the gap between them.

"Vincennes."

"They let such a beautiful young girl come to this city alone?"

"They didn't let me. I ran away. And as you can see, I wasn't all that young."

"*Dios mío,*" he said in a sincere tone.

"They were bad to you?"

"I was the one who was dreadful. I knew they would not allow me to go so I childishly left without their blessing."

"Witty, beautiful *and* determined?"

"*Selfish* would honestly be a better word to describe me."

"You musn't be so hard on yourself, *ma jolie*. Ambition is a powerful lure. I was drawn from Barcelona because of it myself. I left home ten years ago. I allowed my own mother to spend all of her savings to send me here so I could paint in the same city as the great Cézanne."

"You and Monsieur Casagemas?"

She saw a flare of pain cross his face at the mention of Picasso's friend from Barcelona who had committed suicide.

"*Sí.*"

"I'm sure by now you have more than repaid your mother with your success," she added, eager to change the subject for his sake.

"You will do the same in time. Mistinguett told us all how it was you who saved her with your geisha costume. I saw the show last night and it was wonderful. She is greatly indebted to you."

"The debt is mine. But I didn't see you in the audience?"

He raised an eyebrow in response. The balance quickly shifted and he had regained his footing. "It is good to know you thought to look for me."

"I didn't look. I mean, not intentionally. You generally sit in the front, don't you?" she asked, hearing her own flustered tone, like an apology, as she gave too much away.

"Almost always. Except last night. We came in late."

"Well, there was a couple there I noticed, that's all."

She could feel tears prick her eyes suddenly. She hadn't expected it and she fought to press them back, but she knew Picasso saw them.

"Something has made you sad, I see."

"Just remembering my parents, that's all. I think of them so often."

"I understand very well," he said sympathetically. "My own family in Barcelona is never far from my thoughts. Have you called them to try to make amends since you've been in Paris?"

She tipped her head. She didn't understand what he meant. "Called?"

"*Sí,* on a telephone."

"I've never actually seen one," she confessed of the new invention, though it made her feel horribly uncultured to admit it.

Again, he had her at a disadvantage.

"That would be simple enough to remedy," Picasso said, taking her hand. His grip was warm and firm, a little like possession. She could not think when he touched her. "Meet me."

She glanced around nervously. If anyone here should see them! She had sacrificed so much to come to Paris, she couldn't risk it all again now. "Where?"

"As it happens, the lobby of the Hôtel le Meurice has had a telephone installed."

"As it happens," Eva repeated. "You want me to meet you at a hotel in the broad light of day?"

"To use the telephone, *sí.*" He nodded cleverly, refusing to break their gaze, which for her had now become incredibly uncomfortable. She knew that her carefree facade was melting swiftly behind desire for an unattainable man. It was causing her to panic again. She honestly didn't know whether to believe him or not. "Do you trust me so little?" he added.

"I don't trust you at all," she countered. "But I do appreciate your wanting to help. It is very kind of you."

"Of course there is a motive, *ma jolie,*" he revealed again.

Eva dearly wished he would stop calling

158

her that in French with that rich Spanish accent. She would probably do anything for him if they were alone again, and she feared letting that happen now that she knew about Fernande.

"To spend even a few moments more with you . . ."

"And what would Madame Picasso think of that?"

"She is *not* my wife, *maldita sea*!" he declared with a hint of anger.

"Yet she is *yours* in the true sense of the word." She knew she was being petulant but she had no other weapon.

"*Sí. Es verdad,*" Picasso conceded, rubbing the back of his neck as he glanced around the room, suddenly seeming to remember, too, that they were in the middle of a crowd who knew him and Fernande. "But she is no longer a happy woman in my care."

"Still, what would she think of me? Of us?"

"I am offering a kindness to a friend. Only that," he said with a growing irritation at being challenged. Eva wondered how often anyone ever challenged a powerful man like him. "Shall you telephone Vincennes or not?"

"My family has no telephone, Monsieur Picasso. They are simple people."

159

"Is your home near the post office?"

"Yes, near enough."

"Then Monsieur Pablo from Paris will request a favor."

Eva wondered if the people in Vincennes would have any idea who an artist from Paris was, no matter his fame here in the city. Yet she couldn't ignore the lure of such a rare opportunity, if he could somehow actually accomplish it for her.

"Meet me in front of the Hôtel le Meurice on the rue de Rivoli, Monday afternoon. You know the place?"

"Yes, of course I know of the *area,* but someone like me would never be able to —"

"Two o'clock," he said, cutting off her objection.

It was then that Fernande placed a hand on Picasso's shoulder. She brushed it, featherlight, yet with full possession. Eva hadn't even seen her approach. Seeing the tall, auburn-haired beauty with her expensive dress of peach-colored silk, Eva suddenly felt self-conscious.

"Ah, Pablo, here you are! Come, *chéri,* I've been defending your work again to Gertrude and Leo, but I am growing weary of the whole exercise without you. Hello, Eva. How good of you to come." She paused a moment, seeming to study her. "You know,

I don't believe I ever really noticed before what a uniquely pretty face you have. Eyes as wide as a doll's. Picasso loves distinctive features like that. They often inspire him to paint. You know, Pablo, come to think of it, you really ought to ask Eva to pose for you. You always need new models and I'm sure she could use the extra money."

Fernande's voice was like warm honey.

The only thing that stopped Eva from feeling guilty about her feelings for Picasso was that she'd seen the discord between Fernande and Picasso at the Circus Medrano, and tonight he did not seem happy at all. Perhaps Mistinguett was right, that Fernande Olivier cared more for the title Madame Picasso than she did for the man behind it.

Eva thought of every reason in the world not to go the Hôtel le Meurice on Monday. But in the end, her curiosity had won out. No matter what Picasso's motives actually were for this meeting, it was a kindness, too. She must not lose sight of that. She only hoped Picasso didn't keep a room there to which he could lure grateful young ingenues to even greater ruin. She knew, of course, that it was a distinct possibility, and it was a possibility she wasn't certain she would decline if he asked her.

Eva borrowed a dress from Sylvette, pretty yellow linen with a cinched waist and rose-colored appliquéd flowers, and she hoped it would give her confidence today. She waited nervously outside the hotel entrance beside two stone-faced doormen in red frock coats and black top hats.

Picasso came through the doors a moment later wearing a trim black suit, clean shoes and an expensive dark hat. Today he looked every bit the celebrity who belonged in a place like this. He took her hand in his and drew it to his lips.

"*Ma jolie,* you look so beautiful," he said, flashing a charming smile with just a hint of devilishness. "I'm so glad you've come."

"I wasn't certain I would."

"I know. But I'm glad you did."

"Will we not be seen, and cause people to gossip?"

She was preparing herself for however he replied. But no matter what, once she saw him again, she knew that she wanted this. She wanted *him.* She would be an adult, and face the consequences. Wasn't that why she'd come away to Paris, after all — to grow up?

"The Hôtel le Meurice is very discreet," he said, and she wondered how he knew

162

that. But she decided not to ask

He took her hand tightly in his own and led her inside the hotel. They walked across a thick Turkish carpet of ruby-and-emerald thread that ran a long path beneath a glittering crystal chandelier. Eva tried not to stare at the rich Louis XIV chairs framed in gold gilding, or the lush tapestry draperies pulled back with gold tassels. They walked past ormolu statues on marble pedestals toward a set of steps leading to a grand stone archway. She wondered if it led to Picasso's room and she felt the breathlessness of anticipation as they turned a corner into an alcove furnished with a velvet divan and a table draped with an intricate tapestry. On the table was what she knew must be a telephone — a heavy green metal box decorated with gold flourishes. The large receiver was not in the cradle but rather lying on the table beside it connected by a black cord.

Picasso looked over at her. She could see that he had placed the call before he had gone outside to meet her. The connection was already made so that she would not have to endure the awkward wait, or possibly have her hopes dashed once they had been raised. Nor could she change her mind now.

"Why are you doing this?" she asked. Her mouth had gone impossibly dry. All of the maturity that she had tried to gather this morning since she had gotten out of bed dissolved.

"I don't know. Trying, I suppose, to be a better man. Your mother is on the line, *chérie.* Pick it up. Speak with her."

The rest of her questions fell away. They didn't matter, anyway.

"It was not difficult to find the parents of Eva Gouel in a town the size of Vincennes. Go ahead," he gently urged. "Take your time. I will be down the hall when you are finished."

Tears pooled in her eyes and her heart was racing. "Now that I'm here, I don't know if I —"

"*Sí,* of course you can. She sounds like a lovely woman. But her accent is as thick as mine so it took us a while to understand each other." He smiled.

Tears fell onto Eva's face as she picked up the heavy black receiver, then glanced back at him with the hesitation of an uncertain child. She felt so much regret and fear. Leaving her parents as she had somehow seemed unforgivable in this moment.

"You will not know, *ma jolie,* until you try," he said just before he disappeared

164

around the corner and she was left alone with the receiver in her hand.

"*Allô?*"

"Oh, Eva!" said the voice on the other end of the line. *"Czy to naprawde ty?" Is it really you?*

Picasso was waiting for Eva around the corner as he told her he would be, and from his compassionate expression, she knew that her face was a mess.

"Thank you, Monsieur Picasso," she said formally in a last, halfhearted attempt to keep a distance from him, even as he drew her into a warm embrace. Her voice was still plagued by hiccups from crying as she wrapped her arms around his neck and hugged him back with gratitude.

"Monsieur Picasso is my mother's father. Surely now you feel free to call me Pablo, I hope?" he asked with a clever grin. "I'm only twenty-nine, you know, and at the moment looking at you I don't exactly feel ancient."

"At the moment, I feel no better than a silly adolescent," she confessed as she wiped her eyes and runny nose with a handkerchief she drew from a pocket in her dress. "Still, that was beyond generous of you to arrange."

"I am tempted to make it seem more difficult than it was in order to solidify your gratitude. But really, it was nothing," he said, pressing a gentle kiss onto her cheek. "Besides, I like you."

"I honestly don't know what to think," she admitted, feeling the flare of connection once again between them.

He pressed a second tender kiss onto her cheek. His lips were warm and full and they lingered there for a moment longer than she had thought they should. "Don't think. *Feel.* That is how one should live, and paint . . . and love."

"You are not free to speak to me about love."

"It is a concept. An emotion that inspires. Of course I speak of it only in the abstract," he replied in a voice that was as tender as it was seductive in its lack of truth about what he really wanted from her.

They were so close to one another, and the corridor was so quiet, that she could hear his heart beating next to her. She was aware of the rise and fall of his chest along with her own, and in that moment she knew that anything could happen.

"I thank you with all of my heart and I will forever be grateful to you," she said softly as she pulled away from him in the instant before he could kiss her. "But I need to leave now."

She turned away from him but he caught her hand. "Eva, please don't."

The charge between them flared and his dark eyes locked on hers.

"I'm sorry, Monsieur Picasso, but I really must. For both our sakes."

And she knew that much was true. She must go. But as she walked away from him then, she felt the painful longing of something deep and abiding, and she wanted to weep. Pablo Picasso was a force as powerful as a whirlwind and today she had gotten close to the glorious center of what she knew would be a perfect storm.

At his apartment on the boulevard de Clichy, Picasso glanced out the window at the treetops, drew off his hat and dark topcoat, tossed them onto a hook and heaved a weary sigh. Frika greeted him from across the parquet floor, her head bowed as she wagged her tail. When Picasso saw a puddle nearby, he knew Fernande had forgotten to take her for a walk.

He had come home with a heavy heart. He hadn't wanted to let Eva go, but he knew that he must. How little it would have taken to make her stay. Oh, those eyes. He could swim in that blue. He could paint it and be consumed by it. But he didn't deserve her enthusiasm or devotion. Even as she rejected him. He had made a life with Fernande and he was going to see that through, whatever that meant, he reminded himself. She wasn't a bad woman, only a complicated one, with more scars and traumas than he had ever been able to help her vanquish.

Ah, but you are a selfish bastard, he thought of himself as he riffled through the mail left in a pile on the mahogany hall table. Part of him wanted both women.

This mess of torn loyalty was his fault.

He saw an envelope from his agent, Kahnweiler, which undoubtedly was the contract for the sale of *Girl with a Mandolin,* for which Fanny Tellier had posed months ago. There were two letters from Barcelona. One was in his mother's lovely, sloping hand, the other was from his friend Juan Gris. He tossed the envelopes aside and picked up the newspaper, which the maid had placed neatly beneath them. Below the newspaper fold, he could see a bold headline. The American tycoon John Jacob Astor had scandalously married his teenage lover to an uproar of disapproval. *Good for you, Astor,* he thought. *Who cares what people think?* Another story revealed that the new French prime minister, Ernest Monis, was to cut short his upcoming holiday due to the worsening political crisis with Germany. A third announced that Marie Curie had just won her second Nobel prize. Now *that* was true success, he thought.

He tossed the newspaper back on top of the letters and patted Frika on top of her head.

"De nada," he said affectionately to the dog. "I'll make her clean that up. That will teach her for next time."

He walked through the rooms with their tall ceilings and grand windows that looked down onto the tree-lined boulevard. Fernande had meticulously decorated them, largely with the profit from several of his recent sales. There was a massive red-and-blue Turkish rug, a black marble mantel over the fireplace and mahogany bookcases. The wall behind the sofa was covered with the paintings and sketches of his that she particularly liked. Many were nudes, or studies of her. He had taken only the very early work back with him to his new studio at the Bateau-Lavoir.

Picasso glanced around at the ornate room, remembering their first studio. It was bare with no carpets, no chairs and only a single iron-frame bed. They'd had very little food or heat.

"Fernande?" he called out. He was suddenly glad to be home, despite the uncertainty he was feeling.

She was in their bedroom naked and sound alseep on the bed with their Siamese cat curled up beside her. Picasso had once thought Fernande's ample curves were the most glorious lines and shapes in all the world. He had been obsessed by them. He lost track of how many times he had painted and sketched her, with clothes and without, back when she had been one of the most celebrated artist's models in Paris. God, how he had loved her then.

Sensing his nearness as he drew close to her, Fernande reached up and twined her smooth arms seductively around his neck. They had been through this dance with each other so many times. Their connection swiftly reignited his longing for her. He grabbed her forearm and brought it to his lips, kissing the delicate skin. Then he stopped just inside of her wrist. *Could he go back? Could they?*

As he sank onto the bed, then arched over her, kissing her neck and shoulder, Picasso found something incredibly erotic about Fernande half-asleep like this. Her thick auburn hair, splayed out on the pillow, framed her face, her eyes still nearly closed.

Only then, as he felt the passion rising inside of him, did he turn and see the empty opium bowl on the floor beside the bed. The pipe lay beside it. Disappointment was a heavy thing, quickly snuffing out the flame of his ardor, and he fell back onto the bed beside her. Picasso realized that he had not been able to smell the sour, cloying odor of opium smoke when he first came into the apartment because he had not wanted to. A larger part of him than he realized had wanted things to work out with Fernande.

As she surrendered again to sleep, Picasso looked over at her, remembering their good days with sadness. He felt a tender rush of love, of longing and regret for her. He probably always would. A moment later, he rose, took a blanket from the end of the bed and gently covered her with it. He pressed a kiss onto her smooth cheek. Picasso then nestled beside her, holding her tightly as if somehow they could outrun the fate that both of them felt ahead. But already he knew that would be impossible.

The next morning, Picasso was sitting at the breakfast table with an open newspaper spread out in front of him when Fernande walked into the kitchen. She had awoken covered over with a blanket, the empty opium bowl still on the floor. It only took a moment for her to realize the state she had been in last night when Picasso had returned and found her.

As their cat sidled up to her calf, Fernande looked at Picasso and she felt a shiver. She pulled her dressing gown more tightly across her chest just as he looked up over his newspaper. There was tension between them. "Sleep well?" he asked.

"You said you would be out late last night."

"It's always a risk around here these days to change plans," he said dryly.

"I thought you would be gone all evening."

"I thought so, as well."

Finally, he put the paper down onto the table and looked up at her.

"Where did you get it, Fernande?" She knew he meant the opium.

"You know where."

"Damn, Max! *¡Cabrón! ¡De puta!* I'll kill him!"

"It's not his fault. I was bored. He took pity on me. You know how charmingly I can plead," she said with a tentative wide-eyed smile, the one that had long ago won his heart so completely. When he did not respond to it this time, she went to him, sank onto his lap and coiled her arms around his neck.

"Let's go away for the summer — get away from Paris, and from Max's temptations," she urged him.

"I need to be away for a while on my own."

Fernande was stunned.

"Pablo, we haven't been apart for almost four years," she said in a kittenish tone.

"I know that. But my friend Manolo from Barcelona, you remember him? He's working on sculptures in a little village called Céret. He thinks the light and the colors will inspire my work, and I need that just now. I need new inspiration."

She stood again and ran a hand through her hair, pressing it back and letting it cascade like a fire fall over her silk-covered shoulders. "It's always what *you* need, isn't it?"

"I think we need a few weeks apart, that's all. We both know that you have some unfinished business here. It might be easier to conclude it if I'm not in Paris."

She saw his eyes flicker and she almost couldn't look at him for the truth there. "He means nothing to me, Pablo. It's just our little game, you know?"

"I know. Let's give it a few weeks, though,

hmm? Then I'll send for you."

"You're not giving me much of a choice. I know that look of yours well enough."

"No, I'm not."

The crippling feeling of being abandoned returned to her with a vengeance. "Please don't go," she whispered.

Picasso stood slowly and faced her. "I need time."

"And *I* need you."

He caressed her cheek gently between his thumb and forefinger, and Fernande closed her eyes at the feel of his touch. *Don't beg,* she thought. *It never ends well.*

She wanted to weep, but there was no point in that. She would win him back, she always did, she thought as he walked out of the kitchen, and then out of their apartment, slamming the front door behind him.

■ ■ ■ ■

Part II

FAME, LOVE, BRILLIANCE

■ ■ ■ ■

I often have this dream, strange and
    profound,
Of a mysterious woman, who I love, and
    who loves me,
And who, each time, is not quite the same,
And not really different: and who loves me,
    understands me.
Because it is she alone who understands
    my true heart.

— Paul Verlaine

CHAPTER 9

Céret, July 1911

Ah, but this was God's country, Picasso thought with a pleased smile — *el país de Dios*! His friend Manolo had been right to urge him to come here to the South of France to get away from everything for a while. Céret, this unpretentious little village, was always bursting with the sweet fragrance of ripe cherries, fresh from the harvest, and noisy with the steady hum of cicadas.

It had been so long since he had been without Fernande. He was not used to a world where her pungent perfume did not linger in every room.

Sitting at an outdoor café in town, he took a heavy drag on a cigarette, letting the hot smoke invade his lungs. He loved the burn. And the freedom to smoke without Fernande's whining complaint. He did not drink enough alcohol to look forward to the effects of that, and he had given up opium early on. But this, yes, this was pleasure.

Céret was a largely Catalan village in the Pyrenean foothills, just miles from the Spanish border. Aged plane trees shaded the courtyards and cobblestone lanes. Beside him at the next table, speaking in Spanish, two old men were arguing about politics. Their accents were like music to Picasso, who cherished the sound now that he had lived for eleven years in Paris.

He glanced down at his unfinished plate of rice and pork, and took another deep pull on his cigarette. They even made an admirable Spanish *bocadillo* here, in spite of the fact that this town was in France, not Spain.

A warm summer breeze rustled the trees around him, signaling the coming intense heat of summer. Picasso intended to be gone, but this place was a slice of heaven. Hidden. Discreet. Calm.

Since he had been down here, other artistic mediums had opened back up to him, welcoming him like old friends. He was sculpting again alongside Manolo, which he had not done in years. And clay felt good to him, pliable, supple — sensual.

And he was painting differently — certainly with more abandon. His palette of colors here reflected his heart. Where Paris

178

had called up to him the grays and muted shades of brown, beige and blue of the city, here he chose vibrant colors full of light. Picasso had begun to play with shapes, as well, and after listening to a quartet out on the square late one evening, drawn by their soulful tune, he began experimenting further with musical instruments — clarinets and guitars — as subject matter. He also incorporated musical notes, which led him to newspaper clippings with words and fragments he particularly liked. It was liberating not to need a model here, or a lover, and all that went along with it.

Yes, the break here was doing him some good already, away from the traffic, the hubbub and the distraction of the city. Yet away also from Eva.

Picasso exhaled and gazed out across the rue Saint-Ferréol where an old dray was crossing. Why the devil could he not forget that girl? It had only been a month but it felt like an eternity since he had seen her. There was a quiet elegance about her, and that heady spark of fire. Frustrated, he flicked the butt of the cigarette out into the street and stood.

Trying to put her out of his mind, he walked toward the dusty lane that led to the old Capucin monastery on the edge of town. Manolo's benefactor, the wealthy young American Burty Haviland, had offered to let them both work there. It had been one of the lures that had drawn Picasso from Paris. The old stone building, with its terra-cotta roof and soaring, whitewashed walls, was stark and isolated. It was perched on a slight promontory above the town. He liked the location particularly because there were few distractions.

Being here, free of distraction from his personal life, left him free to focus solely on his work, and the people in his world who shared that same unique passion. He had not felt this inspired since his first foray into Cubism. That always brought thoughts of his friend, and fellow Cubist, Georges Braque — the only other artist who truly spoke his creative language.

Picasso had begun to think more and more of Braque in the weeks since he had been down here, and he felt his creativity at a peak. How they did argue, discuss and compare when they were together! Only a true rival could make him better, and Picasso longed for the challenge. And now that his idol, Paul Cézanne, was dead, other than Matisse, Braque was it. He was every bit as talented as Picasso, and they both knew it.

"Come to Céret," Picasso had written to Braque in a tone he knew perfectly well sounded like pleading.

But then he had never been above using any means to get what he wanted. In fact, he had been a master of it since boyhood. Long ago, he had realized that being an only son in a house full of women, and an absent father, did have its advantages. And, after all, if he was not going to have the lure of sex for a while, then he needed the powerful draw of competition to tame his ardor.

Braque had said he would come at the end of July, that he would only stay for two weeks and that he had a surprise. Picasso was not a huge fan of surprises, unless he was the one providing them.

As he neared the end of the boulevard, the quartet at the Grand Café struck up a new tune. It was Harry Fragson's wildly popular "Dernière Chanson." Before now, Picasso had not been listening, but this one sailed at him through the bristling trees. Quite to his fury, he knew it only too well. The surprise of hearing the particular words *ma jolie* from the song, when he was so far from Paris, made him instantly angry.

Ma jolie indeed. She was not *his* anything. But that was her choice.

Picasso lit another cigarette and tried not

to think of Eva.

Get here soon, Braque! he thought. *How I need the distraction!*

CHAPTER 10

Mistinguett and Maurice Chevalier were now officially an "item." The beautiful diva wasted no time in telling anyone at the Moulin Rouge who would listen that all of her good fortune was due to Eva's geisha act idea. It was currently the show's most popular number — and also it was Mistinguett's favorite act to perform. Maurice had taken notice. In addition, it was Eva who had provided her with an alibi for Monsieur Oller when she had been ill that evening. Now, several of the other performers were clambering for Eva to enhance their costumes, as well. It gave her even more panache backstage and deepened her friendship with the star.

"Just let me know how I can ever return the favor, and it's done," Mistinguett often declared, and with dramatic flair.

Eva usually nodded and smiled, unable to imagine a time when the celebrated performer could be of any real help to her. Their worlds were still so very different. For now, Eva felt it was enough that she was making a solid career for herself, and making her own way in Paris. She was favored among the cast and crew — and with Madame Léautaud — so that, at last, she might risk asking for a night off to take a brief trip home to Vincennes to finally visit her parents.

Picasso had paved the way with them, and she was grateful. The way he had facilitated her telephone call had eased the sting of his departure from Paris, and his abrupt absence from her life.

She had learned from Mistinguett that he had gone somewhere in the South of France to paint. Her sense of rejection was eased only somewhat by hearing that Fernande Olivier had not accompanied him — and that, presently, she and Picasso were estranged.

"Whatever *estranged* means when it comes to the two of them," Mistinguett had quipped with a toss of her hair as she dressed one evening for a performance.

It was the night before Eva was planning to return to Vincennes, so she was already on edge with the anticipation. The mention of anything to do with Picasso did not help matters.

"How do you mean that, precisely?" Eva asked as she darned the toe of a red silk stocking Mistinguett was to wear in the second act of the show.

The actress leaned in to the dressing room mirror. "Only that Fernande has held sway over him for more than five years now. They fight like cats and dogs, but they always seem to find their way back together."

"So, he has left her alone in Paris like this before to go and paint elsewhere?"

She turned around on her makeup stool as she fastened a pearl earring to the lobe of her ear. "That's the thing. Can you keep a secret?" She lowered her voice. "Fernande told me last week at lunch that this is the first time he hasn't wanted her to join him. It is the first time in years he has told her that he needed time apart. She was rather bereft about it all. Fernande really has taken the name Madame Picasso to heart, and I suspect she is not too eager, at this point, to surrender it."

"But if they have fallen out of love? Or perhaps Monsieur Picasso has come to care for someone else?" Eva tried to retain a disinterested tone as she kept her eyes trained on her needle and thread.

"A woman does not exist who can compete with her beauty, or her charms." Mistinguett chuckled. "If Fernande wants him back, she will get him. You've met her. You know what I mean. She will lure him back in eventually like she always does. Believe me, everyone in the group has seen her do it."

Eva felt a shiver of disdain. It was all a hornet's nest, pure and simple. Why she had allowed herself involvement in any of that she must now chalk up to an *acte de folie*. Delectible or not, she must move on from her incessant thoughts of Pablo Picasso. There was life to be had in Paris. A life that did not involve an affair with someone else's lover.

The next morning, wearing her black cotton traveling coat, a black hat and high button shoes, she boarded the subway car bound for Vincennes. Louis was by her side for support, since Sylvette was required at the Moulin Rouge for rehearsal. Better a friend than no one, Eva thought as they sat silently, listening to the rhythmic clack of the wheels over the tracks.

Eva was eager to go home now, if only for a few hours. She wanted to sit in her mother's simple kitchen again and take in all of the savory aromas, along with the sweeter memories that had helped to define her uncomplicated suburban childhood. Especially now, she needed the memory of security — things from which she once had fled.

After a while, Louis reached across the seat and took her hand, which she had not realized until then was trembling. Against every instinct she felt, Eva did not pull away. Louis was a good friend, he was a good man, and a part of her was glad he was here so that she would not have to face her return alone.

Her father was gruff at first, her mother was tearful. She welcomed Eva back into their small family home, with the faded rose wallpaper, the mismatched furniture and the curtains they had brought with them from Warsaw. Adrien Gouel sat as usual at the small kitchen table, his hand wrapped around a half-full glass of red wine, fingers tapping the base as her mother dried her tears with the end of her apron.

"So, are you back home, then, or what?" her father asked her.

He did not look up from his glass. Eva exchanged a glance with her mother, who quickly looked away. She could hear the tick from a grandfather clock beyond the kitchen.

"It's only a visit, Papa."

187

"Eva, speak to him with respect," Louis urged beneath his breath.

It occurred to her then that Paris had changed her. She was no longer the shy, obedient girl she once was. Picasso had changed her, certainly. But also, she had a career now, ambition, goals and a future, and she had done it all on her own.

Her mother had made a fragrant leg of lamb, and they all sat awkwardly around the kitchen table, small talk filling the air, punctuated by long, uncomfortable silences.

"That is a very pretty dress you're wearing," Eva's mother remarked in Polish.

The cotton dress beneath her coat was of a floral print, with small capped sleeves and a slim fabric belt at her waist.

"She designed it herself," Louis said with a note of pride. "She has already designed a costume for one of the actors, too. The others are clamoring for her help now."

"At your dance hall," Adrien Gouel growled.

"It is not just a dance hall, Papa. It is the Moulin Rouge. The place is famous."

"If they show their knickers and their backsides, then it's a dance hall."

Eva shot to her feet and tossed down her napkin onto the tabletop. Louis glanced up at her. "Nothing has changed, I see."

188

"What did you expect?" her father barked.

"Maybe a little happiness for me that I am making something of myself? I was going to wait until later to give you both this, but apparently there isn't going to *be* a later."

She drew several franc notes from a pocket in her dress, then tossed them onto the table, and left the kitchen. A moment later, her mother followed her outside onto the front porch.

"You know he is never going to change," she said to Eva.

"Well, *I* have changed. Paris has changed me in ways you cannot imagine."

"So tell me about it, then. What is it like to live in Paris? Have you met anyone famous?" her mother asked with a spark of envy Eva had never heard before, as they both gazed out across the yard and to the road beyond. It was a road that always looked to Eva as if it went nowhere.

"Several, actually," she finally replied, thinking suddenly of Picasso. "Mistinguett, too, has become a friend."

"The actress?" her mother exclaimed with a warm little smile of surprise. "I've seen her picture in the paper!"

Eva could see that she was duly impressed, which made her heart swell with pride.

189

"Yes. She had an unfortunate accident and I cleaned her costume. She has been grateful to me ever since. She even took Louis and me to Gertrude Stein's Saturday evening salon once."

"Gertrude Stein, the American art collector everyone is talking about?"

"I had no idea you knew the name, Mama." Eva smiled with a surprise of her own.

"I *do* read the papers, you know. I'm not a complete *péquenaud.*"

They both chuckled as a warm breeze stirred. The sound of bristling leaves filled the silence between them.

"I have missed you, *kochany,*" her mother said softly, switching back to Polish with the term of endearment.

"I know. I have missed you, too."

"So tell me about Pablo, the Spanish fellow I spoke with on the telephone at the post office. My goodness, that was something."

Eva was surprised at the unassuming way Picasso had identified himself to her mother, when he could have chosen to make a far more grand impression. She felt her heart squeeze. Eva caught a sideways glimpse of her mother just then as they sat beside each other out on the porch. The image was of a woman she did not want to become — but one she saw nonetheless sometimes. While her mother had grown a bit stout, she was still delicate enough to remind Eva of the lace she so patiently created from nothing. Her eyes were the same bright blue as Eva's; her mouth the same small bud. Her face, however, was marked by life's disappointments that nothing could mask.

"He's just an acquaintance who told me he knew where to find a telephone," she lied.

"So, there's nothing between you, then? Nothing for Louis to concern himself about?"

"I told you, Pablo is only an acquaintance. Besides, his mistress is very beautiful."

"His . . . *kurwa*?" She said the word in Polish, emphasizing her disdain. "You have met her?"

"Yes, Mama, at the Steins'. They're all doing that sort of thing in Paris, and a great deal more."

"Well, I'm fond of your Louis. You went all the way to the city and found a Pole, anyway. And an artist yet!"

"He does cartoons for the newspaper. He is hardly Picasso."

"Picasso?"

"A wonderful new artist on the avant-garde scene."

"*Avant-garde* is French for defying convention, I take it."

"Defying convention isn't exactly insulting, Mama."

"Then what would *you* call it? I've read about some of those artists, I'm not completely unaware, Eva. Painting naked women, squatting like animals, and I read that now some of them are painting triangles and cubes and selling such absurdities for hundreds of francs."

"If that's true, they must be smarter than the rest of us."

"Don't be petulant, Eva."

"I just look at things differently than I used to."

"Well, I, for one, am glad you have a nice Polish young man up there in the city to watch out for your health and to help you keep your head on straight around all of that debauchery."

"Louis is a grown man, he isn't a saint, Mama."

"Well, he *will* marry you, and see that you stay healthy, won't he?"

"If I wanted to marry *him,* yes, I suppose he probably would."

"Well, what the devil else would you be waiting for? You got the life in Paris you always wanted. You are mingling with celebrities now, and you have an exciting young man from the home country to share it all with."

"That's your vision of things, Mama."

"Well, there is nothing wrong with my eyesight."

Eva wanted to say that she didn't love Louis. She longed to say that she had been captivated entirely by another man — one of the famous painters who flouted convention, who was making a fortune painting cubes — but she dare not speak her heart. Not even to her own mother. Marie-Louise Gouel could not begin to understand how Paris had really changed her daughter. And besides, what she felt for Pablo Picasso was all a fantasy, anyway. And fantasies, like dreams, are private and very fragile things.

CHAPTER 11

Picasso embraced Georges Braque, and was embarrassed at his own weakness when he felt tears sting his eyes. He hated crying and stubbornly willed back the tears with a hearty cough.

"It's good to see you, amigo," Picasso said, clearing his throat.

It was then that he realized Braque was not alone. The sensation was odd, and for an instant, he felt slightly possessive — even a little jealous. The young woman stood beside him like a shadow.

"You remember Marcelle?" Braque asked with a proud smile.

Picasso cringed at the sound of that name, at the irony of it. He had met Braque's paramour before, but had forgotten that her name was Marcelle — of all the names in the world.

Must you throw everything back at me just to prove you are "God"? he thought. But of course, he remembered Marcelle now. Tall and aloof, pert and blue-eyed, with light, straight hair and a smattering of freckles across the bridge of her nose, Marcelle complemented Georges's burly, coarse appearance perfectly. Braque was a tall man, with tight, dark hair, and engaging sapphire-colored eyes. He easily could have dominated any female companion, but *she* was different.

"We're married now. I've made an honest woman of her. Which is more than can be said for your Fernande."

Picasso knew that Fernande didn't like Braque. She found him to be deliberately rough where, to her, Picasso's less-than-smooth edges were more endearing. Or so she had always told him. At least in the early days. But no matter what Fernande thought of Braque, Picasso adored being with him. He lived for their potent exchanges and debates.

"Congratulations," said Picasso as he reached out to shake Marcelle's hand. He did not think it would be right to embrace her. She was too beautiful, and the fact that her name was Marcelle was more than he could tolerate right now. Marcelle. Eva. Whatever she called herself, Picasso saw her face in his mind again then, in spite of his many attempts to chase it away. He had seduced other women, forgotten them, and he would forget this one, as well . . . if his scattered mind would only let him.

Frika lolled at his ankles now, batting her fluffy golden tail as she looked at Braque with indifference.

"I see you've brought the beast," Braque said, his curly black hair catching a glimmer of sun through the skylight.

"I always bring her. She's quite a gentle creature actually."

"So you repeatedly say."

Marcelle bent down to pat the dog's head.

"As it happens, I have another beast along."

"And *her* name?" Braque smiled.

"Your Norman sense of humor appears to be far more appealing to your wife than to me," Picasso quipped as he nodded to Marcelle. "The *she* is actually a *he,* and he is a monkey."

"You're serious — a monkey?" he repeated in French — as if Picasso's Spanish might have gotten in the way of the truth.

"I bought him from the organ grinder outside of la Rotonde. I didn't like the way he was being swatted, so in exchange I gave him a sketch I did on a napkin. I'm sure he sold it that day for far more than she was worth, but I'm not sorry. He's more entertaining than most girls, anyway."

Braque chuckled. It was such a warm, earthy sound. It always reminded Picasso of the deep, rich and abiding sounds of family. Marcelle Braque smiled, too, and Picasso saw her search for her husband's hand. The nuance made him grimace. He knew that Marcelle loved Braque, faults and all — really *loved* him. Picasso wondered if he would ever find such a love.

"Well, come on, then. Show me what you've been painting," said Braque. "I've been back to Normandy and I'm brimming with ideas!"

They spent hours after that in the whitewashed old monastery where once, in the seventeenth century, monks had been charged with restoring the Catholic faith. Now, in that same space, they poured over Picasso's canvases, comparing ideas of shapes and light. Marcelle sat silently off to the side and, from time to time, Picasso thought how sad it was that she and Fernande had never bonded in that strange, exclusive world that held the ones entrusted with the task of trying to love an artist.

Later that night, after Marcelle had gone off to bed, the two artists stood alone in the vast, candlelit studio, their words echoing as they spoke to one another. They had both drunk too much wine, smoked, laughed and argued until they could think no more. Now Picasso was weary of the pretense of trying to *be* Picasso. At the heart of it, when the creative furor had passed and the passion had died away, all he really wanted to be was Pablo Diego Ruiz y Picasso — son of the man who only ever learned to paint pigeons well, but who wanted something better for his son.

It was part of the legacy that never quite left him.

"I like your monkey," Braque said with a weary smile.

"He likes you."

"You're not with Fernande anymore, are you?"

"We've taken a break from each other."

Braque scratched his day-old whiskers, dark and patchy against his pale chin. "I heard there is a German boy."

"Word travels fast."

"Everyone wants you to be happy, Pablo."

"Everyone wants me to be a success. It is a very different thing. And so, I am a huge success."

"A happy success?"

Picasso glanced back at the wet canvas he had just painted — a guitar and a musical note. The note reminded him of the lyrics from that Harry Fragson song, *"O Manon, ma jolie"* — and thus it reminded him of Eva.

"Content, if not happy."

"You seem not even that."

"Much happens when we are apart, amigo. Look at you. You are married!"

"Take a cigar with me, will you," Braque asked as he led Picasso outside onto the gravel-covered courtyard and into a warm, wisteria-scented breeze where the cicadas sang so loudly they almost could not hear one another. There, the two artists sat in painted metal chairs and looked up at the last of the sunset as it mellowed against the horizon.

"Dígame," Braque bid him in Spanish. The phrase was one he had learned long ago from Picasso himself — one that urged his friend toward confession.

Picasso drew heavily on the cigar, preferring a cigarette. "There is another woman."

"Not a surprise," Braque answered. "Have you painted her, then?"

"I unknowingly stole her innocence."

Braque looked out at the hills and drew heavily on his cigar. There was a silence between them as the white smoke circled over his dark hair. "And Fernande in all of this?"

"I told her not to come. She believed I meant it this time and so she has left me alone."

"Was she wise to believe you?"

"*Sí,* I think she was."

"So, you actually care about this other girl?"

"At the moment I am obsessed."

"Oh, dear."

The candle lamps flickered in the moonlight. "It was all too complicated. So I left."

"Complicated and probably unwise."

"*Sí,* that, too."

"Has she a name that I am fit to know?"

"Her name is Eva but, as it happens, in Paris she calls herself Marcelle."

"*Dieu.*" Braque shook his head.

"*Sí.*"

Picasso put his face in his hands and waited for a while to say more. "I made a vow to Fernande," he finally said on a heavy sigh. "I am trying to live by it, but, *Dios mío,* it is difficult."

"You are not married. There is no binding tie."

"She calls herself Madame Picasso all through Paris."

"Wishing does not always make it so."

"And yet I can have nothing. So I left Paris, hoping the need would pass."

"Painted away, down here where there are few distractions."

"Would that it were so simple."

"This girl, Marcelle, Eva — can you truly say she is so different from all the others? You haven't exactly been faithful to Fernande in the past."

"It is the most bizarre thing, Braque. Her real name is Eve and for me it really is as if she were the first woman in the world. I feel different with her, as if I could be the first man. Rather, as if I could be a new man — different with her."

Picasso washed a hand across his face, feeling he had not adequately explained what he felt. Frika wandered out of the studio and circled around. Then she sank and made a bed at Picasso's feet.

"This is not good at all," Braque said, shaking his head.

"What the hell do I do now?"

"We paint!"

"Until when?" Picasso asked on the heels of another heavy sigh.

"Until the deepest part of it goes away. And then we begin to paint again."

They painted together after that, and compared canvases all the next day as Marcelle brought them tea and fruit, and cleared away their ashtrays. Their banter about form and structure filled the studio on the hill overlooking Céret.

The view, fronted by a sloping orchard of cherry trees, with the rooftops of the village beyond, would be a perfect subject for them both. And so it was decided. Both would paint the same scene from their own creative vision, and in the Cubist style, then at the end of the day they would open a bottle of wine and compare their labors.

At five o'clock, Picasso waited alone on the stone terrace for Braque and Marcelle to come down after their nap. Picasso liked Marcelle, but it still irritated him a bit how solicitous his artistic partner was to his new wife. It was distracting. After all, Picasso had urged him to come here to paint, not to take *la grande vacance* with his woman.

He knew full well that he was envious. What was between them was powerful. That was plain enough. But it highlighted what Picasso did not have in his own life and made him recall some of his own dalliances with women, a lifetime ago before he had any idea at all what love really meant.

He lit another cigarette and remembered the first time his father, Don José, had taken him to a brothel. He was just an adolescent at the time.

"Get it out of your system here, my son, not on girls in our neighborhood who matter. That way your art, and your reputation, remain pure," he had advised, standing tall, slim and gaunt, with his long cheeks and dark beard.

Don José's arm was slung across Pablo's slim shoulders as he introduced his son to the various whores. He had meant well.

Unfortunately for Pablo, brimming with unbridled boyhood, the experience that night did not tame his fantasies. Rather it only served to fuel his fascination and his curiosity. The next night, he sold a couple of sketches on a street corner so that he could go to the brothel on his own. Meanwhile, his little sister Conchita, who was ill, was growing sicker, and at night, beside the red glare of the coal fire, his mother made them all pray for the little girl, heightening the connection for Pablo between his own indiscretions, Conchita's health and God. It was the beginning of the guilt that had never quite left him.

Then there was that final night when Picasso stepped out into the alleyway, with the cloying scent of perfume, and the girl, still clinging to him. His older sister, Lola, had stood waiting for him, rigid, angry and heartbroken. Picasso looked up at her, ashamed. Caught in that moment as a hare in a trap.

"If you are quite finished, you must come home. Mama needs you. Conchita is worse. A pity you and Papa did not choose the same whorehouse to save me the trouble of finding you both." Bile rose up from his gut as he tasted the mix of shame, horror and grief. She slapped his head with an open hand. "You are your father's son already."

The two images fused inside his mind until they became a frightening, twisted whole — innocence and lust: his innocent little sister lying ill, and the young prostitute who had worn too much lipstick, staining his genitals a sickening red, leaving her mark as if she had branded him. After Lola had marched off, his stomach heaved and he vomited against the stone wall as brassy gold light, music and laughter poured out of the open brothel door behind him.

A strange moment followed then — one that would never leave him: the glaring images in his mind of the virgin and the whore — his lust, his loathing and ambivalence toward both.

"Well, let's go see what you've got." Braque's heady baritone jarred Picasso from his memories. Picasso jerked forward as his thoughts wound away back into the quiet dark of the past. "I have set up my canvas inside."

He heaved himself out of the chair. "Mine is over there," he said to Braque, pointing to the easel set up on the other side of the terrace. Braque ambled over and studied it as the sun began to set before them.

"*Zut! C'est une folie! Incroyable!* They are nearly identical," he proclaimed with a hoot. "Well, other than that mine has nuance, which is clearly lacking here." His face held a smirk.

"*¡Cabrón!*" Picasso grumbled as Braque draped an arm over Picasso's shoulders. "*Dios,* it is good to do this with you again." Picasso sighed.

"I like your notion of the light just there." He pointed. "The color you mixed for the rooftop here. It's quite extraordinary."

"Of course it is. I am Picasso." He bit back a smile — glad to have something else to think about.

"And *I* am Braque. We shall see whose name is most memorable one day."

"So we shall," said Picasso as he lit a fresh cigarette.

CHAPTER 12

Eva spread the dressmaker's pattern out on the floor beside her bed, smoothed it down at the crinkled corners and slowly began to trim the edges. One of the actresses, Mado Minty, had pleaded for help with a costume and at first Eva had accepted the after-hours job warily. She was happy for the extra francs, and her increasing stature with the cast members, but she was also aware that she had never actually fashioned a costume from scratch. Soon, however, her ambition strengthened her resolve to try it. She loved this new feeling of thriving on her own, of making her way without needing anyone. She still missed Picasso in her life, and the possibility of something between them. But she was grateful for this time on her own. She knew now that she would rather lose him forever than to become indolent like Fernande.

Sylvette sat propped against her headboard, filing her fingernails as Eva worked. Outside, a summer rain shower hit the window, sounding like pebbles tapping on the glass.

"What's it going to be?" Sylvette asked as she filed.

She was barefoot, wearing a violet dressing gown, her knees bent. She had just painted her toes. Her fingernails were next. Eva crouched on the floor over her crumpled pattern.

"I haven't the faintest idea." She sighed, brushing the hair away from her face with the back of her hand.

"What did you tell her?"

"I told her I would think of something."

"Oh, dear. That *is* a risk."

"My father always said, 'The greater the risk you take, the more you stand to gain.' "

Eva felt a pull at her heart as she recounted the memory of her father. The sensation surprised her. She and her father had been at odds for so long, but she felt sadness as she recalled the better times when she was just a girl. This newfound determination had definitely come from him.

"You never said how the visit went," Sylvette said as she opened a bottle of red nail polish.

It was true. Eva hadn't even spoken of the visit with Louis on the train ride back to Paris. That had been such an awkward journey. When she had arrived back at la Ruche, she had opened a little satchel her mother had pressed at her on the porch as she was about to leave. Inside were two pairs of sensible, clean underdrawers, and a dozen *pierniki,* her favorite Polish thumb-print cookies. Even now the thought brought tears to her eyes.

Eva Gouel and Marcelle Humbert were such different creatures. Now more than ever.

"My mother thinks I should marry Louis."

"You don't agree?"

Eva knew what a good man he was and she tried for a moment to consider that. "I wish I could."

"What does your father think?" Sylvette asked.

"He thinks I should come back to Vin-cennes."

"Where does that leave you and Picasso?"

Eva sat back onto her heels. The scissors fell from her hand and landed on the pattern.

"Don't tell me you thought I didn't know." Sylvette chuckled.

Eva was horrified. "Did he tell you? Or

was it Mistinguett? Oh, God. I will be a laughingstock!"

"No one said anything to me. But I see what I see. I was there that night he came into the dressing room with Monsieur Oller. I saw the two of you, and then at the Steins'. Sparks like that don't fly even on Bastille Day."

Eva felt herself blush, hot with embarrassment.

"Picasso is quite the *bon vivant*."

"I know."

"He has Fernande."

"I know that, too."

"Louis is a far safer bet."

"But I don't want Louis," she said achingly.

"What will you do?"

"He's gone now to the South. There is nothing I *can* do."

"Mistinguett says that Fernande sent Picasso a letter of contrition, and that the two of them are talking again. He answered her only yesterday and I suspect she will go to him."

The image of Picasso's face flickered brightly in her mind. The scent of nail polish in the room brought back the way his studio smelled so strongly of paint. . . . Eva remembered everything. She knew she was being naive, but it was so hard to believe that what had happened between them had meant nothing to him. She looked back down at the dressmaker's pattern.

"It's going to be a bird."

"What?"

"The costume for Mademoiselle Minty. I've decided. I will put ribbons on it, though, instead of feathers. They will move when she twirls. I've got to think of my work, not of romances that will never be. At least a costume is something I have control over."

She was resolved, even if her heart was not entirely over Picasso. Eva had been toying with the costume concept since yesterday but suddenly it fit. She had gotten the idea from the dancers at a Polish festival she had seen as a child — brightly colored ribbons moving around the dancers' thighs. Even back then somehow it had reminded her of the grace of a bird. It had all seemed so winsome and free to her then, especially paired with the lovely, spirited folk music. Surely Mado Minty would do something brilliantly creative with it when she proposed the concept as her own to Monsieur Oller, the owner, and Madame Léautaud.

If I were a bird, a real bird, Eva thought, she would soar above Paris and glide on a breeze, down to the South, and she would find Picasso. And when they saw each other, the connection would flare again, as brightly as the time he had taken her to the Bateau-Lavoir. There would be no Sylvette, no Louis and certainly no Fernande.

"You won't tell anyone, will you?" Eva urged as Sylvette finished painting the last of her fingers.

"About Picasso? Why would I? It never would have come to anything between the two of you, anyway."

"No, of course not," Eva agreed a little too quickly. As the costume idea began to further take shape in her mind, she pulled a box of ribbons from beneath her bed and began to pick out the brightest ones.

CHAPTER 13

Mona Lisa Stolen! Suspects Sought!

Picasso crumpled the newspaper, pressed it into his lap and felt the breath leave his lungs. It was miserably hot now in the South of France, which did not help. The dry, gentle breezes of spring had given way to a hot summer wind, and Picasso, Braque, Marcelle and Manolo were forced to leave the outside tables and sit inside the busy Grand Café where the overhead fans only moved the hot air around.

For a moment, like a guilty schoolboy, he thought of hiding the newspaper in order to bury the headline. As if that could make the news go away. In his breast pocket was his latest pleading missive from Fernande, but not even Fernande could understand the implications of what had happened to the famous painting. What he knew. Nobody could.

Picasso knew in his heart that Apollinaire's secretary had stolen the two Iberian heads in his studio from the Louvre. He just hadn't wanted to believe it. For a time, he had convinced himself that the heads were only similar to the Louvre statues because he wanted them.

Selfishly, he wanted to use them for his work. But now the *Mona Lisa,* too, had gone missing from the Louvre.

It was a crime of unbelievable magnitude, and if the police made that connection, too, Picasso himself, not only Apollinaire, could be implicated. His great rising star would plummet.

His career would be over. Pablo Picasso could be branded a common thief.

He shivered at the thought, remembering that the heads were still sitting out in the open, in his studio, big as life, taunting someone to find them, to implicate him. The only one with a key to that studio was Fernande, who might unknowingly let in an investigator. But he couldn't write and ask her to hide the statues. Things were too tenuous between them and he did not want her to have that kind of advantage over him. But if she were down here with him in the South, the studio would be locked — the secret safe, until he could return to hide them himself without incurring Braque's

213

suspicion over a sudden departure. Having her join him here had become a necessary evil.

"Good Lord, amigo, you look as if you have seen a ghost," Manolo said.

They sat all perspiring beneath a whirring ceiling fan.

"Perhaps I have."

He excused himself from their table and went to the bar to order a Pernod. The deep, anise flavor, sharp and biting, drew him in and calmed him. He took a second hard swallow. He was out of cigarettes and he really needed one of those, but this would have to do as a palliative.

Before now, he'd had no intention of asking Fernande to join him in Céret. The break had been restorative to him on so many levels, and he and Braque were painting feverishly, sharing and learning from one another as they always did. But as the weeks wore on, Picasso continued to miss Eva and to be consumed with thoughts of her. So much so that sending for Fernande felt disloyal to Eva. He simply had no other choice.

He hoped she was happy with Louis. No, he didn't. That was a lie.

He despised the thought of another man touching her. Needing to possess was a

Spanish trait of which he could never quite rid himself. Yes, he wanted to possess her in every possible way, and Picasso had hoped that coming here to the South of France would make his longing for her fade. But so far it had only grown more intense. Still, being implicated in a massive crime was not an option. Until the criminal was caught and the *Mona Lisa* returned to the Louvre, he would force himself to reconcile with Fernande.

"What a very odd creature," Marcelle Braque said as she and her husband watched Picasso stand at the bar, crowded with laborers in their overalls. He drank a first Pernod, then a second.

"Not odd, *mon amour*. Only an artist, like me."

"Pablo is nothing like you."

"Well, thank you, *chérie*. But you *are* biased."

"No, I mean it. He is vain and temperamental, selfish, arrogant —"

"And utterly brilliant," Braque interrupted her. "If his demons don't get in the way, I think he could become a legend."

"For his exploits, if not his paintings," Manolo quipped with a wry smile.

"*You* are the one becoming the legend,

215

my love. Picasso only takes your lead. You have subtlety of color and your use of light is something he could only dream of reproducing."

"She may be right about that, amigo." Manolo hunched his shoulders with equivocation. "He really respects your work."

"We respect one another. No one understands the journey but another artist."

Braque picked up the crumpled newspaper then and glanced at it below the fold. The ship they called *Titanic,* touted as the biggest ship ever built, was being fitted today and leaving Ireland in a few months for a dock in England. His mind ran over the story, wondering how news of a ship could have affected his friend so strongly. Then he opened the paper fully and the other headline hit him like a shot. *Mona Lisa* Stolen!

"What the devil? He's not involved, do you think?" Marcelle asked. They were both thinking how troubled Picasso had become just before crumpling the paper and bolting from his chair. Otherwise, she would not have thought to ask.

"He doesn't even relate to that sort of antiquated style. What would he use a painting like that for, anyway? Besides, he's down here with us and the *Mona Lisa* is in Paris.

216

Or at least it was."

"I'm only saying he certainly knew a dubious enough band of people up in the city to make such a thing plausible."

The three looked at one another. Then they all glanced over at Picasso, who was still standing at the bar. He was certainly a complicated young man, Braque thought. And in spite of how long he and Fernande had been together, Picasso always seemed to him somehow a bit rudderless with her, casting about rather aimlessly for something different, or someone. Picasso was the only person Braque had ever met who could seem alone in a crowded room. But although Braque would never express it, no matter how strong their friendship seemed, he thought Picasso needed someone like his own Marcelle. An even-tempered girl with her own mind to challenge him, but who would also support him. Fernande had always been an instigator. Could she have led Picasso to commit such a dark act to impress her or keep up with her demands?

He hated doubting his friend.

He glanced back at the newspaper lying on the marble table between them and he felt a shiver. As complex as Pablo Picasso was, as ambitious and secretive, Georges Braque simply could not fathom that his friend could have been involved in the theft of the *Mona Lisa.* Still, he could not help but question. Indeed, stranger things had happened.

Picasso returned to the Hôtel du Canigou alone.

He wasn't any good at writing letters, especially in French, but he knew what he had to do. He found Frika asleep on the bed when he entered his room but she began to wag her tail, and his little monkey sat in a cage by the window cleaning himself. What an impulsive thing that had been, to buy a monkey, he thought now with a chuckle. Impulsive and slightly foolish. But he had a soft spot for animals. Much of the time, he liked animals better than people.

He would write his letter because he must, and Fernande would lock up the studio. It would be far too suspicious if he went barreling back to Paris himself with he and Braque in the middle of finishing their canvases. He sat down at the little writing table beside the bed. With a sigh of resignation, he drew out a sheet of paper and began.

"Ma chère Fernande . . ."

CHAPTER 14

"I love it. It's beautiful," Mado exclaimed of the unique costume, with the multicolored ribbons displayed on the dressmaker's mannequin. Eva stood beside her, relieved. She had been working on the costume nonstop for two days.

"You know, I really had no idea whether or not you could actually pull it off."

"Nor did I." Eva smiled. Mado Minty was petite, like herself, so it had been easy, once she began, to fashion a costume that would complement her shape.

"Well, you did it in spades!"

Mado, whose real name was Madeleine, picked up her handbag, drew out a handful of francs and handed them to Eva. Eva was sure it was more money than she had ever held at one time.

Later that evening, she watched the opening act from the wings with a new spark of pride. She really was making a life for herself, on her own terms, and she was enormously proud. All of her dreams were coming true. Most of them, anyway.

She gazed out into the audience at the table nearest the stage and wondered if she would ever stop looking for Picasso there. He had been gone for over a month but she had not quite been able to give up the fantasy that something more might actually happen between them, foolish as that seemed. *Fille stupide!* her inner voice chided. And she was just that. A foolish girl.

Mistinguett came up behind her then and squeezed her arm affectionately.

"I see you've done it again. There will be no living with Mademoiselle Minty now," she said, smiling. "I hope she paid you handsomely for that creation, for which she plans to take full credit."

"She did."

"Splendid. Why don't you join me for supper tonight after the show? And tomorrow I will take you shopping for a new ensemble for yourself. It's dreadfully dull in town since Fernande left."

Hearing the name struck Eva like a slap across the face. "Where did she go?" she forced herself to ask, knowing the answer before the question passed across her lips.

"To the South, of course, to be with

Picasso. She despises that whole provincial set down there, but he pleaded with her so she had to relent."

"Then they are back together?"

"Oh, but of course. It was only a matter of time with those two."

"They do seem suited," Eva lied, suddenly feeling weak.

"They are like fire and ice. But I suppose that's why it works between them. And he will need her support now more than ever, what with the whole Apollinaire thing blowing up just this morning. They are all such a tightly knit group. Apparently they took a train back to Paris."

Eva didn't know what she meant and Mistinguett could see that she didn't.

"Surely you've read the papers. They arrested the poet just this afternoon."

"Arrested him for what?"

"He has been implicated in the theft of the *Mona Lisa*. Apollinaire's former secretary confessed to stealing some carved Iberian heads, so they interrogated him and he confessed. Apparently they suspect a link between the two thefts, both from the Louvre."

Carved Iberian heads. Eva remembered very clearly having seen two of them herself in Picasso's private studio. But she couldn't

221

believe it was possible that he was involved in these crimes.

This was madness! There must be some mistake. Of course there was.

"I need some air," Eva said abruptly, heading for the back door that led into the alleyway.

She was not sure what horrified her more: the thought that Picasso and Fernande Olivier had reconciled, or that Picasso might be a thief. Right now with Mistinguett standing before her, Eva could not afford to react to either possibility. She felt her heart break a little as she staggered outside before anyone could see the tears in her eyes.

It was ruined. Everything he had worked for would be over.

As if it were a great Iberian storm looming on the horizon, Picasso could see the tumult ahead. Today, Apollinaire had been arrested in connection with the theft of the *Mona Lisa.* Now that he and Fernande had returned to Paris, Picasso had only to wait helplessly for the inevitable. The fruits of all the years of poverty and struggle would vanish in the blink of an eye because of a stupid mistake. But a bigger mistake had been made by Apollinaire. Why Guillaume had trusted that useless secretary of his with sculptures that were clearly stolen, he would never know.

But that was a lie. He did know. Of course he did. Pablo Ruiz y Picasso was many things — vain, egotistical, selfish and demanding — but he was not a fool. He had played his part. Ambition had driven both of them to break the rules — and the law.

It was yet another example of why he needed to distance himself from the bad influences in Paris. He needed a change, and this was a sign that the time for change was now. Something drastic must happen.

Sending for Fernande had done little to stem the tide of this growing disaster. It had only served to multiply his problems. She believed that they were reconciled, and now that they were back in Paris, it appeared that way to everyone else. But things were quickly disintegrating further between them.

They had returned with Frika to the apartment on the boulevard de Clichy and, for a few moments yesterday, Picasso had even been glad to be there, comforted by the familiarity of his possessions. In the dining room, his father's beautiful Spanish cabinet, inlaid with ivory and mother-of-pearl, held a commanding place. In the sitting room, his collection of African masks, an old Spanish guitar from Madrid and a mandolin shared space with his treasured flea-market finds.

But as much as he had found peace in being home, he couldn't help but feel a sense of unease. As he glanced around the apartment filled with all the things that defined the life he had built with Fernande, he felt a nagging resentment. Thank God Fernande had taken the dog for a walk. The cat and monkey were curled up together on the sofa. They were harmless, guileless creatures. At the moment, he envied them. He needed a moment to breathe.

He ran a hand through his hair, lit a cigarette and tried in vain to slow his racing heart. The pounding in his ears was deafening. He squeezed his eyes, but the blinding whirl of events from two nights ago was only made sharper in his mind. How pathetic all of it seemed to him now. As if he and Apo might actually have gotten away with something so unbelievably wild! He thought now how it had all begun two days ago.

Apollinaire had been waiting at the Bateau-Lavoir studio the moment they arrived back in Paris. He wore the same wide-eyed hunted expression that Picasso felt.

"What are we going to do?" he asked while Picasso unlocked the door. As a Spaniard, he was particularly terrified by the thought of the French police.

"No one knows anything for certain, do they?" Picasso asked.

"Anything implicating the two of us, you mean? Not yet, no. But I'm afraid it is only a matter of time until the truth comes out."

Apollinaire came inside and Fernande closed the door.

"Someone denounced me anonymously. The police have a warrant. They are in my apartment as we speak, looking for something to incriminate me."

"You're innocent. What would they possibly find," Picasso scoffed with puffed-up bravado that he certainly did not feel.

"Géry took the other Iberian head I had. Remember how I had it on my mantel?" said Apollinaire, pointing to the two Iberian artifacts still perched prominently on a stand in Picasso's alcove. "He stole it from me while you were gone and apparently he was just waiting for a way to blackmail me. He gave it to the *Paris Journal* in order to prove how easy it would be for a thief to have made off with the *Mona Lisa,* too. Apparently, he means to indict security at the Louvre. An opportunist like Géry probably could not resist trying to find a way to claim the fifty-thousand-franc reward once the painting is safely returned."

"Merde!" Fernande murmured with fingers splayed across her lips.

"Merde, c'est ça," Apollinaire repeated. "We need to dispose of these other two heads, and fast."

"What do you propose we do with them, Apo? Prance down unseen and drop them into the Seine?"

"Exactement."

Fernande groaned and rolled her eyes.

"Have you a better idea?" Apollinaire countered as panic rose in his voice.

Picasso exchanged a worried glance with Fernande. A steady summer rain began to beat against the studio's wall of windows.

"Why the devil don't you keep any alcohol in this place?" Apollinaire droned as he sank onto the edge of the bed in the corner of the room.

"The noose does seem to be tightening, Pablo. I told you years ago not to accept these," Fernande snapped uncharitably as she shook her head.

"Will you stop — I can't think!"

He should never have agreed to take them. He knew that. But at the time his self-confidence had overcome his good sense. Picasso remembered having deluded himself into thinking that it was his right to own the ancient Spanish artifacts. After all, he

226

was a Spanish artist producing great new work to glorify his homeland. Here in France, they had been stashed into a dusty display case in a back room.

The next hours that day were a terrifying blur. Picasso and Apollinaire stuffed the two relics into a suitcase and hurried out of Montmartre. They took one streetcar and then another, neither of them daring to speak, for fear of someone overhearing, or even sensing their guilt. When they arrived on the Pont Neuf bridge at dusk, it was crowded with people. Neither of them could do it. Picasso was perspiring and Apollinaire had tears in his eyes as they passed an Italian street performer singing a haunting tune called *"L'as tu vu la Joconde?"* "Have You Seen the *Mona Lisa*?" The case had gripped Paris.

At least they had done the right thing after they had come away from the Seine. They'd had the two heads delivered anonymously to the offices of the *Paris Journal* and they prayed that would calm the furor. Apollinaire had hugged Picasso on the street as they parted.

"It will be all right, don't you think?" Apollinaire had asked, dipping his fedora low.

"Of course, amigo. It will all be fine."

"Now can we *please* go?" Fernande droned as she glanced around impatiently. "They are holding our lunch table, and we have got to get all the way across town in midday traffic. Both of you owe me a hell of a lot more than a good meal. Pablo, there's a ring I've been eyeing."

As they turned to leave, Apollinaire gripped Picasso's arm. "Do you actually believe it will be fine?"

Picasso forced a smile. "I always believe what I say."

Picasso could feel the chill of terror now, two days later. Apollinaire had been arrested an hour ago, as they had both suspected he would be. The police would treat him roughly, considering the masterpiece at stake, and Guillaume was a weak man. He would not mean to implicate Picasso but he would do it nonetheless. A slip of the tongue, a desperate plea for his own freedom, and he would give Picasso over.

He took a last drag on a cigarette, tossed it into an ashtray and lit another. He needed to cut down with the smoking, he thought, yet knowing he wouldn't. He drew in a deep drag, feeling the burn in his lungs, and thought what a fool he was.

Picasso had truly tried in Céret to give reconciliation with Fernande a chance, in spite of the pretext on which he had sent for her. But it was there that he realized even more fully that what he needed was a true partner, now more than ever, with his world falling apart and his career taking off. He needed someone who would help him through these challenges, and steer him away from temptation. He could no longer stand to be berated and used for his growing fame. After so many tempestuous years, he desperately needed someone who could allow him to create and flourish. Without this, he would never survive all that he knew was coming.

CHAPTER 15

Eva was continuing to thrive on her own in Paris. At first she had been hesitant, but now she was eager for the challenges of creating and enhancing several of the costumes for the performers. It was a career path she had not initially considered for herself, but she had discovered a hidden talent for dressmaking, and she loved doing it.

She had worked hard and now she was indispensable at the Moulin Rouge. All of the actresses relied on her, especially Mistinguett, and while Eva had initially thought of her as a condescending Parisian, she actually enjoyed her company. They sparred, joked and laughed together, because there was trust between them now. The two women were not exactly equals, but they understood one another, and Eva found that she had a generous spirit and a vulnerability to which she could relate.

Mistinguett had recently invited Eva shopping and Eva had excitedly accepted. Wearing fashionable cloche hats, gloves and low pump heels, the two women strolled companionably down the boulevard du Palais, on the Île de la Cité. As they passed Notre Dame, they giggled and gossiped, free from the rigorous demands of the Moulin Rouge.

"So what exactly are we doing over here on the island?" Eva asked. "Are there shops here?"

"I have a surprise for you," Mistinguett said as they neared the charming storefront across the street from the ancient cathedral of Sainte-Chapelle. They stopped at the glossy black door beneath a red awning.

"I'm about to take you to the most exclusive hairdresser in the world. Sarah Bernhardt is a client here, but you mustn't tell anyone that. Antoine revealed that to me in the strictest confidence."

"Antoine de Paris?"

"You've heard of him?"

It was rather like asking if she had heard of the king of England. Antoine was as much a celebrity in Paris as some of his clients. He was known for his bob haircut, a style that had become all the rage. Everyone wanted one, but few could even think of sitting in Antoine's chair. "I'm sorry but I — I can't afford that."

"I told you, *ma petite,* that I owed you a great debt for all that you've done. You saved me twice with Monsieur Oller, and you didn't have to do it either time. We come from the same stock, you and I. Well, nearly, anyway. You're my friend and I want to treat you."

The small salon was a hive of activity when they walked in. A tall, elegant man with dove-gray hair, bright blue eyes and a slim mustache approached them. Eva thought that he was handsome, in a Parisian sort of way.

"*Ma chère* Mistinguett," he said as they embraced.

Dressed as she was, in a fashionable new dark blue dress with small brass buttons down the front, Eva no longer looked like a seamstress, nor did she feel like one.

"Antoine, this is the girl I was telling you about, my friend Mademoiselle Humbert."

"*Charmant,*" he said appraisingly as he took her hand and spun her around. "But I see what you mean. Time for a change. And she is young enough, and petite enough, to make it work. Yes, the new style will suit her brilliantly.

"Well, then. Shall we begin?" Antoine asked.

Whatever they meant to do to her, she was eager to submit. After all, Eva felt like such a different person now, she might as well look like it. So, for today at least, she resolved to nod, smile and enjoy every moment of this amazing *petite escapade.*

"I can't believe how different you look!" Mistinguett boasted with excitement afterward as they turned the corner onto the rue de Lutèce.

Eva felt light, saucy and incredibly chic, her new chestnut bob shimmering and bouncing in the sunlight as they walked. She felt as if she belonged in Paris now.

As they passed the imposing Palais de Justice, they watched as a Pigalle-Halle-aux-Vins omnibus stopped to let off some passengers. A uniformed police officer, wearing a long coat and kepi held the arm of a dark-haired man in handcuffs forced to endure the degrading ride on a city bus to the police station. They couldn't see his face, but they could see from his slouched stature that he was weary.

"Allez-y!" the officer shouted.

Mistinguett gripped Eva's arm tightly, as if the prisoner might break free and dash at them across the street. It was an absurd thought, but dangerous things did happen in a big city.

As the guard walked the prisoner around the side of the bus, Eva and Mistinguett were able to get a better look, and in that moment Eva felt as if the wind had been knocked out of her. She was glad Mistinguett had hold of her arm because her knees nearly buckled, and it felt as if she were melting directly into the pavement.

The prisoner led before her was Pablo Picasso.

"Will you look at that!" Mistinguett's voice came at Eva as if from the end of a long tube, and everything that happened in the next moments seemed to pass very slowly. She saw his hair first, black as india ink, shining and long across his forehead. He wore baggy gray trousers and a beige corduroy jacket. Then she saw the flash of silver as he stepped onto the pavement. Handcuffs! *Dieu,* it was horrible. Pablo Picasso being treated like a common criminal.

Eva was relieved for him that there were no photographers, as there had been at Apollinaire's arrest. His photo — that sheepish giant with the sad eyes who to her had seemed so kind — was splashed on the front page of every newspaper in France. She could not imagine how degrading that must have felt to her favorite poet.

Picasso couldn't possibly have been behind the *Mona Lisa* theft, but Eva had seen the stolen sculptures. Was it possible that he knew the whereabouts of the missing painting, too? The timing, and the coincidence, did seem quite damning.

It hurt to admit that this was a man she really did not know at all.

The competing emotions inside her flashed like fireworks, the sound so loud in her mind that she could not think.

Then, as if the moment couldn't get any worse, she saw Fernande Olivier huddled in the shadows beneath the overhanging eaves. She was with Germaine Pichot, the girl Eva had met at the Circus Medrano, and they were watching Picasso being marched into the police station.

Of course Fernande was there. She was Picasso's partner — practically his wife. The two women were Picasso's family, and Eva had been naive to think that their reckless *coup de foudre* had been anything more than a moment in time to him.

Her mind suddenly went blank as a blanket of gray fell over her like a shroud. Her knees gave way, and she collapsed onto the sidewalk, and in her last conscious moment all she could think was what an utter fool she had been.

"Will you *please* eat something? Drink the tea, at least," Sylvette pleaded.

"I don't know what happened to me," Eva whispered. "I'm sorry."

It was late — she didn't know how late, but it was dark outside, and the lights from next door cast an amber glow inside their room at la Ruche.

"Well, if you don't eat at least a morsel, Louis will barge in here himself to feed it to you. He has been pacing up and down the hallway since Mistinguett brought you home."

Dear Louis. He was coming up in the world, selling paintings and sculpting now, too. She cared about him. They shared something similar and real, a fragile uncertainty like at least part of what Fernande and Picasso must have shared in their early years, and that was something with which no one could compete in anyone's life.

Picasso belonged to Fernande. What Eva saw today had proved that *she* was Madame Picasso. She seemed to have earned the right to call herself that, and Eva realized she would never stand a chance. She wondered then if she could allow herself to become Madame Marcoussis, after all.

"Ask Louis to come in," Eva finally said to Sylvette.

Perhaps it was time to find out.

CHAPTER 16

Louis kissed her slowly on the mouth. Eva would never grow accustomed to the taste of him, even though she was determined to try. Louis was a safe harbor from her own emotions and she knew now, after that day near the police station, she needed that. They shared a bond. Perhaps she could will herself into sharing her future with him.

They lay together, on top of his bed at la Ruche in the warmth of a September afternoon a week after Picasso's arrest, and he told her news of the *Mona Lisa*'s recovery. They had not made love this time, as they had the last time she had been in his room. Now they just lay together, kissing and holding each other. Guillaume Apollinaire had been exonerated. The newspaper for which he drew cartoons would be printing the story in the afternoon edition. Even though she had only met him a couple of times, Eva felt that she knew Apollinaire a little bit and she was relieved. Louis twined his fingers with hers and then drew her hand to his lips.

"I do like your hair short like this. It's very sophisticated," he said quietly. "It took me a while to get used to it, but it suits you."

"Thank you."

"When will you let me make love to you again?" he asked as she pulled away from his embrace. She sat up, swung her legs over the side of the bed and smoothed down her skirt.

She had come downstairs to his studio earlier today, fully expecting it to happen again as it had after she had instructed Sylvette to let him into their room that day so that he might comfort her. But something had given her pause. In part it hadn't happened again now because she had not drunk any wine this time, as he had come to calm her after her fall out on the street. But also, she did not feel the desperation she had felt a week ago when she had forced herself to accept that someday Picasso probably would marry Fernande, and she would never see him again.

The best way to mend a broken heart, Sylvette always said, was with a new love. God above, how she was trying to believe that, but his touch made her recoil inside every time. She would make love again with him, she was determined to do it, but it would not be today. For now the kisses and caresses she had just managed to give him would have to be enough. When she did give herself to him again, it would be entirely on her own terms. This would be one romance over which she would have control.

"I'm going to be late for work," she replied, turning back to press a kiss onto his forehead with her fingertips and hiding her true feelings away.

"One of these nights I'll have to come to see the wonderful costumes I keep hearing about. Any chance you could find me a ticket for a seat up near the stage?"

Eva cringed at the thought but smiled sweetly. "I doubt it. Those seats always go to celebrities and wealthy people, especially now that Mistinguett's geisha number is so popular."

"Thanks to *you.*" He chuckled, grasping her wrist and trying to draw her back against him.

"All I did was provide the costume. Mistinguett created the dance all on her own."

"Is there singing in that number?"

He seemed very interested suddenly. She knew that he was trying to think of things to talk about so she would remain with him awhile longer.

"No, she doesn't make a sound. It's all done with the movements of her body and the music, but she brings the house down with it every night. I've watched her perform it so many times, I could probably do it myself."

"Now there's a thought. Any chance you would want to give me a private show?"

Eva playfully swatted him, stood up and slipped her shoes on.

"Ah, you are a tease." Louis chuckled again as he flopped back against his pillow in defeat.

She was not at all teasing. But better for him not to know of her ambivalence toward him. That, she knew, would be far more hurtful.

That evening, Eva was engulfed by the regular shouting and rapid conversation that always went on behind the stage in the moments just before the start of a show. The director, who was a bald, portly little man wearing wire-rimmed glasses, yelled at one of the Swayne Brothers because suddenly tonight he was too fat to fit into his first costume, and the pulley above the stage curtain seemed to be sticking. There were workmen, stagehands and ladders everywhere trying to fix it before Mistinguett's opening number. Eva finished mending a petticoat for Sylvette because she was still the best at working with lace, then she glanced up with an authoritative nod, to approve a fringe her new assistant had seen added to Mado Minty's costume as the actress primped in front of her makeup mirror.

Eva smiled to herself when she considered the fact that, after her success with both Mistinguett and Mado Minty's costumes, she had been promoted by Monsieur Oller to Madame Léautaud's wardrobe assistant. Therefore, in turn, now one of the dresser's had become Eva's assistant. Her self-confidence had grown because of a circumstance that was unimaginable only a year ago.

"It's getting kind of late, isn't it? Where is Mistinguett?" Sylvette asked. "She's always here by now."

"She's had another quarrel with Maurice," Mado said blandly as she patted powder onto her face with a fluffy puff. Sylvette and Eva exchanged a worried glance as the stage lights began to come on.

"Do you know where she's gone?" Eva asked.

"I really have no idea. She dashed out the stage door in a fit of tears half an hour ago.

Monsieur Oller certainly won't be happy if she isn't back to open the show. That geisha number has really been setting the tone for the rest of us with the audiences. There is so much expectation now that the crowd won't be very happy if she isn't here to open the show."

The sound of the large orchestra tuning their instruments heightened the tension. Eva looked over at the kimono that she had transformed, as it hung on the end of the rolling costume rack. The yellow silk now had beautiful red ribbon attached to the collar and cuffs. Seeing the garment still always made her think of home and how far she had come.

Eva thought for a moment, then she began to remove the kimono from the hanger.

"What in blazes are you doing?" Sylvette asked as Eva slipped out of her dress.

"I can't let Mistinguett get in trouble for this. Believe me, I understand now how romance can make all of us act a little foolish."

As the five-minute call before curtain was announced by a stagehand, Mado pivoted on her makeup stool to watch what was happening.

"You cannot be serious!" she exclaimed with a devilish little smile. There was an open tube of bright red lipstick poised in her hand.

"What else can I do? She's my friend," Eva asked as she took the black geisha wig from the stand on Mistinguett's table.

"She is not your friend. Mistinguett uses people," said Mado.

"Don't we all use one another, to one degree or another?" Sylvette shot back.

"You will both lose your jobs for this."

"Or Eva will be a hero," said Sylvette.

"That seems an awfully great risk to take unless you are absolutely certain of the outcome," Mado countered.

"Come here and help me with the makeup," Eva bid Sylvette.

"The two of you are absolutely mad. I'll have nothing to do with this! You're not an actress, you're a seamstress, for heaven's sake!"

"As you well know, I'm the wardrobe assistant now, thank you very much," Eva countered with a little spark of fire in her eyes.

Eva and Sylvette exchanged a smile and Sylvette gestured for Eva to quickly sit on the stool next to Mado.

"Are you sure?"

"No, I'm not sure!" Eva exclaimed.

"Which makes it that much better!"

Dancers in their flouncy costumes were collecting behind them, and they had begun to whisper when they realized what was about to happen. There really was a daring bit of folly to it all, and Eva was not even sure she wouldn't freeze up in front of such a huge crowd. But then it occurred to her, as Sylvette powdered her face to a pearlescent ivory, that she wasn't really Eva here in Paris, anyway. She was Marcelle. And because of the makeup and the kimono costume, she wouldn't really be either one of them.

"You *do* look like her," said a willowy blond dancer named Pauline as Sylvette applied the glistening red lip paint that finished off the look.

"She will never get away with it," Mado declared as she turned back to her mirror with a pouty huff.

"Are you *sure* Mistinguett still isn't here? Could someone go check outside the stage door?" Eva asked. Her heart was pounding, and it was becoming more difficult by the moment to decide if going through with this was a good idea, after all.

The costumed dancers had begun making fifty-centime bets on how quickly Eva would be caught and fired for this mad act of daring.

"Madame Léautaud would have both of your heads if she knew about this," Mado observed dryly as she painted on her own bright lipstick.

"But you won't say anything, will you, because it was Eva who created your popular new bird costume, too, and none of us really want to bite any hand that might well end up feeding us," Sylvette defended.

Mado glared at Sylvette, but she did not challenge her because they both knew she was right. Sylvette embraced Eva, then she smiled brightly with encouragement.

"Go have fun. It won't last long so make the best of it. We'll all be watching!"

As Eva prepared to go onstage, she felt an exhilaration that reminded her of when she had first stepped onto the subway car that took her out of Vincennes. It was the same terrifying thrill of the unknown. The tips of her fingers tingled and she flexed them nervously as she began to run through the movements of the simple routine in her mind. This really was madness, but was that not what being young and in the City of Light was all about?

She drew back a small corner of the heavy fringed stage curtain and took a peek at the crowd. As the orchestra struck up the intro music for the geisha number, Eva felt her knees weaken. Her heart vaulted into her throat. He was here. Out in the audience at his usual table in the front, Picasso sat prominently along with his friends. It only took a moment more for her to realize that Fernande Olivier was not with him.

CHAPTER 17

An hour earlier, Fernande stood in the vaulted doorway to their bedroom on the boulevard de Clichy. A grand brass bed was the focus of the room, which was extravagant and feminine with a view of Sacré Coeur from the grand window. There were tasseled draperies and pieces of furniture here that meant something to them both. Here, Fernande displayed all of the souvenirs of their five years together — inexpensive trinkets she did not wish her stylish new friends to know she had kept because they so clearly marked the impoverished years.

A collection of shells from a trip to the sea shared space with a lump of coal she had kept from the winter she had used her charms to get a box of coal without paying. Fernande was still particularly proud of that use of her feminine wiles.

She was leaning against the jamb now, watching Picasso dress. She held a half-full glass of whiskey, but even that was not managing to take the edge off her distaste with how unraveled things felt between them.

After Apollinaire had implicated him in his crime, Picasso was brought into the Palais de Justice, questioned by the police, brought before a magistrate and then released a few hours later. Fernande knew that he felt the trauma of the experience deeply. Here in France, he was still a foreigner. He would always be at risk of being expelled. The reminder of that only made the tension worse between them.

Fury and frustration had dripped from him like rain from the eaves the day she picked him up from the police station. They could barely stand to look at each other after it was all over. So many things seemed to be coming to a head.

"Can't I go with you this evening?" she asked as he drew a new white shirt across his bare back and began to button it.

"You know you detest the Moulin Rouge. Besides, I'm just taking the amigos and we'll be speaking Spanish." He glanced up at her. "I really wish you wouldn't drink so much."

"And I really wish *you* wouldn't smoke so much."

She watched him for a moment more as

he brushed back his black hair with a tortoiseshell comb.

"What's the point of that place, anyway?"

"I like the music."

"And the dancing girls?"

"You wouldn't enjoy it. There are no young German boys in their show."

She knew Picasso meant to hurt her, and he did. Target hit. She felt the blow. Once there was a time when the battlefield had been equal between them. But that was a lifetime ago. Now, he was nearly famous and growing rich. So much had changed between them in the past five years.

Picasso straightened his collar, which was stark white against his smooth, umber skin. Then he turned and reached down to pat Frika, who lounged happily at the foot of the bed. She began to wag her tail in response to his touch. All these wretched animals, Fernande thought. The hair, the fleas and the relentless barking. But she did it for him.

He put on cuff links. They were Spanish silver and they glinted in the late-afternoon light from the setting sun. He rarely wore them. She did not like when he dressed up like this. Fernande saw the way women looked at him. And the way he looked at them. But two could play that game.

Besides, what he didn't know couldn't hurt him.

She looked at him now, shoving his silver cigarette case and money into the pocket of his trousers. He looked so good. She could not quite imagine why he would want to go to that tacky dance hall, after all that had just happened about the *Mona Lisa*.

Pablo had been so angry at having been implicated by Apollinaire that she was sure they would never speak again. He was slow to forgive when someone betrayed him. She really had pushed her luck with that last lover. But it was over now, anyway.

"Let's go somewhere else. Or we could stay in," she offered as Picasso grabbed the house key from the bureau.

"I must go."

"Without me?"

"Sí."

"Then I may as well go out, too." She could not keep the warning tone from her voice. Pride was a powerful lure. Fernande felt it deeply, and she was drawn to its darkness. Pablo had been slipping away for a long time, but she knew she had been the one to move first. They had both been so young in the beginning. Not a care in the world above paying the rent. Or so it had seemed fun to pretend. What had they been

251

searching for? Fame? Eternity? There was a comfort in affluence. There was predictability, at least. Now everything seemed to be disintegrating.

"As you wish." He did not look at her. "You have known your mind for some time now."

"I used to know yours."

"Did you think so?" Picasso said as he kissed her cheek and walked past her, toward the front door.

A little while after Picasso left, Fernande walked alone out into the warm September evening, and across the busy boulevard. On the corner, beneath an emerald-green canopy of trees, was the chic little Taverne de l'Ermitage, lit golden from inside by candles and lights. There were two big potted oleanders flanking the front door. It had become their place — where they went to hear new music and to drink too much. It was a place for Fernande to forget all that went along with growing fame and self-preservation.

She waited outside for a moment, not wanting to enter the tavern alone. Someone she knew from the neighborhood would come along soon — a man, a couple, it didn't matter — and ask her to join them while she waited for whoever they assumed she was meeting. At this hour, it never took long. She paused just inside the door as if she were looking for someone. The place was warm and the band was playing an evocative version of the new song "The Memphis Blues."

"Madame Picasso?"

She heard the male voice just as she felt his fingers casually touch her shoulder. She turned around. Now there was a surprise, someone she did not expect.

"Ah, Marcoussis." She purred the nickname she had given him last spring. Marcoussis — a friend of that unassuming girl. That sweet little seamstress she liked, promoted to wardrobe assistant or something now, Mistinguett had said. Yes, that pretty girl who worked at the Moulin Rouge.

Picasso sat with Ramón Pichot in his usual spot. There was an untouched glass of champagne, and a bottle in an ice bucket set on the table before them. The stage lamps were seductively low and the orchestra was tuning up since the show was about to begin. Picasso did not usually drink — it often did not agree with him — but Joseph Oller, the owner of the Moulin Rouge, had sent over the impressive bottle of Moët, insistent on celebrating Picasso's vindication with the police.

No one here understood. For all of his success he was still not entirely trusted among the discerning French, even those who had begun to celebrate him. Picasso glanced around, wary of those in his midst. There were still many Parisians who were eager to blame him for the *Mona Lisa* incident. How exciting to think a simple Spanish painter might have been somehow involved with the theft of the most famous masterpiece in the world!

The orchestra music flared. Picasso felt the rolling of the base drum, like thunder, signaling things to come. The anticipation. Ah, yes, that sensation was as necessary to him as breathing. Picasso began to feel eager in the moment.

When he saw the girl walk out onto the stage with small, cautious strides, beautifully vulnerable in the yellow silk kimono, Picasso felt his mind instantly clear of any other thoughts but her. This was not Mistinguett. They were nothing alike. This girl was extraordinary, petite, graceful, as she tipped up her chin and went through the moves of the dance flawlessly. Picasso's hands fell limply into his lap.

She turned, dipped, moved to the music.

Stage light fell on the folds of the kimono making the red cuffs shimmer. She knew the steps perfectly. She turned, dipped again. Her blue eyes flashed. The drunken men around him cheered and hollered, "Bring on the cancan!"

The matador within Picasso flared. His hands made two tight fists in his lap. His body began to tighten and an odd sensation came over him then, captivating him. It drew him from the anger. There was something about her eyes, deep blue, endless. He knew then that the girl was Eva.

Since the last time he'd seen her, in the hotel lobby, he'd felt a deep connection to her. Some deeper part of his true self had been there that day, honestly trying just to help her. What must she have thought — Picasso the rising young star, already well-known around Paris, luring her to a hotel, and before that leaving a book at her door-step, as though that particular volume could ever quite explain the complexity of the desires he often felt, as well as the absolute ambivalence toward everything he loved, or wanted to love. Picasso felt that he always lost the things he loved the most. Conchita. Then Casagemas. Loving fully since then, letting go entirely, had been impossible. Even with Fernande.

Picasso sank back in his chair and drank a glass of champagne in one swallow. How on earth had she pulled off this masterful switch with Mistinguett? He was amused and intrigued. As there was with him, there was far more to Eva than what met the eye. The music was seductive. The trombone slide moved in and out and he watched the way she moved her hands, shocked at how aroused he was at the thought.

Picasso shook his head to steady himself, but she drew him back in. The kimono was made more exotic because she was not. Rather it was a role she played. It was like a game, and he loved games between lovers.

The trombone slide went on moving slowly back and forth. The impression the movement made on him was profound. And how commanding was the bow on the violin, poised over the instrument, masterful and in control.

Suddenly everyone was applauding. The dance had ended, yet everything else was just beginning. He had thought so before Céret, but he knew it now without question. *She* was the future. Picasso began to applaud along with the rest of the crowd. Eva bowed, and a tiny victorious smile turned up the corners of her mouth. She had gotten away with something. How delicious that she had dared! What innovative things might he dare to do in life, and in his work, if she was the one by his side?

Picasso asked Joseph Oller where the cast would be gathering after the show. He must see her. He hoped she would be wearing that kimono. He could barely still the fantasy of it. He could not get the image of Eva out of his mind.

Just down the street, Le Palmier — with its red leather banquettes, below enormous mirrors and hazy with cigarette smoke — was already packed with the cast and crew. As Picasso and Ramón walked in, the place crackled with conversation, music and boisterous laughter. It was an easy place to be anonymous, Picasso thought. At least for a while. If it weren't for an old friend.

It was awkward, and even a little suspicious, that Ramón had insisted on accompanying him tonight when he made it known that he generally liked to be home in the evenings with Germaine. Picasso felt certain that Fernande had put him up to it because she no longer trusted him. Picasso loved Ramón like a brother, and he could never repay all of the kindnesses Ramón had shown him through the years when he was struggling, but this made him angry. Especially after the *Mona Lisa* affair, Picasso was feeling more than a little contemptuous of everyone's motivations.

They sidled up to the edge of the long zinc-topped bar so that Ramón could order a rum. As he did, Picasso heard from the dancers standing beside them what had happened. Marcelle Humbert was now the secret toast of the production for having saved Mistinguett during a lovers' quarrel — and for fooling Monsieur Oller and the wardrobe mistress, who grudgingly had already been forced to take on the ambitious girl as her assistant.

It was then that Eva arrived with a pretty blonde chorus dancer called Sylvette. Eva's face, freshly washed of white makeup, was flushed now with triumph, and she was smiling as she accepted embrace after embrace from cast members. She was glowing. Picasso could tell that they were all whispering words of praise because she kept blushing and nodding in acknowledgment as they made their way toward the bar.

He realized then that she had cut her hair into that same bob style that Sarah Bernhardt was trying, unsuccessfully, to pull off. On Eva, the cut looked chic and stunning. He must talk to her. But first, he needed to break free from Ramón.

"*Dios*, I could use a cigarette." Picasso ran a hand through his hair. "I still feel like everyone is looking at me, judging."

"Relax, amigo, no one still believes you actually stole the *Mona Lisa.*" He chuckled as he slung a fraternal arm across Picasso's shoulders.

"Five francs if you go find me a smoke."

"You *are* desperate."

You cannot imagine, Picasso thought. *But not for the reasons you think.*

"Ten francs and I'll go to the end of the block and buy the ones you like."

"Perfecto. Gracias."

As soon as he was gone, Picasso made his way through the crowd toward Eva. She was talking to Mistinguett and that young blond actor Maurice Chevalier. His heart pulsed, and his mind raced as he tried to formulate what to say to her. As he made his approach, he could hear Eva's conversation.

"Do you suppose Monsieur Oller will hear about it?" Eva asked them. She was holding a small glass of red wine and she sounded a little out of breath.

"Probably. But you saved the show. He'll be eternally grateful to you, if anything, and furious with me."

Picasso moved nearer. He felt his heart racing as she looked up and saw him.

"Oller is a friend of mine," Picasso interjected. "There will not be a problem."

"You are very generous, Monsieur Picasso," Mistinguett said with a tone of obvious relief as she wound her arm more tightly with Chevalier's forearm.

"That will not be necessary," Eva replied. Her words were polite, but she was clearly displeased.

"It's really no trouble," he pressed.

"I simply would rather you didn't."

"Marcelle!" Mistinguett gasped. "You mustn't be rude. Monsieur Picasso was only trying to help."

He bit back a smile. She didn't mean it entirely, he could feel it. Eva was angry with him, but not indifferent. He could work with anger.

"It's all right. I deserve it. Mademoiselle Humbert knows her own mind."

Mistinguett and Chevalier glanced at each other, and Picasso could tell that they suspected there was more between him and Eva than a casual acquaintance.

"Will you excuse us?" Picasso asked Maurice in a tone of calm he did not feel.

"Please don't," Eva said.

"Bien sûr," Maurice countered as he led Mistinguett away from the bar before Eva could object further.

260

"Why did you do that? Now everyone will talk."

"They were already talking about *you* this evening."

"But not about *us.*"

"So there is an 'us,' at least?"

"Not with me. You are with Mademoiselle Olivier. I am forever mindful of that now."

"A pity she does not abide by your distinction."

"Well, I'm nothing like her."

"One of the many reasons I am drawn to you. By the way, I like your new haircut. It suits you. How is your mother?" he asked, trying to diffuse the tension between them.

"Things have changed. I'll not talk about my private life with you. I am with Louis now."

"Marcoussis?"

Picasso struggled not to show his surprise.

"That was the name your mistress gave him."

"I remember. As I remember everything that concerns you. Will the two of you marry?" he asked coolly. Even if she said yes, he knew that she would be lying.

A woman like Eva would never marry a man like that, without spirit or talent.

"That really does not concern you."

"Look, I understand why you are angry

261

with me, my life is complicated just now, I'll admit. But have dinner with me, at least. I know a quiet little bistro nearby where they serve the best Catalan food in Paris. We can talk privately there."

"Talking with you is the very last thing I need, since we both know perfectly well where it will lead."

He took a step nearer so only she would hear him. He caught the faint scent of roses, and he could smell the sweet wine on her breath. "We will only celebrate your wonderful adventure on the stage. You really were quite amazing."

He mustn't plead. That would be unappealing. But he knew without question that he could not let her go. Her eyes narrowed, and he could feel her hesitation. His own breathing slowed. She frowned at him.

"Only dinner," she said cautiously. "And only because we cannot stand here like this alone much longer."

Picasso did not want her to see the elation he so keenly felt. He was afraid of any woman possessing that much control. At least for now. Even so, the reality was, at that moment, there really was nothing in the world he would not have done to bring her into his life. She would be his muse, his Madonna, his only mistress.

262

And he fully intended to make her his wife.

Fernande and Marcoussis were on their second bottle of cognac at the Taverne de l'Ermitage as a crowd of locals pressed in around them. It remained to be seen who would pick up the tab. She sat comfortably in her chair, her auburn hair cascading over her shoulders, beneath a stylish hat. She was wearing a lime-green satin dress, and the luxurious fabric clung to the curves and hollows of her body. She was keenly aware of the effect it was having on Marcoussis, whose fingers moved casually over the back of her hand as she held her glass. Her bold almond-shaped eyes met his as his fingers stilled.

"I thought you were with Marcelle now," she said.

"I am. And you are with Picasso."

Her mouth lengthened into a sensual smile. "Indeed I am. But, alas, he is not here with us now. Nor is your Marcelle."

He smiled back at her. "Whatever will we do without them?"

"Have another drink, most definitely. And then I say we shall go from there."

Louis moved his finger slowly up the length of her bare forearm. "I do like the way you think, almost as much as the way you look."

"Flattery, my dear Marcoussis, will get you everywhere."

A moment later, two young Italians approached the table. Fernande knew one of them, an artist named Gino Severini, who had spent several long evenings with her and Pablo last winter discussing art. Tall and slim, he wore a trim black suit and tie. He had unruly coils of black hair and prominent dark eyes.

"Buona sera, bella," Severini said, bowing to Fernande. He held out his slim hand, then saw her fingers twined with Louis's on the table.

"Monsieur Picasso is not with you this evening?" he asked with a note of surprise snaking through his thick yet charming Italian accent.

"As it happens, he is not," she replied.

Severini glanced at his Italian companion. Only then did Fernande notice how strikingly handsome he was, and how deliciously young. He gazed down at her and a powerful attraction flared between them. Fernande moved just slightly against the back of her chair. She was particularly pleased with the impression she was making, since she had no idea where Pablo was at this moment. And she was beginning to care less and less.

"Madame Picasso, may I present Ubaldo Oppi. He has been badgering me for nearly a month to introduce him to your husband," said Severini.

"I have come all the way from Bologna, hoping for the privilege, señora."

She could see him twisting his black bowler nervously in his hands. Fernande found it endearing, and even a little enticing. He was certainly attractive enough. "Join us, please," she said with a slight smile.

She could feel Louis's jaw tighten. Good, she thought, she did so adore a little rivalry among men.

"Do you expect Monsieur Picasso to join you later this evening, perhaps?" asked the young artist. He had begun to lightly perspire at his temples.

It was another nuance Fernande found particularly enchanting. The sensation of control over men had always pleased her. She liked the deep, throaty timber of his voice. And he smelled of cedar and musk, not cigarettes and paint, as Pablo so often did.

A waiter brought over two chairs and Oppi took a seat beside Fernande.

"Gino tells me you were an artist's

model," Oppi said with a thick accent.

"I *am* an artist's model, one of the best in Paris," she replied coyly.

She needed to ease up on the cognac, but the taste was so honeyed and warm and she loved being the center of this much attention since Picasso was all but ignoring her lately.

"Perhaps you will allow me to paint you sometime. You have the most exquisite features."

Fernande blushed at the compliment, though she was used to lavish praise from men. It would take little more for her to sleep with him. Poor Marcoussis, there really was no contest.

Severini laughed and filled his glass from the cognac bottle on the table as the orchestra returned from their break and struck up a rousing ragtime tune. Guests filed onto a makeshift dance floor. Behind it was a small, candlelit garden with an ivy-covered wall. A light breeze through the open doors stirred the air.

"I would be careful with her, if I were you," Severini cautioned Louis in a low tone. "Picasso seems a very jealous young man. All of that fiery Spanish blood. He's quite a force to be reckoned with in the art world, and with women."

"I can't speak for your companion here," Louis said defensively. "But Picasso and I are friends. I have been with him to the Circus Medrano, and even to Gertrude Stein's last spring. Isn't that right, Fernande?"

"The worst kind of betrayal comes from the people you least suspect," Severini said.

Fernande pressed her fingertips against her lips as she assessed the men around her. A giggle escaped, anyway. She really had better make this her last glass of cognac, she thought. She wanted to remember every detail about Ubaldo Oppi. She must try her best to be elusive, but she was already hoping she would go home with him and not the less-than-inspiring cartoonist. It would certainly serve Picasso right if she did.

He spoke in rapid Spanish with the restaurant owner and his stout, snowy-haired wife. Eva stood next to Picasso under a blue canopy just outside the door of the intimate café. She was charmed by how familiar they all were with one another. He must come here often, she thought to herself. She could see that he was not a celebrity to them, just a young man humbled by surroundings, aromas and spirited sounds that took him back to his exotic roots.

267

The place was called Au Tambourin, and with one glimpse inside, Eva could see why. The blue walls of the cozy café were covered with dozens of tambourines on which all sorts of subjects had been painted in distinctive styles by various artists. There were canvases, as well. It was such a quirky little place that Eva quickly felt at home.

"Monsieur and Madame Segatori," Picasso said with a note of pride. "May I present Mademoiselle Humbert."

The lady took Eva's hand and pressed it into her own warm, fat fingers. "You look so much like Evelyn Thaw, the actress, I thought for a moment you were her. We saw her perform once at the Théâtre de Paris, and I very nearly got her autograph. She truly is the greatest, most beautiful actress!"

The little brick of a woman sounded like a flustered young girl as Eva drew back her hand. She exchanged a smile with Picasso, and she thought how Mistinguett might disagree with that declaration. Eva had seen photos of the strikingly beautiful Miss Thaw, so she knew what a great compliment she had just received.

Eva and Picasso were shown to a small table at the back of the restaurant where only two other tables were occupied. The rich fragrance inside the place was heavenly, the scent of garlic, basil, chicken and tomatoes came at her fully as they neared the table, and only then did Eva realize that she was famished.

She gazed up at a small canvas of bold sunflowers as Monsieur Segatori poured each of them a glass of Pernod, then left the bottle on the table between them. When he saw Eva looking at the painting, he spoke.

"Monsieur Vincent hung that very work there himself over twenty-three years ago now. It seems impossible to believe he has been gone from us for so long. Such a tragedy, so much talent." He shook his head where only a skein of silver hair on top remained.

"Vincent van Gogh?" Eva asked with great interest as she studied the broad brush-strokes on the small canvas.

"He was a great friend of the café in his short time in Paris. As is our Pablo here." He smiled with paternal pride as he patted Picasso's shoulder. "All the greats have dined here at one time or another — Degas, Monet, Cézanne, even that eccentric Monsieur Toulouse-Lautrec. Now *there* was a character! They all came here because we offer privacy and the best food in Paris."

"His wife does all the cooking," Picasso said with a smile.

"It's a darling place," Eva replied.

"I had a feeling you would like it."

"And Fernande? Does she like it here?"

She watched the furrows of his brow deepen. "Why must you always do that?"

"Self-preservation. I'm afraid I must. I certainly cannot care for you."

His voice was low. "Is it not too late for that? I know it is too late for me, since I already care a great deal for you."

Eva tipped her head, trying to gauge his sincerity, but he was unreadable to her.

The candle lamps on the table flickered, the firelight dancing in Picasso's obsidian eyes.

"Why would you be drawn to me away from a woman like Fernande?"

"Because you are nothing at all like her. When I am with you, I feel like a completely different man, a better man. I know I want to *be* better. The way you are with me, the way you look at me when I speak . . . It may sound crazy, but I want to live my life to make you happy, and to share your triumphs as you will share mine."

"You're right. It sounds crazy."

"Watching you these past months, the way you have challenged yourself and succeeded, has been thrilling. From the first moment, I have felt invested."

"Invested how?" All of this sounded slightly insane.

"I see your strength of character, your determination, and I want to be a better man because of it. *Dios,* am I making any sense? It probably sounds like a jumble of thoughts and words."

"That much makes perfect sense actually, and I am flattered."

A diminutive, middle-aged man with wire-rimmed glasses began to play a soft tune on a violin in the corner by the kitchen. They both watched him for a moment before Picasso spoke again. "Do you want to know another wicked little truth?"

"If you feel you must tell me."

"I wish I were holding you right now, as that musician holds his instrument — my hand the bow."

Eva felt herself blush and she looked down at her hands in her lap. He was so brash, yet, on his lips, it did not sound as foul as it might have. "Are you making fun of me?"

"Nothing could be further from the truth. But if you can bear the honesty, that is what you will always have from me."

He leveled his eyes on her and she felt a current run sharply through herself as he reached beneath the tablecloth, clutched her small hand and brought it back to the table-top.

"You do look like Evelyn Thaw, it is true. But I have met her and, believe me, you are nothing at all like her."

"I hope that is a good thing?"

"Oh, but it is a very good thing. There is something in your eyes that assures me you are not an image, nor someone false. You are simply you."

"My humble roots calling up to claim me."

"Yet it is not as simple as that. I can speak to you of anything, and I know that you will understand. Somehow I know my heart would be safe in your care."

She thought how, for her, it was entirely the opposite. Picasso was everything in the world to be cautious about, and to run from.

Over wonderful rich plates of Spanish *ajo blanco,* and more wine, he tried patiently to explain how he had come to embrace the Cubist style, but when he spoke of art, his passion took over. His speech grew rapid and he gesticulated boldly, describing the influence of shapes, angles, colors and light. She found him fascinating and she felt a growing desire to learn about art.

"I adore the power of an artist. There alone, I can remake anything by first breaking it down to its simplest elements of form."

"Anything, or anyone."

"Sí, es verdad."

"How do you decide what your subjects will be?"

"I paint whatever comes up from my soul and through my paintbrush. I can't explain it beyond that, really. Anyway, a painting, or sketch, must speak for itself."

She sipped her wine and considered the explanation as the tabletop candles flickered around them.

Sitting here like this, their hands occasionally touching across the table, their conversation on a variety of subjects, eventually relaxed them both. Eva had no idea how much time had passed when she realized she and Picasso were the last patrons in the restaurant. The musician was packing his violin into a case, and the owner and his wife were sitting at a table in the corner quietly talking to each other, clearly waiting to close for the evening.

"Come home with me," Picasso said in a low voice that only Eva could hear.

"You are very bold, monsieur," she feigned.

"Mademoiselle, it is you who are surprisingly bold. I applaud what you did this evening at the Moulin Rouge. That took enormous courage."

"Not really that. It's just that the kimono belonged to my family, so I felt responsible for it. I offhandedly gave Mistinguett the idea for a geisha number in the first place."

"Bold *and* resourceful." His dark eyes flashed again in the candlelight. "Ah, that you might wear that kimono for me one day, privately."

"That is very forward of you."

"You cannot deny what is happening between us."

"No, but I can try to outrun it for as long as possible."

"A futile option, I assure you."

"I don't want to be hurt, Pablo, or to hurt anyone else."

It was the first time she had spoken his given name. It toppled a hidden little barrier between them. She looked down at their hands, now linked on the table, feeling her cheeks begin to burn again with a mixture of embarrassment and desire.

"I like how that sounds on your lips. I have not liked hearing my name spoken for a very long time."

"Pablo is a lovely name."

"It is too much attached to my youth." He swallowed the last of his drink. "My younger sister called me Pablo with the same singsong tone in her voice as you. She died a very long time ago, but I am still reminded of her so often."

"I'm sorry."

"Don't be. I was blessed once in my life to know pure sweetness like that, which Conchita possessed."

"I'm sure she knew how much you loved her."

"She never knew I broke a promise to God, and that it was my fault that she died. Not much matters in my memories of her beyond that."

Eva could hear the sudden anguish in his voice. She tried to think of something to say that might be a comfort.

"We should allow those lovely people their rest," Picasso said, pushing back his chair and collecting himself swiftly.

He was still holding her hand as they walked together out onto the boulevard de Clichy, past the storefronts shuttered for the evening and past a Métro station with its green, scrolling ironwork sign overhead. It was almost midnight, but it was a warm evening, and there were still groups of people out strolling, others leaving restaurants or out walking dogs on their leashes.

Eva saw the amber lights from the Taverne de l'Ermitage spilling out onto the street. She could hear the music and laughter grow stronger as they neared. Mistinguett had told her once that Picasso and Fernande went there frequently since it was just across the street from their apartment, and everyone who was anyone drank there.

Eva felt a chill of distaste at the notion, since she did not want to think of other women. But she paused with him on the sidewalk beside the now-empty tables and chairs of the brasserie. She was sure he meant to kiss her. They could both see the crowd gathered inside, through the huge windows.

When he did not try to kiss her, after all, Eva followed his gaze. She saw Fernande sitting at a table in the center of the room in a beautiful green silk dress. She was surrounded by young men, almost as if she were holding court, Eva thought. With her auburn hair and wide eyes, Eva was still certain she was the most elegant woman in Paris.

It was then that she noticed the fair-haired young man sitting beside Fernande in a gray jacket and striped tie. He leaned nearer to Fernande and seductively kissed the line of her jaw. He lingered there an instant too long for it to have been something innocent.

A moment later, he turned and she saw that it was Louis. Eva had no right to feel even a spark of betrayal, but she couldn't help but feel angry. This man who said he loved her sat openly now, seducing Picasso's mistress.

"I thought you and Marcoussis —"

"I thought so, too."

"I am sure it will come to nothing."

"Like the 'nothing' that is between the two of us?" Eva asked.

She could see that he, too, was thrown off by what they had seen. But then their eyes met as he brought her hand to his lips and very gently and slowly kissed it. "No, *mi ángel.*"

She tried to break free of Picasso's grasp for fear of losing even more of her heart to him, but he held fast to her hand. They stood in a cone of light, and the shadows it made, cast from inside the brasserie. Eva knew he must feel the betrayal, too, even though he did not acknowledge what they both had seen.

"Come to the Bateau-Lavoir with me," he bid her in a deep and sensual plea as he gently pressed a kiss onto her cheek.

"So that you may paint me?" she asked mockingly. "I cannot go with you. You know that."

"I want you. I'll not insult you by denying

that. But I want you in my life more. Come to the studio with me. It is private there, and quiet. We will watch the sun rise, and then I will see you home, I promise, that's all."

He pressed a stray wisp of hair away from her eyes. The last thing in the world she should do was believe his plea. She'd had so much to drink, the night was balmy and she was still flying high from her daring escapade in the kimono earlier.

"O Manon, ma jolie," he said, whispering the song's refrain.

She knew the popular song, everyone did. She remembered he had called her that before and felt her resolve melting. "Only talk, do you promise?"

"When a Spaniard gives his word, he does so with his pride. I will not touch you until it is what you want, too. On that, you have my word. Only please let me be with you a little while longer."

Eva glanced inside the restaurant where Louis and Fernande were still sitting with two other young men.

"All right, yes, just to talk," she reluctantly agreed.

She wanted to trust this man. She wanted to believe so badly that he could be real. In that moment, Picasso was overtaking her good sense, but she was lost already, and she knew it.

A few minutes later, Picasso stood in the doorway of his studio, waiting as Eva went inside first. There were no electric lights here in this ramshackle old place, or even gas lamps, but it was lit well enough by the full moon, which shone through the big picture window. She saw an oil lamp and a few candles collected in various holders on a small wooden table beside his easel.

"May I light them?" Eva asked, turning to face Picasso.

"Of course," he said, careful not to move so it would not seem like an advance. He wanted to give her a moment to adjust to being here again. She was skittish, he thought — still not fully aware of the power she already had over him.

Eva lit the candles, and the soft light cast a shadow throughout the small studio, hiding the collecting dust and trash, old rags littering the floor and the dirt on the windowpanes. Picasso closed the door and leaned against it. He watched as Eva sank awkwardly onto the edge of the small iron-frame bed, the old springs creaking under her slim weight.

"So, were you involved in the theft?" she asked. Her eyes were wide and the expression in them intensely vulnerable.

"The theft?"

"The *Mona Lisa*."

He was surprised at her boldness. She was always catching him off his guard, always making him try harder to keep up with her. "No, *ma jolie,* I was not."

"I saw the Iberian heads when I was here last, so I thought perhaps you were."

"I am many questionable things, but a thief is not one of them. Apollinaire had a friend who was desperate to make alliances, and we both lacked judgment by accepting them. They were so exquisite, and I was swept away with inspiration for the style I was trying to perfect at the time."

"But you were freed while he spent so much time in jail for the same thing."

If she were anyone else, the accusatory persistence would have angered him, but he respected Eva for her ability to challenge him.

"Apollinaire admitted things I denied." Picasso answered her honestly as he finally moved across the room and sat on the edge of the bed beside her, still careful not to touch her. "I'm not proud of that whole affair. I worked hard with Max Jacob to secure Apo's release. But it's not an easy thing for me to trust the police. In Spain, they are feared."

"But you are Picasso. You are becoming so well-known in Paris."

"I will only ever be a foreigner in France, no matter how famous I become, or how long I live here."

"I suppose it is wise to remember one's boundaries, and never grow too complacent."

No matter what he had promised, her coy smile made him want to ravish Eva. Her naïveté drew him in. Her inexperience was so seductive to him.

He knew there was madness in what he was feeling. But then love was madness, really, wasn't it?

He did not care about being understood because he did not fully understand himself.

From the side of her where he was sitting, he could glimpse only one of her eyes, beautiful clear, sweet eyes that had the power to see him, to know him. She did not yet see all of him, metaphorically, nor had he seen all of her — those beautiful dimensions. Her profile was exquisite. He allowed her image to burn itself on his mind. He would paint her from memory — every aspect he held dear — after she had gone because he could not bear to frighten her with the creative frenzy he knew he would feel tomorrow.

Picasso wanted to freeze this moment between them, and capture it. He wanted her to remain his secret, a puzzle that only he possessed or understood. No one need know quite yet what he felt for her. What was happening between them already felt sacred.

He was pulled from his thoughts when she lay back sleepily on the bed.

"It has all hit me finally, I think. I can't actually believe what I did."

"Going onstage like that certainly was bold."

"When I was a little girl in Vincennes, like all girls, I used to dream of being an actress. I suppose tonight my dreams just got the better of me."

He lay back beside her, crossways, careful not to make an intimate gesture of it. "I understand about childhood dreams," Picasso said as they both gazed up at the ceiling, and the shadows that danced in the candlelight.

Suddenly he turned and saw that her expression had changed and he realized she had seen the unfinished canvas propped on his easel. The bold image of a head split in two dominated the small room. He knew it would be odd and unsettling to her, but he would have to reveal more of himself than he thought he might be capable of if he tried to explain it. And if he took the risk, would she think him vile for the thoughts and urges that so often held him captive and found their way into his work? His soul growled out the declaration that he wasn't respectable. It filled his head. And still he felt compelled to reveal to her alone what he told no one else.

"After my little sister died . . ." Picasso heard himself begin.

He was surprised by the sound of his own words. They were spoken as a confession he had not meant to utter aloud. He cleared his throat and began again.

"After her death, they were conscripting young men for the Spanish war with Cuba so my parents, who thought I needed a change of scenery to get over her death, sent me away with my friend Manuel Pallarès to his village, Horta de Ebro. It was isolated, up in the mountains, where Pallarès wanted to hide out. While we were there, there was a storm. A young girl was struck by lightning, and Pallarès said he knew her, so he wanted to go up the mountain to see for himself if it was really her who had died. He took me with him to the grave digger's shed where they had put her body. *Dios mío,*

I was so young. Thirteen. I hated the dark out there. I thought of ghosts and evil spirits, but he shook me off. 'Be a man, Pablito,' Pallarès said."

Eva propped herself on an elbow and focused intently on him.

"The girl was lying on a table. She was white as paste. There was only the grave digger's lantern to light the musty shed. I remember the sound of the wind, and the rain. My heart was pounding with such terror for the first few moments after we arrived that I couldn't even hear what anyone was saying.

"The grave digger was an odd, toothless old man and he was as frightening to me as the dead girl's lifeless body. But it was the night watchman who decided he wanted to cut open her brain to see if it was really lightning that had killed her. It was really so ghoulish to do a thing like that."

Eva still did not speak, but she reached out and put a hand on his arm. The painting on his easel, the girl with her head separated into two halves, was a key to a place he had not expected to explore tonight. But the door was open now, and he could not turn back.

"I just stood there. I couldn't move. I couldn't have left, anyway, because several

284

curious villagers had come up to see for themselves, and they had crowded into the little shed behind me, as if it were a circus sideshow. To this day, I can still smell the night watchman's cigar smoke. The sour smell of it made me ill. The cigar was clamped between his back teeth, and he was puffing huge clouds of smoke that filled the cramped space as he took a saw and cut the girl open from the top of her skull down to her neck, exposing her brain."

Picasso could see by Eva's expression that he had finally shocked her.

"After he did it, mangled her, really, he stepped back and pulled the cigar from his mouth. His fingers were bloody, and so was the cigar. I escaped the shed, just in time to be ill out in the field."

He closed his eyes and felt the featherlight touch of her kiss on his cheek.

"I've never told anyone that story. It sickened me as a boy. But, as you can see, after all of those years, it has become for me something of a demented fascination."

"Under the circumstances, it is understandable."

"It is, really? I have many dark fantasies, Eva. I think you would not find me so sympathetic if you knew about them."

"Do *you* think they are demented?"

He thought for moment. "Not actually, no. Some are my fantasies come to life through art. Others are pure creative passion, of a moment."

"Then they are all parts of you."

"*Sí,* if you like." He was warning her, and he could tell that she knew it.

"I read the book you gave me about the satyr, and I am still here," she offered.

"Ah, that was nothing, *mi ángel,* I assure you. Do you see that folio over there? It is full of sketches — chalk, pencil and ink studies. Many of them were done when I was young. For others, I have no such excuse. After you see them, if you want to leave, I won't stop you."

He knew she had no idea what she was about to see, his erotic fantasies captured on paper. But better to reveal himself to her now before too much more of his heart was lost.

Eva rose, walked slowly across the studio and brought the folio back to the bed. Her silhouette was small and fragile in the dim candlelight. His heart began to beat wildly with anticipation and fear.

He watched as she flipped through the sketches, holding each one between her delicate fingers. They were crude. Vulgar. The sketch on top was certainly the worst.

Although perhaps it was better to begin there. He gazed down dispassionately for the moment at his own work as she held it between delicate fingers. The image was a familiar one. In sepia, he had drawn a large phallus with a face that resembled Jesus. On the scrotum was a naked woman, crouching, arms outstretched. Behind this sketch was a pen drawing of a naked girl, probably Germaine, although Picasso could not remember now, as it was six or seven years old. The woman's legs were spread, her fingers seductively placed on her own genitals.

He felt himself cringe as he saw these works now through Eva's eyes. It mattered to him what she thought. The next was drawn in the style of a cartoon. Another phallus. A woman in service to it. But this was him, and he must reveal himself to her if there was ever to be full trust between them.

"I slept with Louis after you left Paris," she said suddenly.

"I would have assumed."

"Twice." It seemed to him like a tender warning, perhaps her way of putting them on more even footing. He so admired that spark of fire she had, which always flared when he least expected it.

"All right."

"The first time, it was because I was angry with you. The second time, I just wanted to do it."

"I see."

"So, I am not the complete innocent you think I am."

"Es mejor," he said, feeling a sense of relief.

"Better, how?"

"Relationships are a journey but this is one we could not share if I were always frightening or disgusting to you."

"Is there a journey for us to go on together?"

"Oh, most definitely," Picasso said.

"I really cannot see how."

"Just yet, nor can I. But the path will reveal itself in time if we do not press too hard to find it."

"That sounds very mystical."

"Do you think so?"

His fascination with tarot cards, and knowing the future, had begun a couple of years earlier with Max Jacob, who was always studying religions and mysticism — ways to a higher consciousness, besides at the bottom of a glass. Picasso could not yet, however, bring himself to admit how strongly superstition played a part in his life. His Andalusian roots were deep, something not easily explained to a pretty girl from a suburban French town. He must tread carefully with them.

"Even when I was a child, my sisters and I were exposed to folklore and beliefs in Spain that are not easily explained here."

"You had two sisters, then?" she cautiously asked.

"Lola and Conchita." Picasso could hear the catch in his own voice.

"I wish I could have known Conchita since she meant so much to you. Is there perhaps a sketch or a painting of her?"

He chaffed at the French way Eva spoke Conchita's name. Picasso did not like to hear anyone speak it. It made him defensive and angry. The wound would never be completely healed because he had been so young. But Picasso wanted to try to make her understand what of it he could. The sensations with this woman were all so new, and some were raw to him, but he wanted to push through them, anyway.

"I sketched my sister many times. She enjoyed watching my hand fly over the paper. She said it reminded her of a butterfly."

Eva pressed her head into the curve of his neck. It was a small gesture, but at that moment it meant the world to him.

"Will you tell me how she died?"

"I don't know if I can." He drew in a breath. It had been a long time since he had spoken about her. Not even Fernande knew the whole truth. Thoughts and memories swam in his mind. Picasso squeezed his eyes for a moment.

It did not help that whenever he looked at Eva he was also reminded of Conchita's vulnerability and her gentle spirit. The ache of losing his sister when he was just a boy rushed powerfully back now. She had not deserved to die so young, and he had not deserved the burden of her loss to weigh so heavily upon his heart. How he missed her sweet smile. Nothing in the world had changed the essence of him so much as the circumstances of her death had. It had brought with it a nearly obsessive fear now of illness and death tied deeply in with those Andalusian superstitions. He simply could not bear to be around it.

"When she fell ill, painting was already my great passion, but my mother spoke to us of humbling ourselves in our prayers for Conchita's health. She said that God would save her if we were willing to sacrifice. I was so desperate that I offered to God as my sacrifice the only thing of value I thought I had in the world. I made a vow that if the

Lord would spare her, I would never paint again."

"That was really extraordinary of you, being so young."

"Not so extraordinary. I failed after a week. I painted, and Conchita died of diphtheria. My sister died because of me."

After Conchita died, Picasso had stopped believing in God, but he did not tell Eva that. He could not. Nor could he tell her that he had done everything since then to spite Him — anything to challenge a Lord that would do something so cruel.

"You have to know that it wasn't your fault. Diphtheria is a powerful illness, and she was so young."

"That shouldn't have mattered. I made a promise."

"You were a boy."

"She never thought I could do anything wrong, either." Picasso shrugged in an attempt to push back the tears he could feel at the backs of his eyes. "I've never met anyone like you."

"I'm glad we've become friends, Pablo," she said.

"Yo también, ma jolie," Picasso agreed. But he wanted much more than her friendship.

CHAPTER 18

Summer faded and autumn came again.

The air was crisp, the clear sky was a broad canvas and a vast carpet of amber leaves swirled and danced, making a new landscape across the city. Steadily Parisians donned their heavier woolen coats, scarves and gloves, and lately everyone in the cafés and brasseries were chattering about the upcoming Salon d'Automne art exhibition.

For years, Picasso had chosen not to participate because he did not like the commercialization, or the potential ridicule, that seemed always to come with it. The violent criticism of the Cubist movement had put him off. "There is no need to devote much space to an art form that is utterly without importance," one of the papers had said. And that was one of the more generous commentaries.

Still, his curiosity over what his rivals were doing would get the better of him every time

— especially Georges Braque — and he knew this year he would attend just as he had the Salon des Indépendants.

He had not seen Eva for over a month, but a day did not pass when he did not think of her, or remember every word and nuance of their last conversation. He had not pursued her because he had said he wouldn't, and he meant to show her that he could be a man of his word. He wanted to be the good man he knew she believed him to be.

On his easel now was an unfinished Cubist painting of her. She was different from any other woman he had known and so he was moved to create the image of her differently. The colors on his palette, and on the tip of his paintbrush, were autumnal: gold, brown, a muted green. The symbols he used to represent her would be obvious clues to anyone who knew who held his heart. But Picasso was safe in the knowledge that, at least for now, the only person who knew about his love was Eva.

A treble clef signified the music they had heard at the quaint Au Tambourin a month ago. Fingers were *her* sweet fingers touching her glass of Pernod as she looked up at him. The strings of a violin recalled his confession: "I wish I were holding you right

now, as that musician holds his instrument."
And just a hint of her perfect smile; it made
him think of the *Mona Lisa.* At the bottom
of the canvas, he had painted in just two
simple words: *Ma Jolie.*

Beyond the smudged windowpanes of his
studio, a cool wind blew and a kaleidoscope
of leaves was stirring across the pavement.
He could not imagine what Fernande would
do if she knew about Eva. He and Fernande
were growing more estranged every day, but
he had yet to decide how to leave her in a
way that would not devastate her. Yet even
so, Eva was now his sole obsession.

Picasso knew from his friend Joseph Oller
that she was still working at the Moulin
Rouge, though her foray as a stage actress
had begun and ended that one impetuous
evening. In spite of her protest against it,
Picasso had spoken privately with Oller on
Eva's behalf. He meant to protect her job
behind the scenes whether she wanted him
to or not. Picasso told Oller that he would
consider it a personal favor if there were no
repercussions against Mademoiselle Humbert for having been brave enough to help
one of the show's stars.

At first, Oller, with blustering pomposity,
had rejected the plea. Madame Léautaud
was furious and had already reprimanded

her. But not without a certain power of bluster himself, Picasso threatened to take his business, his friends and his rising fame across town, to the Folies Bergère. Two days later, Eva was formally made an assistant to the costume designer, in addition to the position she already held. Madame Léautaud's only comment was a stiff-lipped congratulations. That much Picasso knew through Mistinguett. He wanted the best for Eva, whether or not he would ever see her again.

The sun was setting a brilliant gold and crimson as Picasso glanced beyond the steep steps of the butte, at the view from Montmartre. Before him, the Tour Eiffel was like a great mythical creature looming over the Paris skyline. He loved this view for all that it signified. Picasso exhaled a breath, then turned in paint-spattered shoes and wound his way along the twisting, cobbled streets. His cap was pulled low over his brow, keeping him happily unrecognized. He rounded a corner bordered by a great stone wall, and at last, down the steep lane, he headed toward la Maison Rose intent on stopping by before heading on to Gertrude Stein's salon.

Picasso took a table outside in the fading

sunlight of early evening since they were not due at the Steins' until after seven. Silently, he watched a young waiter light candles stuffed into old wine bottles on each of the small, linen-draped tables. How many evenings had he and Fernande spent here, happily drinking, dining and enjoying each other's company?

The charming pink bistro was the enterprise of his own long-ago lover Germaine and her husband, Ramón. Picasso always took delight in knowing that he had been the one to introduce them. For five years now, their foursome had been unbreakable.

Of course, years ago, before she had been Picasso's lover, he had also introduced Germaine to Casagemas, his best friend from Barcelona with whom he had come to Paris — and she had been the cause of his suicide. But that was another story best buried now. The friendship between the four of them, one that included Fernande, was deep and enduring. There were few people in the world he trusted more completely than the Pichots.

Germaine came outside and Picasso stood to embrace her. She had the most remarkable green eyes, he had always thought, similar to Fernande. Everyone always thought they were sisters.

"I thought you had plans this evening," she said as he sank back into his chair and another young couple took the table beside him.

"We do. I just thought I would have a beer with Ramón first. Is he here?"

"Where else would he be?" She chuckled. A moment later, she looked more seriously at him. "Is everything okay, Pablo?"

"Why wouldn't it be?" He knew he had answered too quickly because she paused before she spoke again.

"I don't know. We just haven't seen a lot of you since the whole *Mona Lisa* affair. We've been worried about you."

"There is nothing to worry about. I'm working. My paintings are selling. Kahnweiler is organizing another show next month for me in London."

Her expression grew suspicious.

"I haven't seen Fernande for a while, either, since right after the two of you returned from Céret."

"She is no doubt somewhere happily spending my money. That does seem to occupy a good portion of her time these days."

He knew that he sounded brittle, but he could not help it. They had known each other far too long. Ramón came out carrying two plates for a group of diners a few tables away. He set the dishes down, then approached them.

"*Hola,* Don Quixote," Picasso said.

"*El hijo pródigo regresa,*" replied Ramón as he sat down at Picasso's table. *The prodigal son returns.*

Tall and lanky with a long, gaunt, bearded face, Ramón Pichot had long been referred to by Picasso's Barcelona gang as Don Quixote, and the name had stuck.

For his part, Ramón had referred to Picasso as the prodigal son since their youthful days, sipping endless little inky *cafés,* amid the blue smoke of pipes and cigars at Els Quatre Gats in Barcelona, arguing about women and art.

A fraternal smile passed between them. "I always return, amigo," Picasso said as Germaine went to greet another collection of diners and Ramón took her chair.

"So, will Fernande be joining you here?"

"No, she has no idea where I am, either. But I'm certain she will be at the Steins' apartment when I get there. She wouldn't miss a chance to be seen there after summer. One never knows what wildly famous person might be there to welcome Gertrude and Alice back to the land of civilized creatures." He laughed.

"Besides yourself." Ramón chuckled as he

leaned back in the wooden chair.

"Ciertamente."

A moment later, Germaine brought them each a glass of beer, gave Picasso a sisterly pat on the top of his cap and went back inside the bistro.

"Anything you can talk about?" Ramón asked in the evening breeze.

Picasso stared at the candle on the table between them. "Not yet."

"I haven't seen Fernande since that time last spring we all met up at the Circus Medrano."

"I'm not sure that I recall," Picasso lied because he could not bear to talk about that evening with someone who would not understand his feelings for another woman.

"You had invited that couple who went with us for drinks afterward, remember?"

"Fernande invited them."

"I see."

He had answered quickly and his tone was too sharp. Ramón caught it. He knew Picasso too well to let it pass. "The girl you sat beside, with whom you were whispering throughout the circus, she was pretty, no?"

"I didn't notice," Picasso lied again, even less convincingly.

"No?" Ramón arched a brow. A small silence followed. "I certainly did. She looked just like that delectable little actress Evelyn Thaw — difficult to forget. Fernande and Germaine were talking all evening about how small and perfect she was, and I'd have to agree. They could be twins."

"You're married, amigo."

"Perhaps. But not dead." Ramón chuckled again with a mischievous little wink. "Do you remember how you and I, Manolo and Juan Gris used to talk all those prostitutes on the carrer Avinyó into giving us half price?"

"*Sí,* and I remember what Juan got for it, too," Picasso quipped.

Both of them chuckled devilishly at the memory.

"We're going to the Closerie des Lilas for Paul Fort's poetry reading Tuesday night, with Ricardo and Benedetta, since Fort is also back after summer. You and Fernande should join us. It would be good to get the whole group together again, don't you think?"

What Ramón had meant was that it would be good to gather him and Fernande back up in the heavy cloak of friendship and tradition that would ever keep things as they were. "I'll think about it," Picasso said as he finished his beer. Then he left Montmartre, trekking down the steep stone staircase at

the rue Foyatier, before he could say anything else to his friends that might show
more of what he was really thinking. Besides, all he wanted to think about — for
now, anyway — was getting lost in some
wonderful debate with Gertrude Stein. She
was the one friend he could count on, for
an evening, to help him forget everything
that was really troubling him.

CHAPTER 19

Going to Gertrude Stein's this time had been Louis's idea. He had insisted. He had run into Fernande Olivier on the street, coming out of the Métro station. She had personally invited them, he told Eva. Louis did not know that Eva had seen him with Fernande at the Taverne de l'Ermitage, so when he had presented the invitation to the salon, Eva had agreed to go as his companion. To do otherwise would have been to reveal that she, too, had stepped beyond the bounds of propriety that night, and to invite questions she would not wish to answer. She didn't know if he had slept with Fernande, but that didn't matter to her. Eva had used Louis, and she was still ashamed of that. She cared deeply for Picasso, and to her that made the act entirely different with the two men.

As she and Louis stood together at the open door to the very crowded salon, Louis took her hand and gave it a squeeze. She was wearing a stylish new dress of pale rose and lavender fabric. Her waist was tightly cinched with a belt she had found at a little shop on the rue Lepic, over near le Moulin de la Galette. She thought she had begun to look just a bit sophisticated, at last.

"Remember now, here among these people I am known as Marcoussis and I've had to try to live up to my mysterious new persona. But if someone were to say something to you about me, no matter how it strikes you, it will all just be in good fun. You are all that matters to me," he said. Eva privately rolled her eyes at his condescension. She knew then that he was trying to pave the way in case someone remarked about his evening out with Fernande. Eva wanted to look over at him, but she couldn't. Her friend, her first friend in Paris, was standing right here, lying to her, and covering his tracks clumsily as he did it.

It may be all the rage in Paris among their young crowd, to pursue pleasure first and foremost, but at heart, Eva wasn't truly one of them. What had happened between her and Picasso was nothing at all like that.

As they made their way into the crowded salon, it was only a moment inside the apartment before she saw Picasso. He looked more magnificent than any man had a right to look. He was sitting at the large table that dominated the center of the room and he was deep in conversation with Gertrude, Alice and a darkly bearded man in spectacles whom Eva did not know.

"There's Picasso over there, talking with Henri Matisse," Louis murmured excitedly to her as he pulled her toward them through the crowd. "What an opportunity! But don't ruin it for me by engaging them in silly conversation if it's not about art."

Eva felt the sting of his directive, even though all she could see was Picasso, so purely male as always, sitting in a natty tweed jacket and white open-collar shirt. His dark hair was smoothed back from his ebony eyes, which were rooted intensely on Matisse. She had hoped he would be here, and she found herself smiling as he glanced up and saw her.

"Marcoussis, Mademoiselle Humbert, join us. You know Monsieur Matisse, of course," Picasso said, waving them over.

"I — We have not had the pleasure. But I do have a thousand questions," Louis replied a little too eagerly as Picasso stood and chivalrously offered Eva his own chair. Louis was left for a moment to stand beside him. Picasso's dark gaze settled on Eva but

Louis was too enthralled by Matisse to notice. Gertrude stood then and before she could offer her chair to either of them, Picasso quickly slipped into it beside Eva.

"Please, Monsieur Marcoussis, take Alice's chair over there. I've bored these two gentlemen quite long enough about my book. I'm sure they will be only too relieved to go back to discussing art with you. Come, Alice, I see Isadora Duncan and her lover have just arrived. We should greet them," Gertrude said as she and Alice left the table.

Eva could feel the energy between her and Picasso and it was unsettling. It was impossible to think clearly when he was this close to her. If Louis only knew, she thought, trying her best to keep her wits about her.

Louis began to pepper Picasso and Matisse with questions about form and technique. As they patiently answered him, Eva was pulled from the moment by the touch of a feminine hand on her shoulder, and a female voice just behind her. She felt a shiver, knowing by the change in Picasso's expression who it was before she even turned around in her chair.

Fernande was dressed in a silky beige dress and pearls, her hair drawn up off her shoulders, enhancing the elegant turn of her neck. Her sensuality remained effortless, reminding Eva yet again of just how different they were. Her presence stopped the conversation.

"What a lovely surprise. I had no idea you would be here, Marcelle. It has been ages. Ah, and Marcoussis." Fernande indulged him with a casual embrace after he rose to greet her. "Now, gentlemen, if you will excuse us, I must steal Marcelle away so that we can gossip and get caught up. I know nothing of what has been happening with the two of you since the Circus Medrano, and I have a few of my own tales to tell."

"Remember what I said, *ma chérie,* things here are all in good fun," Louis whispered cryptically to Eva.

Before Eva had a chance to object, Fernande spirited her through the crowd, and over to a corner of the room near a window beside a large potted fern. She kissed each of Eva's cheeks then and took up her hands as if they were sisters.

"How are you, *mon amie?* You look absolutely stunning. Mistinguett told me she'd taken you to have your hair styled but I had no idea how sophisticated it would make you look!"

"Thank you," said Eva, not entirely convinced it was a compliment.

306

"How have you been?"

"Very well. Working a great deal lately."

"Still at the Moulin Rouge?"

"Yes. I am officially an assistant to the costume designer now, and I also have duties with wardrobe."

"How lovely. Would you like a drink? I certainly would. I adore Gertude, truly I do. She's been such a friend and supporter to my Pablo, but these things can be so tiresome, don't you agree?"

Eva hadn't realized that, beside them, was a large oak buffet lined with glasses and bottles of wine. For the first time in a while she truly did want a drink. The conversation and events seemed to be happening far too quickly and she was determined to keep up with everything and not say the wrong thing. But that was going to take some effort.

As Fernande poured them each a glass of wine, Eva glanced over and saw Picasso watching them while Louis continued chattering away at Matisse. Picasso's expression had darkened. Clearly, he was not amused that she and Fernande were saying things he could not hear. Eva looked back at Fernande just as she handed Eva an overly full glass, for which she was suddenly grateful.

307

"Things for me have not been quite so good. They have been difficult, really," Fernande confessed. "I'm sure you heard about the whole *Mona Lisa* affair."

"I believe I heard something."

"I don't mind telling you, it has been absolute hell, and there are so few women, no one, really, I can speak about it with, and not feel judged."

"Mistinguett?"

"I adore her, obviously. She is one of my dearest friends. But there was something about you that made me trust you from that first conversation between us in the cab."

Eva felt the pressure once again of guilt's heavy hand bearing down on her. She took a large sip of wine and then another, unable to look back at Picasso. She knew her face was flushed. She could feel it burning.

"May I confide something in you?" Fernande asked. "I really feel as if I have nowhere else to turn."

"Our lives are so different. I don't really see how I could help."

Eva wanted to strain against the guilt that had taken hold of her. She wanted to run from the room but she knew that she was as trapped as a bug on flypaper. Leaving now would cause a scene and only make things worse.

Fernande leaned forward and lowered her tone. "Marcelle, it's Picasso. Since the theft and Apollinaire's arrest, he has been so incredibly cold and distant, you can't imagine. Our summer trip was a veritable disaster, and I don't mind telling you he wouldn't even touch me in Céret. Something has changed between us. I am not to be trifled with like this, I'm truly not."

That last was a sentiment on which they could agree. The urge to escape disappeared and Eva was suddenly eager to hear what Fernande would say next. She took another long sip of wine, trying to steady herself. Eva liked Fernande in spite of everything, but that only worsened her sense of guilt.

"By the way, you really are so perfect looking."

"I would say the same of you."

"I understand why Marcoussis is absolutely enslaved by you. I envy you having that complete devotion from a man. I had it once. Or at least I believed I did."

As they both glanced over at the table where the artists sat, Fernande's color deepened suddenly and her expression changed. In the space between Picasso's and Matisse's chairs stood two swarthy Italian men talking with them now. The younger, and more handsome, of the pair had caught

Fernande's gaze. Suddenly she seemed flustered, and Eva realized that she had seen them both before. It was that night she and Picasso had looked through the window at l'Ermitage.

Fernande looked back at her then with desperate intensity lighting her eyes.

"If you are my real friend, you and I are going to leave here in a moment. Later, I need you to say that we went somewhere together — that you needed someone to talk with, and we lost all track of time. Will you do that for me?"

Eva was stunned. She had refused Picasso because of Fernande — and now Fernande was about to be unfaithful to *him*? What if she told Picasso? Would he even believe her? And would it matter if he did? Who truly knew the private world of any two people and what their limits were with one another? The questions circled around in her mind, like bees in a hive. Eva knew she had a choice to make, and none of the available options were good ones. The risks were great no matter how she played it.

She finally drew in a breath of resolve, looking at this strikingly beautiful woman standing before her, her expression piqued by desperation. Eva would go with her now, and she would lie for her later, if anyone asked. She would do it this time. But this war was far from over. Picasso deserved better, she thought angrily. And so did she.

"That's absolutely awful," Sylvette said as she sat back on her heels on her bed in the room they shared at la Ruche. It was late that same evening after Gertrude's gathering, and after enough time had passed to give Fernande a cover for her infidelity. Eva felt sick. An autumn rain came down in ribbons against the windowpanes and even the walls were made cold by it.

"I know." Eva sighed, brokenhearted. "But what can I do about it?"

"I can't think she'll get away with it. Imagine wanting to make a cuckold of Picasso now that he is becoming so well-known! Why don't you go to their place, and talk to him? You know *she* won't be there."

"Oh, Sylvette, I can't."

"You can't or you won't?"

"What's the difference? I don't want him that way, because he is angry with Fernande and simply trying to retaliate. He would resent me soon enough for being the one to tell him about her."

Sylvette shrugged. "You may be right. But then again, would you regret it if you didn't at least try? He won't have any idea if *you* don't tell him. Give Picasso a chance to do the right thing, hmm? He just might surprise you."

"Sylvette, he could break my heart."

"And what will happen to your heart, *mon amie,* if you walk away from this chance?"

Near midnight, plied with enough wine to give her false courage, Eva stood at the door to Picasso's apartment before a sour-faced maid in a black uniform, white lace apron and cap. A puddle of rainwater collected beneath Eva's shoes, and a closed umbrella was at her side.

"Monsieur Picasso n'est pas ici," the maid said with raised gray eyebrows.

Desperately, Eva peered over the old woman's broad shoulder to look inside the apartment. She caught only a glimpse of Fernande and Picasso's private world then. The elegant space, bathed in soft amber light from a collection of dim lamps, was heavily furnished with African masks on the walls, along with paintings, sketches and batik scarves hung as art. There was a Siamese cat lounging on the sofa.

The maid, standing ramrod straight as she held the door, cleared her throat and Eva snapped back to attention. She suddenly felt cheap. Tawdry. It was a mistake. All of it

312

was a grand mistake. She could strangle Sylvette for urging her to do this.

Eva looked down at the book she held in her hand, the racy volume about satyrs Picasso had given her. She wasn't certain why she had brought it here. An excuse, if she would need one? She felt pathetic.

"May I ask when Monsieur Picasso is expected to return?"

There was a painfully long silence as the maid glared at her and, for a moment, Eva thought she did not mean even to reply.

"Monsieur Picasso has left Paris, and he has not informed me when, or if, he plans to return. Now, since it is late, I shall bid you a good evening. You would be well advised to get yourself back to wherever you came from," she said brusquely, her gray eyebrow still raised suspiciously. "Have you a message you wish to leave before you go? Something perhaps Madame Picasso can assist you with when she returns?"

"That won't be necessary," Eva said.

"Go home, mademoiselle. Believe me, it will be better for you that way."

The gray-haired woman then slammed the tall, black lacquered door without further ceremony, cutting off Eva's hope as well as her last bit of pride.

■ ■ ■ ■

"Where have you been?"

Eva heard the sharp edge in Louis's voice even before she was fully inside her room. The place was dark and full of shadows but for the moonlight through the window, and the yellow glow of a single shaded lamp between the two small beds.

Before she could answer, he held up the key to his own studio downstairs.

"Wait at my place," he directed Sylvette in a frighteningly cold tone. "I need to speak with Eva alone."

Sylvette looked back and forth to each of them, then silently complied. Eva set the book from Picasso on the dresser, and took a step closer to Louis. Sylvette closed the door. A charged silence sprang up between them as she wearily drew off her raincoat and hung it on the wall hook.

"Can this not wait until morning? I'm awfully tired."

"I asked where you've been."

The edge in his voice did not soften.

"You know perfectly well I was at Gertrude Stein's with you."

"And then you slipped out in the company of Fernande Olivier, without so much as a

314

farewell. I couldn't help but notice that young, shifty-eyed Italian boy who slipped out a moment later."

Was that what he thought? *She* and Ubaldo Oppi? The irony nearly made her laugh. But she saw by his expression that the moment was far too serious for laughter. Perhaps Picasso had seen them leave and thought the same thing. But to proclaim her innocence now was to open up a Pandora's box, not just about Fernande and Oppi, but potentially about herself and Picasso. Louis moved forward, cloaked in shadows. In that moment, he looked quite menacing.

"Where did you go with Fernande?"

"She took me to Vernin on the rue Cavallotti."

"Did Ubaldo Oppi join you?"

"Of course not. She needed a friend to talk to."

Eva had heard Fernande mention that Vernin was her favorite bistro, so the lie came to her quickly enough. But she could tell he was not finished with her.

"Why *you*? Certainly she has friends more of her station than a theater hand like you."

Louis had never insulted her before, or been anything but kind. Eva took a step back, but he quickly closed the space between them. His voice now was brittle with suspicion.

"She told me that she didn't feel at times that she could trust her other friends to understand."

"Don't lie to me."

He gripped her by the arms, clamping his fingers so tightly into her skin that she gasped. Then he drew her close enough to smell his sour breath, and he struck her hard across the face with an open palm.

The memory of being struck by her father vaulted into her mind.

"I'm not lying." She forced her voice not to quaver as her face began to burn. She couldn't quite process the fact that he had actually hit her.

"All I'm saying, *ma chère* Marcelle, is that you are mine now, body and soul. If you *were* with that artist, I don't believe I could be responsible for what I might do in response."

"Get out."

Louis headed for the door without protest but then he paused and turned back. He stood in the dim light of the hallway. "By the way, Picasso offered us his congratulations."

"For what?"

"For our engagement, of course. Well, our

soon-to-be engagement, since it is all but decided upon. I meant to keep it as a surprise until I had a proper ring to give you, but I went to Vincennes last Tuesday and spoke with your father."

"You did *what*?"

"He was most agreeable since he said it is long overdue that you settle down and made someone a proper wife. Since I inferred that we are already lovers, he had no objection."

"You had no right!"

"I took your innocence, I had every right."

Eva clutched her temples as incredulity beat out an angry staccato rhythm in her head. Her head throbbed as her mind reeled. She wanted to cry out that they were not lovers. She had given him nothing other than a few moments with her body as she tried to forget the man who would always possess her heart. But that was a closely held secret — like so many other secrets that ruled them all — and she would not breathe a word of it. What she had shared of herself with Picasso felt too sacred.

Chapter 20

The next evening, after the show at the Moulin Rouge, when Eva went to gather up her things, she found a man in a dark coat and black silk top hat waiting for her near the stage door. He was tall and bearded, with deep brown eyes, a long prominent nose and a warm smile. She was surprised when he addressed her as a Mademoiselle Gouel, not as Marcelle Humbert, since few in Paris knew her real name.

"I have been charged by my client to deliver this parcel directly to you, and *only you.*"

"Your client, monsieur?" she asked, looking down at the small parcel. It was wrapped in brown paper and tied with string.

"I believe his identity will become clear once you have unwrapped it, mademoiselle. He has gone to Le Havre for a few days, but he asked that I deliver this to you with the utmost discretion."

"Am I to know who *you* are?"

He gazed down at her and offered a small, patient smile as he removed his top hat politely. "I am Daniel-Henry Kahnweiler."

Kahnweiler was something of a celebrity in Paris as an art dealer who had represented such giants as Cézanne and Gauguin. Eva had read about his stunning sales in the papers more than once, and she knew that Picasso was another of his clients.

"Take care with the contents, mademoiselle, since anything by the artist is a thing of great value in today's market."

Suddenly Eva's heart began beating very fast. She glanced around to see if any of the performers or stage crew had taken notice of their exchange, but thankfully everyone was distracted with packing up for the evening.

"You will want to open it privately," Kahnweiler said as he handed it to her. For a moment he seemed not to want to let it go.

"*Merci,* monsieur."

"I counseled him against this, you know. He was leaving town for a few days to clear his head so I didn't believe he had considered the consequences of such a gift."

"Your client seems a rather determined sort."

"Ah, Mademoiselle Gouel, you cannot

know the half of it," Kahnweiler said as he let go of the parcel at last, and placed the tall hat back on top of his head.

Eva knew what it was the moment she opened the package. A collage of shapes and warm colors came together like sweet music on the canvas. She marveled at how whimsical the painting was, and yet how sensual. It was another moment before she saw the inscription. Three small words that defined the canvas were painted into it. *J'aime Eva.*
I love Eva.

She was glad she was alone in her room as she opened the package because Eva let out a sudden yelp of elation. Was it possible that, all along, he had felt what she felt? Then she thought of Fernande and how shamelessly she had bid Eva, of all women, to lie for her. Fernande was making a fool of Picasso.

Eva fell asleep soon afterward, holding the small painting against her breast. She and Picasso weren't finished, after all. This was just the beginning.

The next morning, she woke to the sound of a motorcar idling outside on the quiet passage Dantzig beneath her slightly open window. The sound of a woman's voice followed. The voice was familiar.

"Go and fetch Mademoiselle Humbert,

320

and do not take 'no' for an answer," she instructed the driver. "Tell her I will take her for a lovely *petite déjeuner* at Hôtel le Meurice. Tell her I am absolutely desperate to confide in her. And do be quick about it, before anyone spots me in this pedestrian neighborhood."

Even though it was after ten, Sylvette was sound asleep, but Eva drew herself quietly onto her knees and pulled aside the curtains. She knew the voice but seeing Fernande here now in the open car still brought a small jolt of surprise. She touched her cheek, which was sore. She glanced at the mirror. There was a bruise. Louis hadn't struck her all that forcefully so she was surprised it had left such a painful mark. She would certainly have to cover that before she went out anywhere.

"And make certain she is dressed in something suitable for le Meurice — if she has anything at all."

"*Oui,* madame."

Eva watched a driver in a blue coat and cap nod to the young woman in the back-seat of the car. *I should have known,* she thought even as panic set in and a light mist fell on the impossibly gray Paris morning.

Eva emerged reluctantly from la Ruche ten

minutes later, the darkening bruise well covered with makeup. The driver silently led her to a cab that was waiting for her just past the ivy-covered courtyard. She did not think going to breakfast with Fernande was a wise decision, but Eva had no idea how to say no. There was such irony in the situation that Eva could scarcely look at Fernande as she sank onto the leather seat beside her.

Fernande was dressed stylishly, as always, in a big beige hat with a black grosgrain ribbon that matched her dress. If she had always been this persuasive with Picasso, Eva understood a bit more about the strength and duration of their relationship. Fernande Olivier was most definitely an intimidating force, even when she was being pleasant.

"Thank you for coming, Marcelle. I really was desperate to speak with someone who knows my circumstance."

The circumstance that has you cheating on your lover right beneath his nose? Eva thought to herself.

The taxi pulled out into traffic on the busy rue de Dantzig.

"Your dress is quite lovely," Fernande said. She seemed to Eva to be avoiding the real reason she had brought her here.

"Thank you, I made it," Eva said, and thought how Picasso had been drawn to it when she'd worn it to Au Tambourin.

"You really are quite talented. It's a wonder Marcoussis has not married you yet."

"Everything in good time, I suppose." She looked over and forced herself calmly to ask, "So to what do I owe the pleasure this morning?"

"It's the same thing, I'm afraid. Only now it's all much more serious."

There was a strained silence that filled the cab as it chugged along, weaving through traffic. As she glanced over at her, Eva could not stop from thinking about how many times Picasso must have sketched Fernande, immortalizing her naked curves before making love to her.

Did Fernande have the slightest idea how fortunate she was? Clearly not since she had brought Eva out to talk about another man. And with a woman who would gladly take Picasso's love if she had the chance.

Keep your friends close, and your enemies closer, Eva thought.

"I've been with Ubaldo these past days and it has been heaven, Marcelle. No moods, no angry tirades, no rejection — only unbelievable passion."

"Would Mistinguett not be a better confidante for you in these matters?" Eva asked, still struggling with the absurdity of Fernande telling her, of all people, about this. "I've far less experience in *affairs de coeur* than she."

"Perhaps that is why I like you. Virtue here in Paris is so surprisingly refreshing."

If you only knew, Eva thought.

"Ubaldo is just so delectable. I've never met anyone quite like him." Her tone, and the cadence of her speech, was suddenly escalating, like a train gathering steam. "He's young, not even twenty-two, so tall, without a worry in the world. When I am with him we just laugh and laugh."

You meant to say that he is everything Pablo Picasso is not, Eva's mind taunted her to say.

"He *is* handsome," she agreed, determined not to betray her own anger and ruin everything.

The taxi came to a stop at the main entrance to Hôtel le Meurice, and a doorman rushed over. A burgundy carpet lined the sidewalk and the pathway to the etched glass front door. Of all the glamorous hotels in Paris, why the very one to which Picasso had taken her to speak with her mother? Eva wondered with an unsettling little shiver. Had Fernande discovered something and now meant to confront her?

The breakfast room was elaborately decorated, and they sat at a small table near the window, ornamented by huge potted ferns, a marble pillar and a gilded birdcage full of yellow canaries. Eva thought the room seemed overly full of hats. Elegant women and their hats. Wide-brimmed, feather-trimmed, felt, silk. It was a sea of color and audacious design. Eva, in her handmade blue cotton dress and loose rust-colored neck scarf, once again felt inadequate and small. She still wore her straw hat, since she had not bothered to buy a fashionable one in Paris. Today particularly, she keenly felt the scope of that mistake.

Eva looked across the table at Fernande as the dreary gray daylight through the window softened her lovely face even more beneath her own hat. Her dolman wrap had white fox at the cuffs. They were both trying to live far beyond their means, being in a place like this, but Fernande seemed perfectly in her element here even so.

A stiff-backed waiter served them coffee from a shiny silver pot while another waiter set out a china plate with an array of croissants, brioche and cream. It would have been impossible for Eva to have consumed a morsel under the circumstance, although Fernande appeared ravenous. Instead, she settled for coffee, hoping that her stomach would not reject even that.

"I am not really sure how I can help you," Eva finally said, even after she swore to herself that she would not speak first.

"He wants me to go away with him, and I am considering it."

Eva took a sip of coffee. "Oh?"

"I know it may seem dreadful of me, but Picasso has been off in Le Havre with that painter Georges Braque. They're probably spending all day painting silly circles and boxes, like little children."

Eva did not think their art style was silly at all, especially after Picasso had explained the inspiration behind it.

"Don't I deserve a bit of excitement on my own? And Picasso truly does need to be taught a lesson for the way he has treated me these past few months, doesn't he?"

Eva longed to say she was certain that Fernande was the one who was about to get the lesson *she* deserved, but she held her tongue.

She had learned in Paris that timing was everything.

"Jealousy could certainly kindle that fire in Picasso again, and Ubaldo is the perfect man to help me do that. Picasso has always gone quite mad at the thought of another artist having me. He considers it the ultimate betrayal."

Fernande's green eyes glittered with cold calculation. "Don't misunderstand, Marcelle. I want Picasso — just perhaps a more agreeable version of him than the one I've had lately, not to mention the passionate one I remember."

"What do you want from me in all this?"

Fernande chuckled, and there was a note of surprise in her tone. "Your loyalty, and of course, your friendship. Picasso is returning tomorrow from Le Havre. Ubaldo and I will need someone who we can trust as a liaison — someone Picasso would believe with the story. I'm sorry to have brought you out so suddenly like this. I hope you don't mind. But you see now, I'm afraid, why time really is of the essence."

Eva nearly choked on her coffee. She tossed her napkin on the tabletop and stood, certain that her face had lost all of its color. Fernande looked at Eva with an expression of surprise.

"Oh, dear. Now I've embarrassed you. It wouldn't be anything too awfully wicked, I promise you. Perhaps just deliver a message here and there. Or cover for me if anyone asks whether or not we're together. That sort of thing can be quite a delicious little game, if you don't take it too seriously."

In the next moment, before Eva could even catch her breath, Fernande stood, fluffing the fur cuffs at her wrists. To Eva, it felt like an exclamation point at the end of a sentence. Everything Fernande did, every word she spoke, seemed designed to be a reminder of exactly who was in charge.

"Enough of all this. I'm going to take you shopping for a hat. No girl can ever have enough hats. I know the most charming little shop over on the rue Cambon. I saw a particularly darling cloche style there yesterday. It's absolutely perfect for you," Fernande declared.

One thing was clear, bribery with elegant breakfasts and fashionable hats or not, Fernande Olivier absolutely intended to cheat on Picasso, with or without Eva's help.

CHAPTER 21

The next day, as the first buds of a new spring began to blossom throughout Paris, reviving everything, Picasso returned from Le Havre. He was weary from the long train ride so he went to Montmartre to spend the night alone at the Bateau-Lavoir before reuniting with Fernande. He was just too tired to face her drama without a good night's sleep.

As he opened the studio door and heard the familiar old creak, he saw something had been slipped beneath the door. It was a crude collage — things that had been glued together on cardboard. It looked almost like a talisman but he knew instantly that it was a response to his painting for Eva.

He was glad he had come here alone.

As he picked it up and looked at it more closely, he saw that there was a piece of torn newsprint from *Le Figaro*. Letters had been ripped from the newspaper to form the phrase *Je t'aime aussi. I love you, too.* Beside them she had glued the label from a bottle of Pernod, the drink they had shared that night at Au Tambourin. Tucked beneath the corner of the label was a swatch of bright yellow fabric that Picasso recognized instantly had come from the seam of the kimono.

Although Mistinguett had retired the geisha routine before he had left, Picasso knew he would never forget the sensual yellow silk as Eva had moved through the routine that one daring night. The bleak feeling of futility he'd had when he left Paris was finally beginning to evaporate. *Well, you are full of surprises, Mademoiselle Gouel,* he thought. His heart soared with a kind of optimism for life and art, and love, he could not remember feeling for a very long time.

Springtime was the beginning of so many things — and finally it was to be their beginning, as well. He had no idea what would happen now with Fernande, but Eva had changed him. Picasso wanted that change.

Nothing else mattered to him now so much as that.

He paused for a moment, then he had an idea. He picked up a key from the table near his easel before he walked down the hall toward the studio of one of his Spanish friends. Manuel never had any money and he spoke very little French, so, for a few welcome centimes, he would be perfect for the task Picasso had in mind. In Le Havre, Picasso had thought so often of Eva — how she had invaded his dreams there — and the words of Paul Verlaine's poem "My Familiar Dream" moved through his mind again now as a tender encouragement.

Eva was all of that in his head, in his heart; she was Marcelle, she was Eva, a seamstress, a designer, an exotic geisha, Polish, French, sensual, small, sincere — and utterly perfect. While he had always liked it, that poem had never touched him so much as it did now.

Picasso held out a key to his friend, nervous as a boy for all that was implied. The message, spoken in hushed Catalan, was simple. *Tell her I have returned to Montmartre, and leave her with this, her own key to my studio, so that she may come here when she is able.*

Because it was late, Eva took a streetcar first, and afterward she rode the funicular the rest of the way up to Montmartre. The conveyances were an indulgence, but she knew by the time she had finally trudged all the way up the steep steps of the rue Foyatier that she would have been too warm

331

and too flustered to face Picasso. She was terrified and excited all at once for what lay ahead.

Eva wore a navy blue dress with brass buttons and the simple cloche hat Fernande had insisted on buying for her yesterday. That particular hat she wore intentionally. After yesterday, she no longer pitied Fernande, who did not cherish Picasso the way Eva knew that she could.

Her ankles wobbled in her beige heels as she walked along the uneven floorboards down the corridor inside the Bateau-Lavoir. The heavy aroma of food and turpentine filled the space, and in a strange way, Eva found the combination pleasing. It was the smell of Picasso's world.

At the end of the second corridor, Eva pushed the key into the lock, then turned the door handle. She drew in a breath to slow her heart before she stepped inside. The studio was bathed in shadows cast by a candle set on a table beside the easel. The painting he called *Ma Jolie* was propped there. Picasso held a paintbrush and was pacing in small strides back and forth in front of it. He was naked. The candle flame, and the moonlight, cast his neck and slim torso in such rich shadows that he looked to her in that moment like a marble sculpture. Her body stirred at the sight of him. Eva loved that he could be so free, and so daring. They were both things she longed to become.

Picasso turned and looked at her as she closed the door but he made no attempt to cover himself. Eva could feel the current between them. "Was it very difficult to find a cab at this hour?" he asked.

"They are always nearby at l'Hôpital Saint-Michel, but I took the last streetcar."

"I am very glad you agreed to come."

"I want to be here, Pablo. I understand things better now."

He took a step toward her, then stopped. Eva saw him very clearly now: the planes of his cheeks, his nose, the line his mouth made. Thoughts and fears moved through her mind, but there was a clarity to everything, too, as she gazed into his bold black eyes. She could see that she was safe here with him.

"This won't be an affair between us," he said.

"Isn't that just what this is, though?" she asked, knowing that, as yet, he did not know about Fernande and Oppi, nor had he officially broken things off with her.

Eva had agreed to come here simply because she loved Picasso, and now she believed that he returned her love. For the time being, it would be a secret affair between them. The rest would have to somehow sort itself out in the coming days.

"I no longer want something with you I cannot have fully. I am going to marry you one day. That is, if you will have me, and if you are not already promised to Marcoussis."

Her heart swelled, and she felt herself smile. "Louis was never your competition. No one ever could be. You must have known that. But we have a bit of distance yet to travel before we find our forever after."

"Perhaps. But we will get there because you are here now, and we both know what it means. This is all of me." He held out a hand. "Here in this place. It is the essence of me — my work, my oddities, my superstitions . . . me as your man. It won't be easy — I can be difficult and demanding, so I want you to understand completely what you are getting yourself into."

"You haven't frightened me away yet."

He took a step so that he was near enough to embrace her. Eva felt time stop, and she could feel his heart beating through the thin fabric of her dress. Then he pressed a kiss very gently, almost reverently, onto her forehead.

"Ah, *mi amor,* be careful not to be too willing," he warned as he kissed each of her cheeks and then her mouth, openly and boldly. "My desire for you is wild. I fear it will not be tamed."

He slipped his fingers skillfully down the peaks and curves of her small body, then back up to the fullness of her breasts beneath the dress fabric. As his hands moved, Eva felt him shudder. The silence here in this old place felt strangely sacred. The secrecy of what was between them drew them into a warm, sweet harbor that both of them had waited months to find. They understood the battles yet to come, but there was no need to speak further of that just now.

Picasso tenderly drew Eva onto the bed, then slipped her dress off over her head. The white sheets were crisp and clean against her bare skin. Eva moved with the anticipation of what was to come.

Picasso arched over her and bent his head toward hers in this silence that was becoming a kind of communion. He lingered for a moment there, tantalizingly, before he matched his soft, warm mouth with hers again. Her thoughts spun and she arched her back.

This time, Picasso was careful with Eva,

as though she were something very delicate. She drew in a quick breath, and her eyes widened as he traced the outline of one breast, then the other, with gentle fingers. She tried to be passive, to let him explore the secret bends and turns of her yielding body. The single melting candle beside them pooled liquid wax at the base, and the flame fluttered like a last gasp.

Eva wanted to keep him like this forever. He was a shaman, a priest, drawing her ever more deeply into the light and the dark places of his world. All of them were places she wanted to go.

They woke the next morning wrapped up in one another, and covered with the Spanish quilt. It was quiet, and the cool blue dawn lit the cold studio that was still absolutely quiet.

"I must paint you," Picasso said. "After last night, I am inspired."

Eva held him against her. "Don't go. Not yet."

"Te amo," he murmured to her in Spanish as he kissed her cheek.

"Je t'aime aussi," she answered him in French.

And then he grew very still again. Eva tried to avert her face shyly, but she knew, with her powder and rouge worn away, what

336

had stopped him was the sight of her bruise.

"How did that happen?"

"I must have run into a door."

"Or a hand?" His tone grew angry; she could feel him tensing. He clutched her more tightly. "You're a terrible liar. I can see by your expression it wasn't a door."

"Oh, Pablo, everything that was before is in the past now. None of it matters." She reached up and combed the thick black hair away from his face with her fingers.

"I'll not let you go back to Marcoussis. I never liked him, anyway. He has a sleazy quality."

"You only say that because he isn't Spanish."

"You know that isn't funny. If he hurt you — if I knew for certain it was him who struck you — I think I would have no trouble killing him."

Outside, a light spring rain began to fall. It beat a soft rhythm against the window-panes. When he glanced over at the table beside the bed, her eyes followed. She had not noticed the black pistol there before, only partly obscured now by a painting rag.

"Oh, dear. Don't you think you've had enough problems recently?"

They both knew she meant the *Mona Lisa.*

"You might as well know now that I can

337

become quite angry at times. It frightens people." He stopped abruptly, pulled away and moved onto his elbow so that she would have no choice but to look at him. "But never have I struck a woman. You will not go back to him, or be alone with him ever again. *Entiendes?*"

"You are asking me to change my life completely when you have yet to do the same."

Their eyes met, and held.

"I told you that I intend for us to marry."

"You have Fernande."

"She will never be my wife."

"How can you know that?"

Eva propped herself against the headboard and pulled the quilt over her chest as Picasso rose from the bed. He opened the small drawer in the bedside table and drew out a worn piece of paper. She saw that it was a drawing of a hand surrounded by odd words and symbols.

"You know Max Jacob."

"The poet? Yes, I met him."

Picasso smiled, though he remained serious. "Max is interested in the magical arts. He has really been quite accurate. I grew up in a place called La Coruña, where belief in magic, and the weight of superstition, was strong. I have become a believer in

Max's predictions."

She knew he was waiting for her to mock his beliefs because his eyes narrowed slightly. Eva saw his mouth tighten. In response, she looked more closely at the paper, trying to decipher the handwriting and to make out the details. Picasso began to read the notes aloud to her with an ease that told her he had read this many times before. His finger trailed one of the lines as he explained.

"This is the line of luck. It says there was a brilliant beginning to my life, then many cruel disappointments."

He glanced briefly at the paintings stacked against the wall near the door. Eva remembered that at the back was the image of Casagemas. It held for her a connection to the time he had bravely told her about two of the most cruel disappointments in his life — the deaths of his friend and his sister Conchita.

"But a change of fortune just before the age of thirty." He looked up at her then with a tender expression. "I met *you* at the Petit Palais, not long before my thirtieth birthday, *mi amor.* That was not Fernande. She has not changed my fortune. You have."

He touched her bare breast and then he kissed her with a passion and tenderness that made her feel entirely exultant.

"What else does it say?" she murmured as he cast the paper to the floor and arched over her again.

"Cultured mind, a sarcastic wit —" His mouth was on the column of her throat.

"And?" She was breathless now with renewed desire.

"Perhaps judgment is not protected from the sudden whims of the imagination —"

"Oh, that sounds dangerous."

"I *am* dangerous, *ma jolie.* But I am also a man deeply in love. One surely cancels out the other."

From the depth of her dream, she thought it was butterflies. Eva stirred and tried to rouse herself when she felt the sunlight coming in through the windows. It had been early when they first awoke, so she had fallen back to sleep, but now she could sense Picasso hovering over her, pressing something feather-light onto her cheek. She could smell the delicious musk of his skin, and the scent of wet paint.

"Don't smile yet," he said as she finally opened her eyes. "It isn't dry."

"What have you done to me, you madman?" she purred with a kind of divine contentment that, until this moment, had been absolutely foreign to her.

Naked and glorious, Picasso left the bed and moved gracefully across the room, where he grabbed a pewter-framed hand mirror and brought it back to her. He had a wet paintbrush in his other hand. Eva looked at her own reflection and saw a delicate yellow-and-black sunflower covering the bruise on her cheekbone. It was painted with such skill that it nearly looked real.

"Oh, Pablo." She touched her cheek with the tip of her finger.

"From now on, I want to make everything bad in your life into something beautiful," he said tenderly.

She felt tears fill her eyes. "You really are going to spoil me for anyone else, you know."

"Exactly the idea, *mi corazón.*" He kissed her mouth, then the top of her forehead, before he sat back on his heels. "You're not going back to la Ruche. Joseph Oller keeps a dormitory on the rue Tholozé, for some of the dancers. You will take a room there for now."

Eva turned her lip down in a mock pout. "Can I not just stay here for a while, if you are so worried about Louis?"

"That would not be safe."

341

Eva felt a spark of jealousy she had not expected. She tried to press back the sensation, but it leaped forward again with a vengeance. "Because of Fernande?"

"Because I know what it is for a woman to live here," he growled, growing angry very quickly. It was a tone she had never heard him use before. "The men who inhabit these dark hallways are poor and desperate, not just for money, but for a woman. Most of them are not French, nor part of their own country, either. They are ruffians and hoodlums."

"Like you?"

The two words crossed her lips before she could stop them.

"*¡Maldito emociones, que me persiguen!* I am not like that anymore — not with you! Can you not see you have changed everything for me? *¡Todo, completo todo!*"

"Forgive me, *mon amour,* I am new at all of this," she said softly, wrapping her arms behind his neck and drawing him near in an attempt to calm his temper. "I didn't understand. I'm sorry. I will move to the dormitory for now if it means that much to you."

He drew in a breath, and then exhaled it, as if a great cloud had passed over him. *"Bueno. Mucho mejor."*

Eva still did not know about Fernande —

342

how, or even if, things would finally end between them. But this darker side of Picasso, which he had warned her about, and even showed her in some of his work, she was now seeing for the first time for herself. Pablo Picasso was a complex genius, as capable of rage as passion, and the one thing she knew without doubt was that she was absolutely wildly in love with every part of him.

There was a riotous commotion at la Ruche when Eva returned later that morning. She had told Picasso she would go back only long enough to collect her things. Besides, Sylvette would be there preparing to leave for rehearsal later that afternoon, so there was little chance of having a problem with Louis.

As she walked through the front door of the building, she heard the gut-wrenching wail of a woman coming from upstairs. She ran toward her room.

The door was open and Fréderic La-Marck, who painted in a studio down the hall, was standing with his girlfriend, Célestine, inside the doorway. When Eva pushed past them, she saw Sylvette, crumpled like a rag doll, in a pile on the floor between their two beds. She was rocking back and forth, knees to her chest, keening, and murmuring words that made no sense.

Her eyes were squeezed tightly, as if to push away some great terror, but her face was red and wet with tears. Louis sat helplessly on the edge of the bed beside her, a hand placed gently on her shoulder.

"What have you done to her?" Eva cried, yanking his hand away.

Louis sprang to his feet. He had tears in his own eyes. "It's not like that. She just received news this morning that her pregnant sister, Marie, and her lover were on that massive ship that went down in the sea — the *Titanic.* They were going to America to start over. . . . Neither of them survived."

Eva glanced down at Sylvette and was swept up instantly by the tragedy.

Last night on the streetcar riding toward Montmartre, Eva had heard people talking about a ship having sunk, but it wasn't a French ship, they'd said. It didn't concern her, she had thought. Eva cringed now as she tried to make sense of the horrifying thing that had happened. She and Louis had spoken of that ship moments before she first met Picasso. She remembered that conversation so clearly now that she shivered. Unsinkable, the newspapers had said.

"There must be some mistake," Eva whispered.

"No mistake. They were both listed among the lost. Their names were printed in the newspaper this morning."

Louis reached for the crumpled edition of *Le Figaro* lying on the bed beside him and handed it to her. She dashed at the tears that were running down her cheeks.

The Disaster of the Titanic.

Eva could not comprehend the vastness of the tragedy. Nearly 1,500 victims.

"God Almighty," she heard herself say.

Eva set the newspaper back down. She could not bear to read any more or look at the portraits. The faces, images of those who had died, haunted her: young, old, some beautiful, some smiling. She saw a photograph of an elderly man with a white beard and kind, sad eyes. He had looked directly into the camera.

"What are we to do?" Eva asked helplessly as Sylvette kept rocking back and forth.

Great ribbons of tears were on all of their faces now. Louis had been here for Sylvette, and Eva was just glad that her friend had not been alone. The rest — all of it — was forgotten. She clamped her hand down on Louis's arm, then gently squeezed it in support. Picasso would be angry, but she could not leave la Ruche just yet. She closed her eyes. *Sainte Marie, Mère de Dieu,* she thought in the space filled with the sound of weeping. But even the Holy Mother Mary could not comfort Sylvette right now.

CHAPTER 22

Tales of human tragedy and heroism — others of great irony, gripped Paris and the world in the days following the *Titanic* disaster. Newspapers and cafés were filled with the stories. Sylvette was so grief-stricken that she was taken to a hospital to be sedated. When she left la Ruche, Eva moved to the dormitory with the dancers, as Picasso had asked her to do.

The Hôtel des Arts was no longer a hotel, but it was a charming place on a cobblestone lane around the corner from the Moulin Rouge. The walls inside were paper-thin, and it was brimming with girls from the show.

Picasso had arranged for her to have a room to herself because so much had happened. She was enormously grateful to him for knowing that she needed privacy just now. Eva certainly needed time alone with her thoughts. But she hoped the move to

Montmartre would be temporary, and that she would soon be with Picasso.

Eva stood alone, feeling small and inconsequential, on the vast expanse of the Pont Neuf, considering the choice suddenly before her. She leaned over the railing, and peered into the murky green waters of the Seine. The springtime sun was warm on her neck and the sky above was bright and cloudless. She could hear crowds of people laughing and talking as they strolled past her. This was her favorite part of Paris — the ancient bridges, the parks and, in the distance, always the grand Tour Eiffel. But the real city was something very different from the image that had drawn her here. It held secrets — like the one in her hands now. Earlier that day, a note had been left for her at the dormitory. She had picked it up along with the rest of her mail when she returned and thought nothing of it at first. The envelope had borne Eva's name, the note itself did not. Now, standing on the bridge, she glanced down at it again.

I am being closely watched. Perhaps Picasso feels guilt himself for something. I don't know. Either way, it is impossible for me to slip away with Ubaldo unless I have an alibi. He wants to take me to Lille for a few days. Will you say that I am with you? I really need a friend in this who will help me teach Picasso a lesson. Fernande

The decision about what to do now should not have been a difficult one for Eva. But she did not know if she had the strength to make certain Picasso would see the damning note, even though something so concrete had the power to finally sever his last ties with Fernande. And if she couldn't do it, could Eva live with herself if she threw away this chance to be rid of her rival and have Picasso's heart exclusively?

A sudden breeze off the water tossed her hair. Love changed people in ways she could never have imagined as the naive young girl she had been back in Vincennes. The triangle in which she found herself had changed her forever.

In her heart, Eva believed that the romance between Picasso and Fernande had run its course. She had seen that for herself on both sides and she had given it time to disintegrate on its own without her help. In a way, Eva was glad Picasso still cared something for Fernande. She would have thought less of a man who could walk away from such a deep relationship without a second thought. But if Eva gave him the note, might he come to resent her one day for pushing him to an end that he knew would have come, anyway? The answer came to her even as she asked herself the question.

She could not give it to him.

But if Picasso were to come upon the note on his own somehow — perhaps find it among his things — then would Eva not only be allowing fate to take its course?

Surely neither Picasso, nor God, could judge her too harshly for that.

Gertrude and Alice were about to leave Paris for Fiesole for the summer, as they did every year. But before leaving, Gertrude always liked to pay a visit to Picasso, to bid him an official farewell. It was a ritual between them. He attended her Saturday evenings on the rue de Fleurus and, in return, she paid an annual visit to the Bateau-Lavoir.

Gertrude wore a green velvet kaftan; Alice wore her favorite olive-and-rust-colored batik print dress, and a straw hat. Both of them wore leather sandals that always caused people to turn and stare.

"I hope he hasn't forgotten," Alice said as they trooped up the great series of steps to the village of Montmartre.

"We'll leave a calling card if he is out. Half the fun is surprising him, just to see if he remembers our deal. You know how Pablo and I have always been with each other," Gertrude said.

"Surprising Picasso, of all people, could make for an inartful encounter, you know. Everyone said last Saturday that he and Fernande are not getting on at all well. There are rumors she is with that handsome young Italian painter this time."

"Our Pablo usually gives as good as he gets. He'll not be outdone if they are taking lovers again."

"That's precisely what I fear," Alice said as they came to the top of the stairs and then walked to the shaded, sloping cobblestone place de Ravignan.

A group of young Spanish artists were gathered outside near the weathered old front door of the Bateau-Lavoir, and the courtyard around them was peppered in springtime like this with pigeons and stray cats. Gertrude and Alice could hear their throaty laughter and conversation as they drew near. They were sitting on overturned crates and stools as shafts of pale spring sunlight shimmered through the bristling trees. The light cast shadows on their exotic Spanish faces, one in particular. They knew one another. Juan Gris stood to greet them.

"Señorita Stein. You are here to see Picasso, no?"

"Our annual trek up the hill, *sí.*"

"I'm not certain if he is in the studio. I have not seen him yet today."

"Well, we are about to find out."

"If he is there, will you give him this? He does not like to be disturbed if he is working, but I know he would forgive you anything."

He reached into his pocket and withdrew a crumpled piece of paper. "I'm afraid I found it at the top of the toilet, as though someone wanted to dispose of it. When I saw it had been signed by his woman, Fernande, I retrieved it, thinking perhaps it was important."

Gertrude and Alice exchanged a glance. Both of them grimaced at the notion of where it had been found. But when they saw that it was not soiled, Gertrude eventually took it and tried her best to flatten it against her own thigh. The handwriting was full of flourishes and she could see that it was indeed signed by Fernande.

"Alas, I do not read French at all well, so I could not tell if it was important," he said.

"Sadly, nor do we. But we will give it to him, or leave it if he has gone out."

Perhaps Picasso was the one to have disposed of the letter himself, but just in case they would take it to his studio.

"*Gracias*, señoritas," Gris said with a nod.

Inside, they descended an old staircase and were swiftly met by the stench from the single toilet, behind a door with no lock. It was shared by all of the inhabitants.

"Ah! The scent of Paris in the springtime," Gertrude said dryly. "And thus, we get ourselves to Fiesole."

"I almost hope he isn't in so we can leave sooner," Alice said beneath her breath.

Both of them were surprised, after knocking, when Gertrude turned the handle and they found the door opened since Picasso regularly locked it. As always, the profusion of color, and the litter of canvases, struck them both. Gertrude knew that this was a warehouse full of masterpieces. All of Picasso's work she had bought on instinct. It was clear to her that he was a genius. The fact that Leo thought Cubism was an abomination did not dissuade her at all. She found it entirely innovative.

"I'll just leave our calling card, and Fernande's note with it, here near his easel for him to sort out," Gertrude said. "Then I will have played through my part of the game at least."

Both of them stopped when they saw the painting on his easel. It was an odd creation. Muted colors of brown and beige. Jagged shapes. Instruments. They looked more critically at it. There were elements of a woman beneath it and the clearly painted words *Ma Jolie.* Sunlight filtered across the room. What a bold, exquisite canvas, they agreed. Even then Gertrude was thinking of where it might fit in on the crowded walls at the rue de Fleurus.

Alice held her chin. "I don't think this is Fernande."

"You know, I think you're right. Fernande always said she hated that song whenever we played it at the apartment."

"Oh, my."

"Whoever *Ma Jolie* is, she matters to him. Look at the musical note there. He painted it with such care. He meant it to be a clue. I know how he thinks. . . . I'll bet it was something they shared. It's rather a delicious mystery."

"So you think he has taken a new mistress?"

"Quite clearly," Gertrude said.

"But who? There is no one who stands out in the group, is there? And the others, like Germaine and Alice Princet, he has long ago conquered."

They both thought through the great list of candidates — women who had made their availability known, not just to Picasso but to the entire Paris entourage.

"You are right about that," Gertrude observed. "I can't imagine anyone with enough courage to go against Fernande Olivier for the heart of Pablo Picasso."

In the end, Eva could not go through with it.

To have been so near to the thing she wanted most in the world, and yet to be about to lose him, anyway, was a bitter pill. She simply could not summon the same courage she had found that night onstage at the Moulin Rouge. Since Sylvette was still in the hospital, Eva had no one with whom to commiserate, and no one to blame but herself. Once again, she felt like an utter fool.

She sat alone on the window ledge inside her room at the Hôtel des Arts, surrounded by beige painted walls, knees to her chest, and gazed over the mansard rooftops at the Paris skyline. Daylight filtered in, and harsh reality came with it. Her plan, at first, had seemed flawless; she would tuck her newly short hair under a houndstooth riding cap, and pull on a pair of boy's trousers from the costume rack at the Moulin Rouge. She was just small enough to get away with it.

She would slip into the Bateau-Lavoir as a messenger boy and then fate would take its course. Things with Picasso would be as they were meant to be. It had all seemed so simple to her as she had trudged up the endless steps to Montmartre. But when she took a moment at the top of the stairs to catch her breath from the climb, she chanced to glance back across the bright blue horizon, and there they were. Gertrude and Alice were not at a great distance behind her, coming up the hill, too. They were difficult to miss — Gertrude in a long, shapeless kaftan, and Alice wearing a bold African print.

Panic took over her plan as the two women drew nearer. Eva made it as far as the foyer of the Bateau-Lavoir before she lost her nerve completely. With tears clouding her eyes, she had crumpled Fernande's note, desperately tossed it into the single toilet there and then fled.

Now, sitting alone, she pressed back the tears in her eyes for the second time that day. She had done the right thing but she could not help despising herself for it.

CHAPTER 23

Eva had fallen asleep on the windowsill, but the giggles and whispers out in the corridor woke her suddenly. When she opened her eyes, she could see that the sky had cleared. It was such a lovely cerulean-blue day.

"It's him, I tell you! I've seen him before! Look down below, there, in the lane!"

"He's so handsome, and famous! What the devil would he want with Marcelle?"

The voices carried through the paper-thin walls between the small rooms. Eva glanced down then and saw Picasso standing outside the door of the dormitory, wearing a proper dark suit, hat and a red silk necktie. He was holding a bouquet of flowers: daisies, daffodils, lilies of the valley and white roses, tied with a bright yellow ribbon. The ribbon was the color of her mother's silk kimono. She was too stunned, at first, to think. Even after everything, it seemed slightly unbelievable that he might be here for her.

357

Eva skittered onto her feet and glanced at the mirror on the wall beside her bed. She pinched both cheeks, which were already flushed from the sudden shock of seeing him. Then she slipped on her shoes, and pulled open the door with such force that it sprang back and crashed against the wall. The giggles and whispers stopped as Eva tumbled out into the hall and past the catty girls gathered there.

"Do you think it's actually true?" she heard one of the chorus girls say as she scurried down the steep, twisted staircase, through the foyer with the rustic walls and out into the street.

She was out of breath when she reached him.

"Run away with me and be my love," Picasso said tenderly.

"Leave Paris?"

"And all of the drama here."

"But I want to work, I like working. I'm proud of being something on my own."

"I have no wish to impede you. Rather, I want us to help each other achieve all of our dreams. There will be more out there for you to do, even greater things to conquer."

"But I'll need to leave the Moulin Rouge."

"And I will be leaving my past, as well,"

Picasso said, and she knew he meant Fernande.

"Are you sure you are ready for that now?"

"Completely."

He handed the flowers to her, and Eva brought them to her nose. Then he drew her against his chest and pressed a gentle kiss just beneath her jaw. She felt a kind of reverence in it, as if she were something precious to him.

Eva could hear a gathering of dancers above them, hanging from the windows to watch, but she didn't care. There was nothing else in the world now but the two of them.

"Where will we run?"

"There is a wonderful little village in the Pyrenees called Céret. I can work freely there, and we can be together."

"Well, then. I must go back up and pack," she replied with a pleased smile.

"Leave everything behind, *ma jolie.* I will do the same."

Again, she knew that he had meant Fernande and she wanted to ask if he knew about Oppi, or what it was that had finally brought this to a conclusion at last. But whatever the reply, it would have changed nothing. Eva would have gone anywhere in the world he asked her to go, because she believed now that he loved her just as she loved him.

"I've never been to the Pyrenees."

She would make a great partner to him, wherever this new adventure would lead, and she would find a way to keep challenging herself. She promised herself that as he took her hand and led her down the narrow cobblestone lane. And never would she neglect to love him the way he deserved to be loved, as Fernande had. She would be the last, best love of Pablo Picasso. Of that, she was certain.

He held her hand and they walked quickly from the Hôtel des Arts, past the stone church of Église Saint-Pierre and up to the tree-lined square of the place Ravignan, with its benches, streetlamps and profusion of pigeons.

"I thought you meant to take me away," she said as he opened the great door to the Bateau-Lavoir.

"First thing tomorrow morning." Picasso smiled.

She held tightly to the bouquet of flowers, and felt herself blush. Eva could see a hint of amusement in his eyes, but he said nothing as he led her inside. She knew that she was still inexperienced in the ways of the world, even though they had been lovers,

360

and she hoped that he would not tire of her before she learned how to please him.

She sensed that she only understood a little about the power of his desires, but Eva had proved to herself how fast she could learn when she wanted something.

Once they were inside his studio, Picasso closed the door and pressed her against it forcefully. She heard herself release a small, startled gasp and the bouquet of flowers fell to the floor. Instinctively, her eyes fluttered to a close as she felt his breath brush the tip of her ear, followed by a kiss. Picasso's hands moved skillfully down the length of her body, and back up again, touching every rise and turn along her torso. Then he clasped both of her hands in one of his own, lifted them over her head, pressed them against the door and himself against her.

"Dios mío, eres hermosa . . . que te quiero," he murmured against her ear.

When they were both free of clothing, he moved across the room with a kind of strutting grace that made Eva want to watch him. She blinked with surprise when she saw her yellow kimono. It was arranged carefully on the iron-frame bed in the alcove. A hostage to her own intense arousal, Eva struggled to process what she saw as Picasso brought it back to her. She was still standing against the door with her hands willingly joined over her head.

"But how —"

He pressed a finger against her lips, then replaced it with his mouth, open, warm, powerful and demanding. "Wear it for me, *jolie* Eva. Only for me."

The power of knowing that he had seen her wearing it onstage, and that he had found it seductive enough to have somehow had it brought here from the dormitory, and waiting for them, was magnificent. She felt herself melt into the moment, and into every nuance of that. She thought of him again, as she had before, like a great shaman, making magic on all of her, especially her heart.

Picasso slipped her arms through the sleeves for her, but he kept the kimono open at her sides as he pressed himself, flesh to flesh, against her. He kissed her tenderly at first, mouth, cheek, throat, but his kisses quickly grew more demanding, and Eva felt herself quiver.

"You are my everything," he murmured against her ear. "And I mean to be yours."

He lay her down on the bed, then knelt between her legs. "You mustn't close your eyes this time. See what we are together as I do."

Eva complied as, first, he ran his fingers sensually from her neck to navel, then gently pinned her arms over her head. The myriad sensations he was making her feel quickly took her over as Picasso finally pressed himself inside of her. She wrapped her legs behind his thighs, an instinct to bring them as close to each other as possible, yet knowing that for her it could never be close enough. She could feel her body move atop the smooth silk kimono beneath her as they made love, then she felt herself quicken.

His breathing was ragged as he murmured over and over, *"Te quiero, te quiero."*

Afterward, she woke in his arms, both of them sheathed in pearl-gray morning light, and by the cool silk fabric. Eva counted the small pale freckles across the bridge of his nose. She touched the coils of dark hair on his chest, pressing away the nagging self-doubt she'd had before this night and luxuriating in the fact that she alone was now Picasso's woman.

Still, she knew that she could not let down her guard completely. Picasso was never known to be a faithful man.

But could he be that, now with her?

Eva rose from the bed and covered Picasso with the apple-green quilt. She bent and pressed a gentle kiss onto his forehead before she donned the kimono, and walked to the window. It felt so good to have it returned to her from the Moulin Rouge and to wear it again, something that was a part of her heritage, and which now had a legacy of its own. She glanced down at the red silk cuffs she had added and was proud of her resourcefulness. She knew she would need a lot more of that in the coming days. But the prospect of the adventure ahead was more exciting to her now than it was frightening.

She thought of her parents then, and she wanted to be able to tell them that she and Picasso were going away for the summer. For all of her wanting to be free of them, maturity had brought about respect. She now understood their steadfast determination to give her a good life. She was every bit their daughter.

"What thoughts are holding you captive over there?"

Eva turned back to him.

"*Dios,* you take my breath away," he said as the kimono shimmered in the growing sunlight through the window.

He leaped from the bed and moved to the other side of the studio. "I need to take your picture just as you are, to capture how you look right now."

"My picture?"

"*Sí.* I have a camera. After my paint-brushes, it is my favorite possession."

He came toward her with a box, covered in maple-colored leather, with a black accordion center, a brass lens and a leather handle on top. She had never actually seen one like it before. It looked sleek and expensive and was definitely state-of-the-art. She could not help but be impressed.

Picasso kissed her cheek and flashed a wink. *"Más tarde, ma jolie Eva,* of course, *más tarde,"* he said, mixing his languages.

"I have never had my picture made before."

"Well, that is about to change. I am going to keep this one forever," he said as he looked down into the viewfinder. "You cannot imagine how I have fantasized about you in your kimono that Mistinguett wore onstage — once I knew it belonged to you. Then, that night, when you came out from behind the curtain as the geisha yourself — *Dios mío, cómo me queria que . . ."*

She loved that he always reverted to Spanish when French words failed him.

"The light is too strong near the window now. Come, stand beside the door. With the shadows, it will look almost like a painting." She could hear the creative excitement in his voice, so it made her happy to do as he asked. "Now, how about your hand, lifted to your chin, as though you are contemplating a great decision."

"Ah, but that has already been made for me." She giggled very softly, meaning her future with Picasso.

"Still, it will be a better photograph if you pose for me with a slightly mysterious air, no? It's not too much to ask, is it, since I cannot convince you to model for one of my paintings."

"Not yet, anyway." She heard her own softly spoken voice, colored with a note of humor. Then she watched his face react to it. The growing smile, eyes crinkling at the corners beneath a disheveled mop of black hair, and true happiness radiating out from him was a reaction of which Eva knew she would never tire. She posed contemplatively, lifting her finger to her chin as Picasso had asked her to do. She felt utterly beautiful. Then she heard the little click-puff sound from the camera.

"That's it?" she asked when it was over.

"That's all there is to it."

"When can I see it?"

"I will ask Kahnweiler to have the film developed, and send the photographs to us in Céret, with a few of my other things."

She remembered her brief meeting with

Kahnweiler the day he brought her Picasso's painting. "Does he sell all of your work for you?"

"There is also Ambroise Vollard, but Kahnweiler is much younger, and he is excited about Cubism. Vollard has made himself too famous from van Gogh and Toulous-Lautrec, I think, to be bothered by innovation in painting, but he is still interested in my sculpture."

As they spoke, Picasso set the camera down and walked to her. He opened the kimono, pressed his bare body against hers as he had done the last time, buried his face against the slender column of her neck and then wrapped the silk behind himself, sealing them together. Then he backed her against the door.

After they made love again, and were dressed for the journey to Céret, Eva kissed Picasso's cheek. "I need to make two small stops before I allow you to spirit me away."

"We will miss our train but, of course, there is nothing I would deny you."

"I need to give Madame Léautaud my notice, of course. And then I must see Sylvette."

Eva watched his expression swiftly darken, and he moved a step away from her as he began to tie his necktie with the help of the

367

mirror's reflection. "Nothing, except perhaps that."

"I don't understand. I thought you liked her."

"I do not share your ease with hospitals."

"Oh, now," she said dismissively, thinking he would give in. "You know perfectly well it's not really a hospital. It's a sanatorium. She is there for depression."

"But people there are ill, aren't they?" Picasso gripped his head and his expression held sudden panic. "Even if it is just in their minds, I cannot tolerate illness of any kind around me."

His tone had become harsh suddenly, and Eva felt the first sting of rejection from him. For a moment, she wasn't certain how to respond.

"Then I will go alone. I'll meet you at the train station later. But I *must* do this. She has been my dear friend in Paris, and her sister has just died in a terrible tragedy. She's in a fragile state. It wouldn't be right not to say goodbye," she said with determination, pressing back the sharp tone in her own voice as much as she could.

Eva sat down on the edge of the bed and began to put on her shoes. She could feel the tension between them but, a moment later, Picasso heaved a sigh and sat beside her.

"Forgive me, *mi amor,*" he said, and there was a silence before he continued. When he did, his voice was low and heavy, as if he were suddenly carrying the weight of the world, and about to try to explain how it felt. "When I am in those places, any kind of hospital, I feel as if I am being strangled, and I am powerless against it. I cannot control my emotions, nor my reactions."

"Like it was with Conchita," she acknowledged softly.

Because she loved him so much, she felt Picasso's pain in that moment, as if it were her own. She watched his eyes until they were like two great, glistening black orbs, highlighting such a tender, vulnerable expression that Eva wanted to weep.

"*Sí.* I will never stop seeing her lying there, so fragile as she was, after the joyful little girl she had been. The nurse, in her long habit, hovering like the angel of death waiting to take her, and our father sitting beside her, constantly checking his pocket watch to see how quickly he could return to his work, and his whores."

She had seen a sketch of what he described in the folio beneath his bed. He must have used the horrific scenes from his mind as a way to try to vanquish the demons that plagued him.

"All of my life, I have run from illness and especially from death. I just cannot . . . I cannot abide it."

"Death *is* part of life, Pablo," she said tenderly.

"Not a part of mine."

Eva could sense the barrier that flared between them now, and she knew that she dare not press him further.

"It's probably best if I go alone, anyway, girl talk and such," she said, and as she rose from the bed, Picasso grabbed her wrist. She had not realized how strong he could be and she did not resist because she wanted to try at least to understand.

"After Conchita's death, when my parents sent me to the countryside, I suppose they thought it would heal me to be away. I was already so broken by then, though, it made no difference. I hated God. But I hated myself more because breaking a promise to Him cost my sister her life."

"My mother always said that God knows we are all failed creatures. He cannot be vengeful when He knows to expect that from each of us."

"Taking a little girl was awfully vengeful, don't you think?"

He shuddered at the memory, and Eva drew him against herself, holding on to him as tightly as she could. "None of us can wipe away our past, my darling Pablo, but we can choose to be different going forward. I understand there is darkness inside of you, but I *know* you are different with me. You will never hurt me. Such a thing is impossible. I believe that with my heart and soul. No amount of *your* past can change *our* future."

Finally a smile broke across his face. "Tell me, *mi amor,* how have you become so wise?" he asked, then kissed her so passionately that she could not answer.

Picasso slipped the pistol into his pocket. Eva was putting on her hat and had not seen him take the gun. He rode with her in the taxi out to the suburb of Auteuil. Then after he had kissed her cheek and let her out in front of the hospital, Picasso instructed the driver to take him back across Paris to la Ruche.

He hoped Louis had not left for the newspaper yet, since this was a scene not meant to be played out in front of anyone else, but he would go there next if he must. As Picasso walked quietly up the pathway along the passage Dantzig, and through the wrought-iron gate, he pressed his hand against the pocket that held the gun. It was Casagemas's gun — the one that had killed him. He opened the studio door without knocking. Inside, Louis was alone, working on a cartoon at the small drafting table beside the window.

"Picasso?" He glanced up with a surprised smile, and quickly stood. "To what do I owe the honor?"

Picasso was a little thrown off. He had forgotten how affable Louis could be. He was a pasty lizard of a man, with pale eyes, pale eyebrows and thin pale lips. He had always reminded Picasso of the epitome of weakness. As angry as he had been a moment before, he found in that moment that he couldn't do what he had intended — for Eva's sake. Frightening Louis would have to be enough.

"I haven't much here, but may I offer you a glass of wine?"

"I've come about Eva."

Louis's expression fell quickly. "*My* Eva?"

"She isn't yours, Marcoussis, she never was."

The tone between them quickly shifted. Louis's mouth fell open like a little hinge. Picasso glared at him with cold, black eyes.

"*You* and Eva? Surely, you are joking,"

372

Louis scoffed.

It was then that Picasso drew the gun from his jacket pocket and pointed it directly at Louis. "Does it look to you like I am joking?"

"So, you and Eva, behind my back? I thought we were friends."

"We were never friends."

"You deceived me."

"It seems to me that you and Fernande know a little something about that sort of thing."

"But we were going to be married. It was all arranged with Eva's father."

"In your mind, never in hers. You are looking at the only man who will *ever* marry Eva Gouel."

Louis's eyes narrowed menacingly as he captured the spark of hesitation from his opponent. "You won't marry her. You're a rake. Women are only playthings to you."

"You don't know me."

Picasso knew he had answered too quickly. Too much of his heart was caught up in this dark exchange. He had lost his footing, and he scrambled to regain it. He put his index finger on the trigger of the gun, and widened his stance. The two men glared at each other. Slowly, he drew back the hammer with his thumb until it clicked. The sound was like an ugly musical note. "I am glad to see you frightened," Picasso said calmly. "I am very certain it is just what Eva felt after you struck her."

"You don't know what you're talking about. It wasn't like that!"

Fear was quickly becoming desperation as Picasso continued to aim the gun at Louis's heart. Louis began to tremble. His eyes filled with helpless tears. Picasso waited, then eased the hammer of the pistol back down. Louis heaved an audible sigh of relief, but it was just as Picasso lunged forward with a brick-solid fist, hurling all of his anger and feelings of protection for Eva into one, direct blow. Louis reeled back into his drafting table, papers and pens and pots of ink scattering, color pooling on the floor around him.

"If you *ever* see Eva again, much less touch her, I *will* kill you! And no one would suspect me. Never forget that."

Sylvette was sitting in a cane-back chair beneath the shade of a large tree out in the garden of the Val-de-Grâce hospital in Auteuil when Eva arrived. Eva sank onto the stone bench beside her friend, took up her hand and squeezed it.

"You're looking much better," Eva said,

trying her best to sound cheerful.

Sylvette's expression was still very sad and her face was gaunt. Gray shadows hung heavily beneath her pretty eyes.

"It's just been so hard. I miss my sister every moment of the day, and I can't help running through my mind whether or not I told her often enough that I loved her, wondering if she knew how much."

Eva squeezed her hand more tightly. "I'm sure she knew, how could she not? You are the most generous, warmhearted soul I know."

"It was good of you to come to see me. The doctors say I can go home tomorrow."

"I'm sorry I haven't been before now. A lot has just happened very quickly."

Suddenly Eva felt guilty sharing anything of her own happiness after the great loss her friend had suffered. But keeping it from her wasn't fair since she was about to go away. Then she saw a very faint smile of recognition brighten Sylvette's eyes.

"*Mon Dieu,* it's you and Picasso, isn't it? It's written all over your face!"

"He's left Fernande for good this time, Sylvette. We're going away together. It has been such a whirlwind. We are to be married once things have calmed down."

"Married? I can hardly believe it. Picasso

never seemed the type to me who would be tamed by marriage. But I am happy for you. So tell me, how did Louis take the news? Not well, I imagine."

"I don't suppose he even knows yet. We had a falling-out just before . . ." Eva stopped herself. She couldn't make herself say "before the *Titanic* tragedy," but they both knew what she meant. "Pablo does not want me to see him again, and I have agreed."

"Oh, dear. I always told Louis his temper was going to get him in trouble. I don't know what he did but I'm guessing it can't have been good. He was pretty angry with you that last night when he asked me to leave the room."

Eva sat back on the bench. "It doesn't matter now. Pablo and I are each starting a new chapter in our lives, and we are doing it together. He entirely supports me finding a new challenge and a new goal."

"And of course, you will do just that. But I'm sure going to miss you, Eva. The Moulin Rouge won't be the same without you. Who will I have to make fun of Mistinguett and Mado with now?"

They smiled at each other. Then Eva sighed. "I need to speak to Madame Léautaud next. I'm not looking forward to it."

"She would probably never admit it but she really liked you even from that first day. Don't tell her I told you, but it was her idea, not Monsieur Oller's, to elevate you to the position as her wardrobe assistant."

"She certainly had a peculiar way of showing support," Eva replied.

"Good thing you were so determined."

Eva laughed. "I was, wasn't I?"

"Picasso saw the same spark. We all did."

"Thank you, my friend." Suddenly tears were clouding her eyes and Eva felt flustered by them. "Oh, I am going to miss you, too! I hate that I won't be there to take care of you when you get back to la Ruche!"

"I'll be fine. I promise. Just write to me about all your adventures this summer, and promise me I will be the first one you visit when you return to Paris."

"I promise," Eva said, and now they were both weeping.

Visiting Sylvette in the hospital had been emotional, and Eva was not certain she had the strength now to face Madame Léautaud, yet it was something that must be done. The dour wardrobe mistress had given her such an incredible opportunity, one that had changed her life, and she would be forever grateful. Eva was proud of all she had accomplished at the Moulin Rouge, and a part of her hated to leave, especially since she had made so many dear friends among the cast and crew. But she knew that her life and her future were with Picasso. As hard as it was to leave, she had no choice but to put this place behind her.

She found Madame Léautaud on a stepping stool inside the large wardrobe closet behind the stage. She was rifling through hats, feather boas and every color of sequined and bejeweled costumes, and they were flying down like rain. Eva squeezed her hands, opening and closing them several times as she tried to calm her racing heart.

"Madame, may I have a word with you?"

"Not now. I've got to find a bowler hat for our new singer. He's in the new opening act and Alain took his costume with him when Monsieur Oller fired him this morning!"

"There's one in the trunk beside the makeup tables. I saw it just yesterday."

Madame Léautaud glanced down at her then and came off the stepping stool. Her tense expression softened. "You really are a lifesaver, Marcelle. Over and over again, it seems." She sighed with relief and gave Eva a genial smile. "I don't mind saying now that I don't know what we would do without you around here."

"Actually, I'm afraid that's why I'm here, madame."

Madame Léautaud's smile faded as their eyes met. "You want another increase in your salary? Is that what this is about?"

"I don't want more money, just my freedom, with my immeasurable gratitude."

"Don't toy with me. That's not at all funny."

The next words tumbled out of her. "I'm sorry, madame, I don't mean to be funny. I have learned so much here, and I have loved every moment. But I have fallen in love and we are going away together. I hope you can be happy for me." Eva could hear the tone of pleading in her own voice but she could not vanquish it completely.

The older woman chuckled, unable to believe what she had heard. "And along with everything else, have you not learned here that love is a fickle thing? Whoever has turned your head can have little intention of anything serious, much less making an honest woman of you. What kind of man would spirit you away from Paris unmarried?"

"But he has asked me to marry him."

"Women are far more compliant when there is a sweet song to distract them."

Eva felt defensive and her stance had

become rigid. "I'm sorry if that has been your experience, Madame Léautaud, but Picasso is not like that."

"You are going away with Pablo Picasso?"

"And one day I will marry him."

"Have you a ring?"

"Not yet, but I will."

"Promises are only words, Marcelle, especially from a *roué* like him."

She exhaled a breath, determined not to say anything she would regret. She could only speak that way of Picasso because she did not know him. "The assistant you hired for me, Suzanne, is a very capable girl. She will do a wonderful job in my place."

"But she isn't you. We have all come to depend on you a great deal here."

Eva was surprised to hear the sudden hint of pleading break through her anger. "And I have found my true self here among all of you. This has been the first place I think I have ever felt that I belonged, and where I felt truly appreciated. The Moulin Rouge has changed my life, and for that I have you to thank. But I love Pablo with all of my heart, and I need to be with him."

Eva could feel her eyes filling with tears once again as Madame Léautaud looked at her in the awkward silence that fell between them. After a moment, her expression softened again. "I am angry, Marcelle, but I am also a prudent woman. Go, if you feel you must. But the door here will be open. While I am loath to admit it, I am actually a bit jealous of you, taking the chances you have taken in your life. Just look at where that spirit of yours has brought you."

"Thank you, madame."

She took Eva's hand and squeezed it tightly. "From now on, you must call me Charlotte, since I have a suspicion, when next we meet, you shall be called madame, as well. That will set us on equal footing. Good luck to you, my dear. I suspect you have quite an adventure ahead of you now."

CHAPTER 24

Nestled against his shoulder, and lulled by the rhythm of the train as it moved forward, Eva fell into a dreamless sleep. The rhythmic clack of the wheels, and the sway of the train car, had gentled her mind and pulled her into a black peace.

When she woke, she found Picasso reading. Eva could see that it was Gertrude Stein's book *Three Lives* and he was slowly tracing the words with his finger. Reading languages other than Spanish was more difficult for him than speaking them. Eva smiled at the childlike quality he could have when no one was looking. He looked so handsome dressed up in his tweed suit and burgundy silk necktie, with his hair combed and tamed back with hair cream.

A steward in a dark uniform, brass buttons and cap came to them then and bowed. "We will be arriving soon, Monsieur Picasso. There is a car at the station ready to take you and madame into Céret."

He glanced up from his book as they felt the steady pull of the brakes easing the train to a stop. "*Merci beaucoup,* monsieur."

"He believes I am your wife."

"And so you shall be," Picasso said as he closed his book and leaned over to kiss her.

"Not in public, Pablo!" She gasped, feeling the color flood her cheeks. "People are watching!"

"And why not in public, *ma jolie*? Are we not together, and in love?"

"For as long as you will have me."

Picasso kissed her cheek more chastely. "Things are different down here. You will see. Life is more relaxed than in Paris. People will leave us alone in Céret."

It certainly was enticing, having Picasso all to herself for the summer. As the screech of the brakes grew louder, the passengers around them began to collect their belongings, to stretch after the long trip and replace their gloves, top hats and bowlers.

Eva glanced out the window at the vastly different landscape of the Pyrenees, fields and trees and a broad sky untouched by buildings. A glossy navy blue car with gleaming white tires, and white leather seats, sat parked in the gravel yard outside the station. Even in Paris, she had never ridden in anything so elegant.

When Picasso saw her expression, he puffed out his chest and smiled proudly. "You will need to grow accustomed to this sort of thing, *jolie* Eva. This is part of your life now, too."

The Hôtel du Canigou, on the main cobblestone square, was a charming old stone place. Cooled by shady plane trees, with a splashing fountain out front, Eva thought it was the most adorably picturesque place she had ever seen. Everything about Céret was different, and she could feel herself begin to breathe more easily here already.

They settled into a large room in the back of the hotel, with a breathtaking view of undulating fields dotted by ripening cherry trees, fat black-and-white grazing cows and the mountains and blue sky beyond. Eva stood on the balcony, held on to the iron railing and drew in a deep breath. The air was rich with the sweet fragrances of the countryside. She was struck by the incredible sense of peace she immediately felt here.

Picasso came up behind her and wrapped her in his arms. She rested her head on his broad shoulder.

"After we have a rest, there is someone I can't wait for you to meet," he murmured, his lips pressing softly against her neck, as his hands moved seductively down along the lines of her body.

"But I am not tired at all."

"Oh, we are not going to sleep. I have much more interesting plans for our afternoon," Picasso said as he moved around to kiss the warm pulse point of her throat.

The cicadas were already out by early evening when they made their way, hand in hand, up the quaint narrow cobblestone lane. It was bordered by ancient stone houses, their windows trimmed with bright blue shutters, and brimming with ruby-red geraniums. Ahead, perched on the edge of a prominent hill, was a picturesque stone house with a rosy terra-cotta tiled roof. It was surrounded by tall cypress trees.

"The place belongs to our friend Burty Haviland, but he lets me use one of the studios here."

"Haviland, as in Haviland porcelain?" Eva asked with surprise.

"The very same. He's young, rich and bored, but Burty fancies the company of young artists rather than his bourgeois family, since he paints his own Cubist works. He invited my friend Manolo down here to sculpt a few years ago. Braque and I followed along last summer because the vistas are so inspiring."

"Georges Braque, the artist?" she asked as they ascended an old stone staircase leading up to the house. She had heard his name from Fernande.

"Too handsome for his own good, and a far more insightful Cubist than I am. But don't tell him I said that. He would be totally insufferable. For now, he's only a *little* irritating." Picasso quirked a smile. "Braque was exhibiting at the art show last year. I had gone there to see his work, and I found you in the process."

Eva felt herself blush. The wanton way they had made love their first time had surprised her. She could not believe what she was now capable of. He had taken her very quickly, and with a passionate force. Eva had known instinctively he would not hurt her, so when he had overwhelmed her with his strength, she had not tried to struggle against him. She liked the idea of his dominance in their passion. Her body reacted to it before her mind did.

"I can tell what you are thinking by the color in your cheeks alone," Picasso said to her in a seductive tone as they stood in the grand foyer of the seventeenth-century house.

His hand was pressed gently against her

back. His touch, along with his words, ignited her all over again and she struggled to maintain her composure. "Never be ashamed, *mi amor,* of the pleasure we give to one another in private."

"I am thinking only of how long it will be before we can do that again," she whispered as a tall, dark-haired young man in paint-splattered pants, and a young woman in a vanilla-colored dress and long rope of pearls came together down the stone staircase. The woman was holding on to the iron handrail and Eva noticed a large diamond on her finger glittering in the light.

"You *are* a naughty thing. Wait until I get you home," Picasso said quietly.

"Ah, Pablo, there you are at last! You were meant to be on the earlier train," Braque exclaimed as he came to the bottom of the stairs beneath a grand ironwork chandelier that held old melted candles.

All of their voices echoed in the hollow, whitewashed space.

"*Sí.* Before we left, Eva needed to visit her friend from the Moulin Rouge who is in the hospital."

"We are both very sorry about that," said the woman as she stepped forward and extended her hand to Eva. She could see by Braque's expression that they knew about

Sylvette and the *Titanic* disaster. Word certainly did travel quickly among their group. The woman with him had such lovely ash-blond hair, set in perfect finger waves, and her mouth was painted the bold color of Céret cherries. "I am Marcelle Braque. I suspect we will be great Cubist widows together. At least I hope we will."

Eva was surprised how forthright Braque's wife seemed. She was certainly different from the women in Paris, past whose cool indifference one must first pass to find the spirit hidden beneath. If it existed at all. This pretty young woman seemed like a breath of fresh air in comparison.

"What my wife is too polite to explain is that Picasso's former companion did not like either of us very much — me in particular, I am afraid," Braque said.

Eva could not imagine why not. Georges Braque seemed like a gentle bear of a man, with a warm smile, and bright, engaging blue eyes that softened his imposing size. Eva liked them both immediately.

"She was only jealous of you." Braque smiled at his wife.

"Well, that is all in the past now," Picasso said a little gruffly, and she could feel his fingers tighten at the small of her back. "Eva is the only woman in the world for me now.

She has already changed me completely."

"If she *is* the only woman in your world, then she really will have changed you, *mon ami.*" Braque chuckled.

"You'll see. Everyone will," Picasso countered. "All right, Wilbur, now show me what you've been up to since I've been gone. You're long overdue for a critical eye from the *real* Cubist master here," he joked. In response, Braque wrapped him in an affectionate embrace before they all walked back upstairs to the studio.

"Wilbur?" Eva asked in confusion. "Isn't his name Georges?"

"Wilbur is for Wilbur Wright, the aviator. Pablo's nickname for Georges came from some item about Wright in the press that eclipsed a review about Georges work. Pablo knew it was a sore subject, but he found that funny."

"They really are like brothers," Eva said as she watched them.

"They argue like it, as well. I heard you were called Marcelle also, in Paris," Braque's wife said as she played absently with the rope of pearls.

"I was. Everyone there was reinventing themselves when I arrived, so I suppose I just wanted to fit in. But Pablo didn't think it suited me at all, so now I am simply myself."

"Ah, Paris! It's certainly not easy to fit in there. I completely understand. Everyone there thinks they are at the center of some great *nouvelle vague.* Even Fernande had changed her name from Amélie when she met Picasso. I think she thought a Spanish name would entice him more. But perhaps you already knew that, if you have met her."

Something in her tone told Eva that Marcelle already knew about the triangle between her, Picasso and Fernande. When they came to the top of the stairs, Braque and Picasso went ahead, their arms still slung across each other's shoulders.

"We've met," Eva cautiously confirmed.

"People probably think that you broke them up," Marcelle continued. "Their group won't like that. But really, it has been coming on for a long time."

The notion of blame startled her. Eva thought she had met most of the people in Picasso's world over this past year: Gertrude Stein, Apollinaire, Max Jacob, Germaine and Ramón Pichot. All of them had seemed perfectly lovely. Certainly his friends would want him to be happy, wouldn't they?

At the top of the stairs was a big vaulted studio with wooden beams and white walls covered with Cubist canvases. Some were hung for prominence of place; others held position in crowded stacks on the floor. The works themselves looked enough like Picasso's to be startling to Eva.

Marcelle and Eva sat in two rush-bottom chairs, the frames of which had been painted blue marine as sunlight, and a warm summer wind blew up from the valley through a wide set of open French doors. They sipped Pernod from two small, glazed green absinthe glasses as Picasso reacted to the earth tones with which Braque was painting now. They seemed to use a language all of their own, punctuated with laughter and grand gestures that took both of them to a place they alone were welcomed.

"They will be like this the whole time," Marcelle warned with an easy smile. "Braque believes their souls are matched by their art. It is their language. He is very glad to have Picasso back here, since it is a language I cannot speak, and I think he was getting a little bored with me."

"That can't be true."

"Ah, don't be too sure! Believe me, life with an artist is complicated. I have learned that quickly enough. They can be so passionate, but also demanding, and very temperamental. It's always a balancing act to complement their work and not hinder it."

"If we are going to be Cubist widows, perhaps we should develop our own little language just to keep up," Eva said with a smile.

Marcelle laughed in response. It was a sweet, gentle sound, Eva thought. Suddenly she was reminded of Sylvette, and all of the times they had laughed with each other. This was a new chapter with new friends, but she must be careful not to trust too quickly.

Afterward, they all sat outside on the terrace until long after sunset, laughing and arguing to the hum of the cicadas. When they left, Eva felt quite drunk on Pernod — but also on hope and possibility.

The next morning when she woke, there was only the faint dreamlike images of Picasso ravishing her in this same little bed in which she nestled beneath a duvet now. When she finally opened her eyes, drawn by the aroma of warm brioche and coffee, his back was to her at his easel. He stood as always unashamed by his nudity, magnificent in his maleness. Gauzy curtains brought a warm morning breeze in through the open window. The sinewy lines of his broad back and tapered torso would always remind her of something Roman and perfect. Hearing her move, Picasso turned, his long paintbrush wet with umber-colored paint, catching the light as his face lit with a smile.

"Here you are with me again, *ma jolie.* Ready for something to eat? I've had a little something sent up for us. You must be famished," he said with a devilish wink.

And she *was* famished. As she sat up in bed and reached for a pastry, Picasso set down his paintbrush and pressed his hands onto his hips, as if he were suddenly studying her like a subject for one of his paintings. "*Dios mío,* but I adore your breasts. I have decided they are the most perfect thing about you."

"And the rest of me?" she asked, biting back a smile.

"You are delectable," he said simply.

He went to her then, sank on the edge of the bed beside her, and she offered him a morsel of the warm brioche. He took it into his mouth, along with her fingers. Eva heard her own breathing change as she felt a host of sensations bombard her again, hunger having only been the prelude. She knew they would make love again and she found every time now that she wanted that as much as he did. He drew her to her feet,

393

and when he reached around, grasped her bottom and pulled her against himself, Eva felt her body eagerly respond. The yearning to have him coursed deep and low inside her. There was never enough of him for her now, never enough of them.

An hour later, they held hands as they walked together down the shade-dappled boulevard toward the prominent Grand Café. The summer air was already warm and sultry, and they were grateful for the cover brought by the huge line of bristling trees as they went to meet Braque and Marcelle.

It seemed to Eva, in that moment, she was living a fairy tale here in Céret, and that the dark parts of the world she had known would never find them here, amid this glorious sunlight, and the rich breeze that she was certain now would press back anything bad.

As they neared the café — a two-story building in a Moorish design dominating the corner of the rue Saint-Ferréol — she could see Braque and Marcelle at one of the marble-top tables cluttering the sidewalk. They were with another young, well-dressed couple. Their presence seemed to surprise Picasso. Although he didn't say anything, Eva felt him squeeze her hand a little more tightly as they approached.

The man was slim, with sleek enameled black hair, and he had a pipe clamped between his teeth that made him look older than he was. The elegant waistcoat and necktie he wore gave him the great allure of Parisian chic. The woman beside him was dark-haired and she wore an expensive dark blue dress, a fashionable wide-brimmed hat and gloves. It was obvious that they had just arrived from the city.

Eva could see that they had been deep in conversation, but all four looked up at the same time. Then the man stood and waved them over. Eva had no idea why she felt an odd frisson of fear, but she pressed it away as the young man she'd never met drew Picasso into a hearty embrace.

"I didn't know you would be down here, too, Derain," Picasso said as he then cast a glance at the woman beside him.

"Pablo." She nodded in a tepid greeting.

"Alice," he returned.

The painter André Derain and his woman. Of course Eva knew the name. She had seen his work at that first Salon des Indépendants, and some of the dancers at the Moulin Rouge had gossiped about their scandalous love affair — one that had begun just after Alice Princet's honeymoon to someone else. André and Alice were one of the young couples with whom Picasso and Fernande were often linked in the papers. Picasso took two chairs from the next table, then he and Eva sat with the group.

"Braque, you didn't mention last night that they would be here."

"I only found out when they arrived at my studio this morning, just before I sent you the message to meet us here."

Eva could see that Braque now, too, was suddenly tense. He was certainly not as carefree as he had been on the terrace last evening. But Marcelle smiled and patted Alice's knee. It was clear that the two women were well acquainted.

"So, isn't it time you introduce us?" Derain asked Picasso as he nodded toward Eva.

It seemed a bit early for wine, yet suddenly she longed for the waiter to bring her a glass. She knew she was at a disadvantage among this group, and Picasso clearly had lost his footing.

"*Bueno* . . . Eva, this is André and his woman, Alice. We all lived and worked together up in Montmartre. Everyone, this is Eva. As soon as possible, we will be married."

"Married?" Alice said the word in a gasp.

Eva was proud of how boldly Picasso had

proclaimed it, but then there were sideways glances everywhere, as though the most unspeakable word in the world had just been uttered.

"Best for the both of us to make honest women of them, as Braque did," Picasso said affably.

A bottle of rum arrived at the table, with six fresh glasses. Picasso rarely drank spirits but Eva watched him make an exception today. She did, as well. Amid some awkward banter, the warm Pyrenean wind and the strong palliative of the rum, the tension among them finally seemed to dissipate. Eventually, they ordered lunch, and then wine, and the whole affair felt to Eva like an eternity. She was relieved to sneak away finally to find the toilette.

She splashed her hands and face and tried to steady herself as she gazed into the dirty mirror above the basin. Today, her trendy little haircut, and fashionable dress, could not completely mask the still-uncertain girl who dwelt inside of her, no matter what she did to vanquish her.

As she walked back through the café, toward the table outside, she paused near the door and heard the voices of two women on the other side. They were hidden by a group of men but their voices were clear.

"Well, what do you expect me to do? I don't have to like her but I *do* have to be nice to her. Pablo is Georges's best friend!"

There was no mistaking it. The first voice belonged to Marcelle Braque.

"So, we are all just supposed to betray Fernande? *Mon Dieu,* this one is just so utterly provincial. It can't last, you know. That Picasso should marry *her* is laughable."

The clipped Parisian accent that followed belonged to Alice Princet.

"I am not going to be rude, that's all," Marcelle countered in a gossipy tone of her own. "Georges would never forgive me. Besides, I have made friends with her, and I think she likes me."

"Well, everyone back in Paris is already whispering about it all — how she stole Picasso right out from under Fernande, who had been foolish enough to take her into her confidence. She even took the little thing shopping! You do what you want, Marcelle, but that Evelyn Thaw act of hers doesn't fool me!"

Eva sank back against the wall, hidden for the moment by the collection of men waiting to be seated at a table inside. Along with the rum, and the heat, she felt ill. She had felt so blissful this morning, but now everything had changed. These were Picasso's friends. Even if she told him about what they had said, what then? She was not at all certain, as she stood there willing herself to go back outside, if she was prepared yet to make him decide between his history and his heart.

"What the devil do you mean?" Picasso growled.

"Ramón, Germaine and Fernande are set on coming here to reason with you. I couldn't stop them, so Alice and I took the first train down from Paris to try to warn you," Derain said once the women had left the table.

Picasso raked his inky-black hair back with both of his hands, and slumped into his chair. He was trying to process the news. The day was growing hotter by the moment, and he was in no mood to sit out here on the sidewalk any longer. This was a joke to both of them, Braque and Derain especially. But this was no joke to Picasso — this was his life. He loved Eva — truly loved her — and now she was about to be caught in the crosshairs.

"The three of them can say what they like, but it is over for me. I am with Eva now."

"Then you won't even talk with Fernande?" Derain dared to ask.

"It's broken, André. It can't be mended. That insufferable Italian prig, Oppi, came to me for help and guidance as an artist, and all the while he wanted to screw her. Some things are just not forgivable. My heart has changed."

Braque and Derain glanced at each other. Picasso began to realize how long Eva had been gone and he felt a jolt of panic. Moments of anxiety about losing her had begun to heighten his fears and superstitions these past weeks.

"How different was it really to what Eva did to Fernande?" Derain asked.

Picasso bolted from the chair and charged at Derain. Braque, bigger and more powerful than both of them, jumped to his feet to intercede.

"Eva has nothing to do with this!" Picasso growled.

"Easy, *mon ami*!" Derain held up his hands. "All I'm asking is whether you know that for certain? Women are such different creatures than men."

"I won't hear it! I love Eva. I *will* marry her! That is all!"

"Then you will have to face Fernande tomorrow and tell her that yourself. They are coming to Céret. You can't stop them now."

■ ■ ■ ■

They came like a cloud — three shadows
descending over the bright place of peace
the sleepy village of Céret had so briefly
been for Picasso and Eva. Picasso thought
he was prepared to battle against them. But
there was something about Fernande. There
always had been. Their passionate youth,
their struggles together, reared up and
pressed forward in his memory now. He was
used to the heavy weight of desire that had
pushed so hard against reason whenever he
saw her, but now there was their dark history he felt, too.

Ramón Pichot slung his arm over Picasso's
shoulders after they greeted each other.

Picasso and Eva had just emerged from
the hotel to find the trio waiting out front
in the little tree-lined town square.
Fernande and Germaine remained on a
painted bench beside a fountain as Ramón
approached alone. Germaine's hand was
wound with Fernande's in dramatic fashion.
Ramón did not acknowledge Eva, and
Picasso was instantly defensive. Though he
had been warned, it did not make this
awkward scene any less uncomfortable.

"Come, *mon ami,* let's speak privately."

401

"Anything you have to say can be said for Eva to hear."

The slim, bearded man whom Picasso so long had trusted and loved looked at Eva with an expression of incredulity. Then he shook his head.

"*Mon cher ami,* please. We have come all this way."

"You shouldn't have."

Over Pichot's shoulder, he could see Fernande sitting on the bench. As she began to weep, she drew out a white lace handkerchief and dabbed it at her eyes. Fernande's flair for the dramatic had always been impeccable, Picasso thought.

"She misses you, Pablo. All the way down here on the train all she could speak of was how she needs you."

"So she slept with another artist?" Picasso put his arm around Eva and drew her protectively against himself.

"She said it was only meant to teach you a lesson. She was trying to make you jealous, to get you to pay attention to her. Honestly, my friend, it has seemed to Germaine and me both that she has had a point."

"My lesson has been well learned, Ramón, believe me. It's over between us. It has been for a while now. I've moved on."

"I don't believe that. I know you too well. Can you not recall all the wonderful times you spent together? All the happiness and laughter?"

"I remember it all, as I remember the betrayal."

Fernande stood then and charged forward. Germaine followed.

"Should we go now?" Eva whispered urgently. Picasso knew that this encounter would only get worse, but he needed to test the strength of his conviction. He looked from Fernande to Germaine as they came and stood with Ramón like sentinels, blocking the door to his future.

"How could you?" Germaine asked angrily as she glared at Eva. "Fernande trusted you, she befriended you. She confided her secrets in you!"

"I always wondered why she did that when she had you."

Eva had spoken the retort in such a meek voice that the strength of her words surprised Picasso. She was proving yet again that she was no one's fool. Finally he had a lover who could match him. He'd had no idea, until this moment, that Fernande had tried to use Eva as her alibi, and he enjoyed that it had come back to bite her all on its own. Eva had never needed to say a single word to him. Fate had found its way forward.

"You had no right to steal him from me," Fernande declared. Her nose was red and runny from weeping.

"She didn't steal me, Fernande. I went willingly."

"I don't believe that. You love me!"

"I did love you."

"Pablo," Germaine interjected. Her hand was still twined with Fernande's, and Picasso's arm was still protectively around Eva. "We've known each other for ages. We've been through so much together. It's unbearable to see you like this."

"Things have changed, and there is no sense in discussing why. Just as I did not make you defend why you insisted on leaving Casagemas when you did — and all *that* brought about," he said accusingly to Germaine.

"If you recall, I left him for *you*!"

"I did not cause your breakup with Casagemas, and you know it. I was only there afterward to pick up the pieces — after he shot himself over you."

Picasso felt Eva's body tense beside him, and he knew she did not know the extent of the history between them all. He was instantly sorry he had taken the bait from these two women who knew him so well. It was a mistake that he had stayed in Céret, and an even bigger mistake that he had allowed this encounter.

"Ramón, *mi* amigo, you must choose a side, it seems," Picasso said sadly.

He was trying not to think of all the summers together, the parties, the laughter, so many good times he would be forced now to surrender.

"He is on Fernande's side, of course," Germaine interrupted. "We both are."

"I'm sorry to hear that. I will have Kahnweiler collect my personal effects from the apartment. You can take the rest. But this is the end for all of us. I won't be seeing any of you after today," Picasso announced with harsh resolve.

"She is a complete fake, Pablo! Not even her name is real!" Fernande cried out desperately. People passing them had begun to stop and stare. "Please don't let her do this to us!"

"Eva has done nothing but pick up the pieces *you* left behind. It is you who destroyed everything. Is there anyone you *haven't* slept with?"

"*She* is the whore, Pablo, not me!"

"What *you* are, Fernande, is my past," he said icily as he stepped around Fernande without looking back, still holding protectively onto Eva's shoulders. "And by the way, when I get back to Paris, I am taking Frika and the cat. You were never good to either of them, anyway. I found the monkey a new home. But you probably did not even realize he was gone. That monkey and I had a lot in common."

Picasso tightened his grip around Eva and turned with her away from his friends. At least they had been his friends once, but no more. He would never forgive any of them for the scene they had just made, and for forcing him to choose between friendship and love. Then again, where love was concerned, there was no choice at all to be made. It was Eva. It always would be her.

"How long were you lovers with your friend's wife?" Eva asked him later as they lay in bed, their legs threaded together.

Picasso brushed a strand of hair from her eyes. "Not long. We were all young, and poor. It was very foolish."

"And Ramón was not jealous?"

"I met Germaine first, but we all knew one another. They made sense together — there was nothing to be jealous of," he explained as he kissed her tenderly. "But there is something else I should tell you, just so there are no more surprises like today. I am not proud, but I once had an affair with Alice."

"Derain's mistress?"

"She wasn't his mistress then. They didn't know each other. The whole thing was very brief."

"And Marcelle Braque?"

He felt himself smile. It sounded more ridiculous to him, describing it, than it had been at the time. He had always been proud of his conquests, but not with Eva. Bravado came naturally to him, but now it all seemed tawdry, and he wanted it to be a part of his past.

"No. But I did introduce her to Georges."

Eva looked away from him. "I see."

"But do you really see? Lust is not the same as enduring love, Eva. Because of you, I know the difference now. The fire of lust cannot sustain itself any more than any fire can. Eventually, it just burns out."

"Will that happen to the two of us? You have had so many lovers, I just don't know how I can ever be all that you desire."

His first response was to kiss her with all of the overwhelming passion he felt, in a way he hoped would reassure her. But he could hardly imagine how it might seem to her. Eva was right. There had been so many lovers, so many affairs. Friends, whores and strangers. Luring women had always been as easy for him as painting. There was an instinctive quality about mastering both. But for the first time in his life, Picasso wanted to be completely faithful. He wanted to marry Eva, to have children with her. He wanted hers to be the last face he saw before he died. Picasso had never felt this way about any woman.

Eva drew him closer against herself.

" 'I often have this dream, strange and profound, of a mysterious woman, who I love, and who loves me . . . it is she alone who understands my true heart.' "

"*You* are quoting Verlaine?" she asked as his words trailed away. She knew "My Familiar Dream" very well.

"I am not only a man who paints squares. It's you in the poem, you know."

"Well, I am very glad about that."

"I am going to paint you when we get to Avignon, whether you want me to or not."

"We are going to Avignon?"

"We can't stay here. I don't think Fernande plans to leave. I hope Braque and Marcelle will join us. And perhaps André and Alice. The light is good there, and it's a little more lively there than it is here in Céret."

"What will we do in Avignon?" she asked him.

"Paint, eat . . . and make love continuously. Is there anything more glorious?"

CHAPTER 25

Picasso and Eva were in Avignon for only two days when they were stopped on the street by a tall Scandinavian-looking artist who Picasso introduced as Kees van Dongen. He was out for a walk with his wife and little golden-haired daughter when they ran into one another. They had known Picasso and Fernande in Montmartre, his wife explained to Eva with an insincere smile after they were introduced.

"Well, this is a surprise," van Dongen said tepidly after nodding to Eva. "We wondered why you left Paris but we never imagined this was the reason. I always thought you and Fernande would work things out."

"Well, life is full of surprises," Picasso said.

In the awkward silence, he embraced their little daughter, who had leaped with abandon into his arms, then he gave her back to her mother. The display of affection did little to ease the tension between all of them.

410

"Perhaps we can meet one evening for supper," said Augusta van Dongen.

"I doubt we will be in town long enough for that," Picasso quickly replied.

"Perhaps when you're back in Paris, then."

"I thought we would be far enough away from all of them here," Picasso muttered to Eva as they walked away.

"All of who?"

"People who knew Fernande and me together."

"I doubt we will ever outrun everyone, Pablo. You were together for a long time."

"I suppose. I just wish it had been anyone but them, in particular, just now. I don't want anything to spoil things for us here."

The jealous part of Eva, against which she did battle, forced her not to ask for details. But she was beginning to wonder if there was anywhere in France at all that she would really be given a chance to be seen as Picasso's partner.

The next evening at dinner, out in the gravel-covered garden of the elegant Hôtel d'Europe, near the Palace of the Popes, a bald, well-dressed man with a heavy golden beard, and a well-dressed woman with a plain face, dark hair and thick eyebrows, approached their table shortly after they were seated. Eva remembered seeing him at Ger-

411

trude Stein's apartment. It was Picasso's friendly rival, Henri Matisse, and he was with his wife, Amélie. Eva silently watched the artists' cool but courteous exchange, and she saw the way Madame Matisse regarded Picasso. Eva realized then that this was the woman who had been depicted in that daring portrait she'd seen at the art show where she had first met Picasso. Clearly, Matisse had idealized his wife, Eva thought.

"What brings you to Avignon?" Picasso asked as he tossed his napkin onto the table, and stood stiffly to greet the couple.

"I'm sure you've heard, it's been in all the papers. Vollard has just sold my painting *The Dance* for an exorbitant sum, so I am taking my wife to Morocco for the rest of the year. There is a lovely old sultan's palace there, and I have rented out the entire thing. It should all be quite decadent." He turned to Eva. "And may we infer that your lovely companion is Madame Picasso?"

Eva was nervously twisting her linen dinner napkin into a knot beneath the table-cloth.

"Not yet," Picasso said, "but very soon, she will be. First, I must take her to Barcelona to meet my family. Monsieur and

Madame Matisse, may I present Eva Gouel."

"Good heavens." Matisse's wife sniffed and pursed her lips. "Your mistress, then?"

It was the first time since Eva had met Picasso that she actually felt brazen. She could not recall what things were said between the three of them after that in the moments before Matisse and his wife were shown to their own table. Eva was too busy pressing back the tears that would only have embarrassed her further.

"Matisse is the one man who always manages to make me feel inept," Picasso growled, still angry an hour later as they climbed the stairs back to their room across town at the more modest Grand Nouvel Hôtel. Eva sensed that the exchange with Fernande and Pichot was weighing on him. Running into the van Dongens and then the Matisses certainly had not helped.

"I'm sorry you've had to face such unpleasantness since we left Paris."

"Matisse is far from unpleasant, but he is one of my greatest rivals, even more than Braque. Both of us know he has found more success, and he loves to taunt me with it."

"No artist rivals you," Eva said meaningfully. "Your work is brilliant."

"Clearly, *ma jolie,* you are biased."

413

"Perhaps, but it's still true."

"I'm liable to grow accustomed to your flattery, you know," Picasso warned her.

"I hope you do."

The next morning when she woke, Picasso was standing over her with a plate of fresh croissants in one hand and a long iron key in the other. "What have you got there?" she asked sleepily as she lifted her head from the pillow.

"It is the key to our new home. I have rented us a summer house in a place where we won't be bothered. It's outside of town in an uninspiring little village not far from here called Sorgues," he said with a proud smile.

"You certainly are making this an adventure."

"A good one, I hope. I want us to have time to ourselves and not to be upset by what others say or what they think. I feel as if half of Paris has followed us down here and I just want you all to myself for a while."

"You are a greedy man, Monsieur Picasso."

"When it comes to you, I am guilty as charged."

Eva had to admit it did feel a bit as though they had been followed and she was frightened at who else might turn up if they didn't find a new little hideaway. She'd never heard of Sorgues but there was a certain excitement in the mystery, and in the notion of being spirited away. Every single day since they'd met had brought surprises. Even though she had no idea what would happen next, Eva found that she liked the sensation.

That afternoon, they took a trolley from Avignon to Sorgues. The brightly painted open-air bus, which the locals had nick-named the Buffalo, snaked along the path among tall grass fields and past an endless grove of trees in the six-mile journey north to the suburb. Picasso carried their two bulging carpetbags as he and Eva walked from the trolley stop beneath the warmth of the summer sun. They made their way through an old gate and a gravel-covered courtyard with an old olive tree, and when they arrived at the house, he bid Eva to open the tall front door. The heavy old thing gave a low squeal as it moved back on its hinges.

"It is called Villa des Clochettes. I was assured by the mayor that it would be quite suitable for us. No one will bother us out here," Picasso explained as they stepped inside. There were lovely blue-and-white mosaic floor tiles and a whitewashed foyer. The house had a Moorish design, which seemed so popular outside of Paris.

There were heavy shutters that were closed against the warmth of the summer sun, so the place was cool and quiet, and the air smelled faintly of oranges. There must be a fruit tree outside in the garden, Eva thought as Picasso pressed back the shutters, and light poured into the vaulted room, bringing everything into view.

She was happy now to have left all of the drama behind in Céret and Avignon. Picasso was right; there was nothing picturesque about this little suburb. But what it appeared to lack in charm was more than made up for in a palpable aura of peace. Picasso could heal here from the horrendous scene with his friends, and he could create. For her part, Eva planned to foster a warm, nurturing world that would be a safe harbor for him, and to find her own path so that she would not merely be swallowed up by his. She was surprised how much that had come to mean to her.

"This seems a perfect studio for you," Eva said of the large room beyond the foyer that was full of sunlight.

She wondered how long it would take Picasso to fill all of these plain walls with his work, the way they were at the Bateau-Lavoir.

"I think it is, too. I am inspired already." He put the suitcases down and poised his hands on his hips as he took stock of the place. "There is a maid who comes with the place, and a competent cook, as well."

"I would rather be the one who cooks for you. My mother says it is the greatest show of a woman's love," Eva said softly, feeling the catch in her own voice — the hint of insecurity — that she always tried so hard to press away when something really mattered to her.

She closed her eyes as she felt his mouth graze her neck. "I can think of another," he murmured seductively, and she could feel his sly grin against her skin.

When she looked at him, Eva could see how his eyes had softened. It was easy now for her to see the devotion in his gaze, where a few short weeks ago she had been uncertain that such a thing was actually possible.

On the opposite side of the room near a bookcase, she saw an old embroidery stand half-covered over with a sheet. As Eva went and drew off the sheet, she felt a wave of nostalgia.

"My mother had one just like this," she said. "She taught me how to embroider when I was just a girl. She made the most beautiful table cover. I remember, she let me make the rose at the center."

"Why don't you make a table cover for our home here, then?"

The idea surprised her. "Oh, I don't know. It has been years," she demurred.

"Well, I know there is nothing you can't do with a needle and thread. Perhaps you could sell them in town, or we could send them up to Paris."

"The tiles and the colors outside do inspire me," she cautiously acknowledged. "They make me think of so many possible designs. But I'd rather design an elegant skirt or a lady's cape perhaps."

Picasso pulled her into his arms. "There, you see? Creating things is as natural to you as it is to me."

"I wouldn't go that far." Eva chuckled. "But it might be fun to try. Maybe I could do a Cubist design. That would be something, wouldn't it?"

"Let's not go getting carried away," he teased.

"Do you really think I could sell my designs?"

"*Ma jolie,* I think that, together, there is nothing we cannot do."

"Well, if I do decide to try, it will have to

take a backseat to my first task."

"Oh? And what would that be?" Picasso asked.

"I intend to learn more about art while we are down here, make a real study of it."

"Ambitious girl."

"Don't tease, Pablo. It's important that I know everything I can so you can talk to me about it."

She could see that he was touched.

"Do you suppose there is a bookstore in one of the towns nearby?" Eva asked.

"If there is, I have a suspicion you will find it. I see how you are when you set your mind to something."

"You'll come with me, of course. To help me choose the best books."

"Your humble servant." He gallantly nodded.

Picasso kissed her, then he glanced around the room. "So do you think you can be happy here in this hidden little Eden? It really is remote."

"So long as I am with you, I can be happy anywhere," she replied, and Eva knew that was more true than anything else she had ever said in her life.

Inside the house, a week later, sheltered from the heat of the summer sun, they lounged leisurely together on the sofa. Earlier, they had gone into town to the market, with its host of vendors from the surrounding countryside selling fat berries, ripe figs, cheeses and breads. Picasso had dutifully held the shopping bag as Eva went from shop to shop, debating which herbs to buy, and haggling with a proprietor over the price of a chicken. Then she selected a local wine for their supper, like any other proper country wife. She reveled in the simple tasks.

Now as they lounged, Eva wore her slip and Picasso only his trousers. Their heads were on the opposite ends of the velveteen sofa, their bare feet entwined in the center. Picasso was covered in a litter of newspapers. Some of them were from Provence and others had been sent down from Paris. Eva was surrounded by heavy art books that she had been pouring over for days, marking them intently for things she wanted to learn more about. The books she had found in the various villages around Sorgues were on her lap and covering the floor around them.

"You do look adorable right now," Picasso said. "Did you realize that your nose crinkles up when you concentrate?"

"Shh!" she playfully scolded. "Learning

takes concentration."

"What are you learning?"

"So far, I've learned that you are not being paid nearly enough for your works."

Picasso bit back a smile. "Is that so?"

"Absolutely. Kahnweiler should be demanding more for your paintings. Not only will it create far greater notoriety for you, but if the overseas price for your paintings goes up, so will your credibility in France. The world will take notice. Plus, you cannot have things just sitting around galleries for too long. They need to be seen flying out the door as fast as you can paint them."

"You got all of that from those books?"

She tipped her head to the side. "Are you making fun of me?"

"Not at all. I'm just surprised that you are so interested."

"Everything about you interests me, and this is *our* world now. I want to be a true partner to you."

"I know you do, and I love you for it." He pushed the books and newspapers onto the floor and slid, snakelike, across the sofa to her.

"So tell me," she said as he laid his head on her thigh, "do you love me enough to help me make dinner?"

He pulled himself up farther along the

curves and length of her body until their mouths met. Then he kissed her sensually. "If you promise to cook wearing only your apron, perhaps this time I might have to help."

"What if someone sees us!" She chuckled as she stroked his hair.

"No one will see us. We have only each other way out here in the middle of nowhere. And it really is just like our little Eden."

On that they agreed. Eva could not imagine being happier anywhere else. Nor, she knew, could Picasso.

That summer in Provence was filled with a magic that was new to them both.

Eva read every book about art she could find, and she began to embroider a piece she intended to make into a dressy cape. Meanwhile, Picasso steadily filled the walls with his art. He worked with gouache, and ink on paper, as well as oil on canvas, for hours at a time. The medium did not matter. He was inspired here, and the happiness he felt manifested itself in the bright colors he was using.

For her part, Eva began to find real joy once again, in both sewing and the calming art of embroidery, just as she had as a girl in Vincennes beneath her mother's patient guidance. And she reveled in the challenge of learning about the world of art. It struck her, as the sun grew more intense, beating down on the little suburb of Sorgues, and they spent more time inside of their lovely shelter, that everything she had wanted to escape to in Paris she now embraced here in Provence, and she had never felt so challenged.

Eva doted on Picasso, and he thrived beneath her tender care. The past seemed very far away to them both as she made him spinach soufflé, and loin of veal, as his mother had done for him in Barcelona. And she believed that whatever dark spirits and superstitions that once had haunted him now had finally been put to rest.

"Kahnweiler finally sent everything," Picasso said late one morning as he painted.

Eva sat on the floor beside him, spreading out a pattern for a dress she intended to make and send as a gift to Sylvette.

"The box was sitting outside when I went to fetch the newspaper."

"I know how you've missed your special brushes, and your old easel."

"And your very enticing yellow kimono. In my rush to leave Paris, we left without that, too," he said devilishly as he drew the garment from the box and handed it to her.

What a full life that kimono has had, Eva thought happily. From Poland to Vincennes, from Vincennes to the Moulin Rouge — and now to Sorgues. She slipped her arms through the sleeves once again, luxuriating in the cool comfort of the familiar silk. She loved how sensual it felt.

"There was something else in the box," he said as he handed her a folded copy of the newspaper *La Vie Parisienne* he had stuffed behind the canvas on his easel. Prominent on the page was a cartoon. "I hate this, but I must be honest with you."

Eva recognized the drawing even at a distance, because she knew the artist so well. She could see that the disparaging drawing was attributed to Marcoussis — as Louis called himself now. *Oh, Louis, how could you?* she thought, feeling a sliver of sadness work its way up through her. There was a time when they were close, but he had changed so much that she could no longer see any of the goodness in him that first had drawn her. Warily, Eva read the derisive title Schéhérazade au Bal de Quat'z Arts.

Louis had drawn her in comic form as the storyteller who seduced a king by her creativity. He was using a public venue to mock Eva. Beside her, he had drawn Picasso with a ball and chain around his ankle. Louis had depicted himself, dancing for joy. Beneath the sketch was the caption "A gentleman who has lost his illusions. The happy bachelor and the newlyweds."

Eva sank onto a footstool beside the easel, crumpling the paper in her lap. No matter where they went, they could not outrun their past.

"Why did Kahnweiler send this?"

"I suppose he wanted us to be warned about what kind of gossip awaits us when we return to Paris," Picasso said with a sigh.

"Oh, Pablo, then must we return? Why can we not just stay here, where we are happy?"

"Ah, *ma jolie* Eva, love of my life, because this is not the real world. Sooner or later, I will need to be where Vollard and Kahn weiler are, if I don't want Matisse, Braque or even Derain to outshine me."

She felt tears prick her eyes, but she forced them back. He was looking absently at the floor, at the dress pattern she had placed there and the pieces of it she had cut away where there were meant to be sleeves and the neckline. Eva could see his mind working. Picasso knelt on the floor and began randomly arranging the scraps of paper. Then he picked up her scissors and cut the newspaper into shapes.

"I used to do this when I was a boy in Barcelona. Since the women in the apartment beside ours were seamstresses they were always cutting patterns, leaving scraps of paper for me to think about shaping into other things, little collages."

"Was one of them your mistress, too?" Eva asked with a half smile as she watched his spontaneous design now take shape.

Picasso glanced up. She could see his surprise at the little spark of spirit behind her question. "Better I keep some bit of mystery from you about all of that, I think!"

She laughed. He was probably right, so she changed the subject. "You need glue for that, to make it a true papier collé."

He had worked a piece of Louis's cartoon behind an ad for Savon du Nord. Then he cut a heart out of the pattern material and put it on top of the cartoon face Louis had drawn of himself.

"I might have to start doing more of these. Papier collé," he said, as though saying it solidified the idea of it for him. "This is surprisingly relaxing to me."

As if atoning for things he knew she would never fully understand about him, Picasso moved on his knees toward Eva and buried his head in her lap. She watched him savor the feel of the rich silk she wore. She touched his cheek, then bent forward and tenderly kissed the top of his head, struck once again by the depth of her love.

The sound of a barking dog broke the moment between them.

Picasso sprang to his feet as his expression lit with boyish excitement. "I would know that bark anywhere! Frika!"

Picasso ran to the door, where the big shaggy dog yelped, and playfully wrestled Picasso to the floor beside the driver who had brought her down from Paris. She wagged her tail and licked his face as tears filled Picasso's eyes. It was the first time Eva had ever seen him so emotional. Who would have guessed a man with such bravado could be so softhearted, Eva thought.

He laughed as Frika nestled onto his lap a big overgrown puppy, her furry tail passing back and forth like a broom. "The only thing that could make the summer more perfect would be for Braque and Marcelle to move in right down the road!"

Ah, Eva thought with a cringe of disappointment. Indeed, what could be more perfect than that?

They were no longer his friends, yet there was a time when he had trusted each of them. He could not abide traitors, yet he felt their loss deeply. As Eva slept upstairs, Picasso felt a quiet fury in these still hours, alone in his studio, lit with lamplight, shadows and the glow of the moon. At this hour, his demons were at their strongest.

He made little to Eva of the disappointing scene in Céret with Fernande and the Pichots, or of the encounters with van Dongen and Matisse in Avignon. They had not spoken further of Marcoussis's crass cartoon, and Picasso had not told Eva how he had threatened Louis before they left Paris. Picasso did not like the idea of keeping things from Eva because it seemed like betrayal. But the depth of his obsession, and the need to protect her, made it necessary to move on now and make something positive of his powerful emotions.

He knew that he must leave a tribute to Eva here in this special place — not paint a canvas, but make something immovable — a fresco that would forever bind them to this place, whatever else the future held.

He had pulled two newly completed canvases from the large wall near the front door. He was surveying the space on the wall and the shapes he had lightly drawn in the place where he planned to paint the fresco when suddenly he saw Eva leaning against the doorjamb, wrapped in the yellow kimono. He had been so possessed by his thoughts that he had not heard her come downstairs. Picasso sank back onto his heels, stunned at how exquisite she looked in this light. She had no idea what little effort it would take her to completely destroy him, he thought. If anything should ever happen to her . . . But he could not think of that.

"Shouldn't you come to bed? It's nearly dawn," she asked sleepily as she rubbed her eyes.

"I will be up in a little while. Go back to bed."

"Not without you."

Using her fingertips, she traced the large circle Picasso had drawn on the blank wall. Inside the circle, he had begun to fashion the shape of a guitar and a bottle of Pernod like the one they had shared with the Braques. And prominently in the center was the familiar term, *Ma Jolie,* which he had used in his painting. Here, it was written boldly, a declaration, as if on a piece of paper.

She regarded the outline with wonder. "What does it mean to you?" Eva asked as she came up beside him and touched his shoulder.

"It is a piece of us forever in this place."

He loved how free with her he felt to explore new mediums without judgment or criticism. Picasso had never wanted to share the essence of his creative spirit so fully with a woman before. Eva really was the new muse he had hoped she would become.

"And so, metaphorically speaking, do you see me as a guitar?" Eva asked, gazing back at the wall.

"I don't see you that way literally. But sometimes, it is how I feel you. It is the life I feel throbbing through you when I touch you. To paint you traditionally right now feels perfunctory to me, like an insult, because the depth of my love for you is not traditional at all."

He studied her for a moment trying to gauge her reaction. "I want to capture the passion that exists between us and keep it forever. *That* is the essence of us, not a face I could reproduce as if I were in art school."

Picasso stopped then and waited. Her puzzled expression made him regret how much he had revealed. He was certain it made no sense.

Eva turned back toward the fresco again and touched the outline of the shapes.

"I would like to watch you work."

"It can be tedious," he warned, secretly

430

hoping, even as he said it, that she would not be put off.

"It won't be tedious to me, because it is us."

He watched as her eyes narrowed, and her cheeks colored. He understood what she was thinking, and he smiled for how tentative they still were with each other's fantasies.

Picasso walked over to his easel, took up a pot of paint and a brush, then returned to her. He dipped the brush in color, handed it to her and slipped his hand over hers. Touching her warm, soft skin kindled not only ardor but Picasso's creative passion.

"Help me paint this one," he bid her.

She laughed. "My name is not Picasso, I can't do that!"

"Soon enough, it will be. *Jolie* Eva Picasso. Now, let's begin our masterpiece."

Over that summer, Picasso tried to smoke less because he could tell Eva did not like it, although she never complained. He took up smoking a pipe instead of cigarettes because it was all the rage for people their ages who were trying to add some gravitas to their youthful images. Picasso would clinch the small burl-wood pipe on the side of his mouth, then study himself in the mir-

431

ror. When Eva giggled at him, Picasso would push the pipe between her lips and make it into an erotic game between them.

They had only become more deeply besotted with each other in Provence.

In July, Picasso's wish came true. Braque and his wife came to Sorgues. Braque told Picasso that they were on their way to the cooler coastline to buy a summerhouse there. But the Braques stayed as their guests in the Sorgues house near the town square until August. Then the Braques invited them to go to Marseille for a few days.

Still Eva said nothing to Picasso, nor did she confront Marcelle about the conversation she had overheard between her and Alice in Céret. But she would be on guard from now on. She was not a fool, but she was a realist. This was Picasso's world, and she was determined to remain at its center.

What she kept from him he would never know.

But what she was to him, she meant for him never to forget.

One of the things she could not tell him yet was about the wave of nausea she had begun to feel the past few days. At first Eva thought she had eaten something bad. But as the days went on, the nausea kept returning. She would worry Picasso if she told him

432

so Eva kept silent.

At dinner one night, Braque told Picasso about an area in Marseille along the waterfront where they sold African tribal art. Picasso had a collection of masks that fascinated him at his former apartment in Paris. He had used them as inspiration for many pieces, particularly his favorite, a canvas that he called *Les Chicas de Avinyó.* Kahnweiler wanted him to change it to a more respectable title, *Les Demoiselles d'Avignon,* so for now artist and dealer were at an impasse and Picasso refused to sell the bold and shocking canvas.

"Is it all right if we go with them to Marseille?" Picasso asked her as the heavy sound of the cicadas filled the warm night air.

" 'Wither thou goest,' " Eva said.

"Trumping Verlaine with the Bible, are you?" Picasso chuckled.

Eva missed the church — the smell of incense, of candle wax and the great sense of restoration when she was sheltered inside the walls of a *maison de Dieu.*

When they returned to Paris in September, Eva would find a parish near wherever they lived, and she hoped Picasso would go to Mass with her. It would be good for him to find some peace through God about some of the things that still haunted him, like the deaths of Casagemas and his little sister Conchita. And she had been praying again privately. She prayed for Picasso and for her own health, as well. Eva had never felt so ill in her life, and it frightened her. Most days, the nausea was unbearable. There was little else to conclude but that she was pregnant.

She wanted to tell Picasso, yet a sliver of doubt remained. Would he be happy about it? Did he even want children at this demanding and challenging time in his career? Would he resent her for burdening him? Until she knew the answers for certain — and until he formally proposed marriage, Eva meant to keep it a secret. But when they arrived back in Paris, the first order of business would be to see a doctor.

CHAPTER 26

Picasso and Eva stood together inside the foyer of Villa des Clochettes, with Frika dutifully by Picasso's side, as they prepared to leave for Paris. There were tears in her eyes, and Picasso's, as well, as a cold and unforgiving mistral stirred up the dust and leaves in the courtyard beyond the open front door. Eva had come down with a deep rheumy cough, which did not help the persistent nausea. Her mother always said she had a weak constitution. She had certainly developed enough cases of *petite angine* in her youth to know it was true. But she did her best to suffer this episode alone. Picasso's earlier declaration about illness made her wary.

"I'm sad to leave this place," Eva said softly, not wanting to ignite another fit of coughing, since they were becoming particularly difficult to hide from Picasso. So far, he believed her when she said it was a reaction to the dust that the wind had stirred. "This has been a wonderful home."

There was a car waiting for them out past the rusty iron gate, with their luggage stowed inside, but Eva needed a moment more here.

As she looked over at the fresco he had painted for her on the wall in the foyer, she thought of a dozen other small touches they had added to make this place special. There were the gauzy curtains with the delicate lace edges she had sewn for the kitchen, and the set of locally made crockery they had bought on an excursion to Tarascon, proudly set out on the antique sideboard. The walls in the sitting room had been adorned with the wonderful masks they had bought in Marseille, ten days earlier, along with several of Picasso's papier collé creations that Eva had inspired — and two new Cubist canvases.

A number of the works contained the words *J'aime Eva.* Or *Jolie Eva.* Most of the messages were hidden, however, so only she might know they were there. Picasso told her that he envisioned them as a tribute to the woman who once had been hidden in his life. He told her he was pleased with the irony, since he could proudly proclaim her now.

"I thought I would like that the mural would remain here after we'd gone," she said, for the last time touching the words *Ma Jolie* painted there.

"Yet now it's like leaving a piece of us."

"That's it, exactly." She wiped tears from her eyes. "I'm sorry for being so hopeless."

"You're not hopeless, you're sentimental. Among the many qualities about you that I adore. As it happens, my father might actually like you."

That had sounded so strange and intimidating. "Oh, dear," she said.

"We have had a difficult relationship for most of my life. When I was growing up, he wasn't a particularly likable father. Mainly, he was self-centered and neglectful."

"The relationship with fathers can be a challenging one," Eva said, thinking of her own father.

"There were times I actually hated him. But I learned to paint from my father and he completely invested in me as an artist. He believed in me from the beginning. Too much of him is deeply rooted inside of me to deny that what he thinks still matters to me. Being with you here has made me reflect, and to think of family."

"Love does many unexpected things," Eva said.

"He is getting old now, and lately I find, in spite of our troubles, that I would like to see him."

"You were worried he wouldn't like me?"

"Don José doesn't like many people. At least he is set against showing it, if he does. He has become a gruff, self-centered old bull, but you will need to meet him, anyway. My mother and my sister Lola, as well. Don José won't tell you to your face, but he will like your softness because he will think his son has finally found a woman over whom I will become both master and slave at last."

She wiped more tears away as he kissed her. "That sounds positively medieval."

"No, just Spanish." He chuckled. "But you will see for yourself when we get to Barcelona."

"When will we go?"

"I was thinking at Christmas, if that's all right. My sister will adore you, and she will be quite open about it. She is recently married, so I think she would value a sister's companionship from you, since she will never have Conchita for that. Her husband is a well-known surgeon in the city, quite a wealthy man, so Don José caters to him as if he were King Alfonso himself."

A silence fell between them as Picasso kissed her again. The word *married* had made her hopeful, in that moment, for the natural progression of the conversation which she hoped would again turn to them. Although she had heard him speak to Matisse of their marriage, it had not yet manifested into a proper proposal. With the prospect of a pregnancy, Eva's fears only grew stronger.

But Picasso said nothing more about it.

Was it his father, she wondered, or perhaps it was really that he still had feelings for Fernande that caused him to delay asking for her hand in marriage? She knew she was being overly emotional lately but Fernande was, after all, so beautiful and sophisticated. The fleeting thought brought a new well-spring of tears to Eva's eyes, which Picasso assumed was about leaving the villa.

"Don't worry any more about the fresco, *mon amour.* Besides, you need to concern yourself with our new apartment in Paris. It was supposed to be a surprise, but I learned just this morning that Kahnweiler has found us a flat in Montparnasse, and he says it has plenty of room for my studio. You remember him?"

Of course she remembered him. Daniel-Henry Kahnweiler was the ambitious young art dealer who had brought her the gift of Picasso's painting and turned the tide of their relationship.

"Will you see Fernande when we return?"

Eva pressed a finger to her lips, as though the words had escaped accidentally. And she had truly not meant to ask the question. Picasso's eyes narrowed. A new wave of nausea swept over her so strongly that she was certain she would be ill or faint, or both.

"Apollinaire and Max Jacob are sentimental types, as you are. Max found her a job at the Maison de Poiret, assisting one of the dress designers. She also has the paintings and sketches I did of her that she can sell, so she is no longer my problem. You are the only woman in my life now. You and Frika, of course."

Eva could not help but recall, with a pitiful sense of irony, that first lunch with Fernande Olivier a year ago now. Fernande had seemed to Eva that day the most elegant creature on earth, with her trendsetting hobble skirt from the Maison de Poiret. Now she would be required to work for the very establishment where once she had been a valued client.

But Eva could not think about that as she tried to steady herself in the doorway, and to smile as if nothing was wrong. Picasso wanted to marry her. They would marry. She knew that. Now that she felt confident about the tie being broken with Fernande, there really was nothing stopping her from being the real Madame Picasso.

The first surprise for Eva was an evening at the theater. On the night they arrived back in Paris, Picasso took her as a guest to the very show at the Moulin Rouge behind which she once had toiled with needle and thread. The change in her circumstance was not lost on Eva.

"I thought you would enjoy a front-row seat from now on, instead of the view from backstage."

Picasso squeezed her gloved hand as he helped her from the car. She was wearing a new dress he'd had waiting for her in their hotel room. It was a fashionable empire waist creation made of burgundy silk, complete with a faux jeweled hair band, fox stole and silk gloves.

It also did not go unnoticed that, for their first night back in Paris as a couple, Picasso had booked them a room at the same elegant hotel where they had once met to telephone her mother. Hôtel le Meurice was a place of princes and kings, so she knew even this one night would have cost him a veritable fortune. "It is my dream to have our wedding dinner here in this place," he had told her.

For so much male bravado, Picasso really did have a tender heart, and she knew that he intended to spoil her, little by little, as he could increasingly afford to do. Just a few more sales of his art, he promised, and they would live a life of unimaginable luxury together. He was on the cusp of that; he told her that he could feel it. And Max Jacob's horoscope readings had foretold great success and wealth beyond his wildest imagination. But Eva didn't need any of it. All she needed was Picasso. When she told him that, he just smiled indulgently and kissed her cheek. Their fate, he had said, and his success, was already written in the stars.

A moment after their arrival, as they stood beneath the bright lights outside, they were greeted by several of the costumed players: Mado Minty, Maurice Chevalier, Mistinguett . . . and Sylvette, back at work.

In that moment, leaning protectedly against Picasso, Eva tried to take in all of the changes life had brought her. She did not feel like the same girl who had first come here to the Moulin Rouge to plead for a seamstress job. That was a day that had changed her life forever in so many ways.

Sylvette was first to plunge forward from the group and embrace Eva as they arrived. "Welcome back!"

"The same to you, *mon amie.*" Eva smiled.

"It's so good to be back," Sylvette said.

Eva saw that her spirit was dampened, but her lovely eyes still had their spark.

"Hello, beautiful!" Mistinguett beamed. She was the next to draw Eva into a hearty embrace. "*L'amour* certainly agrees with you, can we say! Such a wonderful little minx, you are! None of us had a clue. Did you have a clue, Sylvette?"

"Yes, Mistinguett, I had a clue," Sylvette drawled as she rolled her eyes.

Everyone laughed.

The crowd beyond the rope line was swelling and spilling out into the cobblestoned place Blanche. They were excitedly cheering as more of the actors gathered with Picasso and Eva out in front of the theater with the great defining windmill overhead. Only celebrities gathered with the actors and dancers near the door like this before a show.

"I'm so glad you're here," Sylvette whispered to Eva as they linked hands.

"Oh, me, too. You have no idea. You must come to dinner next week, promise me. I'm not sure yet where we will live, but I will

443

send you a formal invitation when I have our new address."

Sylvette smiled but Eva noticed how much weight she had lost. "We never had formal invitations at la Ruche. Why start such an antiquated system now? Just tell me when and where, and it's a date."

Madame Léautaud came out of the theater then. Still such a stiff, intimidating presence. Eva did not see her until she was standing beside Mistinguett. She was wearing the same severe black dress as always, her posture ramrod straight.

"Monsieur Picasso, it is an honor to have you back with us," she fawned as her frosty exterior thawed. In this light her lined cheeks were like a pale road map, edged with too much rouge. "Monsieur Oller will be so happy to know you are returned to Paris."

Madame Léautaud then turned to Eva and their eyes met. She had held Eva's entire future in her hands, and she had given her a chance. Instead of feeling intimidated, as she once had, Eva now felt only gratitude.

"Mademoiselle Humbert," she said with a curt nod.

"It is Mademoiselle Gouel," Picasso corrected her firmly. "Eva Gouel is this beautiful woman's real name."

"You've got a real jewel there, Monsieur Picasso, let me tell you. She is a girl who surely knows her own mind, and has the focus to get whatever she likes."

"It does take all of my effort to keep up with her, but I enjoy the challenge."

"I don't mind telling you that we would take her back here in a heartbeat, so be good to her, will you?"

"Thank you, madame," Eva said proudly, feeling invincible.

After the show, Eva and Picasso joined everyone for drinks at la Rotonde. Eva could not bear even the smallest hint of wine just now, as the nausea that began in Provence never quite fully left her — nor did her accompanying cough. The pregnancy must have weakened her system and brought about another *petite angine.* This baby was certainly taking most of her energy. She needed to find a doctor in Paris to confirm what she already believed, but it must be someone discreet, until she was ready to tell Picasso.

"You're *what?*" Sylvette gasped.

She and Eva sat with their heads together as the music and laughter in the busy brasserie swelled around them.

"I'm not certain. That's why I need to see

a doctor."

"Some of the girls have seen the one over on the rue Frochot." Eva knew the doctor Sylvette was referring to. He was notorious in Montmartre. One of the dancers had even died after his procedure. She had bled to death.

"Sylvette, if I *am* pregnant, I plan to keep this baby," Eva declared with conviction.

"You're not even married."

"I will be. You'll see. He loves me."

"He loved Fernande Olivier, too."

"That was cruel."

"I'm sorry. You know I didn't mean it to be. I just want what's best for you." Sylvette covered Eva's hand on the glass-strewn tabletop with her own as Picasso sat across from them, puffing a cigarette, and conversing animatedly with the young art critic he had introduced as André Salmon. "Picasso has quite a reputation in Paris. You must be careful with your heart, *chérie.* That's all."

"It's far too late for that. I am fully devoted to his happiness," said Eva. "No risk would be too great to keep him happy, I'm afraid."

Picasso was so eager for them to go to Gertrude Stein's salon the next evening that he couldn't stop talking about it. He considered Gertrude one of his dearest friends in the world, even more so now, after what had happened — first with Apollinaire, then with Ramón and Germaine Pichot — and he was anxious for her and Eva to get to know each other.

"Gertrude and Alice have only just returned to Paris, as well, so there will be much for all of us to discuss," Picasso said as they made their way in the back of a cab, across the busy boulevard Raspail toward the new apartment Kahnweiler had leased for the two of them.

"Gertrude will adore you, once the two of you have actually had time to speak."

"She's awfully intimidating, Pablo."

"She will be impressed with your knowledge of poetry and your growing interest in art. You could begin with that."

"And Miss Toklas?"

"Of course, she is much more quiet. I suppose she would have to be in order to coexist with Gertrude." He chuckled. "But she has a good heart, and she is as loyal as you are, so you will have that in common."

Eva cleared her throat into the back of her hand, staving off a cough. She was trying her best to keep from sounding unwell, or particularly contagious. Whatever she had caught, probably from that cold mistral, certainly was not leaving her without a fight.

"Almost there," Picasso said.

She was struck at the sight then beyond the car window as they passed through the crowded intersection of the boulevards Raspail and Montparnasse. There was a vibrant café on each corner: Le Dôme and la Rotonde held most prominence of place — beacons that had signaled "real Paris" to the wide-eyed girl she once had been. Now here she was, moving into an address right around the corner! It was difficult to fathom. It felt like a fairy tale.

They saw Kahnweiler standing in a navy blue suit, white collar and bowler hat, outside the Norman-style building on the boulevard Raspail as the car pulled over to the curb. He held a walking stick in one hand and an iron key in the other. She felt a spark of relief as Picasso stepped out of the car after Eva, then put a hand around her waist.

"Good to see you, Kahnweiler."

"And you, Monsieur Picasso."

"I hope you have found us something splendid. Sorry about the short notice."

"It's on the first floor, I'm afraid. But it has large windows, a private sitting area and, most importantly, room to paint, as you requested. I took the liberty of having your canvases, paints, brushes and easel brought down here from Montmartre so you can begin to work at once."

"Taskmaster," Picasso quipped, and Eva chuckled as Kahnweiler opened the front door of the building.

The eighteenth-century town house apartment looked to Eva as if someone already lived there. Kahnweiler had seen to even the smallest detail in order to make the dark rooms appear charming. Picasso's paintings, and a few of his African masks, already decorated the mahogany-paneled walls. The wood floors were in a parquet pattern and were covered in several places by elegant carpets, and there were vases full of fresh flowers placed everywhere. The only thing the space lacked was adequate light. Even in the afternoon, as the sun shone through the windows, the rooms held the heavy burden of darkness and shadows.

Kahnweiler flipped on a light, as if he sensed what Eva was thinking. At least the place had been fitted with electricity, she thought. Picasso explored the various rooms with purposeful strides as Eva waited in the foyer.

"Is it to your taste, then, mademoiselle?" Kahnweiler asked. He held his walking stick in one hand and the rim of his bowler hat in the other.

"To be honest, I'm not really certain yet what my taste is. But if Monsieur Picasso likes it, I'm certain I will be happy here."

A relieved smile broke across his face. He was handsome, she thought, but his ambition had produced frown lines on his forehead, and beside both eyes, that were far too deep for a man his age.

"You really are different, aren't you?" he said.

"I can only hope he finds me so."

"Perhaps the two of us can work together? Picasso can use some convincing, now and then, about which pieces it is time to part with, since the market for his art is really heating up.

"Like that large one over there, for example," he indicated with his eyes.

Picasso heard him. "You know better than that. My *Chicas* is still not for sale."

"Well, you know you can call it that whenever you *do* decide to sell it. But this is France. They have *demoiselles* in Avignon, not *chicas,*" Kahnweiler teased.

"I didn't set the work in Avignon, either. They're the whores of Avinyó in Barcelona, but I know you don't think that sounds very romantic."

As they bantered, Eva looked more critically at the large, boldly painted canvas propped against the wall. She wasn't certain what to make of the five nude women Picasso had painted, two of them with masks instead of faces. But she could hear the vulnerability in his voice about the painting. No matter the words he spoke, she had learned that his voice usually gave him away. Whatever they ended up calling it, that strange, massive painting seemed as if it was meant to be important. Maybe she could help Picasso see that, too.

Eva still wasn't certain of her full place in Picasso's life, but she gained a little more confidence every day, especially the more she learned about art. She would help Kahn-weiler if she could. Perhaps ahead, there really was a greater role for her to play than just an artist's mistress.

When they arrived that evening, Gertrude's salon was packed with the same crowd of young French luminaries that Eva remembered. But this time, when she entered the room on the arm of Pablo Picasso, everyone stopped to stare with a kind of admiration she had never felt before. She knew she looked *très soigné,* as they said in Paris, dressed in a new green lamp shade tunic studded with rhinestones, and a matching hair band plumed with an ostrich feather. It emboldened her with a measure of confidence to make the entrance she knew Picasso wanted for her as his partner. Still, he must have felt her hesitation because he squeezed her hand tightly as he drew her inside the room.

"Into the lion's den." He chuckled beneath his breath.

Eva was too nervous to laugh in response. The last time she'd had so many people looking at her, she was onstage hidden behind white makeup and a geisha costume, and she still wasn't certain how she had managed to pull that off. From now on, she would always be compared to Fernande, and Eva realized that her task was to exceed everyone's expectations. The prospect was daunting. Like at the Moulin Rouge, once again it was showtime.

She and Picasso were quickly engulfed by a crushing wave of ingratiating guests who came to welcome the artist back to Paris after the summer holiday. She heard a man's voice behind her.

"Well, I do believe grace has just walked right in that door. Will you look at that stunning new girl with Picasso? How does he get all the loveliest ones?"

Eva glanced at Picasso and she could see

by his smile that he had heard. He was pleased! She felt so proud of herself, even in spite of her nerves. She had transformed herself, made something of herself on her own, and now she belonged here with Picasso. In this small moment of triumph, the insults of the girls at the hotel in Montmartre, and Marcelle Braque, suddenly seemed very far away.

Throughout the evening, Picasso answered questions about the upcoming Salon d'Automne, and talked about the new stage play starring Sarah Bernhardt in the title role. A young American actor, who introduced himself as Al Jolson, asked Eva what she thought of the composer Erik Satie, whose music was quite, as he said, avant-garde. Everyone in Paris was talking about Satie.

Eva easily answered Jolson that she found Satie's work bold, rather than trite, and she was relieved that he agreed with her. This was her world now, too. Not simply one of hemlines, recipes and insecurities. To a large extent, she had made that happen on her own. Eva was glad to have spent the summer reading, not only about art but music, as well. She loved the banter, and the notion that anyone here actually cared what she thought.

As Picasso offered up his own opinions to a growing collection of eager guests surrounding them, Eva felt the gentle press of fingers on her shoulder. When she turned around, she saw Alice Toklas standing behind her, wearing a bold blue-and-green caftan, and holding a large gold goblet. Her frizzy black hair was pulled back loosely, and beneath her prominent nose was a thin but noticeable mustache. Eva thought the facial hair gave her a slightly comical appearance, but her eyes were gentle and warm, which set Eva instantly at ease.

"Well, aren't you a vision," Alice said kindly. "Look at you, so stylish now. I almost didn't recognize you. That dress is absolutely stunning."

"Thank you, I made it yesterday."

"My, you *do* have quite the flair for fashion. It looks as grand as anything from one of the Paris fashion houses. And the fox stole, the way you are wearing it, adds such a wonderfully elegant touch."

Eva stifled another cough. "Thank you, Miss Toklas. But no matter what I'm wearing it's still a bit overwhelming, being back here, and being with him — as his partner now."

Alice smiled. "Poor Marcelle. Fernande left you rather large shoes to fill."

"I'm actually Eva. But, yes, she certainly did at that."

"So, it's not Marcelle, then?"

"It was at the Moulin Rouge but Picasso prefers my real name."

"Well, we are all about being our real selves here, if you hadn't guessed." Alice took a sip from the goblet, which looked medieval, then she met her gaze directly.

Eva understood what Alice meant without her needing to explain. Alice and Gertrude were a couple. After all the things Eva had seen in Paris, it didn't surprise her, and she liked Alice.

She stubbornly resisted the urge to cough and lifted her hand to her mouth; still, Alice noticed.

"May I offer you a glass of wine, my dear? You look as if you could use one. You're a bit green around the edges, honestly."

She was certain the mention of alcohol only made her look more green. "No, but thank you kindly."

"Have you seen a doctor? You wouldn't want your cough to worsen."

"I don't have a doctor here in Paris, I'm afraid."

"Gertrude and I know a perfectly lovely one right over on the boulevard du Montparnasse. I'll fetch you his card, it won't

455

take a minute."

"Thank you, Miss Toklas."

"You must call me Alice. All of my friends do."

Eva struggled against the powerful reflex to cough again. It was difficult to breathe, especially in a room so crowded with smoke and guests. "Might it be possible to ask you not to mention it to Picasso? He really does not do well around people who are ill, so I wouldn't want to worry him unnecessarily."

Alice paused for a moment, then she gave Eva's arm a gentle squeeze. "That's true. He always had a particular mania for that sort of thing — all of those Spanish superstitions feeding into it, I imagine. Of course, my dear, I do love a good secret, so yours is safe with me."

"You are definitely not pregnant, Madame Humbert. But I did find something rather troubling during your examination."

Eva squeezed her small black leather handbag tightly on her lap beneath the physician's sleek mahogany desk. She could hear the cars and carriages passing by outside, beyond the office window.

Another bout of bronchitis. Eva could almost hear him say it. She had let the cough go on too long. She knew better. Her mother had made an art form of *I told you so*. Fortunately, her mother would never need to know about this one.

Dr. Rousseau was a trim, silver-haired man with gold-rimmed spectacles and a sharp silver goatee. He leveled his steel-blue eyes at Eva and then removed the spectacles.

"There is a lump in one of your breasts."

He delivered the words dispassionately and Eva's heart began to race. "I don't know what you mean."

"A tumor is most likely."

"Could it not be something else? I haven't been taking the best care of myself recently. We've been traveling and I've been tired. Could it not be some sort of temporary inflammation because of the fatigue?"

The doctor leaned back in his green leather chair and steepled his fingers beneath his chin. "I suppose there is a small chance that my initial diagnosis is incorrect. I'll have to do some further tests, but I really do advise you to bring your husband in to discuss this."

"No."

I adore your breasts . . . they are the most perfect thing about you —

Picasso's voice filled her head but the sound was not pleasing. Why did she have to remember that now? At the moment it

457

was not the sweet utterance it had been, but now it sounded like crows circling overhead. She pressed her hands against her ears and turned away from the desk so she wouldn't cry. She had come so far with him for this to happen now. . . . Eva knew in her heart that Picasso loved her for far more than her breasts, of course he did. It was almost vulgar to doubt that. He was such a good man. She knew that the love they shared was deep and abiding. It was wrong, even insulting, to assume the worst of him over something like this. He would be furious for her doubting him. But even so, she could not entirely chase the fears from her mind. The shock would not allow it. Picasso had made the declaration, and the insecure part of her she thought vanquished these past few months remembered it. He was such a passionate artist, one who revered the female body. His last lover had looked like a goddess. Could she ever fully escape Fernande's shadow? Many of Picasso's sketches idealized women and their breasts, their sexuality. Eva wasn't being fair to him with this doubt, especially with what they were building together, but she simply could not help the fear that was taking her over.

Why this threat particularly? she thought desperately.

458

Discordant thoughts skittered around in her mind. The crows of insecurity circled. Eva looked around trying desperately to collect herself. This man had so many books. Books everywhere. She hadn't noticed that before. Had he read each volume? Did he know about life, and passion, and obsession, beyond what lay beneath all of those red leather bindings, with their perfect gold lettering and scrollwork titles? Perfection was not her life. Passionate determination, zeal and loyalty made up who she was.

Eva could not quiet the incessant noise in her head. *I am Picasso's muse,* she thought, *not an ill woman in need of pity!*

She could not think another thought or listen to a word more. She gathered as much self-possession as she could and stumbled toward the door. "Madame Humbert, I really do urge you to reconsider. Perhaps if I spoke to your husband . . ."

Eva pivoted back. All of the determination she had ever felt in her life lit her eyes like fire now. "Thank you, Doctor, but that is out of the question," Eva said before she dashed tearfully away from the office.

CHAPTER 27

As autumn came and filled Paris with shades of red, rust and gold, Eva kept herself busy designing dresses for some of the Moulin Rouge cast who loved her style and commissioned something unique for them to wear socially. She turned a piece of embroidery she had made in Sorgues into a stunning cape for Mistinguett and in her spare time she also decorated the new apartment on the boulevard Raspail.

Eva was trying to lighten the impossibly dark first-floor rooms with handmade embroidered throw pillows and cheery chintz curtains, and to make the best of the place, while Picasso worked. Along with the boulevard de Clichy apartment, he had given up the studio space in the Bateau-Lavoir in order be nearer to Eva while he worked. She understood how important Montmartre had been to him, and so she felt it was more essential than ever to make their home a welcoming space, and a peaceful environment, in which he could create.

Kahnweiler was happy with Picasso's new papier collé style, which he had developed in Sorgues, and he was able to sell several of the works to foreign buyers — many in Germany. Picasso's price, and his notoriety on the world stage, was steadily growing, and he confessed to Eva that he had begun to feel the increasing weight of expectation to produce. Knowing how he felt only made stronger Eva's determination to become a full partner to him. He needed her and she knew it. In Paris, she continued educating herself about the art market. She fully intended to be able to offer him informed opinions about how he should manage his career, whenever he asked her.

The other thing upon which she was absolutely intent was making herself a great friend to Gertrude and Alice. After what she had witnessed in Céret with the Pichots — and how hurt Picasso was by their rejection, she knew what it would mean to him to have peace among his supporters. Besides, she really did like the two women, and she looked forward to getting to know them better. Of Picasso's friends, they seemed the least judgmental, and they had never made her feel they were comparing

461

her to Fernande. She even planned to seek out Marcelle Braque when she could, and to be gracious to her. *Keep your friends close and your enemies closer,* she thought again and again.

She must love who Picasso loved, no matter the obstacles.

She had decided to host a dinner party in their new flat, and while it was a daunting prospect for Eva, since she was still so new to Picasso's private world, she was determined to do it. Picasso was completely charmed by the idea.

In addition to Gertrude and Alice, Picasso added Max Jacob to the guest list. He was not prepared, however, to include Apollinaire. Instead, Picasso rounded out the guest list to four by including Juan Gris, who he explained to Eva was a Spanish friend from the Bateau-Lavoir.

As Picasso worked, Eva spent the day preparing all of Picasso's favorite dishes for the party. For dessert, she made her mother's special Polish cookies. With tears of nostalgia in her eyes, Eva gently pressed dough onto the baking sheet, relishing a dozen memories that always came to her in the kitchen. She wished she could talk with her mother, confide in her about all of the things that were happening in her life. So much was changing, and it felt as if it was changing so swiftly that at times it was difficult to keep up. Eva loved her new life, and was challenged by it, but there was also the fear for her health and what Picasso would think if he knew. It was hard to face so much alone like this.

"What is it, *mon amour*?" Picasso asked when he caught her standing over the sink, crying.

"It may sound silly, but it is everything in the world, and nothing at all," she said with a tearful smile.

As he drew her into his arms, Eva wished more than anything that she could say that it was her emotions getting the better of her because she was pregnant. She so badly wanted that to be true, rather than worry over what the doctor suspected. For now she would focus on their new life here and the dinner party ahead. That, she decided, was enough for one day.

In the end, it was Max Jacob who made her forget her fears, and helped her to enjoy the evening. Eva did not expect to like him so much or to covet his friendship as she quickly did. But he was dear to Picasso, they shared a long history and she was determined one day to win him over. He was quirky and had a rapier wit, albeit fueled by alcohol, and he was filled with stories that had them all peeling with laughter late into the evening. When he recited some of his own poetry, she found herself rapt. Eva knew his allegiance was to Fernande so she accepted that it would probably take a while to get to know him, but she was eager for the challenge.

Juan Gris, another guest Eva had not met before tonight, was far more quiet, and his French was only passable. He and Picasso spoke in Spanish, from time to time. Then, occasionally, one or the other of them would suddenly laugh at something the other had said that no one but the two of them understood.

"Another of those Polish cookies and Gertrude will need to wheel me home in a barrel," Max exclaimed as he leaned back in his chair and rubbed his abdomen. He was quite drunk.

"We will probably need to do that, anyway," Gertrude said dryly.

Alice stood and picked up two plates. "Let me help you with the dishes."

"That's not necessary," Eva nodded. "We have a girl who comes in the mornings, and she is always quite desperate for something to do."

"That's because my darling Eva has yet to

realize she is not the *femme de ménage.* There is someone else to do the cleaning now," said Picasso as he lit his pipe.

Everyone laughed as Alice followed her to the kitchen. Eva put the dishes in the sink. She knew what Alice was going to say. She unlatched the window and a cold breeze filled the space, making the lacy curtains dance.

"So, did you see Dr. Rousseau?"

Eva turned away and scraped the plates into the trash. "It was a silly concern. He said I am a perfectly healthy young woman. I just need to get a bit more rest."

"Good luck there, with a robust lover like Pablo."

Eva blushed. "I will bear that in mind."

"He is happy with you. We can both see that. He is calmer lately, and he has a focus that he never had before. It is quite obvious."

"Thank you for saying so."

Eva suddenly felt like crying again. It happened so often lately and she struggled to keep her composure. She couldn't help but feel overwhelmed and saddened all at once, just as she had earlier that evening. In the silence, the conversation taking place out in the dining room drew her attention.

"She is certainly nothing like Fernande,

Pablo, I'll tell you that," said Max.

"Precisely," Picasso returned.

"She seems rather meek. I just don't know about her."

"But you will," Picasso countered. "And Eva is a tigress for things she believes in. She isn't meek at all."

Max was speaking loudly enough so that they could both hear him from the kitchen, even over the clinking of silver and china. Alice smiled in response.

"Max can be rather persnickety and judgmental but he is intensely loyal to those he loves. Will you be all right that we are all still friends with Fernande?"

"He is Pablo's friend so I had better win him over one way or another. I actually think I'm ready for the challenge," Eva said. "Besides, I can't pretend the past doesn't exist and neither can any of you."

"Not with Picasso, we can't. His past defines much of him. So do his friendships."

"I was there when Germaine and Ramón confronted him in Céret," Eva admitted.

"Oh, dear. We heard about that nasty business."

"I'm sure they thought they had his best interest at heart."

"Even so, he will never forgive them," Alice said.

Eva felt tears pressing at the backs of her eyes. That was happening so often lately that it had begun to concern her. She still wasn't feeling particularly well in spite of the successful evening, and she was always tired. Inside, she felt like an emotional pendulum, but no one would have known it. No one accept perhaps Alice.

Her warmth and nurturing way made Eva think of her own mother for the second time today. She had been remembering home so often lately, and regretting things. She had an overwhelming desire to confide in Alice about what the doctor had said. But she resisted it. For now, no one must know anything.

"I did not break them up, I swear I didn't."

"No one can tame a horse that does not want to be tamed, without entirely breaking its spirit," Alice offered. "Before Pablo met you, Gertrude always thought his spirit was close to being broken. He is a whirlwind, and he is on the cusp of even more massive stardom than this. It will be a great storm when it happens. She has always believed he is a genius, which the whole world soon will see. Take care of yourself, *ma chère*. Try not to get too caught up in all of that. He will need your support more and more every day."

"I will be right there beside him. We will help each other," she promised as Picasso came up behind them and affectionately encircled Eva, who was still standing at the sink. He pressed an affectionate kiss onto her neck.

"Our guests are beginning to leave. Can I tear you two away from your conversation to come and say good night?"

"Of course." She and Alice exchanged another brief glance. They could both see that Picasso was happy that they were talking as privately as if they were already close friends.

"Eva is a perfectly wonderful hostess, Pablo," Alice said. "Everything was so lovely this evening. You really should be so proud of her. We can be quite an intimidating group but she charmed everyone."

"She's already my good-luck charm, so I never had a doubt the rest of you would see it," he said proudly as they all walked back into the dining room together.

Picasso had always loved the light in Céret.

It was winter now, and he wanted to stop there on the way to Barcelona for Christmas. He told Eva he wanted to secure a house for the summer, and he had heard of one that was perfect for painting, and not too far from the center of town. Eva was ready to go anywhere he liked when they left Paris the next week, but she was disappointed they would not be returning to Sorgues in summer. It was a place that would always be so special to her.

They were dressing for the ballet, which Eva wanted to take him to, when he told her of his travel plan. She had never been to the ballet in Paris, which was an elegant affair, but this evening was to be her surprise for him. She had organized the tickets with Alice and Gertrude's help. Picasso had introduced her to so many new and wonderful things over the months, but this was a world she had loved all her life from afar. As a young woman, Eva's mother had performed in a local ballet. There was even an old brown-and-white photograph of her in costume, placed over the mantel in her parents' home in Vincennes. It looked nothing like the sturdy woman she ultimately became, Eva always thought. But she never forgot her mother's face in the photograph — bright with youthful dreams.

"I was hoping we could rent our lovely house in Sorgues again," she admitted.

Frika watched the conversation suspiciously from the top of the bed.

"The landlord is selling it, I'm afraid."

"Your wonderful fresco! What will become of it?" Her expression was suddenly stricken, remembering what they had left behind, and feeling emotional about its loss.

"Well, now that is another story," he said with a wry smile, taking her by the hand as he drew her into his art studio. "I had planned to make it a surprise for your birthday, but now seems as good a time as any."

He motioned for her to pull a large slip of canvas back from a place near the wall, and when she did, Eva gasped. It was the last thing she expected to see.

"How did you possibly . . . ?" Her words trailed away as she was struck with awe.

"Kahnweiler had it removed for me. The landlord was not happy that I painted it on his wall in the first place, and he fully intended to charge me to paint over it."

"Oh, no!"

"I decided to save him the effort. Kahnweiler thought I was a bit mad to go to the expense of removing part of the wall and having it sent here. But then I suppose some would say I'm a bit mad, in general."

Eva knelt in front of the great slab of plaster, protectively framed in wood. "It is beyond precious to me, Pablo."

"I knew you loved it. Therefore, money

was no object to save it. You know I would do anything to make you happy."

"As I would you."

"Then marry me, Eva. It's high time I asked you formally, even though I hope you knew I would."

"Yes, yes, a thousand times, *yes!*" Eva flung her arms around his neck and kissed his cheeks.

"I was hoping you would say that."

"I will say it until my dying day!"

Picasso's eyes widened, and he stepped back, as if he had been struck. "*Dios,* don't ever say that again."

"Say what?"

"Do not speak *ever* of your own death!"

"Pablo, I only meant —"

"It is bad luck! Don't you understand? Come, quickly. We'll go and say two Hail Marys, and then light a candle!"

Eva looked at him curiously. She wanted to remark that she thought he loathed God. How could such a thing matter in the face of the contempt he held for the Almighty? She knew about his superstitions, but it was another thing to see for herself how deeply they ran. Eva shook off a sudden chill. Yes, he had finally formally proposed, and she was thrilled. But it also felt, in that moment, like someone had just walked over a grave.

CHAPTER 28

Before they left for Barcelona to meet Picasso's family, they spent a few days with Georges Braque, who was back in Paris. Eva loved to watch them argue and discuss art, especially when they were gathered at Gertrude Stein's, where all of the conversations were interesting to her. She had a great thirst to learn, and his Paris group were wonderful teachers.

Eva was certain Picasso never looked so happy, surrounded by his friends and with her at his side, in those days before they left Paris for Céret. Although he had represented them for years, both artists had only recently signed official contracts with Kahnweiler, and Picasso was pleased to have cut a better deal with the art dealer than his rival had. It kept Picasso far more affable with everyone, on those evenings, than he might have been where a competition was involved.

At least, until he heard that Kahnweiler had also included Juan Gris in his stable of artists. Gris may be a friend, but he was an inferior artist, Picasso told Eva on the train from Céret to Barcelona after their brief stop. It was a rainy and gray winter day, and the landscape reminded him of a watery Monet painting, he told her as they sat in a little first-class compartment and watched the scenery go by.

"Juan seems nice enough," Eva said, touching his knee as they gazed out the window.

"That has nothing to do with art. He has always tried too hard. Talent cannot be forced."

"It's a lot like love that way."

Picasso smiled. "Wise beyond your years, *ma jolie.* You would have to be in order to deal with me. So tomorrow, my wise girl, you meet Don José."

"You're scaring me." For weeks, she had been dreading meeting the great family patriarch with whom Fernande had spent time. There was just so much past to rise above.

"I only want you to be prepared. The old man can be quite daunting when he wants to be."

"I can hardly wait."

He kissed her cheek tenderly in response. "You will charm him as much as you've charmed me. He will say you remind him of my mother. If he says that, you've won him over, no matter how gruff he seems."

"Did Fernande remind him of your mother, too?" Eva asked softly as the train car swayed and clacked over the tracks.

"No. He knew she was married when I brought her to meet them, so neither of my parents were very impressed." He quirked a smile. "You're not married, are you?"

"Not yet. But I hope to be very soon."

"How do you feel about a spring wedding?"

"This spring?"

"Why not?"

She wasn't entirely certain why it seemed like such a long time in coming, but it did. It felt like such a long time in coming.

"There is a church around the corner from our new apartment, the Abbey de Sion, and I'd like to have our wedding breakfast afterward somewhere utterly glamorous for you. How about the Hôtel le Meurice?"

"We couldn't! I thought you were joking when you mentioned it that once. It would be scandalously expensive!"

"Kahnweiler assures me that, with my last

German sale, we can afford it. I will use the profit."

She laid her head on his shoulder. "It sounds really lovely, Pablo."

"I thought it was important that you knew the plan before my parents did. I hope you will feel a little more comfortable meeting them that way."

"That does help."

"I am going to ask my mother for my grandmother Picasso's Spanish silver ring. My grandfather gave it to her when they married. I want it to be your engagement ring."

"Oh, my love."

He took her hand and held it tightly in his own. "And I'm sorry about what happened back in Paris. I overreacted about you speaking of your dying day, and I know that I frightened you — proposal or not. It's just that I cannot bear the thought of something bad happening, now that we are finally together."

"Bad things do happen, though, Pablo, no matter how we all wish they wouldn't."

"Well, they don't happen to me. Not any longer. You are my talisman. I told Alice you were my good-luck charm and I meant it," Picasso declared with conviction. "Look how you've inspired me with papier collé.

475

That's all because of you. And my colors are bright again. I've gone away from all the browns, because I don't feel them any longer — and I made a far better contract with Kahnweiler than Braque did because of your advice."

"Well, you certainly *are* the master. You *should* have a better contract," she said.

"I like the way you think. But it really *is* you. I'm telling you, you bring me luck."

He squeezed her knee as the train pulled into the station. "Remember now, no matter what my father says, he really will like you, eventually. So just be yourself."

What a horrible man he must be, Eva thought, a self-centered man, an artist himself, ultimately overshadowed by his more talented son. At least the intimidation and expectation had fostered a genius. But in these moments when she couldn't stop her heart from hammering, that rationale of her fear seemed cold comfort. She would have to go through with this, no matter what, if she wanted to marry Picasso.

They rode in a horse carriage, not a motorcar, because it was so cold that there were no taxis left at the train station when they arrived. But it was warm enough inside for the ride down the wide tree-lined Las Ram-

476

blas, one of the main streets of town.

Eva was not certain what she had expected of Spain, but Barcelona was a beautiful city, far more cosmopolitan than she had imagined. The tall, buttery limestone apartment buildings, with their scrolled ironwork balconies, were as elegant as any in Paris but with their own unique flair. Women strode arm in arm, with a pride that was captivating to see.

As the black carriage moved toward the sea, the landscape and the buildings steadily changed. The streets narrowed. This was the older part of town. The houses near the harbor were darker, the paint peeling on some of them. There were lines of laundry hung between the buildings, and blue-black puddles on the cobblestones in places where the sun rarely shone.

The carriage stopped at a street corner that held a small, dark café with an ancient sign overhead. Picasso opened the carriage door. He got out and held his hand out for Eva as the driver fetched their two large carpetbags.

"This is it. Just down there," he said, motioning with a nod toward the narrow street framed by apartment buildings. "I have tried for two years to get them a larger place, but my mother refuses. She says she has moved enough in her life, and that this is home."

Eva was glad to see pots of bright red geraniums spilling over some of the balconies, bringing in a bit of life, despite the winter air. She could hear a baby cry in one of the apartments, and there were children playing stickball up ahead. It certainly wasn't Montparnasse, she thought. But this was Picasso's world, the place he grew up, and she wanted this part of him, too.

She anxiously straightened her hat and skirt. "Do I look all right?"

"Absolutely ravishing. But, of course, ravishing you will have to wait. My mother, no doubt, will have her rosary out the whole time."

"Now who's nervous?" Eva asked with a smirk as they held hands and climbed the steps.

Picasso's sister Lola greeted them at the front door to their second-floor apartment, and from the moment of their embrace, Eva saw his tension fade. Lola had large brown eyes, a pursed mouth, and there was a touch of early gray at the temples of her elegantly swept-up hairstyle. Eva saw their resemblance to each other immediately. The ease between brother and sister was palpable, and happy smiles brightened both of their faces as they engaged in another round of embraces, and whispered Spanish endearments before she turned from her brother.

"*Bienvenue,* Eva," said Lola in French with a thick Spanish accent. Eva found Lola's efforts to speak to her in her own language endearing, and she could feel her tension ease. "Please make yourself comfortable with us. They are waiting for you in the salon."

Picasso set down their two bags and an elderly housekeeper came out from another room to whisk them away. She watched Picasso smooth back his hair nervously. Then they followed Lola through a small archway framed by heavy green velvet draperies. The smell of camphor in the apartment was very strong.

Picasso looked over at Eva briefly but he did not try to touch her again.

In the small salon, dominated by a fireplace with a white marble mantelpiece and stuffed with heavy dark Italianate furniture in the Renaissance design, two people sat on the edge of a velvet-covered sofa. A fragile, elderly looking man sat beside them in a cane-back wheelchair. He had a daunting presence, so she knew instantly who it was.

Picasso's father's face was drawn. He had

a long gray beard and his hollow blue eyes were glazed. He did not smile as the other two people approached them. A stout, silver-haired woman, who was clearly his mother, reached out to Picasso with an expression of adoration. She drew him to her and whispered something softly in Spanish as tears filled her eyes. Then she kissed both of his cheeks. She held his face for a moment longer, as if to make certain he had truly returned.

"*Madre,* this is Eva. We will speak French with her since she does not understand Spanish," Picasso instructed.

"It is an honor, Señora Picasso," Eva said, feeling suddenly as if she were stuttering.

"It is not Picasso, however," he gently told Eva. "My mother's married name is Ruiz. Picasso is her family name. It is her name that I use professionally."

"Forgive me, I . . . I didn't know." She understood that his relationship with his father had been a difficult one, but Eva found herself wishing that Picasso had warned her of these details before they arrived. She so desperately wanted to make a good impression.

"And this is my brother-in-law, Juan Vilató."

"Dr. Juan," his mother proudly corrected.

"My daughter's husband is a surgeon!"

He was a middle-aged man with a wave of umber-colored hair and a prominent widow's peak low on his forehead. He smiled affably and reached out to take Eva's hand. *"Bienvenue,"* he said in French, also with a thick accent.

Picasso then turned his gaze toward his father. As he did, Eva heard him heave a painful sigh. She could only imagine what he felt. She watched him exchange a glance with Lola then, and move a step nearer to her. "Why did no one warn me?"

"It is not a thing one writes in a letter, Pablito. He has been frail like this for a while, but you haven't been home in a long time."

"Can he even see me?"

"He sees very little now, mainly shapes and shadows. But he knows you are here, and that you've brought a new woman."

Everyone remained silent as Picasso approached his father. He crouched down and spoke to him in Spanish. Eva heard her name amid their quiet banter, and the tick of a large clock on the wall. There were only a few other words she recognized. Her heart began to race as she looked at the formidable old man who did not smile or reach out to embrace his son.

Finally, Picasso looked back at Eva as Don José summoned her with the weak wave of a forearm, his elbow balanced on the wooden arm of the wheelchair. Picasso stood again, with a vague expression of concern, as Eva approached his father.

Suddenly, to her horror, she realized she was not certain what to call him. She knew now it was not Señor Picasso. She knew him from Picasso only as Don José. Her knees went impossibly weak, and the nausea flared. Everyone was looking at her, expecting for her to somehow charm this intimidating old man who could not even see her.

"He wants you to sit on the sofa beside him," Lola said. "He wanted all of us to leave but Pablo told him you don't speak Spanish, so he is allowing me to remain in order to translate."

Eva tried not to show the panic she felt as she glanced up at Picasso. His mother and brother-in-law were already moving, without objection, out of the room. There was silence until Picasso followed, and closed the door behind them.

"He bids you to sit," Lola explained once the three of them were alone.

"*Gracias,* Monsieur — Señor Don José," Eva nervously fumbled, and she knew the sound she had just made was more like a croak than anything close to acceptable Spanish. His slim gray lips turned up just slightly.

"He welcomes you to our home, as Pablo's guest, but asks, now that he is becoming so famous, if you plan to steal his son's money — or only his heart."

Eva was surprised by the frankness of his question. For a moment, she lost her footing and was not sure what to say. She didn't want to make things worse for herself. Finally, she summoned all of her conviction, drew in a breath and exhaled it. Eva would not be undone by this moment. She had come too far. Her spirit flared.

"*Por favor.* I will steal neither. Nor would I want anything other than what is freely given. I love your son with all my heart."

"My father asks if you will give him sons?"

"Once we are married, I would like to give him many. Daughters, too."

A full smile broke across the old man's face, even before Lola had fully translated, but he still did not move his head to look at her.

"My father says that the last one could never have given our family proper heirs because she already had a husband. He did not respect her for depriving Pablo of that which is natural and right to a decent Spanish man. He says Pablo deserved better."

"I would like to hope I am good enough to deserve him," Eva said. "I know that I will spend the rest of my life trying."

"He is pleased to know that you and Pablo plan to marry. He says he will be honored to attend your wedding. I will be, as well," Lola said. "And he wishes me to tell you how much you remind him of his wife."

Relief washed over Eva like water, and she gave herself permission to smile. Ten minutes before, she had not expected his blessing and, by her expression, his daughter Lola had not expected it, either. In that moment, Eva was more proud of herself than she had ever been.

Don José went to bed very early after that while the rest of them ate dinner, and talked late into the night, to the soothing strains of a Spanish guitar someone was playing out on the narrow street below.

Later that night, Eva woke to the sound of Picasso softly weeping in a bedroom across the hall from hers. She knew that the tears he shed were for his father, a man for whom he had once had as much respect as fear — and who had made him an artist.

They stayed in Barcelona for almost two weeks after that. Eva thought it was a wonderful Christmas, and they all celebrated the Epiphany together in great Spanish style. Picasso even attended Mass without complaint, and it seemed to Eva that perhaps he was beginning to make his first bit of peace with a God who he had feared as much as loathed these past years.

He trusted enough in the bright future ahead to finally ask his mother for his grandmother's Spanish silver ring on their last day in Barcelona. As Eva was in the drawing room saying goodbye to Don José, she heard Picasso out in the foyer make the request. When Eva heard his mother's small footsteps pass by, she knew she had gone to get it. Eva joined them near the door a few moments later, almost unable to contain her joy, but did her best not to reveal anything because she did not want to spoil the surprise.

"Thank you for everything," Eva said, stifling a cough as Picasso's mother drew her into a warm embrace.

"It is sad to let our Pablo go again, but it brings me such peace to know he will have you beside him. I think he is finally ready to make a good husband."

Madre, por favor," Picasso chided as if she had revealed a secret. Then he drew his mother away from Eva and tenderly kissed her cheeks.

"Be good to her, Pablito."

"I will spend every day trying to do just that," he said. "And, you are right, I am finally ready now."

When Eva woke their first morning back in Paris, she was disappointed to see that Picasso was not beside her. At first, she was afraid she might have disturbed him in the night with a fit of coughing since she knew she was battling another bout of bronchitis. She had felt sure she had convinced him that it was only a small virus brought on by traveling.

The apartment was quiet. But there on Picasso's pillow was a single long-stemmed red rose set beside a small green leather box. She realized at once what was happening. As her heart raced, Eva drew on the kimono from the foot of the bed and scrambled onto her knees. She was charmed by how carefully Picasso had arranged the items but she wasn't sure she was meant to open the box without him.

The apartment was still quiet as she rose, tied the kimono at her waist and went barefoot out into the wood-paneled drawing room where the draperies were still drawn. Picasso was standing beside the fireplace in a formal black suit and tie, his hair neatly combed. He was surrounded by candles that lit the shadowy room like the nave of a church, and over the mantel now was his painting *Ma Jolie.* He'd had it framed so that it dominated the room in tribute.

Tears clouded Eva's eyes. "You could not wait for me to be dressed as beautifully as you are for this?"

"On the contrary, I wanted you exactly as you are now. It is I who must impress you." He stepped toward her and took both of her hands. She could feel that he, too, was trembling. "I want to honor you entirely with this moment. You have put so much of yourself into loving me, standing by me and supporting me. You have charmed my family, been patient with my friends and entirely won my heart. You are everything to me, Eva."

"Oh, Pablo . . ."

"Will you do me the great honor of formally accepting my proposal of marriage now?"

"Of course!" When she began to weep, he wiped her tears with both of his thumbs and then took her chin in his hands. "But I think the ring is in the other room."

"Only a way to lure you back to bed, my love," he gently teased.

"That will never require any lure. I am

yours devotedly."

They went to the bedroom and he took the box from his pillow and placed it in her hands. "I hope you wouldn't rather have something new," he said as she opened it to find an elegantly detailed silver ring highlighted in the ccntcr by a large ruby.

"Oh, Pablo, it's exquisite!"

"As you are, *ma jolie.* My mother was so pleased to know you would be the one to have it." He slipped it onto her finger, then kissed her passionately. "Tonight, we will meet Gertrude and Alice to officially celebrate our engagement. They're both so eager to see your ring."

"They knew?" Eva asked with a note of surprise.

"Well, I needed to tell someone. Besides, they've both been so excited for us."

"I'm happy they like me."

"They adore you," Picasso said. "Just like all of my friends will, once they get to know what a wonderful woman you are, and how happy you've made me."

Eva secretly thought that might take a while, but even so she was on the right track now. In spite of the constant bronchitis, and Dr. Rousseau's dire suspicion, she was in love with the man of her dreams, he loved her and they would be getting married soon.

Those were the wonderful things she needed to focus on. The only things that mattered.

CHAPTER 29

By spring, Eva and Picasso were back in
Céret. Amid a mistral that was wild and bitter cold, Picasso worked feverishly on a new
series of Cubist canvases. Since his work
kept him busy most of the day, Eva tried to
rest in order to heal her constant fatigue
and the cough that never seemed to leave
her completely. In the shuttered daylight by
a warming fire, she kept busy writing letters
to her parents, and she even sent a postcard
to Alice and Gertrude. Alice wrote back.
Eva wrote again. It became a routine.

It was nice to have a pen pal, and sometimes Gertrude wrote, too, although most
of her letters were addressed to Picasso.
Their friendship ran deep, so Eva took no
offense. But she loved reading Gertrude's
well-crafted words, and her wry sense of
humor.

In the evenings, when the winds calmed a
bit, Eva and Picasso walked alone out into

the endless grassy fields, and they planned their wedding. Sometimes they relaxed at the Grand Café in town after sunset, beneath a string of twinkling lights, and they read their letters from others back and forth to each other, happy for the friendships they still had. Life seemed beyond idyllic. And then one day, the wind stopped, the air grew warm and very suddenly everything else changed, too.

"It's my father," Picasso announced as he sat with a newly opened letter from Barcelona. "Lola says he is gravely ill."

"Oh, Pablo."

"I suppose I shouldn't be surprised, but I am. He was such a force when I was young. I was angry with him for how he pushed me to paint. He wanted me to be all of the things that he wasn't. I didn't realize for such a long time that all the old man could paint were pigeons."

"He gave you such an amazing talent. That is reason enough to love him."

"Will you come to Barcelona with me?"

These past few days, Eva had begun to feel ill and weak again, though she had not yet told Picasso. When he had caught her coughing yesterday, she had convinced him, as she had in Paris, that it was nothing but another virus caused by all of their travel-

491

ing. She certainly did not feel well enough to endure the lengthy train ride to Barcelona in this early heat wave. Besides, it would be good to have time alone until she felt truly well.

"I can't leave you alone," Picasso said when she told him of her intention to stay behind. "Max has wanted to come to Céret to see what all of the fuss is about. He'll be great company for you. I'll wire Kahnweiler instructions to pay for his trip down. You will hardly know I am gone."

"Oh, Pablo, that really isn't necessary."

"I can't be worried about you and my father at the same time. And you like Max."

"Yes, I do," she said, but that was not the problem. She knew Max's loyalty remained with Fernande. She was still determined to win him over, but she definitely had her work cut out for her, especially when she wasn't feeling well.

"Then it is settled. And when I return, you will be rested and everything will be new again. We will go back to Paris, and set a date for the wedding. But I deserve a healthy bride."

"And so you shall have one," Eva promised.

While Picasso was in Barcelona, the spring

brought a torrential rain. It rained for so many days straight that the ground everywhere was sodden. The sky was a heavy gray, and Eva's cough worsened. But through the many long days, she and Max Jacob were forced to coexist in the same house in the suburban town. Initially, the house was made smaller by their inability to escape it. But out of duty to Picasso, at first, Max began to sit with her more often in the drawing room beside the fire to keep her company — even if it was mainly in silence.

"I truly am sorry about this," she said one afternoon amid the steel-gray light of another afternoon rainstorm. Both of them had books open on their laps.

Max glanced up. "What have you to be sorry for?"

She saw a subtle hint of irritation in his expression, but she was determined to press past that. "I asked Pablo not to insist that you stay here with me in his absence."

"He is a very persuasive man. Stubborn, as well."

Eva smiled. "On that we can easily agree. Would you tell me something, Max? From a man's perspective?"

"That *could* prove a challenge, depending upon the subject matter."

She knew he enjoyed poking fun at his

own sexuality, so she smiled and went on undaunted. "Beyond her obvious beauty, what is it exactly about Fernande that draws people so powerfully?"

"Might you be a bit more specific?" She heard a note of defensiveness in his tone.

"I don't mean to be insulting, but for someone who seems a bit self-serving, I find it surprising that so many of Pablo's friends were willing to give up their friendship for her. After all, they were friends with Pablo before they even knew her."

"An excellent question." He studied Eva for a moment before he drew off his small, round reading spectacles. "Have you a concern that she may win him back with these mystical charms of hers if you don't understand them?"

"I suppose," she conceded.

"You really are two very different sorts of women."

"She was the sort he wanted for a long time."

Eva could see that he was struck by a thought. He exhaled deeply and then leveled his eyes on her. "We are all rather tied together, in our own odd little way, aren't we? All of us bound to Picasso — thus, to one another. Even you and Fernande."

"Exactly. The point, I suppose, is that I

did not entirely dislike her. Yet I don't understand the fidelity she engenders from all of you."

"We are a loyal group and most of us, for one reason or another, felt pity for her, I suppose. Fernande had a difficult early life. Picasso never told you about that?"

"He doesn't like to speak of her."

"Fernande was abandoned by her parents, so she was raised by a rather neglectful aunt and uncle. To escape them, she married a man who beat her. She ran away from him to Paris. Poor little bird was too frightened of reprisals to divorce him, so she and Picasso could never actually marry. All of us who were there at the beginning knew the story. It made her deficiencies a bit more tolerable."

A log broke in two inside of the hearth and a brilliant cascade of sparks lit the room. "Then there were so many hungry years for us all," he continued. "That sort of thing forges a bond."

"I can see how it would. But then he cut her off so completely."

"Ah, well, that which exists between lovers is a very unique thing. I shall deny it if you say I am the one who told you, but our dear Fernande was unfaithful, not just that once you knew about but rather habitually.

In the end, she tried to manipulate Picasso's affections one too many times. The fact that the last one was an artist was for Picasso the ultimate betrayal."

"Max?"

"Hmm?"

"Thank you for trusting me with that."

"Much to my dismay, I find that I am growing quite fond of you, after all. Perhaps it is no more than this solitary and incessantly rainy countryside that softens my reserve."

"Yes," she replied as the corners of her mouth lifted. She looked down into the pages of her book again. "I'm sure that is what it is."

In the days that followed, Eva and Max spoke for hours about art and poetry, and also about faith. Eva asked him about his interest in tarot cards and palmistry, and although she was not certain she believed any of it, she was interested. She also found that she truly liked Max, as she had known from the first she would.

"If we marry in a church will you come?" Eva asked him. Even though he was Jewish, he had told her that he didn't have much use for organized religion.

"A bolt of lightning might well strike us

all if I do," he joked.

"Pablo and I will take our chances."

"He said you were a bold girl, but I think I am just beginning to see that for myself."

"I'm glad. We wouldn't want to marry without all of our friends and family around us."

He paused for a moment. "You would have me there even knowing of my allegiance to Fernande?"

"Oh, I have every intention of stealing some of that allegiance between now and then," Eva declared sweetly.

They both laughed. "I'll think about it."

The fit of coughing that came upon her suddenly then was severe. When water could not quiet it, Max was forced to pick her up and carry her to her bed. She was pale and so weak. Each day, her condition had seemed to grow a little worse. Max told her he feared pneumonia.

"We must write to Picasso and ask him what to do," Max insisted the next day.

He sat beside Eva's grand mahogany bed, an antique that seemed to swallow her up, as he laid another cool cloth across her forehead.

"No!" she cried.

"But a cough like yours is a very bad omen."

Suddenly she was not so charmed by Max's preoccupations. "I said no."

"Then let me send for a doctor on my own."

"You are making too much of this, Max. It's only a cough."

"Picasso would have my head if he knew I hadn't gotten you help."

The lights flickered in response to a new clap of thunder.

"You've had word from Fernande since you've been here. I've seen the letters arrive in the mail. How is she?" Eva asked, cutting into the silence with a sudden change of subject.

Max looked critically at her before he replied.

"Not very well. But Apollinaire found her a job reading poetry at Au Lapin Agile."

Eva knew of the modest tavern in Montmartre. Everyone did. It was hard to imagine how vastly their circumstances changed — both Fernande's and Apollinaire's. She pressed the cool cloth against her own cheeks. She wanted to ask about the poet, too. She wanted to know about the man she once had idealized, who had found times difficult after the *Mona Lisa* scandal.

"I thought Fernande was working at the Maison de Poiret."

"Yes, well, that didn't pan out. She can be rather a proud woman."

Eva handed him back the cloth. He ran it through the water again, rinsed it and gave it back to her for her forehead. He had become surprisingly patient and gentle with her.

"You have a kind heart, Max. Fernande is fortunate to have you as a friend."

"Actually, I have had to make a choice about that these past couple of days."

The rain fell in long sheets against the windows. They had been alone in the house long enough now that the revelations came easier for them both.

"I cannot be loyal to you both and keep Picasso's friendship, so, unlike the others, I've chosen you."

"Oh, dear, I would never ask that of you, at least not so soon. I expected it would take time between us."

"No one asked. It is simply the way it is with Picasso. I will have to be completely loyal to you or to her. He is demanding that way. And like the rest of us, I love him in spite of it. I suppose I knew that was what he was after when he chose me to come down here and keep you company."

"Don't tell him I was ill, Max. Please. You know how much illness frightens him. And

499

I'm getting better."

"You're not getting better. But I respect anyone who can put on a costume at the Moulin Rouge and pull off what you did, so for now I will honor your wishes. If Picasso can't tell by the time he returns, I'll not be the one to reveal it to him."

"Thank you."

"I think it's a mistake, mind you. But I've made a lifetime of mistakes myself, so who could begrudge you a misstep of your own?" His laugh filled the silence. There were echoes everywhere in the old house. "Picasso would still love you, you know, even if you were ill."

"I'm just not sure that I am ready to take that chance," she said as another clap of thunder rattled the windows.

In May, Don José died. He had been a force in the life of his only son, and Picasso felt the power of things unsaid — and the inability now to ever set them right. He did not speak for several days, and in the end he decided to go alone to Barcelona. He wanted to bring Eva with him, but it would not have been proper to bring to the funeral a companion to whom he was not yet married. As much as she wished to be there for Picasso, Eva was relieved to have another period of time alone to grow physically stronger.

In his absence, Picasso had sent for Juan Gris, bidding him to join Max in Céret to keep Eva company. His friends would provide her a diversion, he wrote from Spain, and soon enough the two of them would be reunited. Eva trusted Max to keep her confidence. She knew she needed to trust someone. While Gertrude and Alice were once again in Italy, Max Jacob had been duly elected. Picasso's friendship with Gertrude was too enduring for Eva to have trusted her about her health, even if she had wanted to. When she wrote to Alice, it was about frivolous things.

The rain had ceased by early June, but two dark clouds remained: there was a proper Spanish mourning period of one year, during which time Eva knew no wedding ceremony could properly take place — and the tiny lump in her breast felt larger.

CHAPTER 30

July in Céret was warm and dry at last. The boulevards, ancient Roman ramparts and walls, were finally ornamented by the new growth of summer, and the plane trees once again gave shade to the city.

After his return from Barcelona, Picasso did not speak at all of his father, or of the funeral, but images in some of his works showed how deeply he had been affected. Eva was at a loss for how to help him heal, until she came upon an idea. To surprise Picasso, she arranged to have Frika sent down from Paris.

The huge shaggy dog yelped and wagged her tail as Picasso rolled with her on the ground in the back garden of the house in Céret, their usual dance of rediscovery.

The remaining summer days were happy, all four of them living in the fine stone house in town. Picasso and Gris painted, with Picasso authoritatively supervising what he called his friend's "inferior Cubist work." Max tried to write, and with Eva's health improved she cooked for all of them during the long peaceful days. Picasso even insisted on taking them all to a bullfight in the Catalan city of Figueras. Experiencing the passion and majesty of such an event, he told his two friends, could only enhance their work, and it would make him happy if Eva would join them. She sat with a hand over her eyes most of the time, and willed herself not to cry at what she found a barbaric end. But as she had told herself many times since they had met, if this was a part of Picasso's world, then she would learn to appreciate it.

In the late afternoons, Picasso and Eva would take Frika for long walks through the rolling countryside when the air cooled, and a light wind stirred. They would hold hands as they hiked through the tall grass, Picasso blazing a trail with a Spanish walking stick, and Frika trotting up ahead.

"I'm sorry about our not being able to plan the wedding for a while," he said one evening as they made their way together down a grassy hillside.

It was the first time since he had returned from Barcelona that Picasso had referenced his father's death and the inability to marry for a year following the funeral. Eva squeezed his hand in response, glad that he was finally willing to talk to her about the loss of Don José. The sun began to set more swiftly, crimson and gold ahead of them along the horizon. "There will be another spring for us," she said with a gentle smile.

Suddenly there was a yelp, then a plaintive cry. A wild growl followed by barking.

"*Dios,* no! Frika!" Picasso cried out as he gripped the walking stick like a weapon and took off at a sprint down to the bottom of the hill where Frika had gone on ahead.

Eva ran after him, and in the line of grass she could see two dogs tousling, one black as midnight, smaller than Frika, but in fierce control. The sound of Frika whimpering filled the evening air as Picasso hollered and whistled, trying to frighten the mongrel away from his dog. It did not work soon enough.

An hour later, Picasso hired a farmer in town who owned a motorcar to drive them to the nearest veterinarian. He had been forced to promise the man a signed sketch to tear him from his supper. Traumatized and wounded, Frika curled on Picasso's lap in the backseat and only now and then let out a small whimper.

Picasso did not speak at all as they rode

504

along the seemingly endless country road, miles from Céret, well after dark. As he gazed ahead, with his hand on the neck of the gentle beast he had loved for so many years, Eva thought how he looked to be having a silent conversation with God — his lips moving now and then, his dark brows furrowed.

She knew Picasso was devastated, but she was powerless this time even to offer helpful support. The veterinarian was not able to give Picasso a positive prognosis. Frika would die from her wounds, and they could only hope to make the dog's final days comfortable.

Near dawn, Eva woke to the sound of Picasso murmuring in the darkness. "I knew I shouldn't trust you!" he said. "I knew it all along."

Eva struggled for a moment to understand what he meant. But then she knew. Picasso was definitely speaking to God.

Eva touched his cheek. It was wet with sweat. Thankfully, she thought, Frika was asleep in a basket beside the bed, comforted for now by medication.

"It's not God's fault," she whispered. "The other dog was wild."

"God always has a choice! He takes whoever He likes — love be damned!"

Eva could not find a way to argue with that. It broke her heart to see him like this.

"That dog has been my touchstone. When things went wrong, Frika was always there. . . . How I have loved that gentle beast." He sank into the pillows and ran his hands through his hair as he gazed up at the ceiling. "It's foolish, but I thought I would always have her."

"We're going to take care of her."

"Eva, you heard him. She won't recover. She can't."

"Then we will be there with her, help her at the end."

"I cannot do that. I can't be there, witness an agonizing death like that again — and be so helpless like I was with my sister!"

"Pablo, there is an end to everything. We all will die."

"I can't listen. I won't have death around me. It's done!"

The next morning, Picasso paid the farmer to put Frika down. A single bullet, he told Eva with a cold resolve that frightened her. It was more humane than letting her suffer. He and Eva stood in the field at a distance, waiting for the sound to ring through the air. Picasso needed to hear that it was done. Then he insisted on digging the grave himself on a hillside beneath an old

506

cherry tree.

Twice, Picasso had tears in his eyes since she had known him. That night, he wept openly for the first time, safe in Eva's arms. He did not speak directly, only murmured over and over into her hair that he despised a God that could do something so terrible as take away the things he loved most.

Everyone tried to do something to cheer him after Frika's death, but nothing helped to tear him from his grief. Juan Gris surprised Picasso with tickets to another bullfight and Max and Eva took him to a poetry reading in town. Eva wrote to Gertrude and Alice, desperately seeking their advice. Gertrude seemed to know Picasso so well. If there was an answer, surely she had it.

"Bring him back to Paris where he can work and be among friends," she advised. Eva agreed that he needed a change from the place where something so horrible had happened. Now that they were engaged, they needed a new scene, and a new apartment — a home for them that she would choose on her own. The apartment on the boulevard Raspail was not only dreary and dark, but it would be a haven of memories of Frika. Dog toys and blankets would be everywhere when they returned. The new apartment would have a woman's touch — and finally, hopefully, nothing of the past.

To lure him back to the city, Eva read Kahnweiler's letter aloud to Picasso one evening as they sat together out in the back garden. The enthusiastic young art dealer promised exciting news, but he would give no details until they returned. Hopefully, Eva thought, it signaled the final turn toward massive stardom she knew was on the horizon for Picasso. When it came, she secretly prayed that he would be recovered enough from his horrendous summer of losses, to meet his fame head-on. And she would be recovered, as well.

Right now, Picasso needed her to be the strong one and to take charge. From the moment they'd met, Eva felt she had been educating herself and growing steadily more comfortable with her ability to make decisions. She found a perfect apartment all on her own, and she went back with Picasso to show it to him. She had told him in Sorgues that she intended to be a full partner to him and to her this was the first real test of claiming that place in his life.

"So, what do you think of the apartment? We won't take it until you approve, but personally I think it's spectacular and vast, and with such wonderful views."

"It has a view of the Montparnasse Cemetery," Picasso said quietly as they walked up the tree-lined boulevard toward Gertrude and Alice's apartment later.

She twisted the Spanish silver ring around on her finger as they walked through a cool autumn evening, aching to have back the spirited man who had given it to her. "Oh. I hadn't thought of it that way. Well, then, of course I will tell the landlord 'no.' "

"It has good light and a lot of windows."

"It does have that," she carefully conceded. She had toured half a dozen apartments over the past two days since they had returned to Paris, and she had fallen in love with the large studio on the rue Schoelcher. "And the street is quiet."

"Let's talk about it later," he deigned a little too harshly as they arrived. He pushed past a throng of people waiting to get in for Gertrude's now-famous Saturday salon.

As they went in, they could hear people whispering Picasso's name.

"All right, we will talk about it later," she conceded.

The room was already full when they walked in, and as they came through the door, a crowd surged forward to welcome them back. Gertrude and Alice and Leo

Stein were all there, of course; Max had returned to Paris after the summer, and so had Georges and Marcelle Braque.

People who once had so intimidated Eva now seemed as if they were almost her friends as well as his. They asked with real interest how she had found the countryside, what she thought of the bullfights and what her opinion was of the new French potential for war that seemed to be looming.

It hadn't been spoken of greatly in Céret, where people seemed more interested in the price of the cherry harvest, but in the city everyone was talking about the rising political conflicts and the possibility of a conflict with Germany. Eva felt the *Titanic* tragedy had been hard enough for the world to bear. Such a thing as war seemed unimaginable. But Eva was pulled from thoughts of those grand issues and directed quickly to something more immediate here with Picasso's friends as she assessed the behavior of Gertrude's brother. "Mr. Stein seems so changed," she said to Alice after Picasso had gone off to find a drink. "There seems some new tension between Miss Stein and her brother since we last were here."

Alice looked at her thoughtfully.

"It seems that Leo is not a huge supporter of my relationship with his sister. They've

510

quite come to blows over me," Alice said with a reserved smile.

"How dreadful."

"I'm not supposed to tell anyone," Alice said more quietly. "But Leo and Gertrude are going their own separate ways. They are in the process of dividing their massive collection of art, even as we speak. I think Mr. Stein is only here this evening to keep an eye on his investment."

"Oh, Miss Toklas, I'm so sorry."

"Don't be. Gertrude is getting all of the Picassos!" she said with a devilish little laugh that Eva found endearing. "Well, actually, there are three they have both agreed to consign back to Kahnweiler, who will certainly get far more money than was gotten the first time for them. That will be a nice little nest egg for you both. It will more than pay for your wedding breakfast that Pablo talks so excitedly about."

Eva could not imagine anyone wanting to separate from these two divine ladies. They had been so open and welcoming to her, never the least judgmental. It was sad they were not to be given the same courtesy by family, she thought.

"I do hope there will be a wedding breakfast," Eva said.

"Oh, my dear, why would there not? Pablo

is wild about you, and that gorgeous ring certainly reinforces the point."

For an instant, Eva was sorry she had said anything, but to have a woman to confide in who knew them both outweighed her regret. "It's just that things seem to keep getting in the way."

"Ah, yes, the period of mourning. But that will be over before you know it."

"I've been a bit ill, anyway. I don't know if I'd have been up to planning a wedding earlier."

Alice smiled kindly. "Yes, Pablo wrote from Barcelona that he was worried for you, but you look fit enough now. Still, that awful event with Frika must have been a shock to you both. We are just so happy to have you back in Paris with us. Things will get better from now on, you'll see."

Eva and Alice watched Braque and Picasso standing nearby as they embraced and spoke with their usual animation. "Ah, Wilbur! It's about time you came around to pay me your respects," Picasso deadpanned cleverly, using his affectionate moniker for Braque.

"There, you see?" Alice said. "Being around friends is the best medicine for you both."

Eva thought how it was the first time in

weeks she had seen even a small glimmer of light in Picasso's eyes. This was his home, among these people who loved and understood his great talent. She felt certain that now he could finally begin to heal from the past.

At the very moment the thought came to her, Guillaume Apollinaire walked through the door.

"Oh, my," Alice murmured when they both saw the poet. "Perhaps I have spoken too hastily. I didn't realize he was coming this evening."

"Neither did Pablo," Eva said.

Once they saw each other, there began a dance between them, both full of too much pride and bravado for a public encounter to end well. They had not spoken since the theft of the *Mona Lisa,* and their friends watched them to see what would happen.

"Apollinaire," Picasso finally acknowledged with a curt nod when it was impossible to avoid one another any longer.

"Picasso." He nodded in return.

Eva could feel the tension. She motioned to Picasso but Alice gently stopped her. "Let them to it, my dear. The wound between them won't heal if they don't cauterize it first, and that is bound to hurt a bit."

The two men spoke only briefly, and Eva

would have given anything to hear what they said but the crowd in the room was growing and the chatter was too loud. When Picasso moved to join Gertrude across the room, leaving Apollinaire standing alone, Eva had an idea.

"Oh." Alice chuckled. "I can actually see the little wheels turning inside your head. You're going to play peacemaker, aren't you?"

"Pablo misses him, Alice. I know he does. We came back to Paris so he could heal, and I know that part of his pain is the heartbreak over Apollinaire."

"You have a point."

"But he's still an awfully intimidating figure. I have loved his poetry for so long. Even the thought of talking to him makes my knees weak. Come with me while I speak with him?"

"Of course."

Apollinaire embraced Alice and then shook Eva's hand. "Ah, I remember you. The resourceful costumer who also likes poetry," he said affably. "I heard about your little escapade as a geisha. It's a pleasure to see you again."

"And you, Monsieur Apollinaire."

"You must call me Apo. All my friends do. I understand you are with Picasso now."

"We're engaged."

He lifted his eyebrows in surprise. "Well, congratulations are in order, then. Hopefully, you will be a good influence, soften some of that harsh exterior of his."

Avoiding his comment she said, "Monsieur Apo, I'm going to host a small luncheon next Tuesday to celebrate our return to Paris. Everyone would love it if you would come, too. Isn't that right, Alice?"

"Oh, my dear." Apollinaire frowned. "I don't know that Picasso would be quite so welcoming, considering the circumstances."

"Of course he would. Besides, you would be my guest."

"Pretty *and* bold," said Apollinaire. "I must admit, I'm tempted."

"Gertrude and I would certainly enjoy your company," Alice said in support.

"There, it's unanimous," Eva said brightly. "Well, nearly so. But Pablo needs his friends more than ever, Monsieur Apo, even if he hasn't fully realized it yet."

"And you're going to see that he has what he needs."

"You can count on that," Eva declared.

Afterward, when they were home, she waited for Picasso beneath the bedcovers while he undressed. "Did you have a nice time tonight?" she asked.

515

"It was good to see everyone."

"Even Apollinaire?"

"He can hardly be avoided, now can he, giant that he is."

While it was only there for an instant, Eva heard the hint of tenderness in his voice. She must seize the moment then. It was up to her.

"I invited him to lunch here on Tuesday. I hope you don't mind. Alice and Gertrude are coming, as well."

For a moment, Eva wasn't certain if he was going to lash out at her for going behind his back. He still wasn't himself since the death of Frika. She held her breath through the silence. Her heart raced. Instead, Picasso left the bedroom and returned with a sketch pad and a nub of charcoal. Eva did not say anything as he drew back the covers so that he could see her lying naked.

"What time will they arrive?"

"One o'clock."

He did not speak further. Rather, Picasso seated himself, cross-legged, at the foot of the bed and began to draw. She tried her best to lie still, but it was difficult beneath his intense gaze as he settled into the task, and his eyes moved back and forth, from her to the paper. She watched him draw and shade silently, until she could see the form

516

of a woman taking shape on the page. It was the first time she had felt true intimacy between them for weeks.

"Lift your arms above your head on the pillow. It will give a nicer turn to your beautiful curves."

Eva did as Picasso asked, then he tossed aside the sketch pad and came to her. Eva glanced over and saw the delicate classical way he had drawn her. There was nothing of the Cubist style about it.

"I don't know why I haven't insisted you pose for me before. Your body really is quite inspiring."

"I am happy that you think so."

"Oh, I do," he said, just before he arched over her and kissed her deeply.

She thought how long it had been since they had kissed or touched sensually like this as a prelude to passion. Since the death of Frika, Eva felt they had only been going through the motions. She didn't realize how much she had missed the things only Picasso could make her feel. He artfully traced the column of her neck, the turn across her shoulder, and she felt herself melting into him. He grazed one breast with the tips of his fingers, then moved across to the other. As their passion increased, his touch became possession. He cupped her breast tightly as his tongue swept into her mouth. Suddenly his hand stilled and she could see his expression change.

"What's this," he asked, pressing his fingers deeper into the side of her breast.

"It's nothing."

"It's a lump!"

"It's nothing," she declared again, drawing the bedcovers up to her chin.

A silence stretched between them and Eva knew what was coming next.

"You *knew*? How long have you known it was there?"

"It's my body. Of course I knew."

"You *lied* to me?"

"You expected me to be perfect."

He pressed his face into the palms of both his hands. His black hair fell over his fingers. "You *are* perfect. I love all of you."

Eva wrapped her arms defensively around her body, the long months of hiding things from him now springing forward, taking on a life of their own. "Leave me if you want. I can't take any of it back. I can't change it. The doctor thinks it's cancer. And yes, I kept it from you. There, you have it. A reason to leave me, like you did Fernande!"

She began to weep then, uncontrollable tears, for all that she had longed for and dreamed of, for all that she had and knew she would soon lose if it really was cancer. It was fear, and such an enormous weight, she had borne alone all of this time.

"You knew how I felt about illness," he finally said. He did not look at her as he spoke.

"The bronchitis I was battling seemed enough to burden you with, especially after your father became so ill!"

"No one else has ever known as much about me as you. You should have trusted me."

She did not want to tell him about Dr. Rousseau, who had so fervently pleaded with her to have further tests. But in the end she confessed it all.

"Well, first thing Monday morning we will see Dr. Rousseau together, and we will do what we must for you."

"I'd be ashamed. He thinks I am Madame Humbert. If you go with me, and say who you are, he will know that's not true. He'll know we are unmarried."

"Well, Monday he will hear that you are Madame Picasso, since you very nearly are. I've never been so angry in my life, Eva, but, I swear, I'll not lose you now, too! God and I may despise each other, but He cannot add *you* to my list of punishments!"

Whether it was a statement or a challenge

to God Almighty, she did not know. But when morning came, Picasso told her he needed to be alone for a while. He rose, dressed and left the apartment without kissing her goodbye. She heard the door slam, and Eva let him go because she understood the part she had played. She did not blame Picasso, because she knew, given half a chance, there was nothing she would have done differently, for love of him.

Now, hopefully, Dr. Rousseau would say it was only a cyst, that she was fine, and her sacrifice for Picasso's concern had been worth the heavy price she had already paid.

The surgery to extract the tumor for testing was a brutal procedure but removal of the mass and surrounding tissue was the only option to determine whether or not it was cancerous. Eva knew in her heart that it would be, yet she and Picasso told no one, not Gertrude and Alice, or even her family. She could not bear to worry them. And something involving such an intimate part of her body still felt intensely private to Eva. In spite of how hard she tried not to think of it, and to tell herself she wasn't being fair to Picasso, she could not stop herself from seeing all of the idealized female bodies he had drawn, sketched and painted. No matter how he denied it to her, on some level it mattered to him.

The results were delivered with harsh indifference as Picasso sat beside her hospital bed two days later, holding her hand.

It was definitely cancer. If Madame Picasso did not wish to risk the spread of the disease, the doctor advised them that there was no other choice but to remove both breasts and the lymph nodes surrounding them. The procedure would be followed by a course of radiation, administered daily for several weeks.

As Dr. Rousseau stood over them droning out the details of the plan to butcher her body, Eva grew so hysterical that she had to be sedated. Once the doctor had gone and Eva was finally resting, Picasso left the hospital, went alone around the corner out of view, sagged against the building and wept.

CHAPTER 31

Anger covered Picasso like a shroud. Through it, he could see the good things in his life but feel little. Only the anger touched him. In spite of the cold weather, he had been standing outside on the wide steps of the Abbey de Sion for nearly an hour, gazing up at the ornately carved church doors and arguing with himself about whether or not to go inside. A spray of dead winter leaves blew across his black shoes as he murmured epithets in Catalan. He did not want to set things right with a God capable of such cruelty. Had Conchita not been enough?

Picasso was not certain whether he hoped to appease God, or reason with Him. As he stood contemplating that, one of the great doors suddenly swung open. A dark-haired altar boy stepped out wearing a black cassock and white surplice and he was holding an ivory rosary.

For a moment, their eyes met, and Picasso had the bizarre feeling that he was looking at someone familiar. He shook his head and blew into his icy hands as the boy held the door. "Would you like to come inside, monsieur? I think it is about to rain."

"No . . . Yes . . . I suppose so. *Merci bien.*"

After the boy let him inside, he disappeared, and Picasso wondered if he had imagined him. He sat slumped in one of the last pews, unable to make himself kneel. He was too angry with God for that show of reverence.

How had this happened? They had been so happy, so in love. Eva was young and vital. He had done such a great volume of innovative work since he had known her and she had tamed his wild side. Picasso truly had believed she was his muse. He needed her.

How could she have kept the truth from him all of these months? Eva had forced them to live a lie, and that had destroyed something between them. He could not help but feel the sting of betrayal. Was it betrayal on par with Fernande? That he did not yet know.

Picasso loathed being this angry with her, but it was far beyond his control. The vision of his love lying weak and vulnerable in a hospital bed had made him feel weak himself. It made him want to run from everything. Even from her.

He lost track of time, sitting there in that great vaulted space that smelled of beeswax and incense, and Picasso became transfixed by the brilliant details of the stained-glass window above the altar. The Slaughter of the Innocents, from Exodus.

"All right, then, God. I am here. I've come back. What would You have of me?" he finally asked with quiet desperation. "It has been a while since we have spoken. But I am ready now to make a deal."

After what he thought of as an attempt at appeasement and reconciliation with God for Eva's sake, Picasso finally left the church. He did not see the boy again who had let him in, or anyone else.

Amid a wintery downpour, Picasso headed for the Métro station. He moved along anonymously with a parade of Parisians under the city and onto the subway platform, not quite ready to go back to the hospital. He needed to be alone for a while longer, to catch his breath.

By the time he walked out of the station near Montmartre, and trudged up the steep steps beside the funicular, it had stopped raining, but winter had left the air gray and very cold. He wandered alone around the familiar narrow, winding streets without thinking of where he was going. He walked past la Maison Rose café, shuttered at the moment. Fitting, it was closed off to him, as his friendship with Ramón was now, too. He was surprised when he ended up on the rue des Saules, in front of the quaint Au Lapin Agile Cabaret.

With a sudden wave of nostalgia, Picasso drew back the front door. It gave its familiar low squeal. Thank God some things did not change, he thought. He would say hello to Frédé, the beaver-bearded owner, have one beer and then be on his way back to the hospital.

The place was as small and dark as Picasso remembered. It was still early, only late afternoon, so there were only a few patrons. As Picasso took in the familiar sights inside the small tavern, his gaze fell on something he hadn't expected to see. Fernande was sitting alone on a stool in the center of the room. She was wearing a plain black dress as she read aloud from a small red volume of poetry she gripped tightly in both hands. It didn't seem to him that anyone was listening, nor did she notice him come in. Her voice still had that sensual tone, he thought. Once, in another lifetime, that sound alone could seduce him.

Picasso hung back in the shadows, stunned to see her reduced to this. He felt a burst of pity and then wondered if God was testing him. Was his heart so broken that he would open this door to the past?

He could not do it, of course. It had only been a wild, fleeting thought — like so many other strange notions that regularly moved through his mind. He would have given the barkeep a few francs for her before he left the place but Fernande would have made him confess who had left it and Picasso could not bear to give her hope of a reconciliation. There was no one in the world for him, nor would there ever be, but Eva and his love for her.

All of the anger he had felt earlier slowly began to fade away when he thought again of Eva lying in that hospital bed, and seeing in her eyes how frightened she was for the future. His heart could not bear that image now. All this time, she had tried to spare him the worry over her health by bearing the horrible burden on her own. The thought of that was excruciating to him. He was furious with himself for having been angry with her when she had needed him the most. Illness still terrified him. But perhaps God was actually working inside of him, healing his old hurts by giving him another chance to do right by someone he loved.

He realized in that same moment that it was not anger at all that had taken him captive when he had discovered the lump in her breast; it was fear.

I simply cannot lose her, he thought desperately. Picasso was horrified by the thought that followed: he may well one day have to watch Eva die as he had Conchita, and this time, like the last, he would be helpless to stop it.

"We do have to stop meeting in hospitals. People are bound to talk."

Eva opened her eyes and the first thing she saw was Sylvette's pretty smile. She was sitting on the edge of the bed beside her. Eva tried to sit up against the white metal headboard but she felt a sting of pain and decided against it.

"Did Pablo tell you I was here?"

"He asked me to come," Sylvette said.

"No doubt because he cannot bear to look at me himself."

Sylvette took Eva's hand. "Eva — *ma chère amie* — why on earth did you not tell anyone sooner? That's a dreadful thing to keep to yourself."

527

Eva turned her head away, but the truth lingered between them.

"I thought it was nothing. I so badly wanted it to *be* nothing. I know it sounds strange, but I had that horrible cough last summer, and I suppose I had convinced myself that it was just a cyst, my body's reaction to that. I've had weak lungs all my life, but I thought if I healed my cough, the lump would go away."

"Really? And if it didn't go away, what was your plan then?"

"I guess I hadn't thought it through past the panic. Obviously, determination is not the same thing as wisdom. I made a mistake, I know that now. Picasso is furious with me, Sylvette."

"My God, doesn't he have a right to be?"

"You don't understand." Tears clouded Eva's eyes and she struggled not to cry. "The surgery the doctor advises, in order to be certain they cut out all of the cancer, will mutilate me. Dr. Rousseau was quite clear. I will be butchered. I will have a chest with no breasts, only hideous scars. I can wait until the summer to see if they got it all. But if it has spread, that would be my future, and . . ."

"Oh, Eva." Sylvette squeezed her hand.

Now they both had tears in their eyes.

"Dr. Rousseau recommends that I go away to somewhere warm for the rest of the winter, to gain as much strength back as I can. Just in case. That was what he said. Just in case."

"Have you spoken with your family? They really should know. I could go to see them for you, if you like."

"My grandmother died from cancer of the breast. I can't bring myself to worry them over this. And I'm not giving up on the idea that Dr. Rousseau got all of the cancer when he removed the tumor to examine it. It could have been contained. I have a reprieve until summer."

"Will Picasso take you back to Avignon? You liked that area so much, and the little town nearby. That might be the perfect place."

Eva thought of the precious haven they had made in Sorgues. She had never been so happy in her life as that first summer with Picasso. They were so carefree then. Anything seemed possible.

"I don't know what's going to happen. I wish I did. I haven't seen Picasso since yesterday," Eva said sadly. "And when he left here he was none too happy with me."

"He'll be back, Eva. He loves you so much. Everyone can see that. And you're engaged now. Look at your beautiful ring!"

Eva felt it on her finger, the symbol of a unique and precious love between them. Together, they had already weathered so many storms: Fernande, the Pichots, Don José and Frika. Sylvette had to be right. She just needed to give him time to work through the shock of all this. Hopefully, time was something she had to give. Right now, it felt like the most valuable commodity in the world to her.

Eva was still sore three days later, but she was determined to preside over the decorating of their new apartment herself. From a place on the couch where she could rest, she twisted the silver engagement ring around on her finger and delighted in directing the movers with all of the furniture and boxes as they went in and out the open front door. It made her feel so much better to think of things other than the surgery, and their uncertain future. Making this place a real home for Picasso, and a sanctuary for them both, was the best medicine she could imagine, and she had promised him she would take it easy.

Picasso had seemed so distracted since she left the hospital and, while it concerned her, Eva knew the coming art auction was part of the reason. As if he hadn't had enough to deal with, accepting all that had happened, she thought. But she knew he was also using work as an excuse not to fully resolve things between them. They had yet to really speak of it since the surgery.

Gertrude and Alice brought lunch and a potted fern as a housewarming gift. Sylvette came a few minutes later to see what she could do to help out, then Max arrived, clutching a celebratory bottle of Pernod. They all waited for Picasso's return, but Kahnweiler came instead. His dark eyes were ablaze with panic, and he seemed out of breath as he brushed past the front door.

"Is he here?" he asked Eva without ceremony as he stood over the sofa.

"I'm afraid not. I'm sorry about all of the boxes, but do come in."

"I need to speak with Picasso about the show — what reserves he would like me to set on a particular couple of pieces. We're running out of time, and interest is growing fast."

Eva exchanged a glance with Gertrude. But both of them knew where he had gone — because they both understood Picasso better than anyone else. The Bateau-Lavoir was still his retreat when he felt desperate. It probably always would be.

"You need to speak to him. That's all there is to it," Gertrude urged her.

"He worked late last night and was gone first thing this morning," Eva replied.

"I know you are still weak, but if you can manage it, you should go and talk this through, once and for all. Find him, if you're up to it. Don't let this fester. These days, you need each other more than ever."

Eva loved that Gertrude now was as supportive as Alice long had been. Both women had made such a profound impact on her, and on her relationship with Picasso. "I'm much stronger, really. I actually feel quite well."

"Still, I'll ride up to Montmartre with you, and wait in the cab," Sylvette declared.

"Alice and I will watch things for you here," Gertrude said.

Eva found Picasso sitting alone on the little bench on the place Ravignan beneath the trees, outside of the Bateau-Lavoir, as she had suspected. He was surrounded by a profusion of pigeons, but he did not seem to notice them, or her, as she sat down beside him. It was a moment before she gathered the courage to speak.

"Monsieur Kahnweiler has been looking everywhere for you," she said gently. "The auction is tomorrow, you know."

"*Sí.* I know."

"He came to the apartment, brimming with questions about reserves, and different canvases. He says, if you both play it right, this could be the single most significant event of your life."

"I doubt that." Picasso shot back flatly, and then he was quiet again for what felt to Eva like an eternity. "How did you know where to find me?"

"I knew because I love you."

"You should be home resting."

"It's not a home without you in it, too, Pablo."

"I needed time to think. Since you knew where I was, you knew that, as well."

She shook her head. "I only wanted to protect you from worry so that you could work. God, Pablo, I'm just so sorry about everything." They both exhaled deeply and pretended to watch the pigeons on the ground around them. "If I have to have the surgery next summer, everything will change."

"Nothing is so predictable as change, is it?"

She put a hand on his thigh. "Are you ever going to forgive me, or are things going to stay like this between us, until we are just like you and Fernande?"

"You and I could never be like that."

Eva saw a muscle tighten in his Picasso's jaw. There were tears gathering in his black eyes.

"I'm not going to deal with Kahnweiler," Picasso finally said. "It's too much for me, especially right now. I need to work. I'm an artist, not a businessman."

"I was a seamstress, not a dancer. But nothing is so predictable as change, is it?"

"Sometimes, I really hate how clever you are," he said.

"I'm sorry about that."

"You really are a woman like no other."

"My life is you, Pablo."

Picasso looked at her with a serious expression. "Just so you know, the most significant event of my life had nothing to do with art. It was falling in love with you."

Eva wanted to reach out and wrap her arms around him, but she knew she must not push too hard. Not until he was ready to forgive her completely. There was still a journey ahead on the road back to where they had been, still a wound that needed healing. Yet Eva could not help herself from pressing a kiss lightly onto his check. A moment later, Picasso put his hand just briefly onto her knee. It was a small gesture, but she knew it was a beginning.

"What do you want to do about Kahn-weiler?"

"Did he tell you which canvases were in question?"

"*Family of Saltimbanques.* He thinks the sale could be massive and he really needs to speak with you about it."

"I trust you to decide the reserve."

Surely he was joking, but it was not funny to her. "I don't understand."

"You have been studying the market. I sold it six years ago for a thousand francs. Considering the scope of my career, and the increase in prices on the market, what do you think the reserve should be now?"

"Ten times that, at least!"

"Ten thousand francs? That's quite a sum."

"Naturally! It's an amazing painting." *Family of Saltimbanques* was a painting of a family of itinerant performers whom Picasso had met many times at the Circus Medrano, and it was his most evocative work. To Eva, it seemed inestimable but she knew they must set a high bar. She also knew that Kahnweiler had already sold *Young Acrobat on a Ball* to a dealer for sixteen thousand francs, which was a small fortune, but the sale had been a quiet one, not an auction. If she and Picasso could hold fast to the price for *Saltimbanques* in this public arena, she believed, not just the art community and an educated few, but the entire world would at last revere the name Pablo Picasso.

"Then tell him that for me. You have my full support to tell him however you like, not a centime less than ten thousand francs for it at auction."

Eva was relieved to see a smile finally break across his face.

"Do you not think we should attend the auction to see how the sale goes?"

"Ah, but that would surely lessen my mystique," Picasso replied and, for a moment, she could not tell if he was being clever or serious. "But you should go and represent me."

"Alone?"

"You are up to the task. Besides, the truth, *ma jolie,* is that I need someone who I can trust, who will be a buffer for me with dealers so that I can focus on work. It's certain to get awkward when Kahnweiler knows that I am talking to Vollard again about my sculptures. You could soften all of that for me as we go along."

"You would trust me, after everything that has happened?"

"A man must trust his wife, no?"

So many emotions struck her all at once.

536

The peace of forgiveness was the strongest. Picasso put his arm around her and drew her against him as she buried her face in her hands and wept. "I'll be absolutely butchered if I have that surgery. You wouldn't want me as your wife then!"

"If you need it, you *will* go through with it, if I have to fling you over my shoulder and take you to the hospital myself! And you cannot say that I won't want you. I will never want any other woman."

"I can't hold you to that promise. I will look like a monster!"

Eva burrowed more tightly against him, inhaling the musky scent of his skin, and the power of his arms around her. "I want to wait before we marry. Please," she said, almost not believing they were words she had spoken, when all she had ever wanted since the day they'd met was to be his wife.

"*¡Palabras locas!*" he growled in Spanish. "*¡Basta!*"

"It's not crazy! If I have to have the surgery, Pablo —"

"I won't allow you to think like that. It is fine. *You* will be fine. Dr. Rousseau will have cut away all the cancer already, I know it. I went to have a talk with God yesterday. I went to a church, the one where we will marry. I told God that I forgive Him for taking Conchita, because He gave me you."

"Oh, Pablo."

"I told him it was time I forgave Him, so long as he does not take you. What righteous God would be so cruel as to take from me again?"

"If I need the surgery —"

"You won't."

"But if I do, then afterward — if you can look at me with more than pity in your eyes . . ."

"*Mujer,* you are being unreasonable! Why not go through with a simple formality of a marriage, when nearly everyone already believes you are my wife?"

"Because, at the end of the day, *you know* you are still a free man, and that is what's important to me. Until we know how things will go, you still have the freedom to walk away."

"*Dios mío,* no more words like that! My heart has not been free since the day we met!"

"I need to know that I am not your burden."

"Have it your way. But, out of respect to us, everyone we know will still call you Madame Picasso."

Eva could not argue that point, or try to stop it from happening because, more than anything in the world, she so wanted that one thing to be true, and she did so love hearing people say it.

The lunch Eva hosted at their new apartment was a week late due to her surgery. But it went off without a hitch, and Picasso and Apollinaire finally made amends. When it was time to leave, he held Picasso's face while he kissed each of his cheeks, and everyone applauded the reconciliation. He then turned to Eva.

"Thank you for doing this," he said in a low voice. "I fear Pablo would have waited forever without your kind insistence."

"It was nothing."

"Ah, but to me it was everything," he declared, and pressed a small black volume into her hands. "I remember you said you like my poetry. They've included 'The Farewell' in this edition."

"I adore all of them, but that one now especially."

"Then consider this a little gift from a grateful soul."

"Everyone can use a champion now and then," Eva said.

"Picasso is a fortunate man, my dear, to have such a champion as you."

■ ■ ■ ■

Saltimbanques resold at auction for twelve thousand six hundred fifty francs. The French press excitedly proclaimed it a record sale, and they anointed Picasso an artist on par with Cézanne, van Gogh and Gauguin. What the future held for such an innovative young master, they would await with the greatest anticipation. Surely, the future could be nothing for him but bright, they wrote. It was what Eva had been telling him all along.

A week following the sale, and buoyed by her role in it, Eva walked alone into the gallery of Ambroise Vollard, the other dealer who had represented Picasso's work. She had been there a lifetime ago, for Louis. Now, she was wearing a stylish blue coat with a large black fur collar and cuffs, and a black velvet hat, which helped give her the confidence she needed for what she was about to do. It was a vast change from the simple dress she had worn here after the day of her interview at the Moulin Rouge.

A bell tinkled over the door and she took off her elegant black leather gloves as she waited for Vollard to come out of the back room. Her heart was racing but she kept her appearance calm. She had begun her work as Picasso's intermediary at the art auction, and now she was ready to expand her role.

It was obvious from Vollard's expression that he had expected to see Picasso, since Picasso was the one who had called the meeting. Eva stiffened her spine and smiled. This would not be easy. But what in her life had been? Besides, Picasso had asked her to do this. He believed in her ability to promote his work and so she needed to believe it, as well.

They were becoming a formidable team.

"Madame Picasso. What a pleasant surprise," he said. "But naturally I expected to see Pablo."

"Monsieur Picasso has been detained with work at his studio," Eva calmly replied, and watched the eyes of the large, gruff and balding man narrow beneath an accompanying frown. He scratched his dark pointed beard in the awkward silence. She knew Vollard had referred to her as Pablo's wife merely out of deference, but nonetheless she liked the feeling of command it gave her. "He has asked me to speak on his behalf."

She glanced at the many paintings hanging on the walls. Some of the artists' work she recognized. She had learned about them from her own reading, and when she and Picasso visited various museums and art galleries in the South of France and here in Paris. *Teach me everything,* Eva had bid him, and Picasso had taken that to heart.

On a wall in the back of the gallery she saw one of Picasso's canvases, just as he had described it. A brown-and-black Cubist portrait of Ambroise Vollard himself. Eva moved toward it.

"I see you haven't sold Monsieur Picasso's portrait of you."

He followed her cautiously as Eva looked up at the canvas. "Not all of my clients appreciate his Cubist style as I do."

"Ah. And do you?"

Her forward tone seemed to surprise him. "Recently I have had more success with some his earlier blue paintings, and his harlequins."

She pivoted to face him. Her gaze was steady. "Then we would like to buy it back."

"The artist wishes to buy his own painting of me?"

"We wish not to see a masterpiece languish in a dealer's crowded gallery, as though it were an unimportant offering simply there to cover a hole in the wall. We will pay you five thousand francs for the painting."

A tepid smile lifted his heavy mustache. "That is a great sum of money, my dear," he said, his voice dripping with condescension.

"I'm quite certain I can sell it for more. But it needs to be shown properly."

"Are you saying that you know more about the sale of art than the man standing before you who has represented everyone from Vincent van Gogh and Pierre-Auguste Renoir to Paul Cézanne?"

"The painting is still here, is it not?" Eva heard the steely challenge in her own voice. She willed herself not to flinch.

"As it happens, I do have a client in Germany who had expressed some interest in that particular canvas." He scratched his beard again. "He offered four thousand francs, which I declined."

"Well, the artist himself is offering five thousand francs, so he must see value in it greater than what your client has previously considered."

"Offering it through you."

"Yes, through me. Perhaps your German client would be interested to know of a firm counteroffer. Does that not generally spark a sweetened bid from the original party?"

"From the artist himself? I'm not sure of that."

"I don't suppose a businessman, such as yourself, reveals every detail about the identities of his clients when there is an auction at hand."

"Now it's an auction, is it?" he asked with amusement.

"Is that not what you call it when two parties compete for the same painting? Monsieur Picasso and I have made you a firm bid for the portrait."

"Since it has been shown in my shop all this time, I suspect you would like a commission, as well, if I were to sell it elsewhere?"

Eva let only the faintest smile turn her lips. Inside she was shaking. "But of course. Since you have never actually offered a contract to Monsieur Picasso to represent him, that would seem only fair. After all, business is business, Monsieur Vollard."

"You're a shrewd woman, Madame Picasso."

"You may not have intended that as a compliment, but I intend to take it that way," Eva replied as she turned and walked toward the door. "You have a week to sell it to your German client for six thousand francs or we buy it back for five. You will let us know as soon as possible which it will be, won't you?"

Picasso was painting when she arrived back at the studio but when he heard the door he put down his brush and went to her.

Eva fell against him, her heart racing.

"Well, how did it go?"

"It is as good as sold! You should have seen his face!" Eva breathlessly chuckled. "He hated dealing with a woman, I know it. But there was so little he could say out of deference to you. He may not have been willing to offer you a contract in the past, but clearly he does not want to cut all of his ties with you."

"Vollard is a tough old sot. You know I don't want my own painting back. Especially not for five thousand francs when I gave it to him free of charge to try to get a contract out of him."

"Of course not. It was a gamble. But we can't have it just sitting in that shop for everyone to see when you are so close to becoming a worldwide star. There must be a mystique about you. As it turns out, he *did* have an offer on the portrait and he has been dragging his heels. But I think I may very well have lit a fire beneath those feet of his about it. If I am right, you will receive a nice little commission for his embarrassment over letting it languish."

"Such a determined little vixen you are." Picasso wrapped her up into his arms and kissed her. "What in the world would I do without you?"

"Hopefully, you will never have to know the answer to that," she said proudly. Not only did Picasso love her. He believed in her, and after today, she actually did believe in herself.

■ ■ ■ ■

Part III

WAR, ILLNESS, REDEMPTION

■ ■ ■ ■

I have picked this sprig of heather.
Autumn has ended, you do remember.
Never on earth shall we meet again.
Scent of time, sprig of heather
Remember always, I wait for you forever.
— Guillaume Apollinaire

CHAPTER 32

Avignon, July 1914

Six months later, in July, the Great War that everyone had feared descended on Europe with the power of a firestorm and French citizens were eager to take up arms in defense of their country. *Vive la France!* echoed from Paris to Versailles, Céret to Nice, and the carefree years that had followed the Belle Époque were swiftly replaced with a riotous sense of panic, and frenzied cries of renewed patriotism.

The jolly ragtime tunes and boisterous celebrations that had not long ago filled the cafés of Paris were replaced by "La Marseillaise" and hushed conversations about military tactics, approaching airplane squadrons and the sudden food shortages.

When the first shots were fired, and planes strafed Paris, thankfully Picasso and Eva were not there. He had surprised Eva by renting a summer home in Avignon so that she would have a warm place to grow stronger.

He had found a little white house with blue shutters right in the center of town. She would heal there, he said. And so would their relationship. But the dark uncertainty of war set Picasso on edge. He combed through the papers every day. As he worried about his collection of canvases left in Paris, and the safety of his money, Eva started to feel the nausea resurfacing again. But she resolved not to say anything too quickly with all that was going on. Besides, her secret hope was that it signaled a pregnancy at last.

"If people panic, we could lose everything. All the money I have is tied up in the Banque de France in Paris," Picasso declared one morning as he held up a newspaper. "Are you well enough to go with me to withdraw it? There is no time to waste."

He was too anxious about his savings to notice that Eva was barely eating.

"Of course I am going with you," she declared, hoping she could find the strength for the train ride into the city. Now that she was his partner, she meant to be so in every way.

The next day, as they stepped off the train and merged into a crowd, Eva clung to

Picasso's arm, stunned by a city that was so different from the one they had left. Gone were the glamorous Parisians strolling with their beautiful broad-brimmed hats and elegant dresses. Now there seemed to be no one on the streets but soldiers and policemen.

Everywhere they turned were mobilization notices soliciting able-bodied Frenchmen to take up arms. Throughout the city, *joie de vivre* had been replaced by fear.

"Don't worry, I can't be called up. I'm not French," Picasso said beneath his breath as they rushed to the big stone bank near Montparnasse.

There was a huge crowd gathered outside, and there was a line to get in the door that snaked around the block. Picasso clutched Eva's hand more tightly as they approached a stone-faced guard at the tall, iron doors.

"Excuse me, but I need to see to my account," Picasso said. As he spoke, he slipped the guard a silver franc.

"*Messieur-dame, bienvenue,* but you mustn't tarry outside here among this crowd to do your business. It may turn ugly. Please, go inside, quickly!"

Eva felt badly for having pushed with Picasso to the head of the line, and offering the guard a bribe, but she knew that things were desperate and waiting their turn could well cost them every centime they had.

Once they had withdrawn his savings, stuffed it into a bag and checked the lock on their new apartment, they returned quickly to Avignon. Paris was no place to wait out a war, Picasso said. But the conflict found them, anyway. When they arrived back at the house with the blue shutters, Georges and Marcelle Braque were waiting, along with André Derain, his mistress, Alice Princet, and their black German shepherd, Sentinelle. Marcelle Braque, in her familiar rope of pearls, was sitting teary-eyed on the wrought-iron bench near the front door.

"We hoped you would see us off at the station," Braque said somberly. "We've both been called up."

This wasn't possible, Eva thought, suddenly feeling panicked. Between the war and her illness, it was too much to bear. Everything was changing far too swiftly to take it all in.

"My darling Alice here is going to wait out the war in Montfavet with her sister, but she can't have Sentinelle there," Derain said of his mistress.

Stunned by the news, Picasso crouched down and stroked one of the dog's pointed black ears. Eva knew the gesture was designed to keep his composure. He had not allowed himself to show affection toward animals since the death of Frika, but he had known this dog since he was a puppy. Eva saw something in Picasso soften, quite against his will, as Sentinelle wagged his tail in response to Picasso's touch.

Feeling nothing but compassion for her now, Eva sat down on the bench and wrapped her arm around Marcelle's trembling shoulders. "I despise this wretched war already," Marcelle sobbed into her hands.

"What are we to do about poor Sentinelle?" Alice Princet wept. "He's such a gentle beast, and he'll be absolutely lost without André. How can any of this be happening?"

"We could look after him while you are away," Eva offered.

Picasso shot her a stricken glance.

"Please, Pablo. I really could use the company, with everyone leaving us, and with you shut up in your studio working all day."

"I suppose we don't have much of a choice," Picasso eventually relented.

Later, the group gathered at the train depot. There were other families all around them beneath the great iron, steel and glass structure. Soldiers were in their new uniforms. Women were weeping as they embraced them. A little girl waved a small flag. Then a train whistle blew. Eva thought it made a mournful sound. Picasso finally took the dog leash from Derain and the two men embraced.

"Hopefully, it will be a quick war. So we can get back to our easels," Braque said with a wink. He was trying to keep a brave face. They all were. "The Spaniard here will, of course, take full advantage, and grow even more famous in our absence."

"You give them all hell, Wilbur, so we can all be done with this," Picasso said as he gave his friend a mock salute. He could not bear to embrace Braque; that would have been too painful.

"Vive la France!" Eva chimed in a hopeful tone, trying her best to smile through her uncertainty about what lay ahead for them all.

Still weeping, Marcelle Braque pulled Eva into a deep embrace. "I must ask for your forgiveness, Eva," she said.

"Whatever for?"

"Alice and I were not very welcoming to you in the beginning, I am sorry to say. We didn't really give you much of a chance — the ties with Fernande, and all."

"I had no idea," she lied because she knew Picasso would be listening.

"You have really been good for Pablo. We can all see that."

"You needn't say so just because we are taking her dog," Eva countered with a hint of humor, though she could still feel the sting of Marcelle's words that day behind her back. Perhaps she was being overly sentimental because her husband was about to go off to war. Still, now was not the time to nurse old grudges or harbor old anger.

"I'm sincere, Eva, and truly very sorry. When he was with Fernande, he was always so volatile. But there is a wonderful sense of peace about him now. It's really quite striking. Georges sees it in Picasso's work. It is obvious that you are responsible for that."

They all embraced one another one last time before the final train whistle blew. They tried to keep brave faces, but the enormity of war and its costs was too heavy on everyone's hearts for that as Georges Braque and André Derain at last stepped into the train car and disappeared from sight.

In September, they received news that Apollinaire had enlisted in the military. Because of his criminal record, it had taken him twice as long to be approved. Picasso told

Eva he was grateful that he and Apollinaire had reconciled before the start of the war. They had even begun to correspond. He said that last luncheon she arranged had meant the world to him.

Of their closely knit little group, only Max Jacob was rejected for service. But even for those left behind, war dominated everything. There was rationing, and there were shortages, and the newspapers were always full of postings of the wounded and the dead.

Through it all, Picasso did his best to keep working. He produced dozens of new Cubist canvases and he began to sculpt again. He had missed the feeling of wet plaster on his fingers.

Meanwhile, Eva was growing stronger, he told himself. It was time to feel confident again. She was young, and she was a fighter. She was fine, he thought over and over. *They* would be fine.

As he left his latest canvas to dry one morning, Picasso brought Eva breakfast in bed. He had gone through all of his rituals that morning to calm his superstitions, after he had come back from the bakery. He had stopped at the door, paused, turned around, counted to five, turned back around and entered the house. Nothing bad could happen. Not today, at least.

For a few moments, before the scent of fresh brioche woke her, Picasso watched Eva sleep. He relished the vision. Her face, when she slept, was still childlike, and so lovely. He did not believe it was possible to love a person so much as he did Eva, or to feel more devoted. After everything they had been through together, he only worshipped her more. He wanted a child with her — to see the culmination of them both in a pair of bright, innocent eyes. Yet he felt selfish. There was a part of him that was secretly glad he did not have to share her with anyone but Derain's dog, who particularly adored her. True to his name, Sentinelle sat on guard at the foot of the bed, ready to protect her.

"What time is it?" Eva asked sleepily as she struggled up onto her elbows.

"Just past nine o'clock."

"Why did you let me sleep so late? Did you come to bed last night?"

"I was working on something new. I will show you after you've eaten."

He watched her face as she warily considered the tray of brioche, tea and freshly sliced melon.

"Oh, Pablo. You know I can't eat first thing in the morning."

"When we first met, you used to be ravenous for breakfast," he said suspiciously.

"I was ravenous for *you,*" she said with a sleepy smile as he handed her a cup of tea and pressed a kiss onto her cheek. "What's the new painting of?"

"You and your dog. You are wearing that silly fox fur stole." He was referring to the stole he had bought for Eva in Nîmes after they had gone to a bullfight.

"That seemed the least you could do after making me watch that entire gory thing to the end," she said with a mock pout.

"Clearly I failed in my effort to educate you about the majesty of *les corridas.*"

"Clearly you did."

Picasso pressed her hair back behind her ear on one side. "After I have had a little rest, I am going to start another painting of you this afternoon. Of the two of us, actually."

"I like the sound of that."

"Now, with your hair grown out, full and lush as it is again, I am inspired. I have the idea of painting you in the guise of an artist's model. You will have just come from the dressing room, and I will paint myself waiting for you. Actually, I might just leave my own image as a sketch, not paint it in, so that the focus of the piece can be you and your glorious body."

She lifted an eyebrow playfully. "I see. I'm to be naked, then?"

"Of course. And if it is as good as I envision it, I think I will make you a wedding gift of it."

Eva sank back against the pillows. "Pablo, we've been through this. It's too soon."

"It has been a year, *mi amor.* You are as healthy as I am now. All of that dreadful business is behind us, and the mourning period for my father is at an end, so there is no reason to wait any longer to be married. If you still love me, that is."

"Eternally."

"Then it is settled. The newspapers say things have calmed down in Paris for the moment. I am desperate to check on the apartment, and all of my canvases there. Gertrude and Alice will be back, as well, so they can attend the wedding. My family waits only for my direction before they travel to Paris, too."

"You know that the Hôtel le Meurice has been turned into a hospital for wounded soldiers."

"There are other hotels. That cannot be your excuse."

"But that hotel is special to us both. It will be bad luck if we have our wedding breakfast somewhere else."

"Now who is being superstitious? I have it all planned. I'm going to drive us away from the church in high style with Spanish cow bells tied to the back of our motorcar."

"You don't know how to drive!" Eva gaspcd. Sentinelle barked.

"Not yet, I don't, but I am going to buy a car, so I had better learn. I've arranged for a driving lesson with a young soldier for later today. Then I'm going to buy his car. His family is in need of money, but his father won't take anything from me, not even a sketch. The man and his son reminded me a lot of my father and me. I suppose I want to honor that, too."

"You know, you are a very kind man, Pablo Picasso." Eva smiled, and kissed his cheek.

"Don't let that get around." He grinned. "Besides, what I truly am is a man in love with his woman . . . *yo amo a mi mujer.*"

As they walked through town later, Eva and Picasso were reminded yet again about the gravity, and seeming endlessness, of this war. Things had calmed down for the moment, but the conflict was far from over. And in the meantime, Avignon had been transformed into a military encampment. The lovely cobblestone streets were now teeming with regiments of soldiers and crowds of bedraggled and haggard-looking refugees. Hay carts and bicycles were now replaced by trucks loaded with weapons, or filled with soldiers. Troops were installed in the theater, the courthouse and even the historic Palace of the Popes.

They met up with the young soldier in front of a stable near the Hôtel de Ville. He stood proudly in a new dark blue uniform with gold buttons, high black boots and a crisp new kepi on his head. Eva was certain, when she looked at him, that he was no more than sixteen, in spite of a waxy dark mustache designed to make him appear older. Picasso clapped him affably on the shoulder in an effort to put him at ease before they piled into his maroon-colored Peugeot.

Eva was still unaccustomed to the sensation of being in a motorcar, but as they drove, she felt revived by the blissful sensation of sun on her face and the wind in her hair. As the road snaked along beside the silvery river Rhône, and in the shadow of the four stone arches of the famous Avignon Bridge, she felt free of the war, free of fear, pain and worry about her looming illness.

Finally, the young soldier and Picasso got

out to switch places. Eva held her breath with anticipation. Picasso was such a proud man that she knew this could not have been easy for him. The car rolled forward and Picasso tried to release the clutch, but the car jerked to a sudden stop. Eva could see the boy biting back a smile. Picasso tried again, and again the car chugged and jerked, stalling on the narrow dirt road.

"¡Mierda!" he growled, slamming his fist against the steering wheel.

Eva found it so comical that she covered her mouth to hide a burst of laughter. The worst of the pain came with the sudden movement. The intensity was so overwhelming that she gasped for breath. Picasso pivoted toward the backseat, ready to shout — until he saw her face.

"We had better find the hospital, Pablo." It was all she could manage to say.

CHAPTER 33

As winter came, Eva tried very hard to remember what had happened on that terrible day. But for so long there were only fragments. The young soldier speeding through the streets of Avignon toward the Hôpital Sainte-Marthe as she slumped in the backseat crippled by pain. The long, jarring train ride back to Paris buried in Picasso's protective embrace, her mind numbed by laudanum to dull the sharpest parts of everything. There was Picasso's smile. The young soldier's maroon-colored car. Troops marching through the cobblestone streets, a little boy waving at her . . . And their sweet little rented house with the blue shutters, which she had grown to love.

The doctor at the hospital in Avignon had confirmed what, in her heart, Eva had already known. The cancer had spread and the surgical removal of both breasts was now no longer an option — it was the only chance that remained to prolong her life.

Picasso insisted the procedure be performed in Paris, by the best specialist possible. Money was no object, he said. Gertrude trusted Dr. Rousseau, so Picasso trusted him. Eva had surrendered to the surgery passively as winter snow fell all across the city. She could fight her own body's war no longer. Nor did she have the strength to go against what Picasso wished for her, despite her fear that after such a horrendous surgery things would never be the same between them. He was a man who had been inspired by beauty all of his life. Now, and forevermore, she would be like a chipped piece of fine China — a marred version of something that once was flawless.

Eventually, Picasso would be compelled to replace her in his bed — as she once had replaced Fernande. He would not mean to hurt Eva in that way. He would tell himself that she didn't know, and he would take great pains to hide it, as he had, at first, hidden her. He might not even be fully aware of how defiant he was being against illness and death. But for a little while, she had changed him, and inspired him, because of it. Eva was proud of that, and the influence she'd had on at least some of his work.

Endlessly weary, her mind clouded by the

heavy anvil of pain medication, it seemed such a long time before Eva could actually remember everything as facts, not dreams, when she finally opened her eyes. She was in the apartment in Paris on the rue Schoelcher the first time she felt fully aware of everything. As she lay alone, swallowed up by the massive mahogany bed and all of the bedding, the first thing she saw was the huge plaster fresco propped against the bedroom wall. It brought back sweet memories of Sorgues every time she looked at it. She would always miss that house, and the happy time she'd spent with Picasso there.

The Paris apartment was quiet now. Thank God Picasso had finally gone out. He so dearly needed a break. Eva remembered he had not left her side for days. She could hear his voice, the pained insistence that he could not leave her, even for work. Nothing mattered so much as her, he declared. Now all she could hear was the wind whistling through the trees outside the tall windows.

Eva struggled to gain her bearings. Slumber's pull was immense. She glanced around and saw there was a fire in the fireplace, and over the mantel he had hung *Ma Jolie* for her. The bedroom was full of crystal vases of flowers, little bursts of cheerful color among the gray of blankets, bandages and medicine bottles. The flowers had all come from Picasso, except for the hothouse roses from Gertrude and Alice. They were the only ones of their friends who knew about the surgery. Eva had made them swear to tell no one else. The sorrow and pity she saw in Picasso's eyes was quite burden enough. "Tell everyone else that it is influenza or bronchitis again. I couldn't bear their pity otherwise," she had pleaded. "Tell them anything, only not the truth!"

Picasso had held steadfast to his own stance. He would not leave her bedside. Days became weeks. He worked little, and slept even less. He argued with doctors. He pleaded for more pain medication. Especially when her eyes were closed, she could hear the raw anguish in his voice. The sound haunted her.

How odd, Eva thought now as she gazed out the window past the bristling trees, where the Montparnasse Cemetery lay in the distance. She only now grasped the great irony of the view, and how convenient it would soon become.

The macabre thought surprised her. Instead of feeling sad, Eva saw the dark humor in it. What did other dying people think about? She was glad that at least her thoughts were her own. In the privacy of her mind she did not have to accept Picasso's strident optimism that everything would be all right, and his insistence that she not embrace the inevitable.

Paris was still a very different place than the one they had left to go to Avignon. That place seemed as if it had existed an eternity ago. The busy Montparnasse cafés she had so adored were now dim, hollow shells, where few patrons lingered. Air-raid sirens were a common sound in the city and the joyous clinking of glasses was long forgotten beneath the stark staccato cry of this seemingly endless war.

The worst of it seemed to have diminished, but those were still the hallmarks of their day-to-day world.

So many men were in uniform now that Picasso stood out on the streets. Women, whose husbands and sons fought with valor, glared at him with disdain. In their eyes he was just another young man who somehow had avoided serving his country during wartime. They tossed white feathers at him, as any other young man who would not brave the cost of protecting France. A white feather was the sign for a coward.

His work suffered further, as his notoriety did. Thousands of francs worth of his art was locked in Kahnweiler's studio because he was abroad and had not been able to return to France. His shop had been seized by the government, all of the artwork impounded so that it could not be sold. It was left to languish. Kahnweiler owed Picasso a fortune, but the rise and fall of fortunes, like happiness, could be swift and ever-changing, Eva thought. Life certainly had been that way for her.

She forced herself to get up. She was alone, and she was determined to see for herself what was left of her. She swung her legs over the edge of the bed, knowing that Picasso would not have permitted it, but he could not spare either of them forever.

Gathering all of her strength, she shuffled across the room to the wardrobe mirror. It made her suddenly think of the bright makeup mirrors at the Moulin Rouge. Had all of that been real — the lights, the costumes, the excitement?

Eva drew in a breath and exhaled it deeply, then she began to unwrap the gauze and bandages around her chest. She listened again for Picasso, but the apartment remained quiet. Alone, she must face the monster she knew now lived beneath the bandages.

As the gauze fell away she saw the dark

red splashes of dried blood, and the long, angry scars. When she saw what had become of her once-beautiful body, she collapsed like a rag doll onto the carpet and finally allowed herself to weep with primal anguish that until that moment she had refused.

Through tears, she glimpsed the sketch then — that lovely sketch Picasso had made of her that night when all things had seemed possible. She was a delicate beauty in the image, flawlessly and sensually drawn. She had felt like a woman that day, and he had captured that. It was propped unframed, still on the sketch pad, on the top of the bureau, a bit like their life together: not finished. Incomplete. How would his artist's eye see her now? She would never be pretty, never *jolie* again. Eva rose then, took the sketch and ran her fingers over the lines as more helpless tears flooded her eyes. She felt utterly foolish now for all the times that she had urged Picasso to find peace with God or to trust in their happiness.

"Why did You have to do this?" She wept aloud, turning an angry gaze to the ceiling. "It was all such a perfect dream. . . ."

In a paroxysm of grief she could no longer battle, Eva tore the sketch from the pad, turned to the fire and surrendered Picasso's image of her to the flames.

"Perfection is as fleeting as happily-ever-after," she cried angrily. "I was a fool even for a moment to think otherwise!"

November came and the weather turned cold. Alice handed Eva a cup of tea with milk as she rested on the sofa beside the fire at the rue de Fleurus apartment she shared with Gertrude. Eva was still too weak to sit up for long periods of time, but it was nice to get out of her bedroom. The view of the cemetery was becoming too much to bear. And she did so adore Alice Toklas. For a moment, they watched Gertrude and Picasso huddled together over the large dining table in the center of the room. As usual, they were deep in conversation.

"Max should be here soon," Alice said beneath the regular drone of war planes in the sky above them. "You know, he's not one to miss a free meal."

Eva smiled, thinking how true that was of the endearing poet who, that one summer, had been so kind to her. She knew about the continuing addictions that had held him captive since then. Yet he had made such an impression on her, and she missed the loyalty and sense of humor she had only begun to get to know. He would be bringing Sylvette. They had all grown close this past year, and most especially since Eva had finally allowed Picasso to reveal the truth of her condition. Along with Gertrude and Alice, they were such a wonderful source of emotional support.

When they walked in the door, everyone could see by Max's grim expression that he brought bad news. Damn, this horrendous war, Eva thought, wondering if she would ever see its end.

"Is it Apollinaire?" Gertrude asked.

"Apo is fine, thank God," Max said. Gertrude embraced him. "It's not him. But I've had a letter from Marcelle Braque. Georges was badly wounded at Thérouanne. Shot in the head. No one knows yet if he will survive."

"Wilbur. *Dios, Madre María,* no," Picasso murmured, and Max made them all pray aloud with him for Braque's full recovery.

At the table, Eva put an arm around Picasso's shoulders. With tears in their eyes, Gertrude took Picasso's hand across the tabletop.

"I don't know what I'll do without him if he doesn't make it," Picasso said, and there was a catch in his voice.

"You can't think like that, Pablo," Gertrude urged him.

571

"The harder I try to avoid death, the more it presses in."

Everyone knew that he was thinking of Eva, too. The helpless anger flared inside of her again. Sylvette handed Eva a handkerchief.

"Marcelle would be destroyed. She wouldn't want to go on living without him. Her life would be over."

"No one wants to go on living when they lose someone dear, Pablo," Eva said gently. "But there's really no other choice, is there? People have to go on. They have to build new lives. In time, the wounds heal, and the memories become precious ones, right?"

"Not for everyone!" Picasso shot back, angry suddenly. Eva knew he was not talking about Marcelle and Georges Braque, but about the two of them. "Some loves are just too rare for the wound ever to heal."

"I know, *mon amour,*" Eva said softly. "I know."

It really was the only thing for her to say because she knew in her heart that he was right. She could never have recovered from the loss of Picasso.

The mood was somber after that. No one could think of what to say to lighten everyone's spirits, yet still there seemed a comfort in all of them remaining together. They spoke of Braque and each who knew him recounted their memories of him, and happy times they had shared.

Eva wondered if they would all gather one day to do the same for her.

After dinner, they collected around the sofa so that Eva could lie down again. Sylvette sat on the arm of a plush chair by which Max seemed overpowered. He was smaller and so much more fragile looking than she remembered but he and Sylvette were now both smiling with cautiously eager expressions. Clearly tonight there was more to be revealed. By the look on both of their faces, it was better news.

"All right, out with it, both of you, what is it? I don't know which of you is brimming over more than the other," Eva said as, once again, Picasso and Gertrude spoke privately across the room and Alice joined them.

Sylvette answered her first. "It's finally happened, Eva. I'm going to be a real actress. They are giving me a starring role over at the Théâtre des Variétés!"

"Oh, Sylvette, that's wonderful."

"You always told me I wouldn't be in the chorus forever, and now it's actually true!"

"Yes, I did. Congratulations. I am so happy for you."

And Eva was truly happy for her friend.

She was only sad that she would not get to see her triumph onstage. There were so many precious things she already knew she would never see.

"Well, I can't top that," Max said quietly. "Yet I am going to be baptized next week."

"But you're Jewish."

His grin was sheepish and his blue eyes were bright. "I know. But it's time for something drastic. My life is a mess. I've had a vision, and I was told to receive the Lord into my heart."

"I should have guessed by the prayer you led us in earlier," Eva said.

"Picasso has agreed to be my godfather at my baptism."

"You've already spoken to him about it?"

"I wanted to ask you to be my godmother, but Picasso says you're not well enough."

"He's probably right."

"Would you be offended if I ask Sylvette in your place? She is so important to you that it will be like having you there with us."

"It's a wonderful idea," Eva said weakly. "I cannot think of anyone better. I only wish I could be with you on your big day. Where will you be baptized?"

"The Abbey de Sion. Picasso arranged it. Do you know the place?"

It is where we were meant to be married,

574

she wanted to reply. But there was no point in tarnishing his wonderful news. She pushed away the tiny hint of hurt she felt, knowing that Picasso hadn't told her because he wouldn't want to do anything to make her condition worse. Eva was sure he had chosen the place specifically because there was significance to it.

"Yes, it's a lovely church," she said, summoning a smile.

"He is certainly a changed man since you came into his life, Eva," Max said. "To be honest, I never thought there could be anyone better for him than Fernande. They were quite a pair early on. The poet in me would liken her to a bright shooting star — brilliant and fragile. But you, you are like the wave whose depth and force is never ending. Picasso has a kindness now, which has certainly made him a better friend. He has been transformed. For that, you are solely responsible, and personally, I thank you."

"He has changed me, too, Max. I don't suppose I would have done half of what I have with my life if I hadn't met him."

"I hope you will forgive my reluctance with you at first."

"You and I found our way in Céret. I'm glad we are friends."

He leaned forward and his voice went very low. Suddenly she could see tears glisten in his eyes. "You've got to get better, Eva. Not just for Picasso, but for all of us."

"I'm trying, Max. I really am."

Death was a black specter that loomed every day around Picasso. Yet he painted with great purpose, his creativity at last renewed. He bucked against death like a champion matador over a bull. Never far from his mind was the *corrida.* He would always adore the proud ritual of the bullfights, and the determination it symbolized to him.

He painted and painted. Eva slept. It was all tangled to him. The work. The emotion. The anger. Life. Death. Love. Sex. The great longing for it to be as it once was, but could never be again. And betrayal. After all, had God not broken their deal when he had pressed himself to trust again?

Picasso painted on through the war, and Eva grew worse. There were the Cubist canvases, even new harlequins, in the moments that nostalgia took over the anger. He drew, sketched and sculpted as if his own life depended on it. And when the rage flared, he emptied his pain onto the canvas in themes of sarcasm, cruelty and even ridicule of her illness — because ultimately he could not be openly angry with a woman who lay dying. His pain made him declare that *he* would be the god of all emotion. Not God.

But one day, what he had done to vent the rage was too much. A hideous painting of a woman with her breasts nailed onto her chest taunted him from the easel. A monstrosity. He gazed at his creation in horror, as if someone else had painted such a vile image. This wasn't Eva, not the woman of his heart, yet he had painted her cruelly, anyway. Overcome with grief, Picasso surrendered his face to his hands. Then he put a blank canvas on his easel to begin again.

The wounded child hidden inside of him bid him to leave Eva. That would ease this unrelenting pain of seeing her weaken a little more each day, and he so powerless to help her. His feelings about illness and death had always been so complicated. Even he did not understand them, but if he did not work them out soon, he would lose Eva as he had lost Conchita — helplessly and with painful regret.

When finally he could no longer eat or sleep, or even work, Picasso returned to the Abbey de Sion. A heavy rain beat a rhythm against the grand stained-glass windows. He took a seat in the last pew, his shoulders hunched and his hands forming a steeple beneath his chin. He looked up at the huge crucifix suspended in the hollow nave. Jesus in torment . . . He had never felt more helpless in his life.

"Can I help, monsieur?"

Picasso turned with a start to see the same young dark-haired altar boy who had let him into the church that first time. He had not heard anyone approach, yet the boy was sitting beside him. He was wearing the same vestments and holding an ivory rosary. The boy was gazing at him with wide dark eyes and Picasso felt his angry veneer crumble. He could not find his voice at first. Desperate for composure, Picasso cleared his throat, ran a hand across his face and straightened his back. It was then that he realized he had been plaintively weeping. The boy must have heard him.

"Only God could help me now, but He and I are not on the best of terms."

"I felt like that myself once. After my sister died, my parents thought I could be helped by being nearer to the Lord, so they forced me to be an altar boy."

Picasso leaned back against the hard wood of the pew. "They forced you?"

"They were trying to help me reconcile things."

"And did you?"

"Being nearer to the Lord is always best."

Picasso gazed at the boy more intensely then. He looked older now. He certainly sounded older. For a moment, he thought he might be dreaming in this great, shadowy sanctuary. The intimacy was too sudden, as was the coincidence of their loss.

"You must reconcile the things you cannot change, monsieur, past and present, to find true peace for your future."

"I haven't a clue how to do that."

"Perhaps that is the journey our Lord has set you on. No matter how far away we think we are, the past is always there, until we resolve it."

Somehow he meant Conchita, Picasso thought, even though this boy would have had no way of knowing about her. He squeezed his eyes shut against the thought and exhaled several deep breaths. How could he ever resolve her death when he was being forced to lose the only other person he had ever dared to completely love? There was no answer to that. It was impossible.

Picasso stood, preparing to tell the boy that he had no idea what he was talking about. But the boy was gone. Picasso glanced around the church but he had completely disappeared. Or had he been a figment of his desperate mind? *I don't know what You want from me,* Picasso thought. He knew that coming here was a mistake. There was no peace for him here. Not in a church. Certainly not with God.

CHAPTER 34

There was no end to the war as the months went on, and there seemed no place to hide Eva from any of the darkness war brought, or to find her a place to simply die in peace. Dr. Rousseau gave them little hope of a hospital bed in Paris. Wounded soldiers were everywhere, the hotels, schools, private homes. Try the sanatorium in Auteuil, Rousseau advised. For enough money, they may find a space for Madame Picasso there. And so he did.

Every day through the cool autumn Picasso juggled love and duty with art and anger. He would paint throughout the night and the morning, alone in the apartment Eva had chosen and decorated. There were haunting memories of her everywhere there. Then, in the afternoon, he would set out for Auteuil to visit her.

Every single day he descended the subway steps alone and entered the stifling station at Montparnasse to make the journey. In crowded subway cars, the women glared at him; the children pointed. They did not care that he was a rich or important artist, or that the woman he loved lay dying. Picasso always looked away, out the window of the subway car into the blackness of the tunnel. He felt the rhythmic rock and sway as the heavy car clacked endlessly over the tracks. Then always he was jarred by the grinding squeal of the brakes as they arrived at station after station. And every moment of every trip he made to Auteuil and back, Picasso thought of the bright-eyed girl at the exhibition — the one who owned a yellow kimono. And he knew that she had changed his life, and broken his heart, in a way that could never be healed.

Late one afternoon, when he felt Eva stroking his hair, Picasso realized that he had fallen asleep in the chair at her bedside, his head leaning on the edge of the bed. "Are you all right? Do you need anything?" he asked her, quickly shaking off sleep to attend to her.

Her face was so sallow, gray and pale now. The sweet blush of youth had already been eaten up by the cancer that was consuming her.

"Everything I have ever needed is right

here beside me. But I must speak to you about something."

"Is this another lecture about my odd work habits?" he tried to joke, because now it was simply too painful to be serious.

"Pablo, please."

He poured her a glass of water and held it to her lips. She struggled to take a small sip.

"I want you to take a lover."

He bristled and put the glass down. *Dios,* he had not seen that coming. He sat up stiffly, pushing back against the shock that rushed at him. She brushed a hand tenderly along the line of his jaw in response, as if she could almost hear what he was thinking.

"I won't hear this. You're getting better. You will be home with me soon."

"No, *chéri,* I am not going to get better."

"Stop."

"But you are young and strong, and so vital. You have a long life ahead of you."

"Eva, *Dios.* Stop it." He wanted to flee. To be anywhere but here with her forcing him to face the truth yet again about her mortality.

He raked his hair back and pressed both hands against his own temples. Suddenly he felt as if he was going to cry. It was a foreign sensation and it caught him by surprise. He did not want to cry. He could not lose control like that now. Eva needed him to be strong.

"How I hate this."

"I need for you to be happy."

"I was happy. So happy. With you . . ."

"Please, my darling, say you will be happy again."

Eva began to weep softly then as the rain came down more heavily outside the hospital windows. Something, at last, broke inside of Picasso.

"Don't leave me, Eva. Please, don't leave me."

"Oh, my heart. Would that I could give you what you ask. But you have such brilliance ahead of you. No matter who is by your side, you are going to become a legend. I always knew that."

"But I want that to be *you*! You were there when it mattered most, and you believed in me unfailingly. You made so many things possible."

She stroked the back of his hand. "I am grateful for everything we've shared, but even so, I cannot go on with you. When I am gone, don't let people know how I died. I'm so embarrassed."

"Why would you be embarrassed?"

"Vanity, I suppose. A woman's breasts are

part of what makes her a woman." She tried to laugh but only a weak sound came.

"Stop."

"Pablo, I mean it. That is the last thing I will ask of you. Think me foolish if you will, but you knew all along that I didn't want people's pity. Please, speak with Dr. Rousseau. After I am gone, see that he destroys my records. Promise me."

"Eva . . ."

"Please, Pablo." She stroked his hair again.

"*Dios,* why couldn't He have spared you?"

"Oh, *chéri,* I fear that was never God's intention. But I am grateful that you have overcome your fears about illness and death — enough to be here all this time for me. That, I think, was the plan all along."

He looked up at Eva and saw it so clearly then that he could not imagine why he had not seen it before. The boy. The church. It was himself. He felt a cold shiver of realization. Eva had been the inspiration for his healing with God. It was she who had led him to find himself. Picasso had risen to the challenge God had placed before him without even realizing it. In spite of his fears, in the face of her lengthy illness, and now her impending death, he had not abandoned her. Her steadfast love had helped him to become a noble man, and to be there for her in a way he had not been able to be for Conchita.

"I am so sorry . . ." he cried, unable to stop the flood of tears. He hunched over the bed and surrendered himself to the warmth of Eva's weak embrace. He pressed his head to her chest and heard the sound of her faint heartbeat and her shallow breathing. "I'm so very sorry."

"Please don't be, *mon amour.* You have given me the happiest days of my life."

Picasso shook his head, his body racked with sobs. "I should have insisted we marry. Even when you refused me, I should have overcome your objection. You have been a wife to me in every meaning of the word."

"I never refused you. The timing was just never right." She tried to smile but the weak result was only a soft turn of her lips as she reached up and dried his tears with the back of her hand. "Besides, you know our souls were always joined, and forever will be. We didn't need a piece of paper for that to be so. I feel as if I have been your wife all this time."

"I never finished that painting of us. I planned to finish it when you were well again. I wanted to give it to you as a wedding gift. It was meant to hang in our drawing room for our children to have one day."

"An unfinished painting of us seems so fitting now."

"*Dios,* don't say that. You are killing me, and I am dying with you."

"Ah, you will not die for a very long time. The best gift you could ever give me now is to take what we have built together and embrace the magnificent future that is about to come to you. If I have one regret, it is that I won't be here to share that with you. I know it will be amazing."

Picasso hardly heard her last few words. As she spoke them, he slid onto the bed beside her, nestled as tightly against her as he could, buried his face at the turn of her neck and wept for what he knew would be the last few fleeting days ahead that they would ever share together on this earth.

CHAPTER 35

For four years, Fernande had wanted Eva to die. Yet, now that it was actually about to happen, she did not know what to feel. So many things had come full circle for the two of them. This was the fifth day she had come out here and stood in the little courtyard outside the front door of the sanatorium in Auteuil, unable to go inside to speak with her. As she gazed up at the row of windows, memories of her own years with Picasso — and then of her years without him — crisscrossed through her mind. Sorrow filled her but there was a bit of cold comfort to her, in that moment, knowing that with Eva's death, Picasso might finally suffer as she had. Although she had heard through Juan Gris, since they still knew many of the same people, that Picasso had quietly taken a mistress now at the last. She knew him well enough to know that he would have done that for his own emotional survival, not because he didn't still worship Eva.

Fernande was not sure what she had hoped to find by coming here. She had heard from Apollinaire, who wrote from his hospital bed after being wounded like Braque, what lengths Picasso had gone to for her rival, since the start of the war. She never would have imagined him capable of such devotion to a woman. It was not a part of himself that he had revealed to her. Fernande cringed, remembering how she had once made Eva her confidante.

Fernande was lost in her thoughts of the past when a man approached her.

He insisted on leading her beneath the eaves of the sanatorium because it had begun to rain and he could see she had not noticed. "You don't recognize me, do you?" he asked.

His eyes were familiar but she could not recall where she knew him. He looked very old and tired as he stood beside her in a weathered military uniform, his arm in a sling.

"I am Louis Marcoussis. You gave me that name yourself once." They embraced then like long-lost friends, and she glanced down at the sling. "I was wounded so they sent me home. When I heard about Eva, I had to come here."

"He is with her," Fernande said. "I saw him go inside about an hour ago."

A flash of pain lit his blue eyes more brightly, and it struck her then how Pablo Picasso had changed them all. She could see that he had always been in love with Eva, but he had never really had a chance with her heart once destiny struck. Fernande felt the same about Picasso, and she realized going forward that she would never be able to compete with a ghost.

What had become of them all? She wondered if any of them had ever actually been so young and carefree, so wild with abandon, as she remembered. Each of them had been intent on defying convention, in their own unique way. To be bold, wild and romantic was everything. Ah, but then that was the dreamworld of Paris. Such a long-lost dream now.

As she stood there with him, the rain began to fall harder, and Fernande wanted to tell Louis the truth of what she was really here to say to Eva. But even after everything, Fernande could not hate her. Picasso had become a better man because of Eva's love, and as much as she was loath to admit it, she knew that Eva had been better for him.

"He will leave soon to return to his studio in Montparnasse. It is the same every afternoon," she said. "I've tried for days to find the courage to go inside once he leaves. But seeing her again might just do me in."

"I came here because I thought I wanted to see Picasso feel the same pain that I did," Louis said. "But I've seen too much death to take satisfaction. What I need now is to ask Eva for her forgiveness."

"I don't know what to say to her," Fernande added as they began to walk toward the door.

"Me, either," Louis replied. "But I suppose it will come to us. Who shall we tell the nurses we are?" he asked her as they began to walk toward the door.

"We will tell them we are her friends from the old days," Fernande said simply, which, once upon a time, had been true.

As Eva lay wrapped beneath blankets, in the wonderfully soft yellow silk kimono Picasso had brought for her, she thought how much, in wintertime, bare tree branches resembled skeletons. She had gazed for so many endless hours out the window at the gnarled, twisted shapes and pitied the people out there in the cold this time of year. It would be Christmas soon. She knew she would not see spring. It was fitting how her most recent favorite Apollinaire poem, "The Farewell," kept moving in and out of her mind.

> I have picked this sprig of heather.
> Autumn has ended, you do remember.
> Never on earth shall we meet again.
> Scent of time, sprig of heather
> Remember always, I wait for you forever.

The worst of the pain was gone, but in its place was a numbness from the medication that she could not escape.

A few days after Eva entered the sanatorium, Picasso invited her parents to visit. Eva was angry at first because she hadn't wanted them to suffer by seeing her like this. But when she saw them she remembered every good thing about her childhood, and how much she had missed them. They spent hours together lovingly recounting the past, and forgiving one another for all that had happened between them. Picasso had done for her what she had done for him with Apollinaire.

Her mother sat on Picasso's chair beside the bed, her father stood beside it. "I'm sorry that we tried so hard to get you to marry Monsieur Fix, and later your friend Louis," her mother said as she held Eva's hand.

"There was only one man who was ever right for me," Eva weakly replied.

"Your Pablo has been good to us, too. He brought us here and he has assured your father he will take care of everything."

"Then you can believe him."

"Oh, Eva, why didn't you take better care of your health?" Her mother began to cry. "I pleaded with you to get more rest and —"

"Hush, Marie-Louise," Eva's father urged as he pressed a gentle hand onto his wife's shoulder. "That won't help things now."

"I'm sorry the way I left home," Eva whispered. It was difficult to speak. "I know I worried you."

"We pushed you too hard. I just can't help thinking this is all our fault."

"Please don't think that. I couldn't bear to die knowing you did." Eva brought her mother's hand to her lips and kissed it. "What you both gave me was such strength, and an inner core that made so many things possible. That was all from both of you. I have had the best life ever, I really have."

Her mother said a Polish prayer with her then, the way she had when Eva was a child. Then her father kissed her forehead with great tenderness before the nurse came back and told them that Eva needed to rest.

After they had gone, she knew there was nothing left unsaid between them, and she felt ready to give herself over to sleep with only the happiest thoughts in her mind.

To cheer her later after she woke, Picasso told her he had painted a new harlequin. It was a boy sitting on a stool with one of the stool legs broken. He said the boy was himself, and the bandage used to hold the stool leg together symbolized his broken heart. He had embedded secrets in the painting, about himself, about them, just like always, because what she meant to him was simply too precious to share outright with the world, he whispered to her. Eva tried not to imagine how sad the face of the boy probably was. He had always put so much of his soul in his harlequin images. As he had into his love affair with her.

"Do you recall that time we went to the Circus Medrano?" he asked. "I have wanted to paint another harlequin since then."

"Will you bring it with you tomorrow?"

"Of course," he said weakly as he tucked the blankets around her. "I should go now and let you rest."

"Yes, I know you have so much to see to. I don't want to keep you. Don't forget to take Sentinelle for his walk. You know how he loves that."

Picasso smiled. "I'm not giving him back to Derain after the war, you know."

"I know."

"He's your dog."

"He is *our* dog."

"Sí."

"And don't forget to check the mail when you get home. Kahnweiler still owes you a fortune. You should hold him to that, even if it takes until the end of the war."

"He owes it to *us*. You know you inspired many of those paintings," Picasso said as he squeezed her hand, which had become too thin and frail to wear his grandmother's Spanish silver ring.

"Forgive me, Madame Picasso," interrupted a nurse. "A man and woman are here to see you, but I have told them to come back another time."

The nurse was dressed all in white. Eva thought she looked like an angel.

Eva smiled, thinking how lovely it was that someone else had come to visit. But she was so very tired. As she closed her eyes, she felt Picasso press a tender kiss onto her forehead. It felt like butterflies.

"Pleasant dreams, *ma jolie, mon coeur . . .*" she heard Picasso whisper. "I will be back tomorrow."

AUTHOR'S NOTE

Although this is a work of fiction, I have taken the greatest care to respectfully recount events as they are known to have occurred. Various subplots, and the motivations of some of the characters, however, could only be fictionally drawn since Eva left so little of herself for the world to know. Filling in the blanks came, in part, by studying Picasso's work, but also by pouring over every word and nuance of Eva's correspondence with Gertrude Stein and Alice Toklas. I am grateful to the Beinecke Library at Yale University for granting me access to them.

There is no greater clue left to history than what remains in one's own handwriting. Woven poignantly throughout her beautiful sloping penmanship, and the spirited underscoring of her signature, I was moved by her sense of humor, her tender heart, her determination and, most of all, her great enduring love for Picasso.

On many occasions, Eva and Picasso shared postcards and stationery, playfully adding to each other's thoughts, just as they shared their lives. It was Picasso himself, on one occasion, who added "Picasso" to her simple signature "Eva," helping me to bring about the title of this work.

During my research for this novel, there were two facts that touched me especially, and encouraged me to be a voice for the elusive Eva. First, the possibly unfinished painting of Eva and a character resembling Picasso, mentioned toward the end of the novel, was found half a century later, only after Picasso's death. Even after a life marked by other loves, it remained hidden among his private things. Second, was a comment by Picasso's friend and biographer, Pierre Daix: "When we spoke of her two-thirds of a century later, tears came to his eyes. They had truly lived together, and Pablo, when success came, needed her."

With *Madame Picasso,* I have hoped most of all to honor that notion.

ACKNOWLEDGMENTS

First and foremost, I wish to thank famed French photographer Lucien Clergue for helping me to understand Picasso the man, not the myth. A personal friend of Pablo Picasso for over thirty years, Monsieur Clergue met with me at his atelier in France and gave me the great gift of anecdotes and personal stories of Picasso's generosity, private kindnesses and enduring friendship, which I hope helped to humanize an icon in this work.

I also owe an enormous debt of gratitude to Valérie Gillet, Media Liaison, Vaucluse Tourist Board, for her many hours of help with research, arrangements, interviews and translations. On this journey, she began as an expert and guide, and she has become a friend. All poetry and lyric translations in the novel are an original and collaborative effort. For her help with those I am also indebted.

My thanks also to Laurence Minard-Amalou in Sorgues, for help uncovering rare documents and long-hidden key locations; to Anne-Marie Peilhard, Director Angladon Museum, Avignon, for generous information about Picasso's time in the area; to Marie-Pierre Ghirardini, Director Hôtel d'Europe Avignon, for sharing a wealth of local details; and Francine Rioux, Arles Tourist Board Director, for graciously facilitating my introduction to Monsieur Clergue.

I am indebted also to Sònia Marín, Official Guide of Catalunya for revealing details of Picasso's Barcelona. When Picasso speaks in the novel, it is through her extensive knowledge of the history and languages of Spain.

Thanks also to Andrew Kozlowski, President of the Polish Center of Los Angeles, for his assistance with the language and Polish references.

My continuing respect and admiration to the fabulous Irene Goodman, a literary agent unparalleled in support and encouragement of her authors. And many thanks to my editor, Erika Imranyi, for belief from the first few pages in the idea of *Madame Picasso*. Her keen insights and enthusiastic commitment to this book have been invaluable to me.

Finally, my deepest thanks go to my unfailingly supportive dream team of family and friends who keep me inspired and keep me wanting to tell these wonderful true stories from history: Ken, Elizabeth and Alex Haeger, Meg Fried, Rebecca Seltzner, Karen Thorne Isé, Kelly Stevens Costello, Maria Mazzuca and Sarah Galluppi, your love and encouragement have always been my greatest inspiration. I do dearly love you all.

I have also been enormously assisted in this endeavor by several literary sources, including John Richardson's *A Life of Picasso: 1907-1917: The Painter of Modern Life;* Pierre Daix's *Picasso: Life and Art;* Norman Mailer's *Picasso: Portrait of Picasso as a Young Man;* Patrick O'Brian's *Picasso: A Biography; Gertrude Stein on Picasso,* edited by Edward Burns; Jaime Sabartés's *Picasso: An Intimate Portrait; The Moulin Rouge* by Jacques Pessis; *Paris on the Eve: 1900–1914* by Vincent Cronin. And last, but certainly not least, *Loving Picasso: The Private Journal of Fernande Olivier* by Fernande Olivier.

■ ■ ■ ■

MADAME PICASSO

ANNE GIRARD

■ ■ ■ ■

READER'S GUIDE

QUESTIONS FOR DISCUSSION

1. Fernande Olivier and Eva Gouel were both, for a time, the object of Pablo Picasso's obsession. How were the two women different? How were they similar? What do you think were the elements that drew him to each of them? Discuss.

2. In the novel, a fair amount of attention is paid to the poetry of Guillaume Apollinaire. What do you think Eva found so appealing in it?

3. At one point in the story, Eva finally sleeps with Louis. Did you sympathize with her motivation, or did you feel sorry for Louis, who was being misled? Do you think her actions were more self-preservation or defiance? Did you find Louis Markus a sympathetic character? Why or why not?

4. The setting of this book is Paris just after the turn of the century. While it is often depicted as an exciting time, Picasso's world, especially at the Bateau-Lavoir studio, seems less than glamorous. Were you surprised that Eva was not dissuaded from her attraction to Picasso after seeing it that first night? Were you surprised that she was not dissuaded, either, by the base and sexual nature of some of his artwork in 1911?

5. A tense conversation takes place in Céret between Picasso, his former mistress Fernande and their friends, who side with her. Did you find yourself sympathizing with Fernande at that point in the story? Did you believe that she truly had learned her lesson and wished to reconcile with him? If so, what made her a sympathetic figure for you? If not, did you think Picasso should have engaged in a confrontation at all?

6. Eva faces a heartbreaking decision when she is told that her doctor suspects cancer. How did you feel about her decision to withhold that information from Picasso?

7. While Eva was immortalized in several of

Picasso's Cubist works, there is no known classically painted, or sketched, image of her by Picasso himself, yet there are many of Fernande and every other prominent woman in his life before and after. What are the possible reasons for this?

8. What did you make of the way some of Picasso's friends, such as the Pichots, refused to betray Fernande for Eva, even knowing that Fernande had been habitually unfaithful, while others, such as Max Jacob, Gertrude Stein and Alice Toklas, warmed to Eva and even became her devoted friends? Is it impossible to be an impartial friend in that sort of circumstance?

9. If Eva had not fallen ill, do you believe she and Picasso would have married? If so, do you believe he would have remained faithful, when he had never been faithful before her? How might their marriage, and years together, have changed his art?

10. Religion is a common theme in the book. What do you make of Picasso's troubled spiritual journey, from his feelings of anger after the death of his sister to his feelings of betrayal over the impend-

ing loss of Eva? Was the intensity justified? How do you think his feelings of spite toward God contributed to his actions throughout the novel, particularly during Eva's illness?

11. While therc are numerous theories, very little is known about what disease ultimately claimed Eva's life. Though there is circumstantial evidence, documentation and medical records seem to have been destroyed. Do you suppose, as the book infers, that Eva herself did not want the information left to history? If so, what might her reason have been? Does it seem logical to you that shame might have played a part in an era where affairs were rampant and sexuality pervaded art and literature? If not, what might some other reasons have been?

12. Prior to reading *Madame Picasso,* what were your perceptions of Pablo Picasso as a historical figure? Were those perceptions informed by the many biographies of his life, by popular culture (i.e. movies or television documentaries), or his art? How, if at all, were those perceptions changed by reading this novel?

A CONVERSATION WITH ANNE GIRARD

Picasso was known to be a womanizer who took many lovers. What was it about Eva that stood out to you above the other women in his life? Independent from Picasso, what drew you to Eva?

I was struck by the aura of focused determination Eva had. At the time they met, Picasso was young and on the cusp of stardom, and he had become disillusioned with the tumultuous relationships of his past. I believe he saw Eva's focus as a stabilizing influence, and that was immensely attractive to him. Picasso needed a woman who could make him want to be faithful, and Eva was that woman. He was ready to change completely for true love, and with her he certainly did.

What drew me most to Eva's story, and made me know I had to tell it, was a photograph of her wearing a kimono, referred to in the novel. In spite of how demure she looked, I could see the spark of fire she possessed. It just radiated from the image, and I was inspired to find out about this elusive young woman who had been the underdog with many of his friends, yet who became the most important influence in his life. Eva must have been an amazing woman to have made such an impact in such a short time, which certainly would have made her loss that much more of a devastation. It is my belief, after researching and writing the novel, that it was a loss from which he never fully recovered.

In Madame Picasso, *you explore art and culture in turn-of-the-century Paris. What drew you to this time period and setting?*

I have always been intrigued by the "City of Lights," and particularly as it was at the dawn of the twentieth century. The young artists and writers who found fame there, in an age of possibility and new thought, is just so delicious to write about! But I am also intrigued by the clash between mannered society and the bohemian world that rose up to challenge convention. Having lived in Paris for a while, and having traveled extensively throughout France, I do love all things French, so couple that with my academic background in literature, art and history, and falling in love with this particular story was a fait accompli!

It is known that Picasso took a lover during Eva's final days, yet you've chosen not to focus on that detail aside from a passing reference from Fernande. Is there a reason you handled this element of history in this manner?

During my research for the novel, I came to believe that the ill-timed affair was Picasso's way of cushioning the heart-wrenching grief he was enduring and the helpless sense of loss that was coming at him full speed. I did not want to divert the focus of the story from the great love he and Eva shared in order to highlight something seemingly of far less consequence in his life. As awful as the reality of that affair was, people cope differently with personal tragedy, and we can't judge another's decisions too harshly unless we have been not only in that place, but in their mind and heart. For me, Picasso's devotion to Eva during her lengthy illness speaks volumes about the depth of his love for her.

What was the greatest challenge in writing Madame Picasso? *Your greatest pleasure?*

Finding accurate information about the elusive Eva, and then weaving through those facts the necessary assertions about her life with Picasso — that was a challenge! Then, of course, any novelist must take the utmost care to add just the right dose of fictional elements to craft a good strong story while remaining as true as possible to history. My greatest pleasure was spending time with one of Pablo Picasso's last living friends, a man who was able to share stories with me about Picasso the tender and generous man, rather than the mythical figure he seems to have become for the world.

Can you describe the writing process? Do you outline first or dive right in? Do you write scenes consecutively or jump around? Do you have a writing schedule or routine? A lucky charm?

I begin by reading everything I can get my hands on about my subject, as well as the times in which they lived — history, politics, fashion — so that I have a framework established in my mind. I do make a general outline of where I think the story will go, but then I dive in. I write scenes consecutively, but oftentimes the story veers completely away from the outline I intended it to follow as I get to know the characters and allow them to tell their story through me. That really is the best part of the process. My schedule is fairly strict. First coffee, and then I write at least something every day, almost always mornings, so that I don't lose the flow of the story. My lucky charm is a coin, a 1551 douzain from the French Renaissance I found on my first research trip. I keep it on my desk to remind me that the people I write about were once as real as that coin, and so I have a duty to be respectful with the stories I have been entrusted to tell.